D0378714

Winter Sisters

Also by Robin Oliveira

My Name Is Mary Sutter

I Always Loved You

Winter Sisters

Robin Oliveira

VIKING

VIKING
An imprint of Penguin Random House LLC
375 Hudson Street
New York, New York 10014
penguin.com

ISBN 9780399564253 (hardcover)
ISBN 9780399564277 (ebook)

Printed in the United States of America
1 3 5 7 9 10 8 6 4 2

Set in Baskerville MT Std
Designed by Cassandra Garruzzo

For girls and women everywhere

Book One

Chapter One

Two days before Emma and Claire O'Donnell disappeared, a light snow fell from the dawn sky above Albany, New York, almost as a warning mist. Later, people would recall that the flakes were mistakenly perceived as a lark, a last dusting in what had been an unusually cold winter. The year 1879 was already proving to be a surprising one: on March 3, the first woman lawyer had argued a case before the Supreme Court, and despite the wretched cold, there had been an abnormally scant snowfall. Just a foot since November, which had then melted away on three strangely warm days in early February, though the thick ice on the Hudson River had not yet broken.

Emma and Claire O'Donnell were ten and seven years old, respectively. In concession to the snow, they wore boots, but because the day was already warming they donned only a light coat over their spring dresses. Their parents were similarly attired: boots in lieu of lighter, leather shoes, a woolen coat for Bonnie, a thin cloth work jacket for David. The O'Donnells lived in three rooms on the first floor of a row house on Elm Street. Every morning they left the house together, Emma and Claire for the Van Zandt Grammar School, Bonnie to her millinery shop on State Street, and David to the Lumber District.

Their farewell on the morning of March tenth at the school doors was unremarkable as farewells go: a brief wave, an affectionate reminder for Emma to take care of Claire, and noisy reluctance from the sisters, for it was annoying to have to go inside on such a splendid day. There was little reason, any of them believed, to mark the occasion: they would see one another at home for their midday meal, as they always did.

David and Bonnie walked on together through the light, powdery snow the five blocks to State Street, Albany's wide boulevard, which was graced at its summit by the new capitol building, still unfinished after twelve years of construction. It was modeled after the Louvre Palace in Paris, but its outer walls had only just been completed, giving it a faintly apologetic mien, as its facade was still missing a promised grand stairway and a plethora of decorative friezes and gargoyles. Its interior third and fourth floors were still barren hollows of scaffolding and echo. The exasperated legislature, tired of waiting, had preemptively moved into the first two, anticipating years of noise and headache ahead.

The businesses of importance—with the exception of lumber and railroading—proceeded apace below the capitol, on State Street. A languorous hill, it eased from the capitol heights down to the Hudson River, spanned here by two railroad bridges, one north and one south. The waterway had first been named the North River by the Dutch, because it allowed passage northward from the Manhattan harbor, but it had long since been renamed after its discoverer, though the early moniker persisted in Manhattan City, whose centric gaze rarely extended to the wider world.

Albany's principal economic engine was that it offered a decent port on the only navigable river a steamboat day's voyage from the bustling trade center. A stubborn Flemish perseverance had long characterized the city's public personality, which had sustained the founding Dutch through the threat of native unrest, the encroaching French, and finally the conquering English, who captured New Netherlands—essentially all of northeast America—in 1664 and renamed the inauspiciously named yet tenacious city of Beverwijck, Albany. That same perseverance had also sustained the city through year after year of seasonal floods, for though the river was an economic boon, it was also Albany's watery Achilles' heel.

But today, Monday, March 10, it was snowing, and the river was still frozen, and merchants, bankers, printers, engravers, tobacconists, reporters, druggists, lawyers, and one milliner were all converging on State Street to empty mousetraps, sweep refuse from thresholds, and deposit money into their empty tills. The mercantile neighbors waxed convivial with one another about the snow shower. Smiles, all around, and a shaking of heads. *Albany.*

David O'Donnell accompanied Bonnie to her shop at 59 State Street, as he did every morning. His pride at her success was exceeded only by his pride in his daughters, Emma and Claire, though if pressed, he might confess a partiality toward Emma, whose stubborn spiritedness he encouraged perhaps more than he ought. But the pressing thing now was the snow drifting lightly from the skies, and the question of whether or not it had been advisable to have erected the new awning over the mullioned shop window. Under too much accumulation of the white stuff, it would founder. But as they assessed the sky for clues, a patch of blue opened above the river, settling the issue. David kissed Bonnie's cheek, and taking his leave, descended the slippery sidewalk toward Broadway on his way to the Lumber District, where his work as a stevedore had shaped his strong body into an anvil.

"You'll not forget dinner tonight at the Sutters'?" Bonnie called after him. "I mean the Stipps'!" After twelve years, she still couldn't get it straight. Her beloved adopted family had grown. No one in the city of Albany knew whether to call them the Sutters or the Stipps, either. The O'Donnells were generally believed to be their blood relations, though that was not true, even as much as Bonnie wished it were. "And if you stop for a pint on the way home," she threatened, "don't bother to come calling. I'll bolt the door against you."

Turning, David raised his arm in salute, a teasing grin skittering across his weathered face. "Dinner?" he said. "What dinner?"

"David O'Donnell, it's your fault, you know, that Emma is such a scrapper." But Bonnie stood under her green-striped awning and admired the man as he sauntered away. David was her second husband. Her first husband, Jake Miles, had disappeared in the War of the Rebellion, and none too glad had she been to see him gone. For a brief time, she'd been in love with Christian Sutter, Amelia's only son, but he had died early in the war. And then David had spotted her on the street one day, and made a pest of himself until she fell in love with him. He had given her Emma and Claire, whom she cherished. She crossed herself to honor the two children she'd had with Jake. They had died as infants, a sadness from her unlucky past. And she made a last cross to honor Elizabeth Fall: Amelia Sutter's grandchild, whom she loved just as much as she loved her own daughters, and whom she missed, for the brilliant girl had gone with her grandmother far away to Paris to study violin at the conservatory there. Bonnie was worried about her. Lately, Elizabeth's letters had confided great sadness.

"Six o'clock! Remember!" Bonnie called after her husband.

After turning and waving, David cut down Montgomery and dashed across the tangle of railroad tracks at Spencer, then followed Water Street into the Lumber District, crossing the narrow lock bridge that separated the terminus of the Erie Canal from the port basin. A sudden, sharp gust of wind chilled the two thousand laborers pouring into the fifty lumberyards on the hundred-acre island, carved between the Erie Canal and the Hudson. David worked for Gerritt Van der Veer, the preeminent lumber baron in the city. Gerritt S. Van der Veer, it could be said, ruled Albany. Advertisements for his white pine shone down from nearly every brick building lining the grand commercial boulevards of Western Avenue and State Street. THE BEST WHITE PINE IN THE WORLD IS AT VAN DER VEER & SON LUMBER! While Van der Veer was a fair employer, his temper could rage when things went wrong. This year, an unanticipated excess inventory of milled white pine had wintered over, and Van der Veer wanted to ship it the minute the frozen river opened to navigation, which he believed would be soon. His overseer, James Harley, a more reasonable man, nonetheless shouted over the rising gusts to the assembled hundred laborers of Van der Veer Lumber that this morning's first task was to clear the accumulating snow from the stacks. So David and the other longshoremen climbed the towers of plywood and joists and four-by-fours and got to work.

In their classroom at the Van Zandt Grammar School, Emma and Claire were seated two rows apart. They had been gazing out the windows at the snow, which was beginning to turn heavier, but Emma, the oldest, sighed and exchanged a despairing glance with Claire before turning her attention back to their teacher, a recent graduate of the State Normal School, who was teaching some complicated math to the older students. Claire studied Emma from the corner of her eye. It pleased Claire that people said they looked alike, with their cascades of copper hair and bright blue eyes, but that was where their resemblance ended, Claire believed. Emma was so much more clever that she was. As Emma leaned over her paper to solve a raft of division problems, Claire pretended to do the same, but instead she was secretly thinking about the party that night at the Stipps'.

Five long blocks away, Bonnie was contemplating the party, too. It was their annual celebration of the opening of her shop. This year was the sixth, and it was she who ought to be hosting since Amelia Sutter was away with Elizabeth in Paris, but Mary Stipp had insisted on continuing the annual tradition of hosting the party at their home, even in the absence of her mother and niece. It was Amelia who had provided the initial funds. Bonnie had repaid her debt long ago, but the party had become a celebration not only of Amelia's generosity, but of the families' long friendship, close ties, and remade lives. And then there was the fact that Mary Sutter Stipp had delivered both Emma and Claire, and one of her babies from Jake, who had died. Their tight bonds could never be broken.

Outside, the light dimmed as the fluffy flakes turned beady and began to pour from the sky. Casting a wary eye toward the window, Bonnie resolved to leave her shop earlier than she usually did to pick up the cake at Mariano's Bakery for tonight, but she wasn't really worried. It was March, after all, nearly spring. The snow had to let up soon. And she had work to do. She finished dusting her showcase and arranging her worktable, permitting herself a small smile of self-congratulation as she sat down to put the last touches on the hat she had been decorating for her best customer, Viola Van der Veer, the wife of Gerritt Van der Veer, David's employer and the richest man in Albany. Not that long ago—was it really twenty years?—Bonnie had been an ignorant farm girl, and now she was making hats for a woman whose patronage had ensured her success, because when Viola Van der Veer wanted something, the rest of Albany society did, too, not so much out of affection for her, but as a mark of financial equality. That collective desire had provided for, among other things, the excess funds to purchase the cherished awning. Despite the snow, Bonnie expected that Mrs. Van der Veer might stop in today, as she often did, to chat with her as she worked. The society woman's loneliness had come as a revelation, especially given Mrs. Van der Veer's standing in the community, which recently Bonnie had learned Mrs. Van der Veer considered more a chore than a position she prized. Mostly, Bonnie was honored to be the recipient of Mrs. Van der Veer's sometimes mournful confidences, and more than once she had offered the tearful woman her shoulder.

The new wide-brimmed garden hat, a style that would set to advantage Mrs. Van der Veer's tiny figure, was already laden with white egret plumage and exuberant silk peonies. Bonnie marveled at how her customers seemed oblivious of her tricks. All she had to do was juxtapose a pair of complementary colors, offer the surprise of a new pattern, or more importantly, disclose which of a client's friends—or enemies—had purchased a far superior quality of velvet, and the sale was done. In Albany society, Bonnie had learned, superiority mattered. Hard won, reaped with unsheathed claws and an enigmatic smile in ballrooms and dining rooms across the city, who was who was the business of those women, and if she, a former farm girl, provided ammunition to the struggle, then all the better. She paused and took stock. The addition of a hummingbird would finish the hat well. It was an embellishment that Viola Van der Veer loved, and Bonnie often finished her hats with that signature detail. Now she tested first one, then another of the featherlight birds, setting them in a tiny nest of straw, choosing finally a ruby-throated one, its wings aflight.

Bonnie was still holding it up to admire when a violent burst of wind pushed open the door and the iridescent bird flew out of her fingers and up toward the ceiling. So much snow was suddenly spilling from the skies that she could hardly see a thing. She fumbled for matches to light the gas jet, but a curtain of darkness had fallen. The snowfall was no longer a mere sprinkling, a last reflexive fit of winter. It was a blizzard. Bonnie instantly thought of Claire and Emma. Would they shut the schools for a storm this foul, or keep the children instead? It didn't matter. She would go get them. Unthinking, she jammed Viola Van der Veer's unfinished hat on her head and fled outside, pulling on her thin coat. Instantly, the churning wind spun her around. She regained her balance and bent low, taking first one step, then another, into the maelstrom.

In the Lumber District, James Harley, the overseer, hollered above the roar of wind for everyone to get out. Hearing Harley's cries, David leaped to the ground from the top of the stack he'd been clearing and headed toward the Lock Bridge with hundreds of his fellow laborers, each one doubting his ability to find his way home in the sudden whiteout. Despite growing panic, the men worked together, linking arms and edging across the narrow Lock Bridge, made hazardous by the accumulating snow. The snaillike pace of escape was excruciating. When it was finally his turn, David bowed his head and shuffled across, praying not to be blown into the canal. But once he successfully negotiated the bridge, it soon became impossible to know what was ground and what was sky. Gravity lied. Senses failed. By blessed dumb luck, David navigated the twelve long blocks back to State Street, staying to the lee of the buildings and marking his path by memory, his collar turned up against the frigid cold. He blundered on, finally reaching State Street, where he traveled perhaps a dozen steps up the sidewalk before he lost his sense of direction and veered into the street. The blinded driver of a heavily laden dray never saw him, nor did he grasp that the cry he heard and the sudden jolt of his sliding wheels meant that he had crushed a man.

A few steps away, Bonnie heard a man's cry but was in too much trouble to help. In the blinding conditions, she had turned right when she should have turned left, and left when she should have turned right, and since leaving her shop had traveled only in circles. She lunged toward the cry and tumbled into a pillowy drift from which she struggled in vain to free herself.

In Emma and Claire's schoolroom, wild bullets of snow were striking the window, terrifying Claire, who searched for the comforting vision of Emma in the rising darkness. Their young schoolteacher interrupted her lesson on long division to kneel and shovel more coal into the stove, a fractious, unreliable thing she had battled all winter. A burst of air whistled down the updraft, sending a cloud of ash into her face. The soot would dirty her face for three days, but the children would be too frightened to enjoy the comic spectacle. The teacher managed to relight the fire and distract the fifteen children in her care with books until she could no longer outshout the howling wind. Day passed into late afternoon and then evening, and the school's principal raided the cupboards but found only a tin of crackers to serve all three classrooms. No parents arrived, and so the children and their teachers slept in a huddle around their classroom stoves, blanketed by the thin outer garments they'd worn that morning. Drifts buried the flues on the roof and exhaust backed into the classrooms. Woozy, the principal, acting on instinct and little else, stumbled down the hallway in the darkness and cracked open the front door of the schoolhouse, saving them all from asphyxiation but not from the poor judgment and illness the odorless fumes induced. Throughout the next day, Tuesday, as the storm continued to rage, children and teachers alike vomited and shuffled about, poisoned but alive.

On Wednesday at noon, when the storm finally abated and a sheen of brilliant light flooded the city, the befuddled principal spilled forty-five poorly dressed and sickened children into five feet of glittering, blinding snow. Their frantic parents had bolted from their homes the second the snow tapered off, and now they waded through enormous drifts to reach their children, whose befogged minds were clearing in the fresh air. Child after child was scooped into welcoming arms, but no one claimed Emma and Claire. Stunned by the cold, the two girls shivered on the iceberg of snow blown up against the school steps until Emma took hold of Claire's hand and forged a mountain goat path over frozen drifts in the direction of their home.

Just about the time that Emma and Claire started out, the doctors Mary and William Stipp, in their home a mile away on Madison Avenue, discovered that the blizzard had buried the doors, making egress to the wide veranda or the backyard impossible. After some consideration, they dropped to their waists into the deep snow from their parlor window instead. Outfitted in woolen hats, thick gloves and coats, wide mufflers, and lined boots—fitting attire for the daunting task ahead—they were nonetheless unprepared for the breathtaking cold. The air crackled. They blinked and pulled their mufflers above their noses.

Mary wore a pair of William's flannel pants cinched up by one of his wide belts, a new hole punched into it by a scalpel. At forty years of age, Mary Sutter Stipp was much younger than her husband. They'd met during the War of the Rebellion at the Union Hotel Hospital in Washington City, where William had hired her as a nurse. He taught her as much medicine as he could, falling in love with her in the process. Separated in the middle of the war, they lost track of one another. Mary went on to medical school. It wasn't until afterward, in 1867—when William had given up hope of ever finding her—that they found one another again. They had married soon after, because time was a thief, he'd said, and he needed her more than he needed air. William knew it was said in alehouses around town, where men gathered to talk like that, that Mary Stipp was taller and larger-boned than was considered attractive, but the opinions of idiots mattered not one whit to him. Mary exuded an intelligence and determination he'd found intoxicating, as did most anyone who met her. Prematurely silver-haired, frank, and to him, lovely, Mary Sutter had been persuaded to become Mary Stipp, to his everlasting gratitude.

For his part, William Stipp had long passed the age when dropping out of windows into drifts would have been considered a good idea. Sixty-three years old, he was not as nimble as he had once been, though he managed to keep them both from falling as they turned to get their bearings. Ramrod straight, he had aged in the fourteen years since the war, as many other veterans had, exposed to punishing years outside in the elements. His face bore the deep lines of the stress of that cataclysm, as well as the exposure.

When the storm arrived, they had been seeing patients: William in his clinic in a converted downstairs bedchamber, Mary in the dining room, a sunny, windowed cloister that overlooked the back garden. Their well-appointed but plainly furnished parlor served as their waiting room, where from dawn till evening a crowd of tired shopgirls and ill-dressed factory workers corralled their hordes of restless children and waited for their turn with the famous woman doctor. William's patients—crippled veterans complaining of their ill-fitting wooden legs, factory workers hobbled by various ailments, men and women suffering complex fractures—bided their time on the lower stairs or milled about in the wide foyer. Despite the home's location on the relative outskirts of the city, the horsecar line went past every half hour. The morning the blizzard began, when the bright light spilling through the east-facing windows had darkened into night, furious whispers of panic had arisen. The doctors consulted: they would allow no one to leave. Thus, for the last fifty hours, seven women, nine children, and five men had been the Stipps' unexpected guests, bedding down on the divans and floors and exam tables, sharing blankets, and in the case of at least one man and woman, a noisy conjoining that had unnerved everyone.

Now everyone was hungry. The grand dinner of roast beef and brussels sprouts and pudding they had planned for the O'Donnells had barely stretched to feed everyone that first night. Their patients then exhausted the pantry and consumed every last potato in the root cellar, to say nothing of decimating the stores of butter and milk. They had finished all the bread, too.

Mary and William were leaving Harold Bloom, their driver, in charge. Bloom, a wiry man with a thin twig of a mustache, was paid to be ready at any hour and could harness a horse faster than anyone. Married to Vera, a gruff Russian immigrant of immense proportions, the two lived above the carriage house. Vera's English was poor, but she was as flexible as her husband, producing meals at all hours without question, unless there was no food to be had. She leaned out the window now to remind her employers to find butter, eggs, and salted meat, and to not forget milk for the children.

Behind her, Harold's face was knotted in worry. "Be careful. And now I'm shutting this accursed window before we all freeze to death."

Confronted with a white wilderness, William and Mary calculated the effort it might take to reach an open store, if any were open at all. None had yet been established this high on the hill, with the exception of a butcher on Lark Street. Already, Mary's toes burned from the cold. It seemed madness to push on, but they needed food. And they were worried about the O'Donnells, who would have been separated when the storm began—David in the district, Bonnie at her shop, the children at their school. They feared that the children may have been let out of school to fend for themselves at home. And so they plunged into the blank, bristling quiet, holding hands, William forging a path through the high snow one step at a time. They were already winded when they reached the street, but they pressed on.

Their home bordered Washington Park. In the deadened landscape surrounding it, only the Stipps moved. Drifts splashed up against trees, inundated house porches, and buried wagons abandoned at the onset of the storm. They sidestepped down the hill of Madison Avenue toward downtown, alternately hurt and helped by gravity. In the lee of some buildings, the snow was a manageable two or three feet deep, and here and there paths had already been cut, but in the middle of the avenue the drifts reached the unscalable height of eight feet. Still, even keeping to the sheltered side of the street, it took them a good hour to reach Elm Street. Normally a lively residential lane, in the aftermath of the storm it was a deserted wasteland, though here, too, a sleigh had cut through the shallowest depths. At the O'Donnells',

William climbed a drift to the frosted windows of their front room and banged, leaving off only to peer in, his gloved hands cupped around his eyes. The upstairs residents hollered at them through their unopened window that none of the O'Donnells had returned home. Concerned, Mary and William then trudged the several blocks to the Van Zandt School, where they found the doors bolted shut, the school empty. Here, more paths had been trodden through the drifts, and they followed one winding trail toward State Street.

Along Eagle Street, not a single shop had opened, but in the window of the Oyster House, one candle burned a small yellow hole in ferns of frost. They went inside and huddled next to a glowing coal stove. The Stipps thawed and dried their wet gloves and wolfed down a plate of cheese and crackers and mugs of beer in lieu of real food. The restaurateur lived in two rooms above and bemoaned the fate of his expensive daily shipment of oysters from Manhattan City, fearing the bivalves frozen in some stranded railcar. The clock rang three, and William paid an exorbitant sum for the man's last wheel of Vermont cheddar and four tins of crackers, which he obligingly packed into burlap bags. Thus provisioned, they headed again into the biting cold. More people had ventured into the white void on foraging missions of their own. Mary and William tramped block by block toward Bonnie's shop, which they had seen from afar had been stripped of its awning. A wedge of snow three feet high had forced the door open, and inside a crystal white carpet blanketed the floor. Scattered hummingbirds, dyed feathers, spools of ribbon and lace were half buried and strewn about, but balanced on the trim above the mullioned window, a single ruby-throated hummingbird flew above it all. Mary and William waded into the back storeroom, tamping down a rising panic, hoping to find Bonnie wrapped against the cold in a roll of velvet or gingham. No snow had penetrated the small room, but Bonnie was not there.

At the sound of a strangled cry from the street, they dropped their bags and rushed outside. A man had fallen to his knees at the edge of a towering drift, from which protruded a single hand. He and William bent to the task, using bent forearms to sweep aside the dry crystals, which flew back into their faces and bleached their eyebrows and mustaches. Together, they uncovered first an arm, then a torso, then a garden hat, and finally Bonnie, facedown and lifeless, clad in nothing but her soft-spun day dress and one shoe.

William pulled her from the drift and cradled her in his arms. Mary sank to her knees beside them and touched Bonnie's glaciated face, which was icy blue with cold. Snow clotted her curls, and her eyes stared, unseeing.

They carried her corpse to the coroner's office, where Dr. Starkweather would spend the next few days batting away the black humor that attended the confluence of his name and the devastation of the storm. He led them down a steep stairway to a makeshift morgue in the basement, where sandbags already buttressed its street-level windows against snowmelt, and makeshift beds of plywood and sawhorses already bore a dozen unidentified bodies. Notes pinned to their clothes indicated the location of their discovery. They laid Bonnie down on an empty slab and reluctantly turned their attention to the others.

Even for William and Mary, veterans of the War of the Rebellion, the sight of David's battered body brought them both to their knees. A quick examination revealed a head injury and a broken leg. The cold would obscure any internal injury he had likely suffered, but they took no comfort that he would not have survived the accident, blizzard or no.

"Have any children been brought in?" Mary said, making a second, rapid turn of the room. "In another room, maybe? Somewhere? Our friends have—had—two children. We've been looking for them. They weren't at home, they weren't at school."

The city physician was a laconic man, grown unimpressed with death in his years as coroner, but his red-rimmed eyes softened. "No one's brought in any children yet."

"Two little girls. Red hair, blue eyes. If someone—"

Starkweather touched Mary's hand. "I'll send for you. But more than likely, they'll turn up somewhere safe and sound. They were at school when the blizzard came?"

"Yes."

"Then a friend might have taken them in when no one came for them. A thousand things could have happened. Your friends"—he nodded toward Bonnie and David—"that's terrible luck, but it's unlikely to befall their children as well."

The Stipps dragged themselves home in the pale light of a rising gibbous moon.

They had completely forgotten about the cheese and crackers they'd left at Bonnie's shop. Upon hearing they'd have nothing to eat, their ravenous patients wrapped their children in borrowed socks and hats and blankets, and dropped one by one out the parlor window and made for home.

Before the parlor fire, thawing their hands over cups of hot water, Mary and William reassured themselves. Dr. Starkweather was of course right. The girls' teacher or one of their friends would know where they were. And when they found them, they would break the terrible news of their parents' deaths and give them a home with them.

Bonnie and David would want them to.

"Ought we to telegraph Amelia and Elizabeth?" William said. Lately, he'd grown worried about their niece, Elizabeth, who had written to him every week from Paris, but whose letters had recently carried a vague, distant tone. He considered Elizabeth his daughter and had since Thomas Fall, her father, had died. William's face, with its landscape of deep hollows and high crests, was always a reflection of the implacable severity of his war years, but now the firelight, his grief, and thoughts of Elizabeth deepened every crevice.

"I don't think so," Mary said. "Not yet. We ought to spare them as much pain as we can. Let's wait until we know something more."

It was impossible to get warm. They went to bed. William cradled Mary as he had cradled Bonnie, and after a while she stopped shivering.

Chapter Two

The O'Donnells were not related to the Sutters and Stipps, but their ties went just as deep. Theirs was a familiar, if convoluted story in a nation that had of late known too much death. Fourteen years since the end of the War of the Rebellion and the nation was still counting the dead: 600,000, 800,000? An estimate, only. And the toll among the civilians who had starved would go unsung forever. In the wake of the devastation, new families had been formed by tenuous ties: cousins distant and more distant banded together, sad widows married even sadder widowers, brothers and uncles and aunts and friends and orphans clung to one another to assuage their enduring pain.

The Sutter family's story of change began when the war did. In 1861, the Sutters took in the then Bonnie Miles after her second baby with her first husband, Jake Miles, died. Later, after Mary's fraternal twin sister, Jenny, died giving birth to Elizabeth, it was Bonnie who mothered Elizabeth in Jenny's place, even after Elizabeth's father, Thomas Fall, returned from the war. In 1863 they all moved to Manhattan City so that Mary could study medicine with Elizabeth Blackwell, the first woman to graduate from medical school in America. They all continued to live together in Manhattan in the same house even after the war, even after Mary married William. The two families separated only when Bonnie married David. Then, a few years later, both families moved back to Albany.

The weight of this deep and enduring bond pressed on Mary and William the next morning as they ventured out again, following the path that they had forged the previous day. The city was already coming back to life. Many people were daring the cold, shoveling great mounds of snow, but mostly accomplishing only a rearrangement of the white stuff. Frustrated, people set bonfires in an attempt to melt it quickly, but that succeeded only in creating lakes of ice too treacherous to negotiate. A few businesses had opened. Enterprising chestnut roasters had fired up their braziers and were doling out small rations in paper cones for a penny. A dry goods store shuttered the day before was doing brisk business in sacks of flour and cakes of butter. A baker had shoveled his sidewalk early in the morning and was proferring hot rolls. Mary and William bought both rolls and chestnuts and consumed them standing on a corner before pressing on to Elm Street, where they knocked on the doors of David and Bonnie's neighbors and had the same conversation again and again.

"We're looking for Emma and Claire O'Donnell. Did you happen to see where they went?"

"No. Didn't Bonnie or David retrieve them from school?"

Sharing the sorrowful news was exhausting when they had not yet become reconciled to it themselves. And not one of their neighbors knew where the sisters were or even that they were missing. Those who had gone to the school recalled seeing Emma and Claire at the school doors, waiting. Surely someone else had realized they were alone and taken them home? Try the Atkins. Try the MacIntryes. Try the Brunos.

But neither the Atkins nor the MacIntryes nor the Brunos nor anyone else knew where they were. People joined in. By midafternoon, an army was knocking on doors on all the side streets to no avail, though they did learn that the principal, who had forded two miles of drifts to her home in North Albany, had been admitted to City Hospital with frostbite.

"No," the principal said, her eyes widening with confusion and horror. "No. It can't be. I checked the whole school. No one was left behind, no one."

On the hope that perhaps the girls may have been admitted, too, Mary and William swept through the hospital, looking for them. They searched Saint Peter's Hospital, and Child's Hospital on Hawk Street, to no avail.

"Emma and Claire?" their young teacher said at her rented room on Eagle Street. "They're missing?"

And at the morgue, an exhausted Dr. Starkweather, now presiding over twenty bodies, shook his head. "Not yet. But they're still coming in."

That night, Mary and William tried again to reassure themselves that little girls didn't just disappear. But they would soon learn that the storm had devastated the whole of the Northeast, not just Albany. The official count of the dead would total four hundred, with thousands more injured, and a hundred unaccounted for. In Albany, twenty-three people died, and five had gone missing, among them Emma and Claire.

By the next morning, their driver, Harold, had managed to dig out their sleigh from the carriage house, and he drove them to the police station on Dove Street, located several blocks from the former Sutter home.

The precinct house seemed to be in the process of disintegrating. The dull red bricks emanated a shabby weariness that cast a deep pall on the otherwise well-kept neighborhood. Until now, Mary had never once had cause to visit the station, and the narrow vestibule, where little daylight penetrated, did nothing to dispel an impression of suffocating gloom. A lanky policeman hunched at the front desk, a kerosene lantern flaring on a hook above his head, its sooty ghost smoked into the wall. No gas jets burned in this hulking building, for it was too old for such modern conveniences. Inside it was so cold that you could see your breath.

"Missing, eh?" Officer Colm Farrell's accent was thick Irish, a product, no doubt, of his Sixth Ward upbringing, where the Irish in Albany had lived since anyone could remember and turned out policemen like a factory. Thin, fair-haired, and long boned, he nonetheless gave the impression of uncommon physical strength, perhaps because of his square jaw and the large size of his hands. He listened to their panicked entreaties with patience and sympathy, soliciting clarification on timelines and the particulars of Emma's and Claire's appearances and where they had last been seen. Dutifully he took careful notes and when he had exhausted his questions said, "They'll likely turn up. You'll see. But we'll be looking for them. You might want to give the orphanages a look on your own. It'll be faster."

"What's this? Someone missing?" came a voice from the hallway in as thick an Irish accent as Farrell's.

Captain Arthur Mantel was less burly than round, less tall than average. But his demeanor gave the impression of an angry bull, with a matching stance that appealed to Mary. He demurred from taking them back to his office for a private conversation, claiming that it was a death trap, piled about with sundry ledgers and papers and too many guns to count.

"Orphans," he said, after hearing them out. "And you say no one's seen them? That's a shame."

"Yes," William said. "What do you usually do in such a case?"

"Keep a keen eye out. Ask the neighbors. But it's not quite the usual, is it, with the snow? And their names are Emma and Claire O'Donnell? You're certain, now?" His voice carried a measured curiosity, as if he were aware how even this routine question could elicit grief from a panicked citizen.

"Why wouldn't we know their names?" Mary asked, incredulous.

Mantel shook his head. "No reason. Have no worries, now. We'll be vigilant. Every police officer will get a copy of their descriptions. We'll ask at churches, orphanages. You can, too. You've already shown good initiative. Keep it up. It can only help. But I warn you, it's possible that they could have gotten confused in the cold and wandered in the direction of the river."

"Why would they have done that?"

Mantel shrugged. "Like I said, confusion. And then some rift in the ice could have swallowed them up. But that's the worst possible outcome. Keep heart. We'll search with every resource we have."

During the next two weeks, Mary and William braved the cold and snow and swept through the rest of the city's hospitals, posted notices, published a daily ad in all the newspapers, and toured the seven orphan asylums multiple times, including three in Watervliet and Troy, their sleigh flying across the frozen Hudson at the marked crossing. One evening, William took the train to Troy and walked the streets with a lantern. Mary took the train to Schenectady and inquired at a dozen churches and orphanages.

At night, they curled into one another in bed, enervated, nearly broken, and carried on a variation of a single conversation, Mary always beginning, her mind mulling the inconsistencies. "The principal said she didn't dismiss them until the storm ended. They were so close to home. The sun was shining. They simply couldn't have gone into the river by mistake. Their school is too far from the river. None of that makes sense, William."

"They may have made it home and discovered that David and Bonnie weren't there. It's not out of the question that they could have wandered off looking for them, attempted to go to the district—"

"But the neighbors said they didn't come home."

"They may have gone straight for Bonnie's shop or to the Lumber District. Misconstrued where the Lock Bridge was, ventured out onto the unstable ice. Just like the police think."

"But it's all such conjecture. And convenient. If the police decide Emma and Claire are dead, then they don't have to look for them anymore."

"But the girls aren't the only ones, Mary. Dozens of others, too. Gone without a trace."

His voice, that low, glorious growl that Mary loved, was grim with sorrow. From the moment she'd first seen him, at the beginning of the war, when she'd overheard him begging the nuns of the E Street Infirmary to send him a nurse, and she'd taken advantage of that need and shown up at the Union Hotel Hospital insisting he take her on, the deep tones of his distinctive voice had not only chastened and challenged her, but also validated the notion that her intelligence was more valuable than gold, and her unexpected presence in his life a blessed, lucky thing. And on one crucial day at Fairfax Station, when thousands of wounded Union soldiers lay on damp, hay-covered hills, needing an evacuation that seemingly could not be accomplished, his impatience and fury had illuminated the inversion that triage was not cruelty but instead mercy, and that pity was not compassion but instead a useless waste of time. Now, he held her in his arms, and in that way they had of skipping a thousand unnecessary words, read her mind.

"This isn't Fairfax," he said.

"But this isn't the war. People don't just disappear."

"They do if they've gone into the river."

"William."

"But where else could they be, Mary?"

Where else indeed?

At the end of those two weeks, Mary was certain that Captain Mantel had grown tired of her. She recognized the signs: the weary sigh of recognition, the overly polite greeting, the fathomless volume of platitudes lobbed in her direction. *How good to. I've been thinking of. I admire your.* She had called on him daily, and once again early on Monday, March 24, after yet another fruitless weekend of searching. Out of necessity, William had reopened his clinic to patients, but Mary, they had decided, would go on looking. Or rather, Mary had decided. She would not let *missing* stand. She would look for Bonnie and David's children forever.

"But there must be something else you can do?" she implored Mantel now, ignoring the slightly disdainful turn of his lip. She noticed a faint smell of rum about him. She'd heard things, too: he lived in a far nicer house and had more money to spend than a police captain ought to. "Surely you can look harder. Surely there is some solution you haven't thought of yet."

"What more do you want me to do?" There was a new, brittle edge to Mantel's voice. "Pick up the cobblestones one by one and inspect their undersides? They're gone, madam. We have looked in every cranny of the city, just as you have. Most times, you'd been to a place even before we'd gotten there ourselves. There's nowhere else to look."

"That's not possible. There's always something else to be done."

"Listen to me. We kept watch for your young ones, we did. Stopped urchins on the street—you know, those ones that live in the hovels near the tracks and down by the gasworks. Asked after yours. We've done more than that, more than you can imagine."

"But—"

"If you don't mind my saying, madam, grief plays nasty tricks on people, especially when it's children that are perceived to be in trouble. I think it's time you come to terms, and if you cannot, you best head to Saratoga Springs to take a water cure, because you've gone out of your mind with grief. You've got to understand. You've got to believe it. They're gone, and no amount of anger at me is going to find them now."

Outside, Mary put a hand to the side of the brick building to steady herself.

In the twelve years of her marriage to William, children had never come for them. As a substitute for their longing, they had instead lavished attention on Elizabeth, and on Emma and Claire, too.

But now Emma and Claire had vanished.

And it seemed the river was the only explanation.

Chapter Three

Two days later, at four o'clock in the afternoon on March 26, in an apartment on the rue de Rivoli in Paris, Amelia Sutter looked out an open casement window overlooking the Tuileries and the avenue below. A finely boned woman, she had grown slightly fleshy at the waist with age, and in this angled light her face revealed deep lines earned by myriad decades working as a midwife. Amelia considered herself very fortunate. She had rented this high-ceilinged, wainscoted apartment from Elizabeth's former French teacher in Albany, Madame Hubbard, who was French and the wife of a former diplomat to Paris. Madame Hubbard was a practical woman who from time to time suspected her husband of infidelity, and she retained the apartment in case she one day felt compelled to return to the French capital, though she had readily leased it to Amelia a year and a half ago when Elizabeth had auditioned for a place at the Paris Conservatoire.

Recently, Elizabeth had implored her grandmother to let her travel to and from the Conservatoire alone, and despite some trepidation, Amelia had conceded. As the mother of Mary Sutter Stipp, Amelia knew when to give in to an intrepid and stubborn young woman, though in Paris, as in Albany, young women ordinarily did not travel alone and they certainly didn't take the omnibus alone. But, as Elizabeth herself had argued, she was a Sutter, or at least the daughter of a Sutter, and Sutter women had been driving themselves hither, thither, and yon for an eon. No adhering to societal expectations for Sutter women—Sutter women took care of themselves; Sutter women bore up at all times.

And so for the last few months, Amelia had awaited her granddaughter's return from her classes not outside the tall double doors of the Conservatoire at no. 2 rue Bergère, but at this window, enjoying a cup of tea, admiring the beautiful view, and reading *Le Figaro,* the premier Parisian newspaper, to improve her French. But she was uneasy today and had been for some time. It wasn't because they hadn't heard yet from Mary or Bonnie since news of the great northeastern blizzard had reached Paris; the mails and telegraph were said to be down, and only essential communications were being transmitted. It was instead because despite Elizabeth's daily protestations of well-being, Amelia had lately detected a new disquiet in the girl.

Certainly, Elizabeth no longer seemed the self-assured prodigy she had been at the end of October 1877, when they had traveled to Paris for her audition. At fifteen, she had stood alone on the stage of the conservatory's U-shaped performance hall—the first of its kind in the world and widely celebrated for its sublime acoustics—and played Viotti's complex Violin Concerto no. 17 in D minor with confidence and verve, earning unanimous high marks and immediate entry to Charles Girard's vigilant instruction. A faculty member, he was the most famous violinist in France—some might say infamous—and brilliant besides, but he was also exacting.

Gradually, over the year and a half under his charge, Elizabeth had stopped practicing as much, an unsettling development. And she had not been sleeping well, either. And though on Sunday she had played with distinction in one of the periodic public concerts in which only the most gifted students performed, and had earned a standing ovation for her solo, afterward at home Elizabeth had turned critical of her performance, dissolved into tears, and slammed the door of her room. It sometimes occurred to Amelia that perhaps Bonnie should have accompanied Elizabeth to Paris instead. Elizabeth adored Bonnie and shared confidences with her, and Bonnie's pride in Elizabeth's prodigious talents pleased the girl the most. But of course Bonnie had her own family and her millinery shop to take care of.

Amelia took a sip of tea, thinking through the problem of Elizabeth's unhappiness. Perhaps a leave of absence was in order—or a holiday. They could travel to Italy or Nice, where the girl could sort herself out. Elizabeth had grown so temperamental that it was often hard to know how to put things, but she would offer the prospect of time away anyway, because something had to be done.

There was a brief tap at the outer door and within a moment the housemaid, Flavie, a discreet, elfin young woman, appeared carrying a telegram on a silver plate.

Amelia opened the envelope, expecting a confirmation from Albany that all was well.

> *Bonnie and David dead in blizzard. Emma and Claire missing. Delayed in informing you in hope of finding them. All hope now gone. We are heartbroken. Will bury at thaw. Sending our deepest love.*

The mulberry trees in the Tuileries, just budding, blurred as if they had been drowned in a deluge. Amelia put a hand to the arm of the chair, tried to get up, sat back down again.

"Madame?"

"Bonnie. And the girls—oh, the girls. And David. How will I tell Elizabeth?" Amelia said.

Flavie knelt beside Amelia, her black dress puddling on the lush threads of the Turkish carpet. *"Êtes vous malade, madame?"*

Amelia couldn't find the words in French, though Flavie was right. She did feel ill. "Emma and Claire. They're so little. *Petites.*"

"Qui, madame?" Who?

Flavie was still holding Amelia's hand when Elizabeth unlocked the apartment door, her rosewood violin case tucked under her arm. She removed her gloves and set them on the marble-topped table by the door, then looked up.

"Grandmama? What is it, Grandmama? What's the matter?" Elizabeth sank into the chair opposite and set the violin case at her feet, her gray eyes widening. The pale afternoon light fell across the smooth skin of her face. Sometimes Elizabeth's beauty struck Amelia with such force that she forgot how young she was. At seventeen, she lacked the showy twinkle of velvet eyelashes or rose-splashed cheekbones, but she unfailingly brought to mind a Botticelli or a da Vinci. Or, sometimes, her deceased mother.

"Darling," Amelia said. She was measuring her words. "Bonnie and David—Mary has written—"

Elizabeth went white. "What?"

How careful Amelia had always been in matters of death, to leave mothers of stillborns in her care under no illusions. But what other way was there to tell the news? The O'Donnells were gone. "Lizzie, darling. Bonnie and David have died."

"What? No."

"I don't know the particulars. It's something to do with the blizzard."

"They died?"

"Yes."

"When?"

"During the storm, I think."

Elizabeth absorbed the news with a stillness that terrified Amelia. Her granddaughter lifted a gaze turned dull and unseeing. "But

Emma and Claire? Are they all right? Aunt Mary and Uncle William have them?"

Amelia hesitated.

"Tell me, Grandmama."

"I am told they are lost."

"Lost?"

Amelia handed Elizabeth the telegram, which she still held in her hand. After reading it, Elizabeth looked up and said again, *"Lost?"*

Within a week, Elizabeth reported that she had negotiated a leave of absence from the Conservatoire, and within another week, Amelia had booked their passage on the SS *France* of the General Trans-Atlantic Company at Le Havre, bound for Manhattan City, to arrive on April 12.

Just before boarding, Amelia sent a telegram to Mary and William from the dingy steamship offices on the windy quay at Le Havre, informing them to expect their arrival in Albany on Sunday, April 13, on the 12:55 New York Central Express, without fail. Later that night, as the steamship plowed through the choppy gray waters of the English Channel, the hum of the indefatigable twin screws reverberating through their small cabin, Amelia would not admit to herself that she had waited until their plans were irreversible to telegraph. She had no doubt that had Mary been chaperoning Elizabeth in Paris, her stalwart daughter would have refused the girl's petitions to return home, naming perseverance and courage and dedication as reasons to stay. But Amelia was not Mary. She had known too much grief in her lifetime not to understand that Elizabeth's inconsolable sorrow over the loss of the O'Donnells was too much for her now. The girl had changed. Something unknowable had rendered this once devoted musician utterly indifferent to her once all-consuming passion.

Asleep now in the small bed in the alcove of their cabin, Elizabeth looked so much like her deceased mother that Amelia, observing Elizabeth from her vantage point at the porthole window, had to grip an armchair to keep herself upright. Amelia would never stop missing Jenny, dead now seventeen years, would never forget the hours of her daughter's complicated labor that had overwhelmed even her expertise. Ironically, Elizabeth, whose birthday they had recently marked with a sugary cake from the tiny bakery in the Palais-Royale, had been born during a blizzard that had delayed a more gifted Mary from getting to her twin sister's bedside to deliver her until it was too late.

Amelia thought now how much she despised winter.

She wiped fresh tears from her eyes. This was how people kept on, wasn't it? You got on with things. If you wallowed in remembrance, every day was a crucible in which your past exploded into your present. It was how she managed to rise from her bed every morning. Why she forgave everyone nearly everything. At sixty, half the people she had loved had left her. Her son Christian, her daughter Jenny, her husband Nathaniel. She lived now for what was, not for what had once been. After all, what was growing older but a reminder of the loss of everyone you had ever loved? But losing Bonnie, too, and those darling girls was more than she thought she could bear, for Elizabeth's sake. Emma and Claire had been like little sisters to Elizabeth.

Mary would have been wrong to deny Elizabeth this break for grief. The Conservatoire—the violin—could wait. In late summer, surely no later, they would return to Paris, and a refreshed Elizabeth would resume her march toward excellence. Exhausted, Amelia washed her face, snuffed the oil lamp, and settled against the pillows just as the ship entered the open sea.

Chapter Four

The 12:55 Express pulled into the NY Central Railroad Depot at Albany with a burst of steam, trailing soot and dirty clods of snow. Mary and William searched the windows of the cars for Amelia and Elizabeth, but all was chaos and disruption as a flurry of porters and passengers converged on the platform. William climbed on top of a crate and spied his mother-in-law and niece waiting sensibly by a pillar near one of the depot doors, calmly surveying the crowd while passersby took surreptitious note of the curved line of Elizabeth's hat and the trim tidiness of Amelia's bustle. Parisian finery in Albany was rarely seen, and the two had not yet donned mourning, having had no time in the haste of leaving to order a black dress from the seamstress or to dye one of theirs.

Amelia folded Mary into her arms as if Mary were the one returning from a long trip, and Mary surrendered to the maternal affection with a convulsive shudder. Only a mother, Mary thought, could render a grown woman or man a child again, even if only for a moment.

Mary pulled away and embraced her mother in turn. Grief had diminished Amelia. Her gray locks had escaped their pins; creases lined her pale face, and her eyes had hooded and wrinkled with age.

"You shouldn't have come, Mama. But I'm so glad to see you."

"Bonnie was as much a daughter to me as she was sister to you. And Elizabeth couldn't stay away. What is the news?"

Mary shook her head, unwilling to lay out the particulars at the crowded depot, or before Elizabeth, who was weeping quietly on William's shoulder. He unbuttoned his topcoat and reached into his vest pocket for a handkerchief.

Elizabeth broke from his embrace to turn to Mary with a defensive, questioning glance, leading Mary to wonder whether Elizabeth had overheard her admonition that they ought not to have come.

Mary had questioned their return, and did still, for the reason that Elizabeth would suffer the same grief in Paris as in Albany, but there, she could keep up her studies, while here she would be mostly idle, and far more susceptible to the ravages of sorrow, reminded everywhere of the O'Donnells' deaths. Still, it was lovely to see them, and she took her sister's child into her arms. As happened from time to time, Mary, like her mother, caught sight of her twin sister's ghost lurking in Elizabeth's sublime features. The resemblance always startled her, but though Elizabeth's cheeks might be more plump than her mother's and her lashes less full, she still resembled her mother so much that Mary sometimes felt haunted.

Elizabeth yielded only slightly to Mary's embrace before pulling quickly away.

"Of course you are tired," Mary said. "Harold is waiting with the carriage."

That night, they took refuge around the oak dining table, long ago sandwiched into the small nook off the kitchen so that Mary could have the dining room as her clinic. They were contemplating a curl of steam rising from a soup tureen that the insistent Vera had deposited in the middle of the table next to a cobalt blue teapot. Candles flickered, lit by Vera, though outside a fine spring gloaming hovered. It was soothing to be taken care of, to bask in the shafts of evening light streaming through the window, to sip strong Russian caravan tea, and to fortify themselves with Vera's meaty borscht. Outside, an early thrush was trilling from a leafless branch of the maple tree, while in the kitchen, the oven door screeched as it opened, a hint of cinnamon wafting in the air. Vera had baked an apple pie, from last autumn's cellared fruit.

Why was it, Mary thought, that beauty and horror always met side by side, magnifying one other?

To protect Elizabeth, Mary and William blurred the specifics as they told of their search, but the hoped-for salutary effect failed.

"I should never have gone," Elizabeth said.

"To Paris?" Mary said. "Of course you should have."

"No. I should have waited. The conservatory could have waited. Going was such a mistake."

"My darling girl," William said. "You could not have known what would happen. We wanted you to go. Bonnie wanted you to go. She was so proud of you. You could not have predicted such a storm."

"But I would have had more time with them. Instead, I wasted my time—"

"How can you say that? You didn't waste anything," Mary said.

Elizabeth ignored her. "What time do we begin looking tomorrow? I'll help."

Mary glanced at William, who shook his head at her, but Mary pressed. "Looking?"

"For Emma and Claire."

"But we've already looked everywhere. We did everything we could."

"But we have to keep looking. They could be anywhere."

Mary recalled Captain Mantel's harsh words, his dismissive, mocking tone when she had uttered the same protestations. "I know it's hard to accept. It was for us, too. But we—and the police—we've looked every single place they could be—two, three times."

"Bonnie and David would never stop searching," Elizabeth said.

The pronouncement came as a slap across Mary's face, echoing her own vow of just a few weeks ago.

"I know this is difficult, but when you go back to Paris," Mary said, "you might find that—"

"I'm never going back."

Mary glanced at Amelia. "That's just the grief speaking. Don't abandon—"

"You don't understand," Elizabeth said. "You're good at everything. But I am a failure."

William met Mary's eyes, and again shook his head. But Mary couldn't let the girl believe such an outrageous thing. "No, you're not. Your grandmother's letters were full of news of your achievements—"

Elizabeth jumped from her seat and threw down her napkin. "That is always what you say. You always say, *We did everything that we could.* You always say, *Don't turn your back on your gift.*"

"Lizzie! What is the matter?"

But the girl swept past Mary and up the back stairs, her footsteps clattering on the polished wood.

Amelia reached an unsteady hand across the table to Mary.

"Did she just say that she quit?" Mary said.

"She told me she obtained a leave of absence."

"Did you verify that?"

"No, I didn't," Amelia said, drawing herself up. "I didn't check up on her because I don't check up on anyone. I am not the one enrolled in the conservatory. Something has been bothering her. She hasn't been herself lately. When your telegram came, I was already thinking she ought to get away."

William looked on, loath to intervene between mother and daughter.

"But did you know what she'd done?" Mary said.

"I didn't, but as Lizzie said, everyone is not you. Leave her be."

With a great swish of her wide skirts, Vera came clucking into the room with the fragrant pie, her hands swathed in a towel against the hot pan. She set the pastry before them and stood back. Taking in their glum faces at a glance, she muttered something indecipherable in Russian and whisked away the tureen. Returning within moments with the sherry decanter, she distributed three crystal glasses, poured far too much into each, and said, "Drink something."

Chapter Five

The Sutter plot in Albany Rural Cemetery occupied a portion of Bower Hill that overlooked a sparse stand of white oaks and Indian Lake, which had been fashioned from damming Kromme Kill, one of the brooks that meandered through the burying ground. It was now six weeks since the blizzard, and still the last traces of snow had not melted, but here and there tulips and daffodils had broken through the warming soil and unfurled their tapered greenery and hard buds. And though this late in April, ice still blocked the Hudson—another unusual circumstance in this surprising year—the cemetery had sent word that the ground had given away enough to allow burials to begin.

Mary was moving among the graves, purging the aging tombstones of stray rhizoids of the delicate, tenacious lichen that clung to the gray slabs. The plot boasted a flowering dogwood, not yet in bloom, under which Christian's and Jenny's gravestones bracketed their father's. Jenny lay beside her husband, Thomas. A granite statue of two entwined cherubs had been placed next to the two open graves into which Bonnie's and David's caskets had already been lowered. Last week, Mary and Amelia had cleaned out the O'Donnells' flat and Bonnie's shop, a bleak task that had plunged them deeper into misery. Lately, everything they did seemed to bear the mark of finality.

The minister waited until Mary finished her tidying rounds and joined William, Amelia, and Elizabeth before the open graves. The metallic scent of the upturned dirt played on Mary's tongue, reminding her of the smell of blood, that lingering vestige from the war that had never left her. On the other side of the plot's low picket fence, two sweaty gravediggers were leaning on their shovels, waiting for the service to end.

The gilt-edge pages of the minister's open prayer book riffled in the cool wind as he began the liturgy. They had placed a notice in the *Argus* that the graveside service would be private, for they had feared that all of the Lumber District would have turned out, including the society women who loved Bonnie's hats, to say nothing of Emma's and Claire's schoolmates. Despite these efforts, they were not completely alone. Since the war, a new rage for cemetery visits had arisen, out of grief or curiosity or both. This funereal tourism had the unfortunate effect of intruding on the serenity of mourners everywhere, who unwittingly became part of a pastoral tableau. On any given day, an endless parade of sightseers traversed Albany Rural Cemetery's serpentine lanes in their carriages, consulting their *Appletons' Guides* on the monuments and mausoleums of distinction, and today was no exception. To the creak of passing carriages, the minister read the burial service, holding one hand aloft when he bestowed a blessing. During the last prayer, the family threw roses they had purchased at the cemetery greenhouse onto the coffins.

> In sure and certain hope of the resurrection to eternal life, through our Lord Jesus Christ, we commend to almighty God our brother and sister in Christ Bonnie and David O'Donnell and we commit their bodies to the ground, earth to earth, ashes to ashes, dust to dust.

There were no bodies to commit for the girls. For a moment, the minister seemed at a loss. Elizabeth broke into tears.

Earlier that morning, when Mary happened on Elizabeth on the veranda, where each had gone in search of a moment alone before the long carriage ride to the cemetery, Mary had suggested that Elizabeth might want to play the violin at the graveside. Since Elizabeth's return four days earlier, her instrument had been collecting dust under her bed. Nor had Elizabeth been sleeping since she'd come back; Mary often heard her creep downstairs in the middle of the night, the rasp of the bathroom door as it shut, and an onrush of water splashing in the sink.

"You might find solace in playing," Mary hazarded. "You know how the girls and Bonnie loved—"

Elizabeth's retort was sharp, abrupt. "No, Aunt. I'm out of practice."

Taken aback, Mary directed her gaze across the street, where beyond a wrought iron fence Washington Park still projected itself as more of an idea than a full-fledged preserve. The land had once housed the city's burying grounds, and at least forty thousand bodies had been exhumed in the fifties and transported to the newly established Albany Rural Cemetery. When finished, the park promised to be a long rectangle of green, its new, man-made lake a magnet for recreational boating and its numerous graveled paths a verdant refuge for a city-weary public. Several acres of the fledgling park boasted decorative parterres for flowers, and dozens of saplings had been planted in the last few years under a preexisting canopy of older elms and maples, but a good portion of it still consisted of patches of weeds and hillocks of dirt. The city was still reclaiming land. Although its eastern boundary of Willett Street was embroidered with newly built brownstones, down the street, a last line of condemned row houses within the park's boundary awaited demolition. At that very moment, men were gathering with sledgehammers and wheelbarrows, milling about the emptied houses, laying bets on who would make the bricks fall the fastest, their deep voices echoing in the early morning air.

"I *said,* I'm out of practice."

Mary turned, astonished. This—and last night's—belligerence was out of character for Elizabeth; she could be temperamental, but she was rarely confrontational.

"Lizzie, I know you're heartbroken. I am, too. We all are. But what is this about? Did something happen to you in Paris? Is that why you don't want to go back?"

Elizabeth just sighed in response and swept past Mary, slamming the front door behind her as the first blows of sledgehammers dinned in the distance. This, Mary thought, was what came from decades of hearing people utter secrets during labor or the last gasps of a suffocating illness. *I love another man, another woman. I can't have another child or I'll go mad. My father hurts me.* It made Mary believe that people always wanted to confide in her.

Now, in the cemetery, sunlight caught the rounded shoulders and wings of the granite cherubs as Elizabeth wept. The minister was frantically turning pages in search of something fitting to say, finding at last a vague prayer of dedication and benediction as they stooped to lay their last roses at the base of the statue. The gravediggers readied their shovels and the minister offered Amelia his arm to guide the group down the hillside, bearing their grief in the practiced, weary curve of his shoulders.

At the bottom of the rise, an open carriage had drawn next to theirs. Standing before it, a diminutive woman was framed by two men, one older and one younger. The younger man bore six enormous bouquets of flowers. As the family approached, the older man came forward, removing a gray top hat to reveal a bald pate.

"We are sorry to intrude, but we saw the notice in the paper. We couldn't stay away. Allow me to introduce myself. I am Gerritt Van der Veer."

Although the Stipps were well acquainted with Albert Van der

Veer, Gerritt's distant cousin and a surgeon at Albany Hospital, the Stipps had never met Gerritt, though of course they knew of him by reputation. In person there was nothing distinctive about the prominent man except a hoarse, gravelly voice—no doubt acquired from years of screaming orders into the vast expanse of his lumber lot—and a bulldog stature that belied his wealth. Dressed less richly, he could have been mistaken for a common laborer, but in his beautifully tailored gray frockcoat and vest, he looked every inch a gentleman.

"I considered David O'Donnell the best man on my lot. We lost a few men in that blizzard, but we will miss David the most. I—we—are grievously sorry for your loss. Please forgive our tardiness. We would have arrived much earlier, but our horse Dolly threw a shoe. We had to leave her at that traveler's livery on Broadway and exchange her for that sorry beast." He gestured to a spotted mare harnessed to the polished carriage, and then to the woman at his side. "This is my wife, Viola, who has told me that Mrs. O'Donnell made the most beautiful hats in Albany. I believe my wife must have spent a fortune in her shop."

One could almost imagine, from the right angle, that Viola Van der Veer was a child playing dress up. Under her wrap, her shoulders were little more than the width of a pair of hands set finger to finger, and her waist could easily be encircled by one arm. A flat chest had been disguised by a flock of ruffles, meticulously placed and gathered to give the appearance of a bust. Her skin was luminous and unmarked by the sun, and her large dark eyes were framed with thick, black lashes. The doll-like woman carried a consciousness of her lingering beauty, as beautiful women always did, certain of acceptance, reliant on the kind of favor that they received because of it. But in Viola, that easy, unexpected elegance combined with a hint of juvenile insecurity, making her seem less than what she was: the wife of the wealthiest man in town and the daughter of one of the richest men in Manhattan City. It was rumored in Albany circles that their engagement had been hasty and their marriage swift, at the behest of Viola's father, a shipping magnate who was eager to marry off his youngest daughter so that he and his wife could finally withdraw from Manhattan's tiresome social scene. It was said that he had discharged his last paternal duty with a booster's admiration for Gerritt's ambition while ignoring his rougher edges. Perhaps that was the reason for the hint of insecurity, but Viola Van der Veer immediately defied Mary's assessment by floating toward them, exuding kindness and concern.

"How do you do?" she said. "Please forgive our family's intrusion, but I adored Bonnie. She was always so kind to me. She used to put the CLOSED sign on the door and we would gossip over tea in her back room while she sketched designs for the new season. I miss her so much. She told me how fond she was of all of you. We really ought to have written you when it happened. And we are heartbroken about Emma and Claire. I never got the chance to meet them, but Bonnie never stopped talking about them, so I feel as if I knew them a little. You have our sincerest condolences." She extended a comforting hand to Mary's wrist before drawing the young man beside her close with a touch to his elbow. "Have you met my son, Jakob?"

Jakob Van der Veer was far taller than either of his parents, and his physique was that of a young man who heaved and cut and loaded lumber into ships on the Erie Canal all day long. It had recently been announced in the newspapers that he had graduated from Harvard with a law degree and was working in the yards to learn the trade before he joined his father at the helm of their prosperous endeavor. The article also said that for three summers running, starting when Jakob had been fourteen, his father had sent him deep into the Adirondacks to learn lumbering, even insisting that his workers take Jakob out onto the dangerous logjams on the rivers to teach him how to clear them. He appeared as strong as David O'Donnell had been, and his black frockcoat pulled at his wide shoulders.

Jakob offered Amelia, Mary, and Elizabeth each one of the large bouquets, which left him still holding three. The flowers were beautiful: white roses and baby's breath and several sprigs of freesia against a spray of light greenery, wrapped in tissue paper and tied with black ribbons. This early in the season, he must have gone to a great deal of trouble to obtain them.

"Please accept our sincerest sympathies," Jakob said. "David O'Donnell taught me everything I know about handling lumber. I would have been with him that day, except that I happened to be in the office with my father, going over the books. We were able to get home, unlike—well, we are sorry." Regret, or maybe shame, clouded his handsome features. He was apologizing for something over which he had no control, and this kindness endeared him to everyone.

"How kind of you to come," William said, tipping his hat. "I am William Stipp. May I introduce my wife, Dr. Mary Stipp, my mother-in-law, Mrs. Amelia Sutter, and my niece, Elizabeth Fall? And Reverend Miller, our minister."

There were more pleasantries all around, though Elizabeth was keeping to herself, comforted by Amelia, who had one arm around her waist.

"It is a great shame that I never had the pleasure of meeting Bonnie," Gerritt Van der Veer said. "Nor those girls. A tragedy, to lose those two. The blizzard was a terrible thing. But flood, you see, that's the real danger, especially for lumbermen. It's odd that it's always flood danger and never fire in the district, given the inflammability of our product, but we've been lucky there. No fires. But when a flood comes, losses like no one's business. We're due for a bad one, I think, after that blizzard. My men in the Adirondacks have told me that the snowpack is deep. A few days more of warm weather and it will flood out of the mountains.

"This won't be a mere freshet, either," Gerritt went on, unaware that everyone was staring at him, taken aback by his odd digression.

"Not like the usual spring flood. This one will be a torrent. It will come to steal our souls. If you own anything of importance near the river, take precautions. We—"

"We keep to higher ground," William said, turning to go, unwilling to endure more talk of disaster. While it was true that spring freshets regularly inundated Albany, Troy, and Watervliet, too, no one wanted to talk of that now.

Jakob, sensing William's displeasure, said, "Of course we won't keep you longer on this difficult day; however, if I may say one more thing? We are neighbors, are we not? Aren't you the owners of the lovely Victorian across the park from us? On Madison Avenue?"

"Yes," William said. "My wife and I work out of the house, too."

"The famous Doctors Stipp," Gerritt said.

"We are hardly famous," Mary said.

"You are in some circles," Gerritt said. "Dr. Stipp, with your Medal of Honor? You expect to hide?"

William nodded stiffly. He never spoke of it. The honor had come to him after Gettysburg, and because he did not like to be reminded of the war, he kept the medal in its velvet box in a dresser drawer. He wondered how Gerritt knew.

"And Mrs. Stipp is especially famous, or at least she was in my mother's view," Gerritt continued. "When Doctor Stipp— It's difficult keeping you two separate, isn't it? When Mrs. Stipp—*Mary*, if I may—left for the war, my mother thought her brilliant."

"And Miss Fall," Jakob interjected, before Mary could again deny any hint of fame, "are you not the young violin prodigy? The girl who went to Paris to study?"

Elizabeth, who had kept herself apart from the conversation, startled and looked up from her bouquet of flowers, too surprised to say anything.

"I thought so," Jakob said, taking her silence as acquiescence. "I read about you in the newspapers. And once, I heard you play at

Tweddle Hall. You were twelve, I think. I was sixteen then, in awe of your talent. I have not heard anything as beautiful since."

Elizabeth ducked her head and looked away. "Thank you."

"Have you finished with your studies?" Jakob said.

"I'm not certain," she murmured, her voice hardly audible.

Mary and William traded glances, and Jakob attempted no more compliments.

Viola said, "We are aware that you are still in mourning, but couldn't we all become better acquainted? Won't you come to tea or dinner sometime? It needn't be soon."

Her offer seemed as much plea as invitation.

Amelia accepted for all of them, but only after a fashion, murmuring vague thanks without being specific, and expressing gratitude for the flowers.

Gerritt lifted his hat, as did Jakob, who stole a last glance at Elizabeth before taking his mother by the elbow to follow his father, who was already striding up the hill toward the graves where the impatient gravediggers were at their work. As their driver, Harold, steered their carriage down the lane, Mary looked back again to see Viola and Jakob laying the remaining bouquets at the headstones, and Gerritt kneeling, tenderly placing one before the granite cherubs.

That night, neither William nor Mary could sleep. The wind had kicked up during dinner, and the maple tree outside was throwing haunting traces in the moonlight. William could see wisps of Mary's silver curls falling across her face. He never tired of the miracle of Mary at his side, the nighttime soft around them, their bed warm with their love. Fourteen years after the end of the war, twelve since they'd been married, and he still could not believe his good fortune. Nothing else good had come of the war for him, except an expertise in orthopedics, but that was nothing compared to Mary. God, how he loved her. Mary Sutter. Mary Sutter *Stipp*. He had to remember the Stipp part, because he always thought of her as Mary Sutter.

Mary broke the silence, speaking, as she often did, as if William had been privy to the raging conversation in her head. He never minded her habit of assuming that he understood what she had been thinking, because he often did.

Her voice caught as she said, "What if something else happened? Something—unimaginable."

It was the first time she'd voiced this darker prospect. She had hedged and gone silent upon leaving every orphanage, had postulated and suggested and wondered, but she had never before mentioned any outcome besides discovery or death. He himself believed that Emma and Claire were almost certainly dead, though he, too, wondered from time to time, waking in the middle of the night to imagine terrible things, achieving sanity again only at dawn. And though Mary had remained calm in the face of Elizabeth's continuing doubts, privately she was unable to lay to rest her own.

"What if we are all making an assumption?" Mary said. "What if Emma and Claire are still alive?"

Not even two granite angels had silenced the bounding unreason of hope. "Mary, where would they be? Someone would have found them."

Stalemate, again.

William lifted his gaze and watched the shadows of the maple branches play on the ceiling. "That Van der Veer boy seemed to be taken with Elizabeth."

"I hope not. She doesn't need another reason to stay in Albany."

"He seems kind enough."

Mary sighed. "She can't give up."

"The girl is suffering," William said. "You must keep in mind how young she is. I think we forget that sometimes."

"She is not that young. And she is on the cusp of greatness. Mother told me that they had rarely seen such promise."

To distract his persistent wife from worrying about her niece, William said, "Gerritt and Viola are odd ducks, don't you think?"

"Yes. So odd. And all that babbling about flooding? What was that about? It was good of them to come, though. But do you know that Bonnie never said a word to me about Viola, which is a little sad, considering that Viola seems to have been so fond of her. I liked her though, far more than I liked him. I suspect hidden depths, though I am not sure why."

From the hallway came the sound once again of Elizabeth padding down the stairs. They heard her up at least once a night, sometimes more, her tentative steps quiet on the floorboards as she endeavored not to wake them.

"Tomorrow," Mary said, "I'm going to reopen the downtown clinic. It's Thursday, after all. And those women have nowhere else to go."

Downstairs, water ran in the sink, the copper plumbing banging softly in the walls.

"I fear you are tempting fate with that other clinic of yours," William said.

"No one will find out. Oh, William, I could not bear seeing those granite angels today," she said, her voice soft against his cheek. "I wish we knew what happened. I'd accept anything, I think, just to know."

William believed they would never know. And he did not know how to carry that pain. How to mitigate the *not knowing.* Not for Mary, not for Amelia, and certainly not for Elizabeth. He lay very still, conscious of the softening rhythm of Mary's breath, the warm cushion of her breasts. For a man who had long ago given up his belief in God, he prayed now that his love would be enough to comfort them all.

Chapter Six

In the bedroom across the hall from Mary and William's, Elizabeth Fall returned from using the bathroom downstairs and slid her rosewood violin case out from underneath her bed and unlocked it. Taking care not to pop the single latch for fear of making a telltale noise, she eased it open as the pungent scent of rosin wafted up. Since her return, the violin had languished in its glossy case, the bow buttoned into its leather sheath. Had she possessed the wherewithal, she would have stuffed the cursed thing into the back of the armoire, or better yet given it away, but such action would have required the resolve that had incinerated in Monsieur Girard's studio.

Would you like to play the violin? Mary had asked.

Elizabeth knew she had sounded like a petulant child this morning, and at the cemetery she had become furious with herself. Emma and Claire had loved to listen to her play—and so had Bonnie. It still seemed impossible that Bonnie and David had died, that Emma and Claire were gone.

But what was *gone*? Gone was not buried. Gone was nothing.

And she hadn't even been able to set aside her embarrassment and shame to play for them one last time.

In Paris, unknown to Elizabeth, the director of the Conservatoire had assigned her to Monsieur Girard without his consent. She'd been thrilled. To study under such a master! But she soon learned that Girard wasn't happy about being assigned to "*la fille américaine,*" as he called her. *The American girl.*

Little by little, month by month, he set about stripping her of confidence.

In session after session, he complained of her bowing or fingering, or if he were especially irritated, her musicality: *Oh for God's sake, don't you feel it? The warmth? The enticement? Give into it. Oh, at least try. Do this*—he would say, placing his hand between her shoulder blades—*Imagine my hand as the sun on the hills of Sienna, the blazing scorch of evening light on Italian stucco, the day's lingering warmth in vineyard grapes. No. Not that way. You are failing the music, can't you see? Play the piece again. And for God's sake, mind the tempo. It is as if you have just begun playing. Can't you hear the shift in tone?*

Occasionally, he dismissed her from her lesson early with a gesture of disgust. She would never achieve greatness, never communicate the warmth of Rossini, the fluidity of Verdi. She was a disgrace and would never excel. He maintained this assessment even though she was held up for admiration in her other classes, selected to play in special school concerts, and often praised by the director.

But Girard's was the voice she believed, and still heard.

His criticism broke her heart, for from the moment she had first heard the instrument, it had become both love and haven. It was William who had introduced it to her, just after her father died.

She had been young, six years old, when her father succumbed to his war wound, his bed awash with fever and infection. No one knew then that the pressure of the wooden legs on the stumps of amputees would eventually kill them. Once, Elizabeth had asked her father why half his leg was wooden. He'd knocked the golden oak of his right shin and grinned. "When I was in the war, after Antietam, your clever Aunt Mary saved my life by exchanging my old, bad leg for this new, wooden one."

Mary later explained to Elizabeth that her father's wound imitated a bedsore, but Elizabeth had had no idea what stealthy trouble that innocuous-sounding ailment posed. It seemed that so many of the medical complications after the war erupted out of nowhere: fixes that suddenly betrayed, unresolved issues that lingered then pounced, infections from embedded, intractable minié balls, digestive impairments that ultimately starved their victims, deformities that hobbled and crippled. Aunt Mary and Uncle William often despaired of these outcomes.

Later, too, they would tell her that she became inconsolable when her father died. They were living in Manhattan City then. Six years old, and she wouldn't eat, not even for Bonnie, whose ministrations rarely failed. So one snowy night, William lifted Elizabeth into the carriage, tucked a traveling blanket around her, told her that a talented woman would play a violin and that the music would help her to forget her unhappiness. But from the moment the first taps of the kettledrums floated into the auditorium of the Academy of Music, and the violin's strains swelled, Elizabeth began to weep and could not stop. Alarmed, her uncle carried her outside, but she cried loudly to be taken back, creating a scene. William returned with her to their seats and held her on his lap, trying to comfort her.

Afterward, she begged to meet the violinist. William fought his way to the proscenium where Camilla Urso, a French expatriate, stood accepting bouquet after bouquet. Elizabeth held out her hand to be touched. Impressed, Urso invited Elizabeth to visit her the next day in her suite at The Fifth Avenue Hotel. There, a steam lift carried them up six floors to a beautiful room full of opulent furnishings and windows that overlooked the avenue.

"I was seven years old when I first attended the Conservatoire de Paris," Mademoiselle Urso said, offering them each a cup of tea. "You are seven, yes, aren't you, Elizabeth?"

"Six."

"You are the only other little girl I have ever met who weeps at music. I am the other. But does your weeping mean that you wish to play, or that you wish only to meet the people who make the music that makes you weep?"

"She is all of six years old," William said. "Perhaps she is not yet certain what she wants."

"Ah, but I know desire." Mademoiselle Urso set her teacup and saucer on the low table between them and coaxed Elizabeth to a corner of the room. She pulled her gleaming violin from its case, put the bow to the strings, and breathed a single thread of beauty into the echoing room: Pachelbel, the Canon in D, a tune as evocative and haunting as the night wind. Elizabeth again began to weep.

"Do you see?" Mademoiselle Urso said. "She weeps at nuance. She knows what she wants. Don't you, Elizabeth?"

Elizabeth didn't want nuance, whatever that was, she wanted her father back. But when Mademoiselle Urso played, her grief found comforting expression.

"When Elizabeth has exhausted her teachers here, as I know she will, I suggest Paris."

William placed a warm hand on Elizabeth's shoulder. "But we don't know whether or not she has any aptitude."

This practical objection did not seem to matter to Mademoiselle Urso. She shrugged and said, "She will play and she will play well. Now, you must excuse me. I need to begin my practice for tonight, and if I go past two o'clock in the afternoon, the napping matrons in the hotel complain." She kissed Elizabeth on her wet cheek and walked them to the door.

Early the next week, Elizabeth began lessons with a teacher at the New York Academy, who, after a year, passed her on to a new instructor when Elizabeth exhausted both his repertoire and skill.

Would that Monsieur Girard had recused himself, Elizabeth thought now.

She had written Bonnie about Monsieur Girard's disparagement, but now Bonnie was gone. And Elizabeth could never tell her accomplished Aunt Mary anything of her failure. And how would Uncle William look at her if he knew the truth about her? In Paris, Elizabeth had tried to tell Amelia, but she had been unable to form the words. Girard's disapproval had intensified, and Elizabeth had pretended that everything was fine, and then had come the reprieve of the telegram.

Even Jakob Van der Veer believed her to be something she wasn't.

She flipped shut the lid and snapped the clasp as a final hint of rosin floated in the air. Unable to even think of sleeping, she slipped out into the hallway and again padded down the stairs. Her grandmother was sitting in the dark in the parlor. She gestured to Elizabeth to join her. Her gray hair was braided down her back, and she wore a warm robe over her nightgown that felt soft as Elizabeth laid her head on her shoulder.

"You haven't been sleeping, have you, Lizzie?"

"No."

"You weren't toward the end in Paris, either, were you?"

Elizabeth shook her head.

"Do you want to tell me what the matter is?"

She shook her head again.

"It's very hard," Amelia said. "I know how much you loved Bonnie and David and the girls. I did, too. Some days I can hardly breathe, thinking of everyone we've lost. But you must try to live, if you can. Do you see?"

Elizabeth felt tears welling in her eyes. "No."

"But, darling. You must at least try. Will you promise me?"

"I can't." Elizabeth's voice broke. "I don't know what to do."

"Practice," Amelia said. "Practice being alive."

"Practice being alive?" Elizabeth said.

"Yes. If you can. Try. Please? Can you do that?"

"I don't know," Elizabeth said, and got up and left the room without another word.

Chapter Seven

In truth, Albany's architectural elegance was concentrated only on State Street and around the capitol building, the vistas that dominated postcards and guidebooks. Since the war, a denser, homelier hodgepodge of five- and six-story brick and clapboard buildings had mushroomed on the lesser streets running up from the river and away from the grand, central boulevard. Down one of these dank, narrow alleyways, just a stone's throw from the elegant Delavan House, the premier hotel in the city, Mary had rented a forlorn room in a marginal state of repair where on Thursday mornings she treated Albany's prostitutes. She had started the practice when they returned from Manhattan City, when she realized that every hospital in the city, including City Hospital, where she and William were on staff, turned prostitutes away from their doors, even when they were in dire need, and especially if they were suffering from a botched abortion. Mary did not perform that procedure, even when the women begged, but she offered to deliver their babies, and frequently did. But because the police considered offering care to a prostitute aiding and abetting a criminal, Mary was the only doctor in Albany who would treat them.

The clinic's only advertisement was a diminutive red cross that she affixed above the door outside, small enough not to draw the eye, but large enough to be a signal to those in the know. Mary was certain the International Red Cross would not mind the appropriation. After all, Mary believed her clients suffered the same need as did any soldier of war.

The room boasted two windows situated high enough to block the view of anyone passing. She had partitioned off a part of the room with a burlap curtain to provide at least the illusion of privacy, a foreign commodity to the women she served. Furnished simply, the room contained several chairs, an exam table, an instrument cabinet, and a wide table set next to the rudimentary sink, into which she had plumbed a line at some expense. The new faucet piped river water, which needed boiling to thwart typhoid, so she kept two kettles simmering at all times on the coal stove.

On Thursdays, Mary always arrived at half past eight to light the stove, boil the water, and resupply her stash of carbolic soap and clean towels before she opened at nine. But today she arrived much earlier, for just as she had feared, her long absence after Emma's and Claire's disappearance had caused the room to go to must. Surveying the exposed brick of the walls, she discovered a cluster of roaches nesting in a damp corner. After battling these with the business end of a broom, she scrubbed the rough stone floor, dusted away cobwebs, and wiped down everything with a soaped rag, even climbing on a chair to wash a film of grime from the high window. But no matter how primitive this clinic was, it still surpassed the facilities of the Union Hotel Hospital during the war, where she had had to be everything—scullery maid, housekeeper, and nurse.

Satisfied with her preparations, Mary lit a kerosene lantern and hung it on its hook outside. Alerted by this signal, it did not take more than fifteen minutes for women to straggle in by ones and twos, clutching woolen shawls over their exposed shoulders. Within a half an hour of opening, twelve women had gathered, and once inside they slouched against the walls, their eyes following Mary about the room. Unadorned by face paint and the cheap satin of their working attire, the women nonetheless wore their hard lives in their sallow skin and rheumy eyes. Their sickly appearance always shocked Mary. Three years ago, when she had first begun, it had upset her to learn that a prostitute's average life span after beginning in the trade was just four years. They aged quickly, and died quickly, too.

"Where have you been?"

This sullen question was uttered by a woman who called herself Darlene—*Darling*—a name chosen long ago after having discarded her real name to save herself from any memory of who she had once been. They all had names like that—*Honey, Sweetie, Clementine*—names crafted of fantasy and sweetness when their lives were anything but. They all said their last names were Addison, a name they gave when they were arrested. So many women named Mrs. Addison had been arrested for prostitution in the past few years in Albany that the police had given up trying to extract the truth from them. Still, it was better than the name Mary Balls, the previous incarnation of a shared name, a sly joke that had infuriated the police when, after many times of carefully inscribing it in the police ledger, they finally caught on.

A plump woman past thirty, Darlene had pinned her hennaed hair carelessly this morning into a ragged snood. "Where?" she said again.

"I apologize," Mary said. "It wasn't my intention to abandon you. But I had something important to attend to." As a rule, Mary told them as little as possible about herself. She was their caretaker, not they hers, and when they pried, she answered their questions as cordially and obscurely as possible. Even now, when she believed they would readily accept her more than acceptable excuse for desertion, she preferred to reveal nothing.

"Seems like you could have warned us," Darlene said, hugging her arms to her chest. A feverish sheen glistened on her forehead. "I traipsed down here three Thursdays in a row looking for you before I gave up."

"Didn't you see the notice I tacked up to say it would be a while before I could return?"

"Well, if I could read, then I would have, wouldn't I?"

"I'm sorry," Mary said. She didn't begrudge Darlene her anger; Mary had been loath to keep the clinic closed, but she'd had only enough energy to keep the house clinic open. And for weeks after the blizzard, snow had made travel treacherous. "Now, who can I help first?"

The door burst open and a thin woman named Glynnis—Mary could never discern whether she was just thin or truly emaciated—hurried in, carrying her five-year-old daughter, Maude, whom she was raising in the whorehouse where they lived. That morning, Glynnis had discovered Maude lying on the attic floor where they slept with the other inmates of the house in cots lined up under the eaves. The listless child was drooling excessively and breathing loudly, as if through a narrow pipe. Within seconds, Mary performed an examination and diagnosed quinsy, a throat abscess that was causing Maude's tonsil to swell.

Quickly, Mary set up for the minor surgery, arranging her instruments and washing the back of Maude's throat with borax. The child was so feverish that she did not protest. With ease, Mary was able to nick the abscess with a scalpel, irrigate the girl's mouth of the draining pus, and deliver her into her relieved mother's arms, the whole thing from exam to execution taking perhaps five minutes.

Only then did Mary notice that her audience was gaping at her. Perhaps, she thought, she ought to have pulled the burlap curtain.

She washed her hands and asked who was next.

Darlene lurched forward and held out her arms, revealing that the reason for her earlier disgruntlement was that she was in pain. A drunken client had slashed the underbelly of her forearms with a razor. This time Mary did draw the curtain before washing the festering wounds with carbolic soap, noting as she did that Darlene's hair was riddled with lice.

"People count on you, you know," Darlene said as Mary scrubbed. "You disappear and we all wonder whether you're ever going to come back. What would have happened to Glynnis's girl if you hadn't been here?"

"I will always come back, Darlene. How long ago did this happen?"

"Saturday. Friday. I can't remember."

Five days, then, at least. If Mary had gotten to the cuts earlier, she could have stitched them, but now it was too late. "You must wash these every day. Do you have any carbolic soap?"

Darlene shrugged.

"I'll give you a bar. Boil your water, then let it cool before you begin. And I'll give you a bottle of Lice-Bane, too. Wash your hair in it twice."

Darlene nodded in a distracted way. "What kind of problem takes more than an entire month to fix? Were you sick? You don't look sick."

"Something personal."

"As if my arms aren't personal. Or my legs. Or my hoochie. All of what you and every man in Albany has seen."

Mary patted Darlene's plump forearms with a clean towel, taking special care with the ridge of heat and redness surrounding the long, jagged cuts. "Soap, do you understand?" she said. "Soap. Wash these every day."

"It's been more than a month, hasn't it?" Darlene said, studying her. "Wasn't that when the blizzard hit?"

"Hold still," Mary said, winding bandages around the woman's forearms.

"You lost someone, didn't you?" Darlene persisted. "I can tell. Anyone who ignores questions has answers they don't want to let on."

Mary tied off the last bandage and washed her hands.

"If it's true, then that's nothing but a damn shame."

No one had said anything as blatant since the girls had gone. Mary shut off the faucet, dried her hands, and rooted out a roll of gauze and the bar of soap and handed them to Darlene. "Get someone to help you, if you can."

"Who?"

Mary shook her head, knowing that Darlene was not asking for suggestions about who should help her.

"Did they die?"

Mary looked up at the window, to the cool rays of the morning sun filtering through the glass. "You come back next week if those cuts get worse."

"Talking to you is like trying to rouse a man's reluctant johnson to happiness. Just tell me, won't you? Did they run away? Die? What?"

Mary turned. "My nieces. Or, rather, children I consider to be my nieces. We don't know what happened. They left school on the day the storm ended, and then—vanished."

"Have you looked for them?"

"Everywhere. All the orphan asylums. The hospitals. We put notices in the paper."

"Is that all?" Darlene scoffed. "For someone as skilled as you, you're not too smart, are you? Did you look along the waterfront? Down the alleyways? In any of the houses? In the Tenderloin? At the far end of Broadway where the lights burn red?"

"No," Mary said. She felt Darlene's incredulous stare and the damp chill of the room. They hadn't even thought to look in the whorehouses. She'd tended these women for several years now and in the past six weeks had never once made the connection. "But who would—?"

"Take them? Anyone thinking they could make some money." Darlene looked at her sharply. "You've lived too easy a life."

She hadn't, of course, but Mary said nothing.

"We'll all keep an eye," Darlene said, reading Mary's panic. "Won't we, girls?" Wincing, Darlene drew aside the curtain. The thin fabric had not muffled their conversation. The dozen waiting women eyed Mary with pity, because they knew things that they never told her, no matter how frank they were with her about their lives.

"Have any of you seen them?" Mary said, her voice trembling. "They are seven and ten. Long red hair, big eyes. Blue? Their names were—*are* Emma and Claire."

No one had seen them, but they promised they would look.

"I hope you don't—"

"Find them?" Darlene said, her voice gone soft with sympathy.

Miserably, Mary nodded.

"Us, too."

Already, Maude showed signs of improving health. Her breathing was regular and deep, her pulse steady and firm; it had taken only the release of the infection to reverse her fever. The girl was just stirring when the door shot open, and Captain Mantel and five uniformed police officers burst into the room.

Chapter Eight

Instinctively, Mary stepped between her patients and the policemen as Darlene slunk toward the far wall and the other women. Mantel tilted his head to one side, eyeing them all with suspicion. Light glinted off the brass buttons of his uniform as he took Mary's measure. She realized what she must look like to him now—her clinic dress, though presentable, was made of gray worsted serge—the fabric of utility—and her hair was pinned up carelessly, without style, though she rarely paid much attention to it on any given day. On Thursdays she dressed this way to avoid attention, easily passing on her way to the clinic as yet another shopgirl, though as a rule she cared little for the geegaws and fripperies of fashion, dispensing with a trip to the dressmakers in as little time as possible, asking only to be outfitted in something acceptable, and taking what the dressmaker made without complaint or comment, though it was often still too decorative for her indifferent taste.

"So, it is true," Mantel said.

"I beg your pardon?"

"The rumors. I could hardly believe them at first. The lady doctor of Washington Park treating prostitutes."

"What concern is it of yours?"

"Helping these degenerates, not reforming them like the genial folks at the House of Shelter, is what we in the righteous business of law enforcement call abetting. I ought to throw you in jail." He leaned to one side, surveying the women gathered behind her. "Or I could arrest them."

"For what? Standing?" Mary said.

"You're the lady doctor that came into the precinct house," one of the policemen said.

Mary recognized Officer Farrell—the tall, sympathetic policeman who had been so kind the first time they'd gone to the precinct house.

"We were on the lookout for those—your girls. Blizzard orphans, right? Drowned in the river, right?" He looked to Mantel for confirmation. "A shame, that."

"Shut up, Farrell."

Mary seized on the interruption. "Officer Mantel. Tell me, of all those places you told me you searched, did you ever go to the red-light districts?"

"Now, Dr. Stipp, what a question." He eyed the women massed behind her. "You're obviously still in a state. Though I understand. I do. After all, the whole of the Northeast is still suffering. It's been one long funeral for all of us. And we'd not got it so bad here in Albany. I got reports of infants froze to death in Boston—"

"Stop."

He affected a pitying smile. "I apologize. Didn't mean to upset you. I forget, sometimes, that as a lady, you've not got the stronger constitution—"

"If you are going to patronize me, do it without that simpering smile."

Mantel thrust his short legs wide. "Fine. Happy to. Let me tell you something. Now that you are consorting with the ladies of the night, it's probably best for you to understand what we men of the force have understood for a good long time. These women will lie, cheat, steal, and say anything in order to get what they want. You cannot trust a word that comes out of their mouths. I expect tomorrow or the next day you'll hear from someone here that she has found the girls. But she'll be needing some kind of payment for the information, and you'll give it to her because you're desperate."

"That's ridiculous," Darlene said, elbowing her way forward.

Mantel ignored her. "You're thinking in wishes, Doctor Stipp. Hope has made you vulnerable to those who would do you harm or toy with your thinking—like that one there," he said, jutting his chin at Darlene. "But I was too hard on you last time. It's a sad thing what happened. You have my pity, you do. But you need to come to terms."

"You didn't look there, did you?" Mary said.

"You're grasping, Dr. Stipp."

"It would take nothing. Two thorough patrolmen, applying real method. The search could be accomplished by tonight."

"You know as well as I do that as soon as a patrolman sets foot in one of those houses, a messenger will be out the back door, spreading the news that we're on the lookout for two girls. And those two girls would be well hidden by the time we get to where they are. Anyway, we're arguing about ghosts. Those girls are dead."

"You're being obtuse," Mary said. "Or lazy."

"Listen to me, doctor, you've done more good work than most of us ever will in a lifetime." Mantel's gaze swiveled around the clinic. "Except for this, of course. But we all know what you and your husband did in the war. A bit of an amazing thing, not what most women would do. And I honor that. I do. But I'll not go charging through the city's dens of iniquity because you've gotten an idea from loose women who want to please you. Or fleece you. Trust me on this: we are in and out of whorehouses all the time. If your girls were there, I'd have found them.

"Now, go home. Get out of this—place. Deliver a baby. Mend people's broken bodies. Go on doing the good deeds that people admire you for."

Though his tone was respectful, it was also patronizing, with an undercurrent of disdain. When people asked Mary about the war, they supposed that it had been a frustrating, awful experience. But in that lawless landscape, when she had wanted to accomplish something, all she'd had to do was to take steps to get it done: climb onto trains going in the direction of battles; talk her way through barriers both prejudicial and material; in some cases, just show up until someone relented. That was how she'd met William. She'd arrived at the door of the Union Hotel Hospital, demanded he hire her, and wearied him into taking her on. Therein lay the advantage of wartime: men were too busy killing one another to take heed of women's activities. But after the war, people's general opinion of her turned; she wasn't quite respectable, her ambitions were unladylike, at best she was a curiosity. She was aware that many society women who asked for her help eyed her with this same suspicion. And people like Mantel felt free to lecture her about what she could and could not do.

And now, somehow, the police had discovered her clinic and were here, for a reason she couldn't discern.

"You need to leave, Captain Mantel."

"How old did you say that oldest girl was?"

"Ten."

He shrugged. "She was of age."

Mary stared at him, aghast. "She is a child." *Is. Was.*

"You know as well as I do that we can't interfere with a girl's rights to do whatever she wishes. If that's the life she's chosen, then—"

"Emma and Claire didn't *choose* anything."

"Madam, they are not alive. That's the end of it. And if I hear of you treating these women again, I will arrest you."

As he turned to leave, a man pushed through the crowd of officers at the door. At first he appeared only in silhouette, a top hat elongating his short stature, a velvet-lined cape flung across one shoulder, a confident cast to his bold stance. He removed his hat and offered a slight bow. "Dr. Stipp."

"Mr. Van der Veer?" Mary said.

Gerritt stepped inside and made a second bow to the captain. The two men resembled one another. Mantel had a broader, more barreled chest, but in the bald head, dark eyes, and even the way they held themselves they could have been brothers. Only Mantel's thick accent distinguished him. Gerritt's tone, while braying, was nuanced by the more aristocratic tones of Dutch Albany. Seen in shadow, though, it would be hard to tell them apart.

"I do hope nothing has happened. Is all well, Arthur?"

"We were making rounds and heard a disturbance."

"There was no disturbance," Mary said.

"Surely you have no quarrel with this fine woman?" Van der Veer said. "This physician to whom we are all so much indebted?"

The captain shot Mary a grim look that could be either apology or condemnation, which he nevertheless quickly wiped from his face. He turned to Farrell to commiserate over The Things He Had to Put Up With, pushed past Van der Veer, and, trailed by his officers, sauntered down the alleyway.

Gerritt Van der Veer said, "Are you all right, Dr. Stipp?"

"He is a loathsome man."

Gerritt glanced around the room, his assessing gaze missing nothing. "I've come with an invitation, but I see that you are busy. May I return within the hour? Or two? Name the time. It's important. Or at least I hope you will agree that it is once we have spoken."

There were eleven more women to see, and the washing up to do afterward. "Two hours?"

"I'll return then." He tipped his hat and was gone.

For the rest of the morning, Mary cared for the women's bruises, ailments, and diseases as they chattered at her, trying to console her. They heard things, they said. Men at their leisure liked to talk. They would listen. Ask around. Mary forced herself to concentrate on her work but was as rattled nearly as much as she had been at Antietam, when the men were bleeding to death in the barnyard and she had only corn husks as dressings. *I'm not afraid,* she had declared to William after their first night of surgery together. He had laughed at her then, incredulous that she would ever think he thought her afraid of anything. Now fury made her clumsy: twice she tripped over her own feet, and once, when irrigating a sore, she knocked over the basin with her elbow and it splashed onto the floor with a loud clatter.

Could what Darlene said be true?

By twelve thirty, when Gerritt Van der Veer again knocked at the door, everyone had gone.

"Is this a bad time?" he said.

"Neither good nor bad. Tell me, how does everyone suddenly know about my clinic?"

"I can't speak for Captain Mantel, but I saw the lantern burning."

"And how do you know about the lantern?"

He shrugged. "Albany talks. I hear things."

"I offer these women medical care, Mr. Van der Veer. Care that no one else offers them."

"That's not completely true. There is the House of Shelter, for one, that offers help if they want to leave the profession, so to speak. But you mistake me. I did not come to pronounce censure, as it appeared Mantel did. Did he threaten you?"

"Yes." Mary untied her sodden apron and added it to the pile of laundry. "He insinuated that I've been performing abortions."

Van der Veer was circling the room, taking in the uneven stone floor, bare walls, and sparse furnishings. He turned on his heel. "Have you?"

"No."

"All right then. I've come to make you an offer and an invitation. Actually, two invitations. I wish to fund this clinic. Move you to a better space. Pay the rent. Give you money to obtain whatever medicines and instruments you require. Get you out from underneath police harassment." Van der Veer's smile widened into a deep grin. With his malleable face and short stature, he resembled an elf more than a lumber baron.

"Why, when Mantel was auguring arrest?"

Van der Veer shrugged. "I hold a deep fondness for the downtrodden."

"If you knew me at all, then you would know that I don't accept glib answers."

"Very well," he said. "Two reasons. One, Albany is my city. I own it, at least as far as commerce goes, and I've little patience for corruption. At least two dozen brothels operate on the waterfront. Elsewhere, they've sprung up like weeds. It's a scourge. And the injustice toward the women involved, which you have boldly confronted in this small establishment, makes me furious. And, second, I'd like to help you."

"By giving me money?"

He shrugged. "I have plenty."

"You wish to be associated with prostitution? You? Staunch Episcopalian, the richest man in the city, with the highest social standing?"

"You honor me, but I don't think that the reigning families would agree with your assessment of my standing. I do not rank so highly on the social ladder; I do not live in their rarefied enclave on Elk Street, amidst their mansions and beloved cathedral. I live on the park, like you do. You are mistaking wealth with position. The two are not always congruent. But yes, I want to take a stand. Will you accept?"

"Your money would attract attention."

"What if we tell no one that I am involved?"

Mary gathered the towels and rags accumulated on the table and began stuffing them into a canvas bag. "That's impossible. Albany lives for gossip. You said it yourself. *I hear things.*"

"I think you are being foolish. This is a good opportunity."

She cinched the laundry bag tight. "Many men have thought me foolish, Mr. Van der Veer. That never has any bearing on what I do."

"Viola says that I can be obtuse. If I have offended you, I apologize."

"I am not easily offended. And now I need to get home," she said, pinning on her hat and herding him toward the door.

"It could be an homage to the O'Donnells," Van der Veer said. "We could name the clinic after them. The O'Donnell Clinic."

"It's very kind, but I can't accept your money."

"Very well. By the way, did I overhear you asking Mantel to search the brothels?"

"Yes."

"Why?"

Mary's gaze strayed to the open door, wishing to be gone. "One of the women thought it possible that the girls might have ended up in one of them."

"What did Mantel say to that?"

"That I am mistaken."

"I'll say something to him."

"It's not important."

"There is that famous courage. Think about what I offered, won't you? I know how difficult things have been for you lately and I admire all"—he opened his hands—"this. But you forget. I also came bearing an invitation."

They stepped into the alley, where runnels of sudsy water rippled among the cobbles from the washhouse up the hill. Dirty piles of snow still banked some of the buildings. Mary handed Gerritt the laundry, enjoying the insolence of burdening one of the most noteworthy men in Albany with a sack of dirtied linens. But he waited good-naturedly enough while she wrapped herself in her cloak, snuffed the lantern, and placed it inside before locking the bolt and thrusting the key deep into her pocket. She directed him uphill toward the washhouse, where she dropped off the laundry, and then turned downhill to the Delavan House, where she had left her carriage with the doorman.

"My invitation is this: I would like to invite you to join the board of the House of Shelter."

She stopped dead. "You are the one who funds the House of Shelter?"

"You see, I can keep secrets: I am already associated with prostitution."

"The house is a wonderful service. Several women I've treated have gotten help there. One of them is married. Did you know? She lives in Coxsackie now. Another works in the glass factory."

"Then you know that I am serious. I would have asked you yesterday at the cemetery, with your husband present, but I felt it would have been an intrusion somehow. I admire you. You seem to be unafraid of anything. My mother was right, all those years ago. Do you know what rumors raced around Albany when you left for the war? You were with child, you'd run away to get married, you'd lost your mind. All of us young men were making bets."

"How disappointed you must have been when I turned up well educated and chaste," Mary said.

"On the contrary. I won the bet."

"Are you really offering me a place on the board?"

"I am. Though I can assure you that the board is made up of a bunch of sanctimonious priests and pastors who threaten hellfire when our charges don't comply with every rule. And one of those Pruyn men heads it," he said, making a face. The Pruyns were first among the prominent families of Albany, and deeply involved in church affairs. Recently, one of its members had served as a missionary to China.

Mary studied the man whose wife thought him obtuse. His top

hat did little to shield him from the sunlight, but his eyes, squinting, seemed without guile.

He opened one hand in a welcoming gesture, implying he had no motive other than concern and generosity. "All right then. If you won't answer me now, consider my offer open," Van der Veer said. "And contemplate this: should you accept you would be the first woman in Albany to sit on a board. I have no idea why you haven't been involved with the House of Shelter before, with such an invested interest as this." He tilted his chin back toward the clinic in approval. "And you must know that Viola was very taken with you yesterday. She loved Mrs. O'Donnell. She is having a tea party this afternoon, one of those obligation teas meant to appease the reigning queens of *old Albany.*" He made another comic face. "Would you allow me to escort you to our home? Viola would be so pleased to have a moment with you. I realize that it may be too early in your grief for social forays. But you have returned to work, and it would mean a great deal to my wife. Follow me in your carriage?"

"I enjoyed meeting Viola very much, but I am sorry, I don't have time."

"Just a half an hour. That's all."

"Another time, perhaps. Do give her my regards, though."

Gerritt waited while the doorman at the Delavan retrieved Mary's carriage from the hotel's large barns, located several blocks away. He didn't want to leave her unescorted. Mary laughed at his chivalry, for if he knew her at all, he would know she'd traipsed far more dangerous paths than the sidewalks of Albany.

Chapter Nine

Two years before leaving for Paris, Elizabeth began taking French lessons with Madame Hubbard, who did not give lessons so much as she gave conversation, and not conversation so much as reveries. Madame Hubbard's husband had brought her to Albany from France under protest, and she relived her days there in long florid descriptions of balls and parties, excursions and entertainments, and divertissements on the general superiority of Paris versus Albany. In these extended musings, Madame Hubbard often talked far beyond Elizabeth's allotted tutorial of one hour, and she never assigned declensions, vocabulary lists, or grammar books. What she offered instead was repetitive exposure to the language, and by listening and conversing, Elizabeth had long ago grown facile.

Now, upon seeing Elizabeth at her doorstep, Madame Hubbard enveloped her in a perfumed haze of bosom, proclaiming herself overjoyed at once again seeing her darling, darling girl. Unable to express herself precisely in English, she frequently fell back on repeating adjectives to emphasize the depth of her emotions, which were often overwrought but always welcome to the recipient of her exaggerated Gallic affections. The Frenchwoman was small, plump, and bright faced, frequently overly powdered, with thinning reddish hair and given to wearing tightly corseted dresses. Elizabeth melted into the shadowy comfort of Madame Hubbard's ample décolletage, feeling as if she'd come home. Home for Madame Hubbard happened to be a large brick mansion situated just west of the capitol building on Washington Avenue, where from time to time thuds from its ongoing construction penetrated the thick walls of her parlor, which did not now prevent Madame Hubbard from expressing astonishment that Elizabeth had left Paris.

"I left Paris for love, but every day I question whether or not that was reason enough to forsake her—especially for this city. I don't know why a young person like yourself would leave Paris, when you had everything before you."

"The O'Donnells—"

"Yes, yes," Madame Hubbard said, leaning forward. "I understand. But, my dear, as sad as it is, you could have grieved there and kept on with your studies."

"I couldn't stay, Madame Hubbard." Elizabeth had brought with her Victor Hugo's novel *Les Misérables.* Previously, it had been their practice for Elizabeth to read aloud in French and ask questions about sentence structure and idiom. The French language was the one thing of Paris that Elizabeth missed: the puzzle of the complicated grammar, the challenges of pronouncing the tricky vowels, and most of all the language's musicality, a lyricism that reminded her of the extended notes of Mozart's most fanciful concertos. She fingered the pages of the book now, hoping to divert Madame Hubbard's attention.

"Tell me the truth, darling mademoiselle," Madame Hubbard continued. "Did they ask you to leave the conservatory? This happens, I am told, especially to foreigners. It is nothing to be ashamed of. You can tell me. I will not think less of you."

Madame Hubbard had come perilously close to the embarrassing truth. But of course Monsieur Girard had never demanded that Elizabeth leave. Instead, she had taken flight. She had failed in courage. Shame hung around her like a noose. There was so little to tell, so little that she wanted to tell.

"I see," Madame Hubbard said when Elizabeth did not answer. "Perhaps it was love?"

"It was nothing like that."

"You make me guess, mademoiselle, when you do not tell me everything. But anyone can see that you are miserable. You miss playing your violin. I can tell at a moment's glance. This will not do at all."

"But how do you know that I am not playing?"

"Your pain is evident. And it is more than your cherished O'Donnells. You are broken, *ma petite.* I am so sorry that this happened to you."

Elizabeth stood, her heart pounding in her chest, stammering excuses as she fled the parlor. She had forgotten how perceptive Madame Hubbard could be. "I'm sorry, but I just remembered that I have another engagement. Will you forgive me?"

The maid held open the front door for her and dutifully returned to report to Madame Hubbard that Elizabeth had been wiping tears from her eyes.

Madame Hubbard brought her teacup to her lips and mused about the complications of youth, worrying for her *petite violiniste,* who had already borne too much in her young life.

Outside, Elizabeth hurried past clusters of men waiting at the omnibus stop. Home was perhaps a mile away, and she walked several long blocks before yielding to her embarrassment. At the corner of Washington Avenue and Lark, a melancholy little corner lacking even a modest dwelling to cheer up the bedraggled empty lot, Elizabeth finally succumbed. Monsieur Girard's voice replayed itself inside her head: *You are nothing. You are an embarrassment to the violin. Why did you come all the way from America to shame yourself?* She pulled a handkerchief from her reticule, turning away so that no passerby could observe her mortification.

"Here, now. What's this?"

Elizabeth blinked back her tears, stuffed her handkerchief into her sleeve, and turned to find a young man hovering beside her. He floated before her, beautifully formed, wide at the shoulders and slim at the hips, possessed of a shock of untamed yellow hair that sprouted from underneath a narrow hat brim. A topcoat covered a fitted jacket under which a paisley vest glinted in her watery vision.

To her blank look, the young man said, "I am Jakob Van der Veer. We met yesterday at the cemetery. Might I accompany you? Escort you somewhere? You seem—as if you might appreciate someone to walk with you." He hesitated, and at length said, "I beg your pardon. I see that you've forgotten. Of course you were in a state of grief yesterday and have no memory of meeting me. Please forgive my intrusion." He lifted his hat and offered an apologetic smile.

"I remember you, Mr. Van der Veer."

"Shall we begin again, then? How do you do? To spark our conversation, I'll share the details of my day. I was just at the capitol, attending to some particulars regarding a delivery of lumber. The foreman is unclear how much he needs and when he wants it. The whole thing is a mess, actually, as has been all of the construction there. I was on my way home when I saw you. But if you like, I will wait a few more moments before I proceed, until you make the turn at the park. Would you like that?"

He did not seem to be mocking her. He was striving to make his expression neutral. What was that biblical term, Elizabeth thought? A lack of guile.

"May I offer some perspective?" Jakob said, when she hesitated. "I am aware that accepting the offer of an escort from someone you hardly know—me—poses the uncertainty that I might turn out to be a crashing bore, which I think is your greatest risk. But I promise that I will do everything to entertain you and thus erase what I believe to be your most likely objection to my presence. I assure you, Miss Fall, that as far as dangers go, the worst offense that I might impose would be a reverential disquisition on the merits of the new ice-yacht that my father recently purchased for next week's regatta. On that subject, I may fail in my quest not to bore you, but at your command, I will abandon any subject that you forbid."

Elizabeth stifled a small laugh. She recalled her grandmother's admonition: *But you must try to live, if you can.*

"I have an idea," Jakob said, when she still didn't answer. "We'll pretend instead that we don't know one another. We will walk together, but apart, as if we are strangers who have just come upon one another. I will speak indifferently of the weather. You will nod and answer something entirely lifeless. No one will suspect anything. And it might even vanquish the awkwardness. Do I offend you by offering you my company?" Jakob said.

Practice, she thought. Practice being alive. "I am not offended."

"Excellent. However," he said, "I insist upon walking you all the way home. It's only polite. What kind of a protector would I be if I didn't?"

She finally relented, and they fell into wary step beside one another.

"Perhaps," Elizabeth said, "I should make clear to you that my unhappiness has nothing to do with you. It is about something—else."

"Of course," he said. "I was very fond of Mr. O'Donnell. He was wonderful—hardworking, funny."

"He was," she said.

"And you came back from Paris for them?" Jakob said.

"Yes." Which wasn't a complete lie, but nonetheless it felt dishonest to pretend that all her unhappiness was centered on losing Bonnie and her family. She cast about for something to lead the conversation away from herself. "You are in law?"

"And in lumber. Though lumber doesn't hold the same fascination for me as it does for my father. He breathes lumber. Most nights he comes home smelling of pinesap."

"Don't you?"

"I will always smell of the lumberyard if my father has his way."

"And what way is that?"

"That I take over for him when he dies."

"But he will be dead. He will never know whether you do or don't." Her unguarded words slipped out before she had a chance to censor herself.

Jakob laughed. "I suppose that's true."

"Forgive me, Mr. Van der Veer—"

"Jakob."

"May I say something to you? I suspect you love something else if you are so willing to give up such a lucrative enterprise."

Jakob cocked his head, rueful. "My father's sole purpose in having me read law at Harvard was to understand shipping and land rights, learn the acquisition tools for obtaining timberland, and master the art of contracts. All of which I find incredibly boring. I love criminal law. Though my father will never let me practice."

"Why not?"

"Because I am his son."

They crossed to the other side of Madison to avoid the dust rising from the razing of the row houses. Blows of sledgehammers rang out like the percussive chops of a bass drum.

In New York State, Jakob went on, the tradition was that new lawyers—junior lawyers—were taken on by more practiced attorneys and apprenticed, but it was only a tradition, not a law. Jakob, if he wanted, could set out his shingle today and work without the advisement of a more senior attorney. But that would mean abandoning his father. His father claimed he needed him, and Jakob liked to think of himself as a dutiful son.

"You must have other interests?" Elizabeth said. "Besides law?"

"Travel. I have always wanted to go to Paris."

"I wouldn't set my sights on Paris. It is a great disappointment, not what one dreams it will be."

"Such weary knowingness," he said, eyeing her.

"I am sorry. You should go," she said. "To see for yourself whether or not it is what people say."

"Perhaps I will," he said.

They strolled up the avenue, easier in their silence now. On the southern edge of the park, only a few houses besides the Stipps' had been built. In the distance, the dirty bricks of the almshouse hulked, and boys playing stickball kicked up shimmering wakes of dust.

"Will I see you there when I go?" Jakob said.

"No," Elizabeth said. "I won't be returning."

"So you are finished with your studies?"

"I have given up playing," she said.

"What a shame."

They'd reached home. She could feel the weight of his gaze.

"So, it was you who loved something once—and now you no longer do?" he said.

A sparrow flitted in the branches of a red maple above her head. She tucked her book to her chest. He had turned her question back on her. The problem with *trying to live*, she thought, was that it was impossible to hide.

He smiled at her. "I see. You may ask probing spiritual questions of me, but not I of you. I understand the rules. If I agree to ask you nothing personal, ever, may I come another day to call on you? Or perhaps instead you would like to go to the ice regatta with me next week, if the ice holds? We would be lost in the crowd. You could pretend you don't know me."

Elizabeth ducked her head and smiled. She couldn't ever recall meeting anyone this charming. "Thank you for the flowers yesterday."

He grinned. "Wear a warm coat. It gets cold on the ice."

Chapter Ten

"No," Amelia said, a look of intense pain clouding her features. "No." She'd been saying *no* ever since Mary had started talking.

Though Mary had had some time to accustom herself to the idea, she still was not able to keep the fear from her voice. In the past few minutes, she had recounted Darlene's suspicions to her mother, along with Mantel's visit, whispering to keep her voice from carrying. Beyond the closed pocket doors of the dining room, the last of William's patients colonized the parlor, waiting his turn to be seen in William's clinic on the other side of the stairwell.

Amelia was pacing, following the pattern of inlaid mahogany in the dining room floor, tracing a path from the glassed-in medicine and instrument cabinets to the exam table, strands of hair working loose from the lilac ribbon holding her silver strands in place. Her dress was muted lavender silk, with a line of simple buttons decorating the neck and wrists.

"No," Amelia said again. "It can't be. We buried Emma and Claire yesterday."

"But we didn't, did we?"

Amelia turned away, looking out the back window into the garden, where a wash of late afternoon light was filtering through a western bank of low clouds. "No."

All those weeks she and William had wasted going from orphanage to orphanage, Mary thought. And now every second, every minute, seemed wasted. She ought to be down on the waterfront right now, going from brothel to brothel, at least the ones she knew. The women would admit her, happily. All that goodwill from her medical care would stand her in good stead. They all knew her, or at least of her. She could count on that.

"But think, Mary," Amelia said, gripping Mary's wrist. "Do you think it's possible that you are merely reaching, out of hope?"

"Maybe. Perhaps. I don't know," Mary said, giving in to doubt again. One minute Darlene's theory seemed brilliant and the next completely implausible.

"And," Amelia said, "do you think it's possible that the captain could be right about Darlene, that she might be planning to extort money from you in exchange for information? Information that might turn out not to be true?"

"I trust her, Mother. She's no opportunist. If she'd wanted money, she would have asked me for it then, wouldn't she have, if she intended to lie? And besides, none of that matters, does it, if we go looking ourselves? The brothels are the single place we haven't looked. What harm can come from looking? I can't understand why Captain Mantel refused. Oh, damn him. The police know exactly where the brothels are. It would be so easy for them."

"But the captain doesn't believe that they're alive."

"But what does that matter—"

Mary broke off at the sound of footsteps and the rustle of skirts coming down the back stairs. Elizabeth emerged from the butler's pantry, her hair tied back with a thick band of striped ribbon. The narrow worry line that had cropped up between her eyes had deepened.

Mary pasted a smile on her face. "Did you enjoy Madame Hubbard's?" She was aware that her voice was far too bright, but Elizabeth flared so easily these days, like tinder, that it was impossible to strike the right tone.

"Not especially. Should I help Uncle William with his patients?"

"Are you well, Lizzie?" her grandmother asked. "You seem—"

"I'm fine."

Not even Amelia could loosen Elizabeth's tongue—Amelia, who could pry anything from anyone.

"Well, then, I'm certain that your uncle would appreciate your help," Amelia said. "He'll be happy that you want to."

Elizabeth padded through the room, opening the pocket doors wide to the now empty parlor as a sudden, brief cry from William's clinic resounded throughout the house. They watched Elizabeth quicken her pace, round the staircase, and disappear down the hall.

"Was that enthusiasm?" Mary said.

"I hope so," Amelia said. "It would be good if she could find something to do. If Bonnie were here, she might be able to—"

"Mother."

"I'm sorry," Amelia said. "Sometimes—"

"I know," Mary said.

But Elizabeth wasn't needed. William was following his patient to the front door, calling after him as he stumbled onto the veranda, a sling supporting his right arm. Soon he was lurching down Madison Avenue in the opposite direction of downtown.

"The other way, Mr. Matthews. The other way!" William yelled, waving him in the other direction. The man swung around, nodded, and trotted back down the street. Just then, an omnibus lurched by and stopped for him, and he clambered aboard and scrambled onto a seat, dazedly staring out the window.

William shook his head as he came into Mary's clinic. "He insisted on going right away, but I don't think he was altogether right when he got here. I've set more than a thousand bones and he's the only one who's bellowed like a cow in heat. And for a tiny fracture, too. He'd never have made it during the war," William said, shaking his head. He turned and looked at Mary. "Good God, what's the matter?"

William was seated, holding his head in his hands. "I'll go tonight. I'll go now."

Mary and Amelia threw one another a furtive look. "We're going with you."

William looked from his wife to his mother-in-law, both of them equally insistent, both of them more than capable of prolonging the conversation beyond his level of tolerance. Though he frequently accused them of being in the habit of deciding what to do and only then informing him of their plans, he rarely disagreed with them. But he did now. "Neither of you is going."

"We know where the brothels are better than you do, William. At least I hope that's the case," Amelia said, shooting a grimly amused glance at Mary. "And they know us. We've helped them. Mary certainly has, in ways that no one else—"

"I shall point out the obvious," William said. "At night, if a man and a woman enter that particular type of—enterprise—together, it will look suspicious. It will be easier for a man alone to make inquiries."

"I'm going," Mary said.

"We don't have to go at night," Amelia said. "Tomorrow morning, instead, then."

"No. Tomorrow is too late," Mary said. "So much wasted time already."

"Mary," William said. "Your going would be broadcast within seconds between the houses. I will draw no special notice. And the chances that they are alive—"

"I know. I know. But what if they are? We have to look again, we have to—"

"Hush," Amelia said, laying a hand on Mary's shoulder. "Where is Elizabeth?"

They could hear the sound of rushing water in the bathroom and resumed talking in a whisper.

"You cannot go alone," Amelia said. "What if something happens?"

William cocked his head. "And just what would you do, Amelia Sutter, if something happened?"

"Alert the police—"

"Because they've been so helpful?"

It was, William stated again, idiotic for either of them to accompany him.

But when darkness fell, Mary climbed into the carriage with him. She and Amelia had scribbled out a long list of the addresses of all the brothels where they had delivered babies. William did not tell them that they needn't have bothered, for a brothel was as obvious a structure as the nose on a man's face. One only had to follow the trail.

Later that night, a full hour after the lamplighters had made their midnight rounds to snuff the gaslights lining Broadway, the thoroughfare began to empty of revelers, whose dissipation belied an uncanny ability to navigate their way home in the early morning blackness. They crept up the slope of Arbor Hill to the west, with its quiet hum of tenements and feral hogs rooting among the blackberry vines, or tripped up Broadway into North Albany, where lumber handlers and their families populated wooden row houses by the hundreds and sour wives awaited their drunken husbands. Some—too inebriated to make it home—bedded down next to the Erie Canal's towpath.

William and Mary leaned against the ridged siding of a stationer's store, watching the nocturnal evacuation. All night William had followed fidgety, purposeful men from one bawdy house to another, where girls far too young to be in the prostitution business were secreted in back rooms. He'd scanned small face after small face for Emma and Claire, trying to see through face paint and bruises and too much of the wrong kind of experience. At the last house, the madam had traded in blackmail: *You asked for young,* she trilled, her hand outstretched for coins.

A dozen houses tonight. How many more were there?

Mary had slipped into the alleyways behind the houses, just in case some madam had been spooked and was shuttling girls out the back to avoid detection, but she found only weary ladies of the night, smoking pipes or fortifying themselves with liquor.

All evening they had prayed both to find and to not find Emma and Claire, a state of intolerable dissonance that dogged their every footstep. Were they alive? Were they not? To hope was to defy reason. To think of them as alive and dead at the same time was to court madness. When the clock struck two, they started for home, making plans to return the next night, and the night after that, though secretly William feared they were chasing ghosts.

Over the next three nights, William and Mary prowled the back rooms of bawdy houses and saloons all over the city, but found no trace of the girls.

Chapter Eleven

After he walked Elizabeth home, Jakob went home, too, to the Van der Veers' Dutch Renaissance Revival home, which sat across Washington Park from the Stipps'. Jakob did not much like the new house. He preferred their old home on Ten Broeck Street, but his father had been the first lumber baron to forsake that old enclave, predicting that others would soon follow them to upper State Street. He had been right. Several lumber and manufacturing barons had also built new homes on the park, albeit far less ostentatious ones, and the former backwater was now gaining in prestige. But the Van der Veer house, boasting five stories, a carriageway, a back courtyard, and a ballroom that extended the depth of the house, far outdid any of its few neighbors in opulence and size.

Now the last of the afternoon light filtered up the stairwell as Jakob tiptoed down the wood-paneled, third-floor corridor toward his mother's bedchamber. The new house was still in the act of settling; underfoot, the wide floorboards creaked, and not even the Turkish runner could prevent the floor from cracking and popping. Upon reaching his mother's door, Jakob hesitated. The hinges often squeaked. He had to be careful; he had not yet once awakened his mother on this errand, nor did he want to now. How his mother reconciled the periodic disappearance of the sherry decanter from its misbegotten residence on her nightstand, Jakob didn't know. But since so much of everything that happened around the sherry decanter in this house was never remarked upon, Jakob found the prevailing silence surrounding its migration back to the butler's pantry not at all mystifying.

The window curtains were drawn. The brocade drapes on the canopied bed were drawn, too, with the exception of those on the side of the nightstand. His mother lay asleep, cocooned in her tangled bedclothes, her head and shoulders propped up on mounds of pillows, her quilted bed jacket hanging askew around her shoulders, her dark hair in pin curls. Everyone who met her believed her younger than her forty years by a decade, whether from her skittish public behavior or her childish features. Her current disarray added to that impression of childishness. Jakob had feared he might find her in this state and he wondered how much sherry she had consumed this time to get through the ordeal of the tea party his father had insisted she give. His mother hated having to put on teas and parties to advance Gerritt's standing in the community. That his mother suffered from acute shyness, preferring small, intimate gatherings with a few people to grander affairs, was of no import to Gerritt, who wished to scale the heights of Albany aristocracy.

On the night table, a stemmed crystal glass kept the sought-after decanter company, casting rose-colored shadows onto the lace doily beneath. Several curio cabinets in the corner contained his mother's beloved collection of Jumeau dolls. His mother had explained to him that they were fashion dolls, meant to show off the new clothes of the French couturiers. Their glass eyes looked on now as Jakob deftly took the empty decanter and glass into custody. The last he knew, the decanter had been more than half full. Stashing it under one arm, he unlatched the door.

"Is he home yet?"

Jakob turned. His mother was playing with the edge of her embroidered sheet. Her speech was slurred, which meant that her last drink had not been that long ago.

If she was surprised to see her son sneaking around in her chambers, she didn't say so.

"Did you have a nice rest?" Jakob said, setting the glass and decanter back down on a marble table near the door.

"He's still out, isn't he?"

"I think he's at the district."

"Or so he says." The alcohol on her breath emanated from her like a fog.

Jakob had no wish to speculate on where his father went in the evenings. He and his mother often took dinner alone together: more recently, she in various and increasing states of inebriation, he attempting to manage the situation. "Would you like to rest some more before dinner?"

"Why would I want to rest?"

As usual, she ignored his subtle allusion to her drinking. He never said anything overt. How this state of affairs had come to be, he couldn't say. It was understood, however, that no one was to say anything direct about it at all, ever. Not even his father, who more than once, in disdainful abeyance of the tacit agreement, had inferred that his wife's increasing inability to hold her sherry was an egregious failure of character, especially since he was more than capable of managing his liquor of choice, which was Scotch. Fine Scotch, too, that took more than a few dollars to buy, but to Gerritt that mattered little. He was a wealthy man, and the money he spent on his own intoxication made no inroads into the family fortune. Scotch and sherry were delivered by the wagonful to 411 State Street.

"You don't have to give parties, Mother," Jakob said. "If you hate them so much."

"Oh, but I do. Mary Pruyn was here and everyone else. It was exhausting." Everyone else was all the other leading citizens of Albany, who had all attended Viola's afternoon tea: the Langdons, Lansings, Parkers, Cornings, Richardsons, Vanderpoels, Ten Eycks, and Schuylers. "It's like running a circus, trying to find something to talk about that they hadn't already discussed the day before, at a party I hadn't been invited to. But do not fear. I am well. I am always well." She fluttered to full consciousness, discarding the sulking mask she'd worn not a moment before, and by this dismissal demanded that he once again collude in the lie of her well-being. It always puzzled Jakob that his mother appeared more at ease when she was befuddled by drink than when she was fully sober, with the exception of the other morning at the cemetery, where for some reason, the imposing Mary Stipp seemed to have set his mother at ease.

He took leave of her without comment, surreptitiously spiriting away the decanter and glass. Downstairs, he stowed them in the butler's pantry. In the kitchen, he instructed a maid to prepare a pot of strong tea and a glass of milk whipped with egg and dusted with nutmeg, a concoction into which he planned to stir acetylsalicylic acid. He had recently discovered this cure while overhearing some of his friends decry their sorrows after a hard night of drinking. Jakob hovered at the door as the maid prepared the tea tray, wondering how much she or any of the maids knew. But even if they knew anything, they would never say. Maids had their own conspiracy of silence, if only to keep their jobs.

Upstairs he stirred the medicine into the eggnog before setting the tray on the bed and gently touching his mother's shoulder to wake her, for she had once again nodded off.

She drank the nog without comment and without evident embarrassment, then poured herself some tea, her hands unsteady but her aim true. Jakob had brought two teacups, and they sat together, steam rising from their cups, avoiding saying anything that would upset the facade of her well-being. This entailed more vigilance on

Jakob's part, but this kind of caution suited him. Sometimes, on his mother's good days, he could forget the spiral into which she had fallen. The change had happened suddenly. One day, she had been temperate, and the next she had fallen into excess and there had stayed. At first Jakob had found himself unable to navigate the uncertain shoals of the mother he adored falling to pieces. The puzzle of *why* remained unanswered. It was more than her innate shyness. And in a house where no one acknowledged a problem, addressing it was out of the question.

He poured them both more tea. He had not come to his mother only to abscond with the sherry. Elizabeth had enchanted him. It had taken him only a moment to realize that the young woman crying on the street was the same stunning young woman he had met at the cemetery.

"Mother," he said. "Do you think we could extend that invitation to the Stipp family for dinner? The one you mentioned at the cemetery?"

"I was planning to. I admire Mary Stipp a great deal. I'd like to get to know her. But why are *you* asking?" She was edging back into sobriety, into the mother he knew before she had become the mother he did not.

"I met Elizabeth on the street just now. I find her charming."

"Do you?"

His father's distinctive, heavy tread sounded on the stairs, and Viola hurriedly rearranged her face from its private to its public mask, the one she used with everyone but Jakob.

"I have to dress for dinner. Send in my maid, won't you?" she said, looking at Jakob with the last bit of her true self that he would see that night.

When his father's bedchamber door slammed shut, Jakob left his mother smoothing the front of her bed jacket, showing little embarrassment at having been disarranged in front of him, but wanting to be put together in front of her maid.

The appearance of happiness in the face of great unhappiness had become her vocation.

At dinner that night, Gerritt wanted to know how Jakob had gotten on with that foreman up at the capitol and all his shilly-shallying. Had Jakob wrangled him into some kind of submission? Jakob assured him repeatedly that he had. When Gerritt's queries dwindled into a satisfied silence, augmented by his third tumbler of Scotch, Jakob reminded his father of the invitation.

Gerritt raised an eyebrow. "That violinist?"

Jakob nodded, grimacing a little at Elizabeth being referred to as "that violinist."

"Splendid. She's quite the beauty. You certainly have an eye. When shall we have them?"

In the wake of this surprisingly hearty reception, it was decided to invite the entire family for several days hence, on Monday night.

Chapter Twelve

A mile or so southeast of the capitol building lay the part of the city known as the Pastures, a low-lying grid of streets adjacent to the Greenbush Ferry Landing and north of Norman's Kill, an area that housed icehouses and foundries and a hundred squat row houses on a floodplain. One of these houses stood at 153 Green Street. Nothing about the whitewashed clapboard or its gaily curtained windows gave anything away, except perhaps the meticulous way that its owner, James Harley, kept two garden boxes partly obscuring the cellar windows that sat at street level. He swore they kept the seasonal floodwaters out. At the earliest chance in the spring months, he planted the boxes with herbs and tomatoes that he then wrapped with chicken wire to discourage theft.

The burly man mostly kept to himself. His brutish bearing—a thick chest and muscled arms—belied a retiring manner, and his round face, while weathered, lately exuded a nervousness that invited sympathy. It was said that he was admiringly reliable in his job as overseer for Gerritt Van der Veer. He was reported to attend Our Mother of Mercy Catholic Church on Sunday mornings. He unfailingly tipped his bowler hat to ladies on the street, even when it was raining. And while he was also known to take a pint in the evenings, he was not considered a dedicated tippler, so he was held up as a model of rectitude to the more dissolute husbands of the street, who protested at the injustice of being compared to a man without a wife and children to spoil his day.

The single odd thing that people noted—but only in passing—was that lately in the nighttime Harley burned candles in his basement windows. The warm glow from the candlelight formed a halo around the garden boxes, attracting attention while obscuring any ability to peer around them to see what he was up to. Foiled in their curiosity, the neighbors decided that if a man wanted to do a bit of fiddling in his basement of an evening, who was anyone to question him? Most likely, he was building furniture. He did that on the side, or so someone had once said.

Harley, however, was not building furniture. He had found a much better use for his basement, which had until very recently served as his root cellar.

He had turned the dark hole into a home.

Emma and Claire O'Donnell didn't think of the basement that way, nor did they know Harley's name. He had never introduced himself, even as he brought them food and water, emptied out the privy he had built for them in one corner, and sometimes brushed their hair, taking care with the tangles, and apologizing for the long gaps of time between grooming sessions, even though Emma and Claire brushed one another's hair all the time. He had to work during the day, he explained. That prevented him from showing his complete devotion, though they should be assured that he thought of them all the time. He was as big a man as they had ever seen, with arms the size of stovepipes and shoulders as wide as the Hudson. He wore a mustache, not a beard, and his head had no hair at all. They could hear him upstairs when he came home from work dragging a tub across the floor, then the sound of water sloshing, and afterward, the splash when he tossed it in the street gutter. Then, he came down the stairs in clean, pressed clothes, smelling of soap and carrying a tray of bread and butter and meats.

They were allowed the run of the basement. He didn't want them to be uncomfortable, he said. They were to make themselves at home on the couch he had fashioned of wood with his own hands, pillowed with a mattress folded in half and covered with a pink-and-brown length of calico he scolded them for not straightening after they wrinkled it. In the far corner, he had laid another mattress on the floor, under a pile of eiderdown and sheets he boiled once a week as he clucked, *Nothing but the best for my girls.*

But the stone walls of the basement, packed with loose dirt in the uneven crevices, exuded a foul odor of sewage that, no matter how many times they took spit baths by the warmth of the coal stove, had settled in the sisters' hair and under their nail beds. They were left alone most of the time, long, painful stretches during which Emma recovered. Day and night, through the narrow slits of window high above them, they could hear the whistles of day boats plying the Hudson and locomotives sounding their horns, the *clackety clack* of passing trains so near that sometimes it felt as if they could touch them. At night those plaintive sounds rolled unfettered through the empty streets, the rush of following air sounding hollow, the way that frightening things always had before. Now what frightened them was the damped hush of must and earth.

"We must be near the river," Emma said, for the hundredth time. They were lying on the bed together, their arms encircling one another, Emma's nose nestled in Claire's long hair. "Father works near the river. He is looking for us, Claire. He'll find us." Emma had long ago lost track of time. Innumerable days had passed since the blizzard. *Time is nothing,* she often whispered to Claire. *Time is nothing; We aren't here; This isn't happening.* But time was everything, Emma thought. It was always the same minute over and over, the same cage with no key, the same dark night, the same eternal present.

Early on, the first time, the Other Man had said that if Emma didn't cooperate, he would hurt Claire. And that if she cooperated, he wouldn't. And he had kept that promise. But she didn't know if he would keep it up. She was grateful when the Man took Claire away, up the stairs while the Other Man made himself busy with her.

"Father works near the river. He is looking for us, Claire. He'll find us. He loves us and he'll find us," Emma said, keeping up the running prattle, though she no longer expected Claire to answer. Little Claire, only seven years old, wiser than she, had stopped talking long ago, having learned better than Emma that silence gave you power when nothing else did. Claire spent most of her time staring at the walls with the fixed, stunned expression that had lately hollowed her cheeks and eyes, worrying Emma, who had done all she could to protect her.

There were two men. The Man who lived upstairs and took care of them, and the Other Man, the one who found them and brought them here and came sometimes after dinner. Before the Other Man came downstairs to see Emma, the Man would whisper a scolding, *Be good,* a flat warning, *Don't look,* and a brief caress, *my little ones.* Then he would take Claire away and the Other Man would come down. But he came only sometimes. They always had to be ready, just in case. It was the waiting that was awful. The anticipation.

Emma would turn her face away, press one ear into the ground, cover the other with one hand, and transform *now* into *before*, *here* into *not here*, *happening* into *not happening.* In the darkness, she would remember the pattern of the walls and the bedspread and the way the lettering on the stove looked, but it was both Claire and Elizabeth who comforted her *during.* Emma would first think of Claire, safe upstairs, knowing nothing of what was happening, and Emma would then be free to imagine that she was listening to Elizabeth play her violin. Elizabeth had always been able to change how Emma felt just by pulling a bow across a string.

Now Emma tucked the edge of a blue sweater over her little sister's shoulders and said, "They never come in the day, Claire. Remember? You can sleep if you want. I'll keep watch, and wake you when they do." Claire blinked once, twice, then shut her eyes, having learned, it seemed, that if she followed orders, there would be less pain for both of them. Emma marveled at her sister's ability to drop away and wondered why Claire still trusted her. She shouldn't. Emma didn't even trust herself. The Man had said that her parents had given up on them. That they didn't care. That Claire and Emma should learn to love him instead, because wasn't he taking good care of them?

She hated him.

Emma began to gulp air, but she fought the rising wave of panic.

Lately, her life was measured solely by her ability to keep Claire safe, a safety that two months ago she had never dreamed she would be responsible for. She suppressed the urge to cry now, an urge that required constant vigilance or it would unleash itself and get her into trouble. Instead, she chewed the edges of her tongue, working the tongue against her teeth. Somehow it soothed her, the hint of pain, the scraping of the flesh, the small bubbles of noise that she alone could hear.

Once, the Other Man had seemed their savior.

On their way home from school that day the blizzard ended, Claire had sunk to her neck in one of the deep drifts. Despite Emma's frantic efforts, Claire kept sinking, and Emma began to wail for help. That was when the Other Man veered toward them in his bright cherry sleigh—as bright as the maraschino cherries at Huyler's ice cream shop—and leaped from the bench. Within moments, he dug Claire out. And before Emma could thank him, he dusted them both off and lifted them into his sleigh, tucked them on the seat next to him under a thick carriage blanket, and slipped a warmed brick between them. Stunned and hungry, they accepted his ministrations, though now Emma remembered entertaining a vague sense that she ought to ask to be taken straight home. But she couldn't think. The cold was a monster, scaring her into silence. And the snow was so deep that they hadn't been able to move. And then he had taken their stiffened hands into his thick leather gloves, his scarf sparkling with snow, and said things like, "I'll help you. I'll take care of you." And, "Trust me." But now he said it just to taunt her. He liked her terror. Observed it with glee. Savored it.

Emma thought that by now her pain would have coalesced, become one large throbbing ache, but every muscle drew attention to itself, every space between bone and sinew vibrated with ache. The cold of the blizzard still lingered in her body and in the basement stones. Until a few days ago, the walls had wept with snowmelt and her bones had felt as if they would shatter from the cold, despite the smothering piles of eiderdown the Man supplied. Even the coal stove, which the Other Man stoked during his nighttime visits, could not battle the damp. He shoveled the coal into the stove as he said, *I am so sorry.*

After, mad with worry, Emma would ask Claire, *What did the Man do with you upstairs?*

Claire would say, *He made me a new dress. Do you like it?* Or, *he combed my hair and carried me around on his shoulders.* Or, *He fed me porridge. He says I'm special.*

"O'Donnell?" the Other Man had said when he first asked their names, rolling the vowels on his tongue, his eyes lighting up a little as he knelt before them in the sleigh. "Well, well. That's quite the Irish name. Emma and Claire? Lovely. Perfect for you. Such pretty, pretty things you are."

Now Emma wished she had never told him who they were, because their names were too precious a thing to have given to him. It was as if she had given the Other Man a key, for he used her name like a bludgeon: *You will do this, Emma. You will.* She hated his voice. It was so cold, and it sounded like the far edge of pain.

Emma wanted to sleep, because when she slept she could forget, but she had promised Claire, so she pinched the bruises on her arms to stay awake. Outside, past the obscuring window boxes, footsteps sounded on the sidewalk, bursts of laughter and happy chatter falling away as the passersby tripped onward, oblivious.

One more sound out of you, he'd said that first night, *and Claire won't live.*

Emma buried her face in her sister's hair, chewed the edges of her tongue, and willed herself into silence.

Chapter Thirteen

The Van der Veer mansion harbored a carriageway that led to a large courtyard, fashioned of intricately patterned bricks, that was filled this evening with a throng of carriages and their drivers.

"Did the invitation say it was a party?" Amelia asked.

"It didn't," Mary said.

William shook his head. "Shanghaied."

The handwritten invitation had arrived in a cream-colored envelope several days before.

"Do you want to go?" William had said.

"It feels too soon."

"I know, but Elizabeth needs to get out." William never directly refuted Amelia or Mary about Elizabeth; instead he made only gentle suggestions from time to time, which they never mistook for anything less than a very strong opinion. So, the invitation had been accepted, and now Elizabeth glowed in a midnight blue dress that Amelia had bought her in Paris. The cabal of drivers gaped when Elizabeth alighted from the carriage and trailed across the bricks, gossiping about her beauty until she disappeared inside the mansion, where an echoing foyer checkerboarded with black and white tiles took up half the first floor. A crisply attired maid in a black dress and starched white apron took their coats, and a footman swept them all upstairs and down a wainscoted hallway. They passed a set of double swinging doors, from which emerged the sound of pots and pans above a steady murmur of chatter and scold, along with an enticing smell of puff pastry. Farther down the long corridor, a music room glimmered with painted murals and a golden harp in a far alcove. And a peek through a door standing slightly ajar gave a glimpse of an elegant dining room. Finally, at the far end of the hallway, in a French parlor that stretched the width of the house, a dozen people stopped their conversations to behold the newcomers. The group represented a select portion of the cream of Albany aristocracy, with the exception of one burly man who stood apart, a confused scowl of disorientation affixed to his weathered face.

Gerritt Van der Veer emerged from a clutch of men already gathered by the large fireplace, its blaze illuminating the women's silken skirts and the high gloss of Macassar oil in the men's hair.

"Viola," Gerritt said, waving a hand. "Come."

She rose from an armchair and glided to his side, a rictus of a smile affixed to her pale face. This evening she was clad in a swath of violet froth, lavishly beribboned and pleated. This plethora of color and light only enhanced her childish beauty, making her seem too young to be the mistress of such a magnificent home.

"We are both so glad you could come," Gerritt said. "Allow me to introduce you to our guests."

He was possessive in his certainty that the Stipp family could not possibly be acquainted with any of them, though unknown to him they were almost to a person the Stipps' patients. Physicians lived in an obligation of social purgatory, one in which they would never acknowledge their patients in a social setting. Gerritt reeled off the gilded names: Mary Pruyn, widowed at the age of thirty-nine and unescorted this evening; Mary and Erastus Corning of the Albany

City National Bank, the word *bank* emphasized; Erastus Corning's in-laws the Amasa J. Parkers, parents to Mary Corning and head of the legal firm Amasa Parker & Countryman; the Abraham Lansings of A. & W. Lansing, lawyers, too; and the Robert H. Pruyns, of the National Commercial Bank.

Albany wealth, rooted in the merchant class—as was all wealth in America—disliked any overt statement of it, and Gerritt, with his propensity for the ostentatious, obviated the very thing his guests were disposed to censure, forgetting that their roots were just as commercial. This unassailable difference was that his guests' mercantile associations were of a certain, august age and long-distanced from their current prosperity, now anchored in vast holdings of property that manufactured wealth without an obvious need to work for it. It had recently been whispered in certain circles that Viola suffered this divide acutely. Any cachet from her elite Manhattan family and inherited standing among Manhattanites had been diminished in Albany's provincial eyes by her marriage to the crass and grasping Gerritt Van der Veer, no matter that his accumulated wealth far exceeded theirs by a good deal more than any of them would ever admit.

Viola's smile now seemed cemented in place, while Gerritt exhibited no consciousness of this social divide. He beamed at them all and gestured to his son at the end of the carved fireplace mantel, where he cut an elegant figure in an evening coat. "And you know Jakob, of course. And may I present my overseer and head stevedore, James Harley."

James Harley bowed stiffly but did not relinquish his square of real estate where he stood alone, adjacent to a heavily draped window. Three enormous windows along that wall opened onto the interior courtyard, where torches licked flickering yellow shadows onto the golden weave of the curtains, and the splash of the fountain muffled the drivers' laughter.

Gerritt beckoned to Harley with a surprisingly thin, delicate hand, and the man skirted the crowd, an untouched glass of champagne bubbling in his hand.

"My dear Doctors Stipp, this is the man I trust most in the world," Gerritt said, whacking Harley on the back with approval. "Do you know that he has worked for me for twenty years? *Twenty.* He manages everything at Van der Veer Lumber. Except the books, of course. And he sails my ice-yacht for me. *Honey Girl.* She's a beauty. No one can skate an ice-yacht like Harley. We race on Saturday—if the ice holds—which I fear it won't."

Harley was not wearing an evening jacket like the other men, but a tight worsted woolen suit stretched across a muscled expanse of chest. If physicians existed in social purgatory, a foreman drowned in obscurity. Why Gerritt had invited both Harley and the Cornings to the same party surpassed even Mary's democratic understanding. Harley murmured *How do you do* and fixed a pleading gaze on Gerritt to be excused.

"I'm a champion of everyone, loyal to the people who are loyal to me," Gerritt explained. "And I like to put people together. Harley, do you know that these doctors are to be celebrated? Celebrated! They went to the war. Even Mrs. Stipp—a woman! Can you imagine?"

Occasionally men discussed Mary's service during the war in this way, as if she weren't in the room. Generally this conversation occurred when they could not bring themselves to admit their own, lesser roles.

"Now," Gerritt said, spouting on in a confiding voice, "I'm not ashamed to tell you that Harley and I labored here, in Albany, in the district. The army needed lumber, and we worked like the devil to sell it to them. I dare say that we were just as instrumental in the Union success as the soldiers—I'll even wager just as much as you doctors were."

"How interesting," Mary said, catching William's eye and raising an amused eyebrow. "Yours must have been a great sacrifice."

At the word *sacrifice,* Harley, understanding Mary's undertone, looked away. But Gerritt was unfazed.

"Have you had any champagne? It's Veuve Clicquot. The best. I sent to Paris for a dozen cases." Gerritt gestured to a footman, who glided over bearing a tray of bubbling glasses. Gerritt handed them around, then steered both Harley and William toward the erect forms of the two bankers, Erastus Corning and Robert H. Pruyn, who were engrossed in a discussion about interest rates that they abandoned at the approach of the outsiders.

Viola, who had retreated into the background, now confided to Mary, "Tonight was meant to be an intimate dinner with just our two families, but sometimes Gerritt cannot help himself. He invited the other guests without informing me. He told the cook only this morning. She had to scramble to find enough oysters."

She delivered this spousal treason with a shy smile.

"You are not privy to your husband's decisions?" Mary asked.

"Not even his whereabouts. I never have any idea when Gerritt will be anywhere. He is never at home during the day. He lunches at the Oyster House, he tells me, and most nights eats dinner at his club. Occasionally, he comes home in the evening, but then he goes out again. The problem for me is that I am very shy, and so I am left alone a great deal. It is difficult for me to be out in company and offer invitations; I prefer quiet chats with a good friend. But you see, society—this kind of society—isn't really about friendship, is it? That's why I liked Bonnie so much—she was a confidante whenever I could get the courage to visit her. She used to hide me in the back room when any other customers came in so that I wouldn't be discovered lurking about so helplessly. She said I helped her business, though. She said I had an eye for millinery, and whatever I asked her to make for me the other women all had to have, but I think she was being kind. She was the one who was brilliant."

Viola let her smile flag and looked furtively about the room, and

Mary felt terrible about her and William's vaguely disparaging assessment of her. Bonnie had clearly liked Viola and even, it seems, taken care of her by not gossiping about her wealthy friend to anyone, even Mary.

"I hate having to be on display," Viola continued. "But this is what Gerritt wants, and so I do it for him."

Mary tried to imagine a life without agency and couldn't. "How long have you been married?"

"I always have to gauge it by Jakob's birth. He is twenty-one now, so—twenty-two years."

"He went to Harvard, I hear?"

"I missed him so much when he was gone. But he's found Elizabeth, hasn't he?" She nodded at Jakob, who had claimed not only Elizabeth's company but Amelia's, too, and had brought them each a glass of champagne. "Is she—she's your niece, isn't she?—back from Paris permanently?"

"I hope not. I expect she'll return to Paris shortly to continue her studies."

"One should always return to Paris as often as one can. It is my favorite city in the world, though I hardly ever get there now. My father used to take the family before he tired of traipsing back and forth across the Atlantic on his ships."

Catherine and Abraham Lansing appeared and, having overheard, announced that they were going to sail the Atlantic in June so that Abraham could attend the International Conference for the Codification of the Law of Nations in London. "We are going on to Paris afterward," Abraham said. "You and Gerritt really ought to plan a crossing soon, Mrs. Van der Veer. And you and your husband, too, Mrs. Stipp. By the way, we plan on taking in a concert at the Conservatoire while we are there. Will Miss Fall have returned by then? We would like very much to hear her play."

Before Mary could answer, a liveried footman struck a triangle with a hand wand to announce dinner. Viola guided her chattering guests down the hallway and into the ornate dining room, where two enormous chandeliers blazed under a coffered tin ceiling, cornflower blue tapers paraded down a long center table decorated with a yellow tablecloth, and splashes of pink tulips and purple hyacinths overflowed cut crystal bowls.

Place cards instructed the guests: Mary was seated in the place of honor at Gerritt's right, William to Viola's left. Jakob anchored the middle of the table, a cavalier in charge of Elizabeth to his right, and the widow Pruyn to his left, who was not thrilled to find that the man to her other side was a bemused James Harley, who held out her chair stiffly before surrendering himself with pained gravity to the brocade silk of his. Amelia was relegated to the care of Erastus Corning, who smiled and introduced her to his wife, whose five children Amelia had delivered over the course of fifteen years and whose astute skill with breech births had ensured that every one lived. Politesse prevailed as the rest of the guests accepted their lesser assignments with resentful grace.

When the first course, *soupe à la reine*, had been served in footed bowls of gleaming gilt-edged china, Gerritt cleared his throat.

"I would like to say something. It's important that these things are acknowledged, I think. Viola and I want to mention that our new friends, the William Stipps, their niece, and Mrs. Amelia Sutter have recently suffered a great sadness, one in which Viola and I share. Some of you may remember that the Stipps were particular friends of the David O'Donnells. O'Donnell worked in my yard as a stevedore. Sadly, he and his wife were among those who died in the storm. I know the ladies will remember Bonnie's millinery shop. And, of course, even more disheartening is that their children—the Stipps' goddaughters, I believe—were lost, never to be found. Before we go any further with the evening, I thought we might wish to give the Stipps our humble regard and sympathies. They chose not to have a public funeral, and so I thought that now would be an appropriate moment to acknowledge their pain."

The awkward pronouncement ricocheted around the room. William projected a silent plea to Mary for forgiveness for having encouraged their attendance. Elizabeth blanched. Amelia's hand floated to her throat. The bulk of the guests looked up from consuming their soup and locked eyes with one another. James Harley held himself perfectly still.

Viola cleared her throat, a deep flush coloring her cheeks. "I adored Bonnie," she said, linking herself with the Stipps in their sorrow, holding fast to the kindness she had already displayed. "I think every one of the women in this room owns at least a half dozen of her creations. Don't we all?"

"It's such a pity," Mary Parker Corning said, tilting her lace-capped head from her distant corner to address Mary. "Bonnie made the most exquisite hats. Now we'll have to go all the way to Manhattan City to get them made."

"Which," Mary Pruyn hastily added, "is a real testament to your friend's artistry, Dr. Stipp."

They knew they had mired themselves in class. Bonnie was nothing to them but their milliner. In the ensuing silence, it was Erastus Corning who set down his spoon on the rim of his bowl and with this authoritative gesture seized command of the situation. "That storm was a terrible thing. We are all sorry for your loss."

"Yes," Amasa Parker echoed, the deep gravel of his voice rumbling down the table, almost as a weapon. He was an elderly man, a former judge and congressman, whose dour face had long ago seared into disappointment when he lost his two runs for the governorship. His wife, Harriett, lifted her chin in response, the high black ruffle of her dress at its neck giving her an ecclesiastical air. "Yes," she chorused. "Yes."

We are. Yes. All sorry. Relieved murmurs of agreement filled the room. Rescued, everyone took up their soup spoons again.

Everyone, Mary saw, except Elizabeth, who was looking into her lap, her head bowed, the startling mass of her glossy curls glowing in the warm light of the chandeliers. They should not have brought her. They had questioned her surprising willingness, but she had assured them of her equanimity, which Mary was now certain had nothing to do with ease and everything to do with Jakob Van der Veer, whose sympathetic gaze was fixed on her.

In the wake of Gerritt's blundering condolence, no one could think of a thing to say. Spoons rose and slipped into the creamy broth, the tender stewed capon occasionally slithering from spoons back into the soup.

The silence became unbearable.

Erastus Corning lofted his glass and made a toast to *Our Beloved Departed,* a second deft intervention. He then remarked that the weather had turned warm, encouraging someone else to opine that the river must soon break up, which caused a successfully distracted Gerritt to again bemoan this year's volume of snowmelt even as he expressed relief that navigation might soon be restored.

"But," he said, "lumber doesn't move unless the river does. Until then, we Van der Veers are living on last year's receipts."

Jakob leaned over to whisper to Elizabeth, "I am sorry about my father. He means well, but he can be clumsy in society. I don't think he even realizes. I'm sure he meant well, bringing up your friends. I'm sure he meant to share your grief. But I am sorry."

"The hazards," Elizabeth said, attempting a tremulous smile and lifting her spoon, "of appearing in society too early."

"You must blame me. I was the one who wanted you to come to dinner."

"You did?" she said.

"Yes," he said, pausing bashfully. "I wanted to see you again."

Gerritt abandoned his loud talk of receipts and turned to Mary, saying of Jakob and Elizabeth, "They seem to be getting on well?"

"Elizabeth is still grieving. We all are."

As Elizabeth managed another hint of a smile, Gerritt boomed down the table: "Miss Elizabeth. We have the most beautiful music room. And I've bought many instruments for when musicians come to visit: piano, violin, even a harp. Will you play for us? Show us what you've learned in the Conservatoire? Accompany us at dinner, perhaps?"

Elizabeth's eyes widened in panic, her gaze darting from guest to guest, finally landing on Jakob. "I cannot. I haven't practiced in weeks. Not since Paris."

"But in one so accomplished, our famous violinist returned from the Continent, what is a few weeks?" Gerritt pressed.

"Oh, do play for us, Elizabeth. How delightful!" This was the widow Pruyn, vying for position.

Abraham Lansing stated that he was fond of Mozart. Preferable, he said, to that unreliable Bach.

"Doesn't our violinist look beautiful tonight?" Gerritt said, directing his question to James Harley, who had said nothing during the entire dinner, and did not answer now. "So young, and so accomplished."

Elizabeth flushed under the attention. "I will not, if you don't mind. I haven't played since I heard about the O'Donnells."

Of course, of course, came the sympathetic murmur, led by Erastus Corning. The fish course—oysters, on a bed of rock salt—sailed in on silver platters. "Oh, look," Corning said. "Oysters."

"I apologize again," Jakob murmured to Elizabeth. "My father is an admirer of anyone of fame."

"I have no fame," Elizabeth's gaze had turned glassy. "None whatsoever."

"Mrs. Stipp," Abraham Lansing said, with a conspiring glance at Jakob, obviously seeking again to divert attention from the distressed Elizabeth, "are you considering retirement from your profession?"

"I beg your pardon?" Mary said.

"Society has no need for women physicians. The war is long since over. There are plenty of men to do the job. I ask because I've heard that in some states women doctors are petitioning the courts to be allowed to practice where they've been denied. The effort seems excessive. War gives license for many things, but a woman's natural province is the home. Why are you so compelled to exhaust yourself with work when you could lead a regular life?"

Mary lifted her wineglass. "What is a regular life? Perhaps you would like it if I stayed home and twiddled my thumbs?"

Viola gave a short laugh, and Jakob rose, eager both to avoid outright war and to save Elizabeth and Mary from the unwanted attentions directed their way. "If you'll excuse us, I am in dire need of some fresh air. Miss Elizabeth has kindly consented to accompany me in a stroll down the street." He turned to her and said, "Haven't you, Elizabeth? With your permission, of course, Dr. Stipp." Jakob directed an appealing gaze at William, who acquiesced with a brief nod. Jakob apologized to his mother, who waved him on his way, and the two young people fled the room.

Eyebrows raised at the impropriety of the young scion of the family and an unchaperoned girl deserting a dinner barely in its infancy—there were still five courses to come—but there was brittle envy, too, for most of the guests wanted to leave but could not, out of deeply ingrained manners that dictated courtesy before sanity.

Later, in the parlor, the women took tea while the men drank brandy by the bank of windows flung open to ventilate the room of their blue cigar smoke. Elizabeth and Jakob had returned sometime during dessert and were being left alone, albeit under the watchful eye of Amelia, who sat nearby, half-listening to their gentle teasing and half-listening to Jane Pruyn discuss her husband's ambassadorial service to Japan during the war.

"We didn't go with Robert, of course, the children and I. And here the War of the Rebellion was on, so we moved to the Continent for four years. The Continent is so much more civilized than the Orient. Don't you agree?"

Gerritt had cornered William by a vase of hothouse roses and said under his breath, "You'll forgive me. I meant no disrespect. I am sometimes an oaf when it comes to delicate things. But I would like very much to extend again the House of Shelter proposition that I made to Mrs. Stipp."

"That is entirely for her to decide."

"Of course, of course. But between men—"

"Mary Sutter makes her own decisions."

"Mary Sutter?"

"I call her that when she is at her most courageous. Which is most of the time."

"I only want to help."

"You can. Do not mention the clinic to anyone else. It was never yours to interfere with in any way. I perceive that in your offer you meant to be generous. But Mary is not a woman to be manipulated. She alone will decide what she wants to do."

In an armchair nearby, Mary smiled. William rarely interjected himself into her fights, but when he did, his machinations generally took the form of orders and not negotiation.

"Of course," Gerritt said. "Forgive me. I invited you all because I thought a party might cheer you. And I thought Jakob and Elizabeth might be able to hide in a crowd and get to know one another. The other night at dinner, Jakob mentioned to me that he was quite taken with her, and I must admit that I am, too."

William opened his mouth to reply when a deafening explosion rocked the house, a flat boom that thundered through the open windows, followed by percussive, shuddering waves. A violent cracking noise reverberated through the air, and then another. The night erupted. Bells began to ring: deeply resonant church bells, sharp, clanging fire bells, and then the awful, piercing shriek of the Lumber District siren.

The sudden clamor startled everyone into silence.

Then the guests exhaled. The river. Yes. That was it, they all agreed. The river ice was breaking up.

But Harley and Gerritt, far from sanguine, exchanged a swift and piercing look. Gerritt jerked his chin to the door, and Harley bolted from the room. Jakob, too, jumped to his feet.

"Get the books!" Gerritt shouted at him, tossing him a key ring from a pocket of his frock coat.

Jakob caught it, lunged for the door, and dashed away without a backward glance.

Chapter Fourteen

With the first warning boom, chaos broke out all over the city. Intoxicated men poured out of taverns. At Tweddle Hall, patrons in fancy dress fled the night's entertainment for their waiting carriages. Merchants who lived above their riverside shops tumbled down back stairwells and thrust themselves into the fraught business of preserving their livelihoods, while their wives herded their crying children uphill. Hoteliers near the river instructed sleepy guests to pack their bags and skedaddle. Railroad engineers scrambled to move their locomotives out of harm's way, adding the incessant screech of steam whistles to the rising din. And stevedores and lumber handlers converged in droves on the district, intent on saving as much lumber as they could. They had maybe an hour, two if they were lucky, before river water inundated the district and washed away the overwintered stock.

The Van der Veer carriage hurtled through the city, carrying Jakob to the district. At North Broadway, several blocks distant from the rising river, he encountered a mounted policeman cantering down the granite blocks of the thoroughfare, shouting over the bells, "Get to higher ground. Run like the devil is after you." The streetlights of Broadway fell away as Jakob exited the carriage and raced on foot toward the river. At the corner of Water Street, he called to a shopkeeper turning the key in the lock of his dry goods store. Jakob plucked a new lantern, a can of kerosene, and a box of carbon matches from the shelves, and threw money onto the counter as the storekeeper begged in vain for help moving his goods into the eaves. Outside, Jakob coaxed a brilliant flame from the fragile lantern mantle. Holding the swinging lantern aloft, he hurtled down the remaining quarter mile to Lock Two, then squeezed into the mass of men pouring into the district. Everywhere was noise—people screaming, horses' hooves clattering against cobbles, and fractured river ice crashing into the pilings of the north railroad bridge, a cacophony that sounded like the end of the world.

The Van der Veer lot thrummed with chaos. Harley had taken off from the party in his little gig without waiting for Jakob, but now Jakob, his lantern swinging wildly, darted between the towering stacks of lumber, searching for the overseer, who he thought had preceded him to the district. But the man was nowhere. Irritated, Jakob abandoned the fruitless search and tried to get a sense of what could be done with the dozens of Van der Veer men who had reported. Underfoot, slush and mud were making the going hellish, and the river ice was cracking and roaring as it gave way.

In Harley's place Jakob directed the men to load the flat barges with as much lumber as the ships could carry. Canal boats that had frozen in the slips during the blizzard could carry 165,000 board feet—a good save, and every board foot they preserved was money in everyone's pocket. The men responded to Jakob's shouted instructions, crawling onto the stacks, manning ropes and pulleys, and leaping onto barges to receive the payloads. They worked hard and fast, wary eyes peering into the darkness toward the river, their backs bent to the job. The only light came from bobbing lanterns and the silver shine of a half moon reflected on banks of low clouds. No one knew how much time they had, or how many hours they worked, but to a man, bones grew weary and sweat poured from them like a fire hose.

Suddenly an enormous cry broke through the chaos as lookouts posted on the river shore shouted, "Now, now, now!"

Men abandoned their work on the spot and bolted.

They thundered past Jakob, vanishing into the night, urging him to follow. But instead Jakob hunted every inch of blackness, and only when he had verified that every last one of their men had vacated the lot did he race to the Van der Veer Lumber office to retrieve the company books, which contained the record of every transaction the company had ever made. This retrieval had been his father's sole aim in sending Jakob tonight, but Harley's absence—and his father's—had forced Jakob to perform the overseer's responsibilities until this last minute.

The office occupied a square of land adjacent to the main road that ran along the river side of the district, but the office was a good hundred feet from the shore. The location was advantageous—close to the Lock Bridge, serviced by the district trolley, just steps away from one of the big sawmills. All day long, the scent of sawdust and the whine of the enormous band saw penetrated the two-room edifice where his father reigned as the king of lumber. His father had built the impressive office a decade ago, when the company's coffers had swelled after the war. With a view to impressing clients, Gerritt had spent eight thousand dollars on an elegant building crafted not of lumber, but of brick—a heretical ode to profitability. Its French roof rose twenty feet, and the walls inside were paneled in black walnut. It was the envy of the other dealers, and his father's pride and joy.

Dredging the key ring from his pocket, Jakob juggled the lantern, fumbling as he unlocked the door. The river sounded like a freight train. He tripped on the raised threshold as he went in, slammed the door, and rushed through the reception room with its high sales counter and overstuffed chairs into his father's office in the back.

There he kept his big combination vault, hidden behind a panel door fashioned to look like the wall. He rounded his father's wide oak desk and dialed the lock, his fingers trembling. Outside, chunks of ice battered the North Bridge, grinding against it. He misdialed and began again, his fingers feeling like jelly. After an eon, the tumblers locked into place. Jakob hefted the bolt, swung open the lead door, and began rummaging, loading ledgers into the crook of his elbow, in all, fifteen volumes of the history of Van der Veer Lumber. He had no idea that his father kept so many. He stuffed them one after the other into a thick burlap sack, scooped up piles of greenbacks, slammed the door shut, twirled the lock, snagged the lantern, and charged out of the inner office and back through the front room with his spoils.

He yanked the outside door open an inch. Black, icy water surged in around his feet.

Heart pounding, he strong-armed the door shut, but somehow, water kept seeping in underfoot

He stood there, panting. There was no going outside. The river would sweep him away. How long had he been inside? Two minutes? Less?

He skidded back through the front room to his father's heavy oak desk and heaved the burlap bag atop, plunked the lantern beside it, and clambered on top, too, breathing hard, making rapid calculations. He recalled his father's warnings at the cemetery. If the freshet turned out to be as bad as his father predicted, the building might fill with water. And fast. And if the river rose above twenty feet—which it sometimes did—rarely, but still—the office would be completely submerged. Gulping air, he fought panic, reeling with fury at Harley. Where was that man? If he'd shown up to do his job, Jakob could have retrieved the books straightaway. He would not now be facing a watery grave. Furthermore, where was his father? He'd thought he was just behind him. Had he said that he was coming? The ominous splash of lumber piles toppling and ice smashing made it impossible to think.

What was essential? Staying alive.

For a brief moment, he thought of Elizabeth. They had not walked far—just down to Willett Street and back under flowering horse chestnut trees, but then they had sat on a neighbor's steps, whispering together about Paris and the Conservatoire. Elizabeth had confided the relentless criticism her instructor had heaped on her, her overwhelming sense of failure, the sadness of everything she had loved vanishing from her life, all of it pouring out of her in a rush. He had taken her gloved hands in his and did not relinquish them until she finished.

A huge crash thundered through the air. Slabs of ice, keeling over.

Underfoot, water already lapped halfway up the solid desk. Where was it coming in? From underneath the floorboards maybe?

Frantic, Jakob took inventory in the flickering lantern light. At some point, he had lost the kerosene tin. Soon, the oil would run out and he would be plunged into pitch-blackness.

His eyes raked the shelves, searching for anything of use.

Then he remembered.

In the front room, his father kept an altar to the lumber business: links of grappling chain, a long cant hook, an even longer, sharp-pronged peavey, a mass of lethal picaroons. And one double-bitted ax.

He lowered himself into the freezing waters and gasped.

He toed forward, uncertain of the flooring. There was little current. A vase bobbed by. An oil lamp. Holding his lantern high, he headed for the front room.

The double-sided ax hung suspended on nails on the wall, high above the sales counter. Heaving himself up, he grappled for it and knocked it off its hooks. It splashed into the water beside him. He grabbed for it, just snagging the curved wooden handle before it drifted away. His legs were already numb. One hand grasping the ax, the other the lantern, he drifted like a ghost back through the water, thinking rather than feeling his way.

Shivering, he lugged himself onto the desk, and pulled his legs up one by one. He was shuddering, cold through. He crawled to his hands and knees, staggered to a stand. The desk was heavy enough to stay put for a while, but water could carry anything away.

For a brief moment, he had a sense of the walls of his heart dissolving. He had just been born, and now he might die. A vision flickered before him—his mother, weeping.

He was not dressed for exertion. He was dressed for a dinner party. He began wildly swinging the ax.

Chapter Fifteen

At the first peel of bells, Emma was on her feet.

She'd been dreaming and now she was awake and she didn't know why.

Earlier, she and Claire had fallen asleep under a new blanket that the Man had promised would ward off the chill of the stone walls. It hadn't. She was always cold.

The dream was her favorite one. She dreamed it all the time. It was about stars in the sky and a ladder that dropped down from heaven and a little man who wore a sparkling top hat who reached over the starry ledge to beckon Emma and Claire to climb the ladder into the shimmer, away from all the pain.

The nearby church bell, the one that rang on Sunday mornings, was banging back and forth in its tower. Above the sound of the bell, the high shriek of the Lumber District whistle wailed, too. The Lumber District siren used to mean that her father was coming home from work. Now it meant that the Man was coming back.

But it wasn't morning. And it wasn't evening. It was dark.

Emma blinked into the blackness, looking first, as she always did, to the top of the stairs to see whether or not the Man was coming down. He always came down first if the Other Man was coming, to admonish Emma into cooperation, to carry Claire away. But the door wasn't opening. On the street, yellow lantern light flashed around the black shadows of the window boxes. Hollow calls of panic and worry floated in the air.

The bell was the one that rang so loudly on Sundays. Yes, for certain, it was the church bell. But it wasn't Sunday morning now, was it? And the siren had already sounded for that night. And the Man wasn't coming down the stairs.

At least not yet.

Claire woke and began to weep, and Emma wrapped her arms around Claire's waist and petted her hair.

Think!

Until this moment, the ringing of the church bell had been a gift. It had given her the ability to mark time. She counted everything now: the number of weeks they'd been gone, the number of stairs to the locked door, the number of times the Other Man came, the number of times he'd forced her to do *that.*

But the bell also meant that one more week had passed and her mother and father hadn't yet come for them. She feared that what the Man said was true. That her parents had given up on them. That they didn't care.

Tonight, neither the Man nor the Other Man had come downstairs, but now that reprieve vanished in importance. Now, more bells began to ring. Was this upheaval a new trick? But how could the Man enlist everyone? Outside, people were yelling. No. This was something else, something the Man didn't cause, though in their new world nothing happened that the Man didn't make happen.

Her mother loved the sound of church bells, except when it was the middle of the night. When it was the middle of the night, the bells signified something terrible, Emma remembered. Her mind churned as she struggled to remember what her mother said they meant.

Outside, flashes of candle and lantern light flickered past the window boxes. People were up. People were awake.

When the bells rang, her mother would leap from her bed. She would throw open the window and call out—what?

Oh, her mind was working so slowly. Too slowly.

Fire or flood!

Cradling Claire in her arms, Emma forced herself to make her thoughts as ordered as the rungs on that ladder to the sky. She didn't smell smoke. But she couldn't be certain. Sometimes the coal stove smoked and sometimes everything smelled of it, and when it did, she didn't smell other, loathsome things.

Emma put away her fear. Because she might need to do something.

Think one thought at a time, she told herself.

Down here, shut up in the basement, she might not smell smoke. So it was possible that the bells meant fire.

But maybe it was just early in the morning. Maybe it was a holiday. Easter was coming. She remembered that she was to have had a new dress for the holiday. Her mother had promised to make it for her. Maybe it was Easter now?

Did bells ring like this on Easter?

No. Easter came on Sunday. It wasn't Sunday.

Outside, wagons were creaking past. Someone set a lantern down near one window box. No one was hurrying. Hurrying would mean fire.

So, it must be flood. In flood, there was always time.

She and her father had once gone to the lapping edge of a freshet on Broadway and watched an eddy carry away bales of hay from an upturned packet boat. But she didn't know whether they were above or below Broadway now. The Man wouldn't tell them where they were. She knew only that after the Other Man had picked them up, he had driven them in his sleigh toward the river, and now train and boat whistles sounded almost all the time, and it felt as if they were so close that she sometimes dreamed that those sounds could carry them away like that eddy.

Claire was still crying.

Had the Man gone out? Sometimes he did at night, when the Other Man didn't come. But she'd fallen asleep. Maybe they were alone. She couldn't tell.

Was he here? Where was he?

Would he save them? Oh, she didn't want to drown. Sometimes people did. That's why they lived up high, her father told her. That's why they lived up away from the river. Sometimes, the man's voice in her dream sounded like her father's. Come up! Come away! it called.

She heard keys jangling in the lock, and a sliver of light from the opening door spilled down the stairs. Candlelight jounced around the basement, glinting off the shiny tip of the coal shovel.

"Hello, doves," the Man's awful voice shrieked from the top of the stairs. "Don't be afraid of those nasty bells. I'm here."

Chapter Sixteen

At dawn, James Harley sputtered and reared upward onto his hands and knees, grabbing at a hellish pain at the back of his head. Wheezing, disoriented, he pulled his hand away. Blood was smeared across his palm. Stumbling to his feet, he took in the strange sight of the remnants of his winter coal bobbing on blackened water, a scrap of blanket drifting toward him, and a bed submerged under the opaque surface of the pooling mess. His brain worked hard to make sense of what he was seeing. He had lost something, he thought. Yes, that was it, something vaguely new and wonderful that had given him so much happiness of late. Woozy, he reached for a pillar. His shirt and trousers dripped with water. At his feet, the tip of his coal shovel protruded from the surface of the water. He picked it up. Staring at it, he tried to understand the odd confluence of seeping water, brutal headache, bloodied shovel, and the dispiriting sense of loss that now overwhelmed him.

Water was rising past his ankles, seeping up from the ground, trickling through the walls, pouring in through the windows. He must get out of here; yes, this is what he must do. Driven by this sudden clarity, he dropped the shovel into the half foot of water rapidly overtaking his cellar and waded the few feet to the stairs. He climbed the wooden staircase on his hands and knees, fighting dizziness. Upstairs, he scrambled across the plank floor of his kitchen, staggering to his feet when he reached the back door. He flung it open. Water coursed down the alley. Two, six inches? More?

Sunlight flickered off the water. His neighbors were spilling into the alleyway. One of them, a short, stout woman in a red kerchief, clung to a weathered fire escape. She had knotted a blanket around her chest, and from it came the muffled wailing of an infant. He knew the woman by sight, though not her name. She lived down the street, one of the many impoverished women whose boys wandered shoeless in the summer and hatless in the winter. Her boys clung to her, the youngest with one arm slung around her neck, his legs cinched around her waist, the older hanging onto the ties of her dirty apron. He was submerged to his waist at her side, wailing. The children's high-pitched screams ricocheted off the water. The screaming finally accomplished what the water had not. It restored his foggy memory.

Stricken, he turned. In his confusion, had he missed them? Left them in the cellar? Had he locked the door? Were they inside, drowning? Or had they somehow escaped upstairs? He replayed his awakening in his mind. Had the door to the cellar been open when he woke? Usually he locked it going in and out, but now he couldn't remember.

"In the name of God, James Harley, you've got to help me," the woman cried.

How would he explain Emma and Claire to anyone? Even if he could get down into the cellar and back again without being drowned, what would the girls do when they were free? Start talking, maybe. Tell everyone. And then—oh God, then—it would be the end of him. He looked yearningly at the door to his house. Water was already breaking over the threshold, pouring in. Surely the basement was nearly full now.

Torn between returning to save them and saving himself, he hesitated, his choice so painful he could hardly breathe.

Surely the girls were already dead.

Or would be, soon.

It occurred to him now that he ought perhaps to have relayed the fact that the Pastures had a tendency to flood when he agreed to house the girls. But he'd not been given much choice.

Harley ventured into the alley, first one step, then another, then scuttled backward and pressed his body against the house. The water was numbingly cold and rising fast. Within moments, it would pass his knees. He had to go now.

Harley struck out across the alley, raising a hand to indicate to the shrieking woman that he was on his way. Twice, the current nearly took him. The woman screamed again and again for him to hurry. When he reached her, she turned so that he could peel the young boy off her back. Nimbly, the boy scrambled onto Harley's shoulders and grabbed at the cut on his neck. Harley's knees buckled from the searing pain. Terrified, the boy reared backward, and Harley lost balance and they both fell into the water. Harley struggled to his feet and fished the boy out by his wrist, warning him through gritted teeth to not touch his neck again or he'd be sorry. The frightened boy nodded. The older boy wrapped his arms around Harley's right thigh, and they all plunged westward, trailed by the woman cradling the blanket and its wailing contents to her chest.

They fought their way up the alley, crossed Franklin and Pearl Streets, forged on. More than a few pounds too heavy, the woman stopped frequently to catch her breath. The boys would not let Harley proceed without their mother at their side. They marched in fits and starts another three blocks up the slow rise of Madison, where the water lapped finally at dry pavement on Grand Street. There Harley plucked the children from his back and leg and sank to the ground, where an ever-growing crowd was seeking refuge.

Exhausted, Harley hung his head between his knees, breathing hard, his neck throbbing. The woman sprawled on the pavement beside him and regaled anyone who would listen about his kindness. He had saved her children, and couldn't they tell the poor man was hurt? A lurking journalist—in danger of losing his job if he didn't come up with an interesting concoction—*story*—sooner rather than later—interrogated the woman, encouraging embellishment, and when she failed to comply, embellished his notes himself, inventing and shaping, hardly noticing when Harley slumped sideways onto the cobbles. Everyone took far too long to notice the nasty welt at the base of his skull. For a moment, the reporter contemplated the possibility that the man's death might provide a more rousing and satisfactory end to his story, but he was too weak a person to lead a life of remorse. He commandeered a carriage to ferry them to City Hospital, and as it jounced up the cobbled hill, the reporter cradled Harley's head in his lap, careful not to touch the gaping wound that would prove his subject's heroism.

Chapter Seventeen

At the Van der Veer mansion, when the bells commenced their interminable peal, the Doctors Stipp and their family extracted themselves from the party, and Harold, already waiting outside, drove them to City Hospital at a rapid trot. The streets of the city seethed with panic. Drays and carts were fleeing uphill, away from the river, their coach lights winking. Harold shouted for news and they were fed bits and pieces: yes, it was the ice; the gas along the riverfront was already out; the water was a devil. At Eagle Street, traffic was stoppered by a bottleneck and Harold could go no farther, and he had no choice but to deposit them into the swirling eddies of humankind.

The hospital loomed at the corner of Eagle and Howard Streets: three stories, a basement, a new wing along Eagle Street, and a hexagonal Victorian tower, its windows lit tonight by candles in lieu of the usual gas. The building was a former jail, and though much money had been spent in fashioning a pleasing transformation, its dark stone facade still put a chill into Mary's heart. They pushed through a crowd to the steep stairs of the hospital entrance. They had already determined that Mary and William would attend to whatever presented itself in the accident ward, Amelia would treat any laboring women, and Elizabeth would be helpful in whatever way she could. Dressed in their finery, they made an incongruous picture among the refugee patients.

"You'll be fine," Mary assured Elizabeth as they donned aprons, telling her niece that instinct would serve her well. Immediately, the nurse in charge put Elizabeth to work, arming her with pen and ink and ledger so that she could record patients' names. Mary and William surveyed the crowded corridors, picking their way around sprawled limbs and sleeping children. St. Peter's Hospital on Broadway usually treated these kinds of trauma because of its proximity to the railroad, where accidents occurred almost daily. But apparently the flood had inundated St. Peter's and dozens of patients were stranded on its upper floors. Any and all victims—no matter how wounded—were being sent to City.

The accident ward was downstairs, flush with Eagle Street, to allow for stretchers to be carried in. So far the injuries seemed to be mostly the result of the general frenzy: cuts and bruises and mild shock from fright. Since there were no women in labor, the same nurse in charge marshaled Amelia's services to perform basic triage; she was to send those with bruised shins, broken fingers, and minor cuts upstairs to wait their turn. The more troubling cases called for immediate attention. These were arriving trundled up from the waterfront in jolting wagons, for the hospital board had yet to fund ambulances.

"Have any other physicians come to help?" Mary said.

"Just you and Dr. Stipp," the nurse said, shaking her head.

They were inundated. The accident ward was filling up. One man had shattered his feet by dropping something heavy on them, and William wheeled him to the operating room. Mary splinted a woman's broken arm and leg, making a mental note to fashion her proper casts during a lull, but she could wait several days if necessary. Mary pulled a sheet over the head of a woman trampled by a runaway horse.

Albert Van der Veer, distant cousin to Gerritt, arrived around one in the morning. He had also served as a surgeon in the War of the Rebellion. His brother, also named Garrett but with the more traditional spelling, had been a lieutenant colonel in the war but was killed in action in the Battle of Olustee in Florida. Unlike most of his compatriots, the younger doctor had welcomed Mary to the staff of the hospital when the Stipps arrived from Manhattan City. He was particularly skilled, like William, in orthopedics. Together, he and Mary operated on an open fracture, using techniques developed during and after the war. William set a broken humerus under anesthesia. In this way, the night lingered on, with complicated cases punctuating ever-lengthening periods of bandaging and soothing, the three doctors falling into the familiar rhythm of the marathon surgery sessions of the war.

At 7:00 a.m., when an entire hour had gone by without a new patient, Albert Van der Veer went home. It was then that Mary and William found themselves at the side of an unconscious man who had suffered an odd blow to the base of his skull, which looked, for all the world, as if he had been hit across the back of his neck by a sword or a shovel.

"Do you know him?" William asked the gaunt rail of a man at his side, who was keeping intense watch.

"Not his name," the young man said. "But he's the hero of the flood."

William and Mary peered at their patient's bloodied face, prominent jaw, and stolid build.

"William, *we* know him. Isn't this Mr. Harley?" Mary said. "Gerritt Van der Veer's overseer?"

It was. The cut had swelled, distorting the features of his face, but it was indeed James Harley. They rushed him into the operating amphitheater. They spent a good deal of time washing out the gash, which smelled of sewer water and railroad grease. The blow had somehow not severed the spine, but the cut was a perfect slice down to the sixth cervical vertebra. The vertebral process was exposed, glistening white in its pillow of red tissue. A chip of the bone had been cut away. Even with surgical intervention, there would be more swelling, and pain, probably for a good long while. He had likely suffered concussion, too, though they needed to wait to assess the extent of the danger. However, they both agreed he would be one lucky man if he emerged from this with only a ripping headache and sore neck. In the end, their task was mostly a matter of careful stitching.

They saw Harley safely upstairs to a clean bed, where the young man from before was writing in a notebook. He leaped up and extended his hand.

"Horace Young. I'm a reporter with the *Argus.* Tell me, how is our hero?"

They answered the young man's questions, repeating several times in different ways that the outlook for Harley's recovery was still undetermined.

"I see. Well, I'm going to write a story about our hero."

"Why do you keep calling him that?" Mary asked.

"Don't you know? He saved two children."

"Two children?' Mary swallowed and exchanged a swift glance with William, allowing herself a moment of hope. "Girls?"

The reporter shook his head. "Two little boys. Mr. Harley helped them through the floodwaters. Isn't that a great story? You saved the life of a man who saved the lives of children."

"But are you certain they weren't girls?"

Young peered at her from under a layer of pale eyelashes. His scrutiny gave off the foul taint of a vulture. "Wait. I know who you are. Stipp. That's your name, isn't it? Of course. You are those doctors who wouldn't give up on those sisters who died in the blizzard. That's why you asked whether or not the children were girls. But you buried them the other day, didn't you? I read the notice in the *Argus.*"

William followed Mary as she turned away and strode down the hallway, sick of the cavalier way people mentioned Emma and Claire's disappearance.

"Wait," Young called. "I want to write about your part in all of this, too. A woman doctor is so interesting. What does your husband think of your unusual profession?"

"Unusual profession?" Mary said, wheeling around. First at the party, from Abraham Lansing, and now this reporter. "As opposed to what? A laundress? Or a prostitute? Is that what you are implying? Or ought I to become a writer so that I, too, could ask idiotic questions while making ridiculous assumptions about what people ought and ought not to do?"

He caught up to them, breathless. Didn't she grasp that they, too, were heroes for saving Harley's life? Didn't she understand that her name would be honored throughout the city? Didn't she realize how free advertisement like this would help her?

William seized Young by the elbow and bellowed, "Ye God man, have you no sense? Leave us alone."

On the way home, the chaos of the night before had subsided, though the traffic was still heavy. It was cold. Outside the thick stone walls of the hospital, you could hear the ice marshaling its forces and pushing ever southward. Mary laid her head against the hood strut of their carriage, exhausted. Amelia had already fallen asleep, and Elizabeth was nodding off opposite Mary. Only William was alert, interrogating Harold on what he had heard of the flood damages. Throughout the night, Mary had glimpsed Elizabeth at her duties, and her niece had appeared competent and engaged, an encouraging sign that Amelia and Mary had acknowledged to one another using the tools of concerned parents everywhere: mute and fleeting expressions of approval and relief, which they assumed their children never saw and which their children always did.

As the carriage crested the hill on Madison, it occurred to Mary that she ought to send a note to the Van der Veers to tell them about James Harley's injury.

She shot straight up, recalling only now that Jakob had left with Harley to go to the Lumber District. At least that was what Gerritt had explained after Jakob and Harley bolted from the room. Something, Gerritt had said, about retrieving the company's books. But if Harley had been hurt, then what about Jakob? Had he, too, been caught in the flood? Too drained by the night's demands, she and William hadn't yet told Elizabeth or Amelia that they had treated Harley. She debated now whether or not to raise the alarm, but she decided not to. It would only cause unnecessary worry and concern. In her note to the Van der Veers, she would ask after Jakob. She would wait to see what they replied before mentioning anything. It was, after all, a good sign that Jakob hadn't been admitted.

When they pulled up to their house, it was Elizabeth who climbed out first and noticed the policeman seated on their front steps.

And another moment still before she saw that his arms were wrapped around two sleeping girls, their heads resting in his lap.

Book Two

Chapter Eighteen

By eight in the morning, the damage the flooding had caused was visible everywhere along the waterfront. Jagged ice piled along the shore had been overtopped by river water brimming with all the flotsam it had dredged along its path—carriage wheels, horsewhips, sidewalk planking, uprooted trees, roof beams, drowned livestock, a child's hobbyhorse, and one spiraling dervish of a cart. In the middle of the river channel, great mountains of ice abutted the North Bridge supports. A house floated past, completely intact until it cracked against the bridge and smashed to pieces. On a smaller floe, a rooster flapped its wings and crowed. A steam tug had gone keel up and jutted against a remnant of the pier. Onshore, roiling water enveloped the buildings along the quay to at least the second floor, making canals of the streets, and even swirling into the gasworks between Lawrence and North Lansing, tearing away piping. The Hudson inundated warehouses and homes alike, wetted grain as well as silk, inconvenienced both the rich and the poor, defied the careful and the careless, swamped the Erie Canal, sloshed upward to the D&H railroad tracks, and sundered the city's main waterline from its anchors.

From his lofty perch on the roof of Van der Veer Lumber, Jakob shifted uncomfortably in his oiled boots. His pants were soaked to the knees, and the cooling breeze that rippled the surface of the muddy, littered sea chilled him to the bone. He'd spent the night huddled in a corner of the roof up against the chimney. From time to time, the moon had come out from behind a cloud, but the silvery light had been insufficient to pinpoint the rise of the river. Chopping through the ceiling into the attic and then onto the roof itself, he'd worked up a good sweat, but in the freezing hours of the early morning his perspiration had evaporated, leaving him wet and chilled through. In the cold, his thinking had sometimes grown confused, and he had to remember not to pace to warm himself, because he didn't want to risk forgetting that there was a hole in the roof. Occasionally he stood and swung his arms and stamped his feet, but for the most part there was nothing to do but to stare into the darkness and wait, terrified and impotent. Fearing that he might lose consciousness in the bitter cold, he relived sitting with Elizabeth on the neighbor's stoop as she revealed her heartache to him about her time in Paris. As she talked he had discovered that she was not as fragile as her delicate beauty made her appear. From time to time, flashes of steely resolve had emerged, rendering her even more attractive to him.

Now he swept his gaze 360 degrees, taking in his watery view.

The world had turned upside down.

The river and its vast cargo of broken ice surged a few feet below him, skirting his father's sturdy building that had so far refused to give way. Only a few of the better-built lumber offices still stood, their steep roofs holding firm against the deluge. The saloon had disappeared. The telegraph polls were all toppled and tangled together, roped by the silver wires still strung between them. The chapel steeple bobbed on its side. The overwintered stacks of milled lumber that had filled the hundred-acre district had vanished, even the board feet that had been rushed last night onto packet boats in hopes of salvaging at least some of the stock. Not a single island of lumber protruded from the river's sunlit surface. Van der Veer & Son—indeed, every lumber merchant—had just lost a great deal of money.

Jakob thought back to Sunday, the night his father had returned late from somewhere and woken him, malt liquor and Scotch mingling on his breath, a vague satisfaction playing across his weathered features. He'd perched tipsily on the edge of Jakob's bed and gone on and on about his plans for the coming year, the money they would make. As gaslight hissed from the wall sconce, Jakob nodded, barely listening, because his father sought not approval but an audience, a function Jakob had performed for him ever since returning from Harvard. He knew his father regarded these sessions as Jakob's real education, which Jakob did not dispute out of a fervent wish to keep the peace, because any conflict only meant more misery for his mother. Jakob recalled that before his father had left, he'd leaned in confidingly, the stale smell of the liquor mingling with the perpetual pinesap. "Just so you know, son—love, regard—these are the most important things in the world. Not even money matters as much." His father had steadied himself at the doorjamb before radiating a beatifying smile of contentedness, which Jakob was certain was not reflective of amorous feelings for his mother. Jakob had only recently become aware of his father's adulterous inclinations. A week ago, at a gathering at his father's club—to which Jakob had recently been admitted on the strength of his father's money—he'd watched his father ogle a young barmaid and remark to a fellow member, "Wouldn't you like to get her up against a wall?" The man had shrugged a half smile, then walked away as Gerritt hitched up his pants. Gerritt turned to his son, a sly grin of defiance blooming across his face when he noticed Jakob watching. In his confusion and revulsion, Jakob had not said anything, but now, facing the possibility of death, he felt ashamed that he hadn't confronted his father.

Jakob shook off the sordid memory. His mother would be frantic, wondering where he was. He searched the shore for any indication that help was on its way; it stood now perhaps three hundred yards distant—double its true length. He shouted and waved his arms, but he knew no one would hear him. The river was too loud. Unbuttoning his dinner jacket, he yanked it off and waved it overhead. He was cold, but the exertion hardly warmed him. He was hungry, too, but that problem could not be solved. He went on like this for a while, pushing away the obvious perils involved in any attempted rescue, but finally he acknowledged with a shiver that the river was too fast, the water too high. Defeated, he wrapped himself in his coat and huddled back against the chimney, his desperate ruminations distracting him enough that he missed the great shudder of yet another icehouse giving way in the basin. The river was a shifting demon. It was impossible to tell what it would do next.

And then, with breathtaking rapidity, great slabs of ice groaned to a stop, then climbed over one another, effectively stoppering all the ice behind it. As Jakob watched, a frozen crust formed suddenly between him and the shore. What had moments before been a raging river was now an ice dam, a dam with incredible weight and force behind it, but solid all the same. He knew at once that it could crush the building he was standing on. Crush him, too. But it might yield passage if he could summon the courage to cross it. Terror rocketed through him, recalling his summers of dislodging logjams, the leaping from one floating log to another, the jabbing at bottlenecks with pikes, all of it a dangerous gamble where one misstep could prove fatal. Those dams broke suddenly, and occasionally men were carried away and drowned. A dangerous business, that.

This dam, too, could break at any moment. But he could feel the mounting pressure of the ice forcing itself against the building. If he didn't chance the river, he might be killed here anyway. Either choice might be suicide.

His foot knocked against the heavy burlap bag stuffed with his father's books, the reason he was stuck here. It would be foolish to take them, far easier to gain footing without them, but then what had this all been for? His father's words: *love is more important than money.* Jakob wasn't convinced his father believed that for a second.

There was the terrible crunch of shattering window glass. Jakob scooped up the bag and hugged it to his chest. In a second, he dropped three feet from the mansard roof down onto the uneven, shifting surface of the temporary, frozen lake. The slab of ice rocked precariously. He sprang off it onto its neighbor then dashed pell-mell toward the city. The treacherous footing shifted from second to second. He juggled the heavy bag and grabbed for purchase here and there, taking hold of the odd protrusion to propel himself forward. At every moment, it felt as if the ice were about to give way. It happened like that: ice dammed, then shifted, and then dammed again, then broke through and became liquid once more. He was breathing hard. Small shards of ice coated his cheeks, making them rigid with cold. As he neared shore, he began to hear shouts of encouragement. From the top of Cammon's Piano Factory, spectators were calling to him, urging him on. He was so close! With one last leap, he hurled himself forward, wrenched himself between two enormous upended slabs, handed the bag through the crevice, then squeezed into the crack just as the river ice broke behind him. One marooned mountain of ice to go. He scaled it and then clambered down the other side, into three feet of relatively still water on Rathbone Street, where he splashed into the arms of a waiting policeman who'd been alerted to his desperate status by the onlookers.

"What daft idiot are you?" the policeman demanded, hauling him upright. "Out on the ice like that? And what the bloody hell is this?" he continued, snatching the burlap sack from Jakob's hands. "Looted goods?"

"No." Jakob, his hands to his knees, was breathing hard. "Van der Veer Lumber's books. My father's books."

"Christ Almighty, boy. You Van der Veers really do like your money."

Jakob was too exhausted to explain. He let the policeman haul him and his bag through the knee-high water to Broadway, the officer shouting that they had been ousted from their own precinct house by the flood and had their hands full without daredevils like Jakob testing themselves. He muttered that looting had broken out at the City Hotel, and that loiterers were taking to fisticuffs over food, apparently not having heard that City Hall had been flung open to the displaced, with mayoral orders to provide everything necessary for comfort. The policeman hailed an enterprising boatman rowing down the flooded thoroughfare and heaved Jakob and his sack into the boat with a hearty pat to his back. The oarsman bore Jakob around the Mattimore Coal and Wood Yard, over the submerged tracks of the NY Central railroad's Tivoli Hollow Line, and past the No. 9 Police Station, then left him off at the base of State Street, across from the flooded post office, where a crowd had gathered, held back by a line of policemen. Jakob sloshed through a foot of freezing water and sank onto a dry square of pavement against the First National Bank building, shivering, with the company's books pressed against his chest.

He heard a shriek, and someone call his name. Then he sank into a dreamless sleep.

Chapter Nineteen

Elizabeth broke and ran toward the veranda, comprehending a second earlier than everyone else. Amelia gasped and followed, and Mary and William ran behind, their footsteps on the flagstone a warning drumbeat they would later remember as the herald of everything that followed.

The girls.

Anyone passing would think the family had lost their minds. And perhaps they had.

Their dead had returned.

The dead never return, and yet *theirs* had.

They sank onto the veranda steps, surrounding the policeman and Emma and Claire. The girls sat up and rubbed their eyes, pulling away from the policeman, who did not relinquish his firm grip around their shoulders. They were still mirrors of one another, with those high cheekbones and wide blue eyes rimmed with thick lashes, like curtains, their long copper hair shimmering in the cold morning light. And they had been fed, clearly, though their hair was tangled. No one but the policeman wondered yet why they were wearing only nightgowns. No one noticed that their bare feet were mottled with cold.

They were seeing only the girls, resurrected.

"I stumbled across them in the alleyway behind Ferry Street," the policeman said, his fair hair glinting in the early rays of the sun. "That's in the Pastures. They were sleeping all alone up against a wooden fence. I'm glad I found 'em when I did. The Pastures is underwater now, most of the basements filled up. The sober citizens were already packing their wagons by the time I started knocking on doors—that was my job. Most got out. God help the others—though I think most folks got out when the bells started. But the Pastures always floods late cause the water gets dammed up under the South Bridge. It's not like before the bridges were built, when the whole city went under at once."

They hardly heard him. Time had reversed itself, and all the rules of the world had been broken just for them. Amelia was petting Claire's hair. It was a raft of tangle and dirt. Elizabeth had reached out and taken a hold of Emma's hand. Mary, her eyes glassy with tears, wiped them away. It was a miracle, a mirage. Everyone was trying to catch their breath.

"They're skittish," the policeman warned, though no one was paying any attention to him. "I woke them out of a sound sleep. The bells were ringing like no one's business and they were sleeping. Then I couldn't believe it when they told me their names. I asked them again and that's when they ran."

They had torn away from him as if he were the devil himself, he said. He'd yelled over the din, *Emma! Claire! We've been looking for you.* He'd chased after them and swung them into his arms and pinned them there while he said how the whole world was worried about them and that people had been searching for them for a long time.

The family was only half-listening; they were intoxicated: *The girls are here. The girls are alive. The girls are back.*

The policeman talked on. "I can usually spot 'em, the little ones on their own who don't like it out there? First, I thought maybe they belonged to somebody—everyone was out on the streets—but I got the picture soon enough." He seemed to be spinning words, not wanting to come out with something, as if there was something they didn't yet understand.

The sleeve of Emma's nightgown inched up her arm, and she seized it and tugged it back into place. It was a small gesture. Innocuous. The policeman buried her up to her shoulders under his great coat. No one was heeding the cold.

"It was bedlam in the streets, you understand." The policeman couldn't get to the point. He was going around it and under it, backtracking, anything but saying it straight out.

Mary noticed that the girls' dazed expressions seemed not to be registering where they were. They were as silent as their granite statue. Vanished was any trace of Emma's spirited confidence, Claire's sparkling happiness. Flesh, yes, here, yes, but they exhibited no exultation. Their gaze focused on nothing and no one. They were blank. Blurred.

"Grandmama?" Elizabeth said.

"Yes, Lizzie. Isn't it wonderful?" Amelia caressed Emma's shoulder and wiped a smudge of dirt from her face.

Emma flinched and pulled away.

The policeman repeated his stories, *Ferry Street, tried to get away,* measuring every word while they all peered at Emma and Claire, studying them as they hadn't before: Was that a bruise? What was that on Claire's collar? It wasn't blood, was it?

"I asked them who they were and I couldn't believe it. Not at first," the policeman said. He was repeating himself. The sisters were saying nothing.

"They talked to you?" William said, his eyes narrowing.

"They did."

"Officer Farrell?" Mary said, finally recognizing him as the policeman from her visits to the precinct house, and then from the day

Mantel had come to the clinic, the one who had remembered about Emma and Claire

"Wondered when you'd notice." Colm Farrell was less effusive now. "They knew their names. I couldn't believe it. Had to ask them twice. When they told me, I thought what the hell, I'd let the drunks drown. I didn't have a wagon with me so I carried them up the hill."

"From the Pastures?" William said, keen now to every detail. "All that way?"

Officer Farrell still had Emma and Claire by their shoulders; it was clear now to everyone that he didn't mean to let them go. "I stopped first by their house. They'd given me the address—46 Elm Street. That's how I knew for sure it was them. 'Cross the street from the brewery, up from that orphanage?" He was stalling. "Another family had already moved into the rooms. I don't know what I was thinking. I didn't know what to tell them. Then I remembered you." He nodded at Mary. "That's when I brought them here."

The story took sudden shape as they all studied the girls and really saw them for the first time. Their skin was sallow and sickeningly pale, their eyes were glazed and blank, and both girls seemed unreachable. Mary marked the dirt under their fingernails, the rigid way they held their arms tight to their sides.

"I didn't know what to tell them," the policeman repeated.

"What exactly did you say?" William said.

"I said we had to come here first. That they needed to see a doctor." Officer Farrell shifted. His voice grew raw. "There's something not quite right. They were asleep when I found them. I've had a chance to study them here while they were sleeping and we were waiting for you." He pulled back the great coat. "That isn't all dirt spattered on their gowns. Something happened, and I'd like to know what, if you can pry it from their lips. I couldn't get it out of them. But if you can . . ." He lowered his voice. "They look badly used to me, and I've seen some things."

Mary and William turned to one another. They had seen this lifeless look before, in the war. It was more than exhaustion. More than disorientation. It was shock.

Mary said, "Officer Farrell, William, could you bring Emma and Claire inside, please?"

William and Farrell bent to pick them up. The girls arched their backs, pushing them away with balled fists and kicking so vigorously that William and Farrell released them. The girls scrambled into one another's arms, silent as stones.

Amelia reached out a hand to them, but Emma kicked her away.

Without a word, Elizabeth turned on her heel and disappeared into the house. No one asked any more questions about where the girls had been since their disappearance, because the answer was obvious.

Clearly, Emma and Claire O'Donnell had been residing in hell.

A wavering melody, barely discernible, penetrated the shocked silence.

Elizabeth was standing at the threshold, her violin tucked under her chin, eyes shut, arm drawing back and forth, her body yielding like a blade of grass, playing Pachelbel, the lyrical canon that Mademoiselle Urso had first played for Elizabeth and William.

Emma and Claire both turned their wary gaze on Elizabeth.

Time slowed. It happens that way, sometimes, when life rearranges itself.

From despair to possibility within a hair's breath.

Amelia nodded to William to lift a becalmed Emma into his arms. William nodded to Farrell, who stooped over Claire like a crane, his long arms gathering her in. The girls allowed themselves to be lifted up, and Elizabeth, seeing this, led them all into the house like a Pied Piper.

Chapter Twenty

"I can tell you've been hurt," Mary said, kneeling in front of Emma. "Someone hurt you, didn't they?"

Emma shook her head, and with her thumb wiped dirt from Claire's upturned face. Emma was still trying to decide what to do. She didn't know whether they were safe. Where were their parents? They were the ones she wanted, though she remembered—a long time ago, it seemed—loving Auntie Amelia and Aunt Mary, and feeling safe in this home. And here was Elizabeth, too, who had been gone so long. Had Emma conjured her into being? Paris, her mother had told her—a city across the ocean. But here Elizabeth was, and she had played her violin. But Emma didn't know what was real anymore. Were they really here? And she didn't know who she could trust. She had lost the ability to trust, to believe in anything. For a moment, Elizabeth's music had reminded her, but when it stopped, she forgot again how to think. She didn't know what to do, what to say. Claire would run if Emma said to. Claire would do anything Emma asked. But Emma was so tired. Where would they go? The clean sound of water tumbling into the bathtub spilled from the other room. She remembered the bathtub from nights they had stayed here. Auntie Amelia was drawing a bath, Aunt Mary said now. Had Emma agreed to take one? Had she spoken? She had learned from Claire to say nothing, but they kept asking her questions. She looked at Elizabeth again, at a loss as to whether to believe it really was Elizabeth. She had forgotten how to ask for help, had forgotten, even, what help felt like.

"We want to help you," Aunt Mary said. "Please let us give you a bath. You'll be much warmer if we do, and you'll be safe, I promise."

Help. Safe. Could Aunt Mary read minds? With the flicker of an eyelid, a gesture so involuntary that Emma hardly knew she made it, she acquiesced. Did she? She didn't know, but she did not protest when Mary took Claire's free hand in hers and led them both into the steamy room. Water was falling from the tap, a cloud of mist hanging in the air. Emma could feel the seductive promise—the memory—of warmth and being clean. She needed that, wanted that, because she smelled of sewer. She smelled of *him.*

"Let's get those dirty nightgowns off you," Aunt Amelia said. Her voice was bright with kindness. Claire turned to Emma for permission, but Emma didn't give it. Instead she backed them both against the wooden enclosure of the tub. She didn't know how she was going to get clean with her nightgown on, but she was. And so was Claire. No one could ever make her take her clothes off again. She sidled out of their reach and boosted Claire onto the bathtub frame so that she could slide into the water. Emma slid in behind her, their nightgowns billowing shields they could hide behind. The water was warm and soothing, and she closed her eyes, yielding to the enveloping heat. The water lapped against her, her nightgown clinging to her wet skin.

It was then that she heard Aunt Mary and Auntie Amelia gasp.

Emma opened her eyes. Her nightgown had turned invisible. They could see her, could see everything.

Emma cried out, and when she did, Aunt Mary's face broke.

It was the only way Emma could think to describe the way the light in her beautiful eyes fractured, the way her mouth dropped open, as if its hinges had failed, the way Amelia and Mary and Elizabeth saw through the watery, transparent cloth what a terrible girl Emma had been: the flowering purple stain that engulfed one entire shoulder, the scratches and deeper cuts that crosshatched her forearms and thighs, the bruising on her hips, all the evidence of her shame. She sank against the warm copper. Now it wasn't that Emma did not want to speak, it was that Emma could not speak, could not form the words to explain what had happened, because she did not want to remember any of it. She felt a little dizzy. What she ought to remember was competing with what she yearned to forget, and it was impossible to keep them straight. Especially after last night. They'd broken free. Done the terrible thing and run. Not even the dark night and clanging bells and swirling river had intimidated them. Not even the pain or the cold. They'd flown like sparrows, the two of them. Taken wing.

Aunt Mary reached for towels hanging on a rod above her head. She was moving slowly, as if she had to tell her body what to do and how to do it. Then Aunt Mary and Auntie Amelia both reached into the tub and pulled her and Claire out. No one said anything. From the corner of her eye, Emma could see Auntie Amelia wrapping Claire in a towel and drawing her into her lap. Aunt Mary drew Emma onto hers. She did not hold her too tightly. Emma felt she could leave if she wanted. She could feel tears wetting her hair. Elizabeth had sunk to the floor between them and taken hold of both Claire and Emma in any way she could.

"We looked everywhere. Everywhere," Aunt Mary was saying. "Orphanages. Schools. The police looked, too. Uncle William took the train to Troy and searched every single cranny. I went to Schenectady. We went out at night with lanterns, we walked up and down the alleys. We took out an ad in the newspapers. We looked in all the hospitals. We looked everywhere. The police thought you had drowned after the blizzard, but I knew you hadn't."

Silence roared in Emma's ears, a heavy quiet that blocked out pain.

"Am I hurting you?" Mary said, holding her close.

Everything hurt, but so much less than anything had hurt in a long time.

Mary said, "The water is cooling."

The taps were opened again and the muffled sound of falling water filled the room.

Amelia and Mary helped Claire and Emma rid themselves of their wet nightgowns. Amelia ran a frantic gaze over Claire's small body. When she discovered nothing—a scratch here, a rash there, but no bruises, no cuts, no intrusions—Emma swelled with pride. At least she had kept Claire safe. The Other Man had never touched her. Not once.

Mary picked Emma up and eased her again into the water. Mary knelt beside the tub at its edge and ran the soap gently over Emma's arms and legs while she eased her body into the warmth. The water was a balm. Claire was beside her, the water lapping at their waists and then their armpits as they laid back against the curve of the tub. Emma wondered whether you could clean time, too, as you could a body, whether you could scrub it of everything that had gone before. She slid down to her neck to let her hair drift in the water.

"Take as long as you want," Amelia said. "Do you understand? As long as you like. We are here."

Mary murmured something about getting her doctor's bag and left the room. Amelia and Elizabeth kneeled beside the tub, and Emma and Claire floated together in the tide of warmth. A long time passed like this. She and Claire locked their hands together and shut their eyes and did not cry. They were together. They were safe. They needed nothing. Only their parents. Soon, they would come for them.

Emma reached for the soap and lifted Claire's arm and ran the square up and down her skeletal limbs. Nudging Claire forward, she washed her back, gliding over the nubs of her spine. Emma then washed herself, the slippery square melting and gliding over her broken skin, getting caught in the tendrils of her hair. She eased Claire back again and made her float until only her round, freckled face showed above the soup of suds and water. She ran the soap through Claire's hair with her fingers, working her scalp.

How much time passed, Emma didn't know. She was lost in safety, lost in the respite of hot water, lost in the escape from vigilance. In the water she felt light, when lately her body had felt so heavy. She shut her eyes. Mary came back. Amelia inspected them and said their hair needed to be rewashed, so they kneeled in the tub as she ran clean water over them and rubbed more soap in to sluice away the last of the dirt. They allowed their hair to be tugged and fought with and tamed. New nightgowns appeared as if by magic. They allowed themselves to be dressed. They allowed this as Emma had been made to allow the other.

They were carried out of the bathroom and up the stairs and tucked into clean sheets that smelled of the sun. Mary gave her and Claire a pill to swallow, then went to the door and opened it and called for someone and asked for food. In a little while, a tray appeared with plates of scrambled eggs and ham and mugs of warm milk, and they ate the food from the tray set on a low table between their two beds. They ate too fast, trying to extinguish the flame of want. When they could eat no more, they let go their spoons and lay back against their pillows and closed their eyes. It had been an eon since they had slept for longer than a few hours at a time. Emma left her bed and climbed into Claire's and spooned herself against her sister's curled body. Light spilled through the windows. The light was so beautiful that Emma did not want to shut her eyes. She had been in darkness so long. She lifted her head and looked at Mary, who leaned forward, her face a question mark.

Still, Emma couldn't speak.

"Ah," Mary said. "Don't worry. I won't leave, I promise. You can sleep."

So Emma did.

Chapter Twenty-One

Viola Van der Veer hurried ahead to open the door to her son's room as one of the servants carried Jakob in and laid him on his bed. She had collected eiderdown quilts from the other bedchambers and now she peeled away Jakob's wet evening clothes, toweled him dry, and piled five quilts on top of his prostrate form.

"Call for a doctor," Viola said to the butler, who had raced up the stairs behind her. "One of the Doctors Stipp—they're just across the park—on Madison. Hurry."

The butler turned on his heel, his coattails whipping behind him as he barked orders to the other servants to bring warming bricks and to stoke the fire. Viola stroked her son's stubbled cheek. It was frigid to the touch. His eyes blinked open and shut. She reached for his hands to warm them, but her own hands were still numb from having spent the entire night on State Street. Though she had worn her fur hat and gloves and hugged the carriage blanket around her shoulders, toward three in the morning she had grown so cold that she left the carriage and began to pace in an effort to warm herself. Gerritt had come and gone after buying a lantern from one of the nearby stores, opened by its proprietor in a burst of entrepreneurial genius to serve the anxious crowds. An enterprising chestnut roaster had trundled his cart to a corner and fired up his brazier, and she had gone and purchased several for herself and her driver to hold in their hands. From time to time, Gerritt returned and reported on the state of the flood. Furious with him for sending Jakob into the district, she pummeled his chest with her fists. Toward dawn, Gerritt departed on another reconnaissance mission and did not return. Alone, she sat vigil another three hours, her heart in her throat, hardly able to breathe as the waters edged up Broadway. And then at nine Jakob stumbled out of the floodwaters like an apparition, carrying those accursed books with him. Now, Viola rubbed her stiff hands together and kneaded Jakob's shoulders and arms and urged him to talk, trying to will him back from the edge of unconsciousness. Servants hurried in with warmed bricks wrapped in towels. Viola nestled them close to Jakob's body. A fire roared in the fireplace. Someone brought hot tea.

"Jakob, please, darling, wake up. Can you wake up and drink some tea?"

His eyes fluttered open.

"Jakob?"

His voice was slurred and raw. "Are you all right?"

"Me?" she said, incredulous. "How are you?"

"I think I will never be warm again."

She gasped with laughter, relieved. "What happened?"

"Father wanted the books, but Harley didn't come. I had to save the lumber—" He shut his eyes again and drifted away.

Downstairs, a flurry of voices, punctuated by Gerritt's roaring bray, carried up the stairwell.

Viola handed the cup of tea to a hovering maid and said, "Make him drink this." She flew down the three flights to the foyer, where Gerritt sat slumped against the wall, his legs thrust out before him. His hands were sickly white, his bald head was moist with sweat, his lips chapped, and his face a ruby blister of chilblains. Slashed above his left eye was a bloody welt that a maid was attempting to stanch with her apron while a footman knelt before Gerritt unlacing his sodden boots. His clothes were soaked through.

"I couldn't find 'em," Gerritt muttered, shivering.

"It's all right. He is home," Viola said, but he appeared unrelieved by the news that Jakob was safe. "Did you hear me? Jakob's home. He's safe. Where did you go? What happened?"

"Slipped. Fell in the water. Knocked my head against a lamppost."

"What were you doing?"

"Searching," he said.

"Call for more help, would you please?" Viola asked the footman, who had managed to yank off the second of Gerritt's boots.

The footman hastened outside and returned with a stable hand. They crossed and linked their arms together and bore Gerritt up the three flights to his room. Gerritt, like Jakob, was shivering uncontrollably, and Viola tugged off his wet socks, then the wet canvas work clothes he'd changed into after the party, and then his underclothes. She threw a quilt over him and leaned out the door and pleaded with a maid to unearth more. He had dropped the apron, and the cut was bleeding profusely. Viola ripped a pillowcase off a pillow and bunched it against his forehead.

"Why didn't you go to the hospital?" she said. "You're bleeding."

Gerritt wrenched the pillowcase from her hands. He stared at the bloodstain, then held it against his forehead himself. "It's nothing. I've had worse."

"I thought you were both gone."

"Well, neither of us is, are we?" Gerritt said, scowling. "You said Jakob's fine?"

"He is so cold. I sent for one of the Doctors Stipp."

Gerritt winced as he raised one eyebrow. "The Stipps? Are they coming?"

"I hope so."

He pushed himself up to one elbow, yanking the quilt to his neck. "Did anyone die? Has everyone been evacuated?"

"I don't know," Viola said. "No one knows."

"Damn," he yelled. "My new ice-yacht. Oh, why didn't I think of her? Damn, she's gone now."

A footman arrived with more warming bricks and muscled them under the covers and set about hunting for a nightshirt for Gerritt. Viola left the footman cajoling Gerritt to dress.

Jakob, thank God, was sitting up in bed. A maid had brought him a breakfast tray of boiled eggs and toast and a full pot of coffee. He had stopped shivering and could speak now without slurring.

"Did I hear Father?" he said.

"He slipped in the water looking for you. He's got a cut above his eye."

"Did he go out onto the ice?"

"I don't know." Her voice caught in her throat. Last night, she had pictured losing Jakob over and over, and now here he was, safe. "Dr. Stipp should be here soon."

"I'm all right," Jakob said, reaching for her and pulling her to him.

"I thought I'd lost you," she said, laying her head on his shoulder. He used to do that, when he was little, when he was frightened.

"I'm here," he said.

"I couldn't bear it," she said. She had been so selfish of late, had asked too much of him. But last night she had made it through the entire party without a drop of sherry, braving the scrutiny of her guests. She was glad that she had, for she had her wits about her when Gerritt refused to take her to the river with him. She had fought him and won.

Jakob let go and fell back against the pillows. "I'll never be warm."

"I'll have them draw a hot bath. Try to eat, if you can."

She floated back and forth between her two patients. For his part, Gerritt was refusing food but had downed two cups of black coffee.

Unlike the noisy flurry of Gerritt's arrival, Viola did not know William Stipp had arrived until he knocked on Gerritt's open door, his bag in hand.

"Despite your misadventure, Gerritt, your brain is intact," the doctor said after examining him. He'd asked Gerritt a series of questions, waved a lit match in front of his eyes. "But we need to stitch that gash." He doused a needle in alcohol and guided a length of catgut into the needle's eye. "I'm surprised you even dared to go near the river, Gerritt. Someone who works as close to it as you knows how dangerous it can be."

"I'm not afraid of the river," Gerritt said, throwing off his covers.

Dr. Stipp pushed him back against the pillow. "Be still and drink this," he said, handing him a shot of whiskey he'd ordered from a footman.

Gerritt grimaced under the pricks and tugs of Stipp's needle as the doctor warned that sometimes deeper injuries took a while to reveal themselves, and that it was best if Gerritt rested for at least the rest of the day, if not tomorrow, too. Wrapping Gerritt's head with gauze to keep the bandage in place, he said to Viola, "If he is not himself, or you cannot wake him, call for me immediately. I'll take him to City Hospital and put a trephine in to lower pressure in his skull. But I'm being overly cautious. I think he's suffered only a mild bump. I put in five stitches, but only out of an abundance of caution. During the war we wouldn't have paid such a slight wound any attention."

"There was so much blood," Viola said.

Gerritt scoffed, "There wasn't that much blood. Viola lives for drama. I tried to dissuade her from calling you, but you know how ladies can be."

Viola flushed at Gerritt's lie and said, "Doctor Stipp, could you come now and see Jakob? He was out on the ice all night. He had only his evening cloak—he was so cold. I still don't know how he got to shore."

"It's been a night," Dr. Stipp agreed. "Mary and I were at the hospital till morning." He hesitated, as if he were going to say something else but then decided not to.

Too distracted before to notice, Viola saw now how exhausted the doctor was. There were heavy bags under his eyes, and despite his efficient competence, he was moving slowly. He seemed distant, troubled.

"Have you heard whether anyone else was hurt?" Gerritt said. "In the city? Anyone missing?"

"No numbers yet, but there were quite a few injuries, mostly from panic. Fractures, that sort of thing. Oh," he said, turning away from the door. "Forgive me, I forgot. Your foreman. Mary was going to send you a note, but things got a little busy at our house this morning. She and I performed surgery on Mr. Harley earlier today. He suffered a gash to the back of his neck. More serious than yours, Gerritt. We stitched him up—he should be fine, if the wound doesn't become infected."

"Harley?" Gerritt's gaze sharpened. "Did he say anything?"

"He wasn't conscious. I have no idea how he got hurt. But he's getting a lot of attention. A reporter is writing him up. He saved two children."

"Children?" Gerritt said. "Whose children?"

"I don't know. Why?"

"I've got a lot of employees who live by the river. They've all got young children, and of course it's them you worry about in a flood, isn't it?"

"It's children you worry about most times."

"Where is Harley now?"

"City Hospital."

Gerritt went as pale as the white walls and sprang from bed and began to pull clothes from his walnut armoire, agile in spite of his injury. "I have to see him. Have the carriage readied, Viola."

"Gerritt, get back in bed. Besides, don't you want to see Jakob before you go rushing off to see your overseer?" she said.

Gerritt turned and scowled, and Viola knew she would pay dearly for her admonition later. He did not like being scolded, especially not in front of anyone.

"Don't be an idiot, Gerritt," William said. "Listen to your wife. Spend at least today in bed. You've had a blow to the head. Drink brandy to burn away the river water. And next time, use a boat, like a sensible person. I will allow you, however, to come with us to see your son." Scowling again, Gerritt followed them to Jakob's room, fingering a cut end of suture that had worked through the gauze.

Jakob, like Gerritt, had donned nightclothes. His breakfast tray had been removed, and Viola was relieved to see that he was no longer a ghostly white.

"Dear boy," Gerritt said. "How are you?"

"I'm fine," Jakob said. "What happened to you?"

"I was looking for you and slipped. Stupid of me. Tell us what happened to you."

As Jakob revealed the details of his ordeal, Viola learned just how close he had come to being killed. As Jakob talked, Doctor Stipp examined him, studying the tips of his fingers for frostbite, ordering him once to be silent so that he could listen to his lungs. Jakob was making light of things, no doubt a show for his father, and perhaps even for the doctor, but Viola detected a wavering hint of fear underneath his bravado, especially when he described his desperate dash across the ice. Jakob ended by nodding at the burlap bag in the corner.

Delighted, Gerritt asked, "You got all of them?"

"I did."

He beamed. "You're a hero. Do you hear, Viola? This one chopped through the roof."

"He nearly died."

"But he didn't, did he?"

William cleared his throat, interrupting the exchange. "Jakob, I think you'll be fine, but Viola, you must keep watch for pneumonia or any sign of fever. He's been chilled to the bone. Now," he said, snapping shut his bag, "if you'll excuse me, I must be off—"

"Who or what could be more important than my son?" Gerritt said.

"Call for me if you need anything. And I most emphatically recommend that you do not go to the hospital, Gerritt. Mary and I will keep you updated on Harley's condition."

"Harley?" Jakob said.

"He's in the hospital with an ugly cut to the back of his neck," Gerritt said.

"He is? What happened?"

"No one knows," Gerritt said, jerking his head at the doctor. "He took care of him and he doesn't even know."

"We've imposed on you too long, Dr. Stipp," Viola said. "You must be exhausted. Thank you so much for coming. Please allow me to show you out." In the hallway, Viola steered William toward the stairwell, but she stopped when they reached it. "I want to assure you, Doctor Stipp, that I do not exaggerate. Nor do I live, as my husband stated, for drama. He sometimes likes to paint me as hysterical. He thinks me flighty and silly. And perhaps I am. But I was terrified."

The doctor's gaze turned soft with kindness. "Mrs. Van der Veer, are you all right?"

"I was terribly frightened," Viola said. She felt her knees buckling. "Jakob is my only child."

"He will be all right."

"I apologize," she said, "for my husband's rudeness."

"Remember that he almost lost his son, too. Strain like that will undo anyone. I've heard worse from other patients. I've probably said worse."

"The war?"

"Violence and fright loosen tongues." He paused and cleared his throat. "Forgive me, but, if at any time you need anything, Mary and I are always here."

"Thank you. That's very kind."

When Viola returned upstairs, she found Gerritt in his bedroom, dressing. He thrust his arm toward a dangling coat sleeve but missed and yanked the whole thing off and threw it on the floor.

"What are you doing, Gerritt? The doctor said you shouldn't go anywhere."

He turned on her. "How dare you embarrass me in front of the doctor?"

"He says you should stay in bed."

"Don't you know that we've just lost thousands of dollars? Maybe tens of thousands. I have to see Harley. I have to know what he thinks we should do now."

"What does money matter when we almost lost our son? What possessed you to send Jakob into the district when the ice was breaking?" There was a new edge to her voice, one she hadn't chanced with him in a long while, reminiscent of long ago, before she started feeling the avalanche of his scorn. Out of the corner of her eye she caught sight of herself in the mirror. The filtered light betrayed age: shallow half moons bracketed her mouth, and her eyes looked hooded.

"Oh, please, spare me, Viola. No one knew the water would rise that fast. It never does. And if it was too dangerous, he shouldn't have gone in. The boy's got a brain. A good one, that I paid Harvard to give him. And he got himself out of that pickle pretty well. Bloody hell, woman. Help me get dressed or get out of the way."

"Didn't you hear Jakob? He thinks the office might have been crushed. He could have been lost to us."

"But he's here, isn't he?" Gerritt bent over and scooped the jacket from the floor and punched at it to remove dust. "You see what I mean about your penchant for drama?"

"I was terrified, Gerritt. I didn't know where you were. I didn't know if Jakob was alive."

Gerritt drew very close. "What? No sherry this morning? Really, for a woman to fall into drink is such a tawdry thing, don't you agree?"

Viola started and backed away. "I've learned not to care about the awful things you say to me. And I've also learned not to care about the other women you see, either."

He snorted, apparently unperturbed that she knew. "For God's sake, Viola, there are more important things than *how you feel*." He stumbled past her, wrestling with his coat and screaming for the carriage.

Viola shut her eyes, fighting an overwhelming desire to sneak into the butler's pantry for some sherry.

"Mother?" she heard Jakob call. "Is that bath ready?"

She turned away from the stairwell and made for her son's room, calling for another tray of tea.

Chapter Twenty-Two

It was two in the afternoon, and James Harley was slowly coming around. He could determine little of his whereabouts, because sandbags prevented him from turning his head. Indistinguishable voices and the occasional groan of agony filtered above a mild buzz of activity. His neck throbbed, his head ached, and his throat flamed with thirst. He lay in the throes of this discomfort for some time until he reared up, grabbing at a searing pain scorching the back of his neck. His hand came away with a white square stained with pale, pinkish fluid that smelled of musk. He stared at the strange object, wondering how such a benign thing could cause him so much pain. He turned his head an inch. He was in a square, high-ceilinged room with three other recumbent men, and seated next to his bed a fourth man in need of a change of clothes slept in a chair, his long legs resting on the edge of the bed, his arms knotted in a loose pretzel of repose around a folded newspaper. Whirling with nausea, Harley lay back down.

The chair-sitter snorted to life, slapping his feet against the floor and throwing his head back in a violent way before coming to full animation with a bracing shake of his head and a scratching paw at his short beard, now drizzled with saliva. He hugged the newspaper to his chest and leaned forward with keen interest.

"You're awake," he announced in a high, reedy voice. "Do you know how lucky you are?"

"Lucky?" Harley said.

"You're at City Hospital. You're a hero." The man waggled his newspaper in front of Harley's nose, aggravating the swells of nausea.

"Hero?"

"Don't be modest, sir. Those little ones would have died if not for you."

"Little ones?" Harley remembered nothing of little ones. "Do you have any whiskey?"

His strange companion laughed. "Thirsty, huh? I'm afraid they frown on whiskey here. All I'll be able to scare up is some weak tea, if that. Think on what happened while I go hunt that down. I want to hear all the details, everything from the moment the waters felled you."

Harley pondered these declarations—*Little ones, Hero, Waters*—as the man shambled out of sight. Harley heard him imploring someone for tea, how he needed it for the hero. Harley wondered whether he might be dreaming. From the hallway, a harried explanation of a problem with a broken water main was followed with a warning about an expected menace of typhoid. But, no matter, a voice said, the man—hero or not—couldn't drink for eight hours after receiving chloroform. And he still had half an hour to go. "And for goodness's sake, keep him in bed. When they wake up, they don't know where they are. They can't remember a thing. Keep an eye on him."

Full recollection, or what Harley believed to be full recollection, came suddenly. His feet hit the cold floorboards. The room reeled. He made it as far as the door before he sank to his knees.

"Hey now, hey," said the high, reedy voice. "You can't be getting out of bed. Ye gods, man, you can't be so brave as all that, can you? Going to look for them again, eh? Don't worry, don't worry. The little ones are fine. They're fine." His strange companion knelt and helped Harley up, then let loose a low, thin whistle. "Dear God, that cut is still ugly. What did you do with your bandage?"

"Where are they now?" Harley squawked.

"The little ones? With their mother."

"No. They can't be."

"Rest easy, Harley. You saved them."

"I saw it in the papers, by God. They buried them just the other day. The whole family."

"No one's had time to bury anyone. And everyone survived. They had good warning. Don't you remember those bells?"

Harley remembered no bells. He aimed for the bed, one knee catching on the disarranged sheets. The room continued to spin as the stranger settled him against the hard edges of the sandbags.

Harley said, "Are they at the house? They shouldn't be alone. They'll be frightened."

"God, man, you're in bad shape. That chloroform plays tricks, doesn't it? They're not at their house."

"But where are they?"

"With their mother. Look. I found you and brought you here. Everything is fine, because of you. Name's Horace Young. I wrote an article. Let me read it to you."

He launched in, oblivious to Harley's protests.

A True Hero

> The wealthy and famous Gerritt Van der Veer will be pleased to know that early this morning James Harley, his stalwart stevedore and head foreman, despite having suffered a crippling blow to his head during the flood, carried two boys on his back to the safety of the intersection of Westerlo and Grand Streets in the low-lying Pastures neighborhood, after which he then collapsed.

> He was operated on at City Hospital by Dr. William Stipp and lightly assisted by his wife, Albany's famous native daughter, the former Miss Mary Sutter who defied the usual squeamishness of her sex to become a doctor. But in a coquettish display of temper, Mrs. Stipp declined to outline for this concerned reporter Mr. Harley's prognosis.
>
> Perhaps such unprofessional behavior is to be expected, for in the past six weeks, it is known that Mrs. Stipp exhausted herself in an endless and ultimately futile search for the two O'Donnell sisters, lost in the winter blizzard. No doubt she is now unhinged with grief, for on Wednesday last, the Stipp and Sutter family finally set a stone in remembrance of them in our magnificent Albany Rural Cemetery.

The reporter grinned, his teeth gleaming through an untended mustache as he tapped the newspaper against Harley's chest. "Good, yes?"

The article had prompted in Harley ghostly flashes of wading through water and a frightening feeling of drowning, but clarity remained a flickering goal, just out of reach. There had been a flood, apparently. And he had rescued not Emma and Claire, but two boys he had no memory of. Harley concentrated on breathing, trying to calm the throbbing in his neck, but all he could think about was the girls. Where were they? Were they safe? Still in the house? Why couldn't he remember? He hoped they were alive, hoped they were all right. He'd often thought he ought to give them back, but that had been impossible, wishful dreaming. He'd grown awfully fond of them in the past weeks. He'd done everything he could for them. It was like losing his own children now, not knowing where they were. A wave of remorse washed over him. What if they were dead? Oh, his darling girls! He rose on one elbow, leaned over the side of the bed, and retched at Young's feet.

"James Harley?" a disembodied voice thundered from the hallway. Never before had Captain Mantel's coarse tones roused terror in Harley. But they did now. He had lost the girls, and he didn't know where they were.

Young rose and stuck his head out the door. "Harley's here. Who's asking?"

"Who are you?" Mantel said, his considerable bulk filling the doorframe.

Young offered his hand. "Horace Young. The *Argus*."

"Could you excuse us? Police business," Mantel said, steering the reporter into the hallway and shutting the door on him. Mantel took Young's seat and grinned at Harley, clearly mindful of the close quarters and Harley's fellow patients, who were staring now.

"I didn't mean to lose them," Harley said. "I love them. Especially—"

Mantel leaned in and whispered, "Who didn't you lose?"

Harley swallowed. "I don't know."

"Goddamn it, man," Mantel hissed. "Do you have those O'Donnell sisters or not?"

Harley tried to remember what he'd said before but couldn't. Words seemed to float out of him of their own accord. But by the look on Mantel's face now, he feared he might have said too much. "Sisters?" he finally rasped.

"The whole of the Pastures is under water," Mantel said, still whispering, still leaning in. "Did you leave them in the house while you were busy rescuing neighbors? Is that where they are? Drowned? Are you responsible for that?"

Tears slid down Harley's cheeks. Oh, his beloveds. His head was clearing, the nausea fading. The back of his neck ached, and he reached for the wound, hoping it would remind him of what had occurred. A murky memory returned, of Emma and a coal shovel. He scrambled to find some explanation now that would appease Mantel, but couldn't. He was terrified of the man, who flared at the slightest provocation. The girls might be dead. Oh, it was too terrible. Had there been water in the basement when he went down to fetch them? Or had he left the door open at the top of the stairs? Maybe they had escaped. That thought was even more terrifying. It was him they knew, him they would recognize. "I remember nothing," he said, hoping to put the police captain off.

Gerritt Van der Veer strode into the room, a rakish bandage affixed above his left eye. Mantel rose and shook Van der Veer's hand, turning affable: a clap to the back, an extended hand, a hearty shake.

"What happened to you, Van der Veer?" Mantel said. "Don't tell me you were mucking around in the water, too?"

"I was down at the river last night. My son was caught in the district. I slipped. What are you doing here?

"Just visiting our hero. I read about him in the paper. Did you see the article?"

"Bought one from a newsboy just as I came in. You had time in the middle of all this"—Gerritt made a gesture that seemed to encompass the whole city—"to pay tribute to my overseer?"

"I just went off duty. Harley will be up for a medal, I say. You should be proud. Such a public display of bravery."

"Two little boys. Display of courage beyond compare. Speaking of courage, my son hightailed it off the ice this morning. He was caught in the flooding—waited on the roof all night. Saved my books," Gerritt said.

"Loyal boy," Mantel said.

A nurse appeared carrying a tray of gauze and bandage scissors, a brown bottle of iodine balanced between them. "Excuse me, gentlemen, but I need to change Mr. Harley's dressing."

Mantel and Van der Veer stepped outside, into the hallway, out of Harley's sight. The nurse was asking Harley whether he was still nauseated. He was, but it was no longer due to the effects of the anesthetic. She set about her work, tsking and fretting as she dabbed his neck and bandaged him, saying he was to keep his hands away. She offered him a sip of sarsaparilla and a pill to swallow—*something for the pain*—and helped him to lie back down again.

The promise of an imminent release from pain soothed his grave worry of whether or not the girls were dead. Or maybe that was the morphine talking. Mantel had been furious, but the captain was furious most of the time. It's what made him so good at his job. After all, through force of will, the man had managed to dissuade the Stipps that their girls were alive. That had been extremely helpful. And Harley would do anything now to keep up that fiction. If only he could stay awake, but the morphine was already warming his stomach and spreading to his bones.

Chapter Twenty-Three

Upstairs in the Stipps' house, Emma and Claire lay asleep under the light covers of a white sheet in the lying-in room Amelia maintained for the odd woman in labor who didn't want to deliver in her own home. The two girls were in Claire's bed, where Emma had crawled earlier, and where they had fallen, as Mary had hoped they would, under the narcotic spell of the morphine pills she had given them. The room had gone humid with their deep sleep. Flung outside the sheets, Emma's bruised and abraded arms encircled Claire's tiny body. Claire's mouth was slightly open, and her hands clasped Emma's.

Their sleep was not so much sleep as an exhausted swoon.

Mary dropped to one knee beside their bed. She did not notice Amelia unlocking a window and cracking open its bottom sash. Nor did she hear William pacing outside the door, impatient to learn the girls' condition but unwilling to breach their modesty. As was she. But she was certain that the girls would not be able to tolerate what she was about to do if they were conscious. They were too devastated, too crippled by fear. But she had to examine them, not only to ascertain the state of their health, but also to catalogue for the police the extent and nature of their injuries. Under any other circumstance, she would never commit the intrusion, but this was no ordinary situation.

First Mary ran a cursory gaze over the sleeping forms, confirming that the girls' nail beds were pink. If either of them were bleeding internally, they would be white. Their skin, though, was as pale as bleached linen, though it was not the alarming pallor of acute anemia; instead, it seemed only as if they hadn't seen the sun in a long while. Their breathing, too, was even and not depressed, indicating that they were tolerating the morphine well. They showed no signs of acute starvation. She and William had treated some of the survivors of Andersonville years after their release from the deadly Confederate prison, but the girls evinced none of the dry, cracked skin, atrophied muscles, or sunken cheeks of malnourishment.

Now Mary began her formal exams. She started with Claire, easing back the top sheet, taking care not to wake either of them as she inched Claire from Emma's protective grasp. She inspected every inch of Claire's body, hunting for clues, taking her time, turning her gently so that she did not waken. Claire's body betrayed no marks, no signs of intrusion, nary even a bruise, only an insignificant rash on the underside of one forearm. Mary, intent on thoroughness, opened Claire's mouth, ran her hands along her scalp, felt along the length of her neck and under her arms for swollen lymph nodes, palpated her abdomen for resistance that might reveal swelling or damage, moved all her limbs in succession to assess for breaks or sprains, and finally propped her legs up in a V and hunted for signs of intrusion. There were none. Claire's body was fully intact.

Mary tucked the soft white cotton of Claire's nightgown around her sleeping body and circled the bed to kneel beside Emma. It took a moment to splice together the specter of Emma's youth with the extent of the assault. As had been clear during her bath, an array of bruising—yellowing and purple—marred one of Emma's shoulders, and the bruising extended to either side of her rib cage, along the crests of her pelvic bones, and down her back, where more abrasions marred her scapulae and spine. Scratches traveled up the length of her spindled thighs. A long splinter was embedded in the flesh of the right inner thigh.

In her life and practice, Mary had grown accustomed to a great deal, bearing witness to more pain than most, but now her hands were shaking. She admonished herself to be methodical, disciplined, objective. She palpated every joint and bone, percussed every inch of Emma's abdomen, turned her neck and head, looking for spinal problems. She auscultated Emma's lungs, worried about pneumonia, reminded herself to do the same for Claire. She turned Emma this way and that, tested her reflexes, ran her hands over the worst of the bruises and discovered to her relief that the bruising, while extensive, was superficial. Luckily, Emma had suffered no broken bones, damage to any internal organs, or bumps on her scalp to indicate concussion.

She still had the last of the exam to do. Again, she propped open Emma's legs and steeled herself.

The tissue was swollen, inflamed, torn, typical of the kind of injury rendered during repeated traumatic entry. No, she berated herself, that medical term was too evasive. She needed to use the real word. During *rape.* She also needed to stay focused. She needed to note everything. No gonorrheal exudate, no chancres indicative of syphilis, something to be grateful for. And Emma was not yet in puberty, a relief of such immense proportions that the cuts and tears seemed a dispensation in comparison to the disaster pregnancy would have been. At some point, Amelia had left and returned with a Dieffenbach needle-holder, toothed forceps, sutures, and gauze. Now Mary took a deep breath, pushing away a sudden wave of fury. From the second she had begun, she had had to stifle her anger, and she still had to now, or her hands would not be able to do their meticulous work.

Shut your mind, Mary told herself. Shut your mind and do not think of who or what this is. Think only: layer by layer, rebuild from the bottom up, use enough but not too many stitches, be conservative, do no further harm, preserve tissue and function.

Mary shot a despairing but determined look at her mother, took up her instruments, and began the work of putting Emma back together.

Chapter Twenty-Four

They had once again taken refuge around the dining table. It was five o'clock, six weeks since the blizzard, twenty hours since the ice had broken, nine hours since Emma and Claire had materialized on the veranda, two since Mary had finished the heart-rending work of repairing Emma. Vera had made a roast of lamb and potatoes, cooling untouched on a platter in the middle of the table. Upstairs, Emma and Claire were sleeping. Mary had given them a second dose of morphine when they began to emerge from the first, and they again fell safely under its narcotic, amnesiac tide. Throughout the afternoon, Amelia and Mary had looked in on them and found them buried beneath the sheets, softly breathing. They were all tired. None of them had slept since returning from the hospital. From the scullery came the sound of Vera washing pots and pans; from time to time, she broke down sobbing. Mary had finally relieved herself of her tight button boots, donning slippers in their place. She still wore the evening dress that she had worn to the party and toiled in all night and day.

William fixed his gaze on his wife. She had relayed the unimaginable details in a desultory way, her usual fierceness dimmed by what he would determine, in anyone else, to be shock. Now, he reached for

Mary's hand and laid down his fork. He could not eat, though he could not remember the last time he or any of them had eaten. Mary was gazing at him with that same flat expression she had greeted him with at the door when he returned from the Van der Veers'. Until today, he had never seen her this way—not when she had assisted him at his first amputation at the Union Hotel Hospital, nor at Antietam, either, where he had taught her to perform the operation herself out of the overwhelming imperative to save men's lives. Mary had seen the worst of everything, and yet this was worse still. War had found them all. Again.

Amelia, as always, allowed them their moment, holding back her own suffering, though her eyes were glazed and red rimmed. She had moved through the afternoon like an apparition. Amelia, whom Albany relied on to deliver their babies, who had worked all her life for good, who tirelessly went wherever need beckoned, now stared unseeing across the table. For women who rushed headlong into the disasters of others, there was no one now to rush headlong into theirs. They had only each other.

Elizabeth was staring into the distance. Amelia had shadowed her granddaughter all afternoon. For a while, Elizabeth had been inconsolable, though more than twice she raged that her weeping was of no help. *Why?* she kept asking. But Amelia had no answer for the perpetual, unanswerable question of *Why?* Nor did William, who had long ago decided that humanity never learned anything at all and that philosophy failed at everything necessary: solace, explanation, reparation. Mary could only shake her head. Whatever presence of mind had driven her meticulous repair of Emma had now deserted her.

The enormity of the abomination had paralyzed them all.

Separately, they were each recalling the events of the last several days. On Wednesday morning, they had buried David and Bonnie and erected the stone for the girls. On Thursday, one of the prostitutes had revived their hopes that the girls might be alive. For four nights running, Mary and William had roamed through Albany's streets, searching for them. Last night, they had braved a social outing at the Van der Veers, worked all night at the hospital, and then this morning, Tuesday, miraculously, the girls had come home. Time had stretched seven days into an illusion of weeks and weeks.

Amelia was picking at a seam on the sleeve of her dress, loosening a thread. "*Our* girls," she whispered, her voice subdued and pained.

"Morphine," Mary said dazedly. Medicine was her comforting familiar. She could face anything in the calm recitation of medical facts. "I'll have to wean them from it." She was speaking in measured, preoccupied tones. "They can't stay on the drug long. I could use chloral, if they need to sleep. Then willow bark tea for Emma until she heals. I'll keep watching for syphilis and gonorrhea"—at this, Amelia shuddered—"but I saw no indication of either, and if they aren't fulminant now, it's unlikely they'll develop. Her molesters must have been fastidious. Safes, etc."

"Mary," Amelia said. "Have a care for Elizabeth."

Elizabeth shook her head. "Thank you, Grandmama, but I am not a child."

"Whatever possessed you, Lizzie," Amelia said, "to think of playing for the girls? We're so grateful to you."

"I didn't think." Elizabeth said she had no memory of disinterring her violin from its dusty case under the bed, or of rubbing rosin on the bow. She had come to herself on the veranda, grasping the violin by its neck, her fingers automatically turning its pegs to tune the instrument. And then music had floated through the air and the blank, terrified look had disappeared from Emma's and Claire's eyes.

"Lost in a blizzard, saved by a flood," William mused. He turned to Mary. "Claire was really untouched?"

"Yes," Mary said. She pushed away her empty plate. "I think it's possible that she was deliberately spared."

They all tried to come to terms with the malevolent deliberation necessary to spare one girl while harming another, and couldn't.

"It's odd, though, isn't it?" William said, shaking his head.

"It's no mystery," Mary said. "Emma is ten. She's at the age of consent."

Amelia removed her spectacles and laid them on the table. She had seen a lot in her years of intimacy with the world. In houses high and low, many private terrors had revealed their secrets to her. But none like this. "The horror of it," she whispered. She looked outside, where the gloaming had burned itself out. "We are none of us innocents, the three of us," she said. "We know what happens. We should have looked harder."

"I wanted to," Elizabeth said.

"But we did look," William said.

His pronouncement was not enough absolution for any of them, though it was hard to imagine how much harder they could have looked without forcing their way through every door in Albany. Still, it was impossible to escape the devastation of having, in essence, buried the girls, when they had been alive and in desperate need. All four privately entertained the appalling notion that they were glad that Bonnie was dead, because they didn't think she could have faced this.

"Where could they have been all this time?" Elizabeth said.

William shook his head. Earlier, before he'd been called away to the Van der Veers, he and Officer Farrell had discussed that very thing. Farrell already had plans to ask around in the Pastures, since that was where he had found the girls, but he warned William that the floodwaters would likely wash away any evidence.

"And Bonnie and David," Amelia said, her voice catching. She felt the need to tally every wrong, to list every insurmountable hurdle ahead. "We have to tell Emma and Claire." She dreaded telling them. They all did. How to tell brutalized children that the people they most wanted, most needed, were no longer alive? Mothers who birthed stillborns asked about their dead infants only when they were ready to hear what they already instinctively knew. When Emma and Claire might be ready to learn they were orphans, no one could imagine. Amelia tried to picture telling them and couldn't even conjure the words.

Mary lifted her head, her gaze direct, new life showing in her eyes. "How did we miss them that day?"

"What do you mean?" William said.

"The teacher said she let the students out around noon. We left the house about then. How did we miss seeing them? They couldn't have made it far, not on their own."

William shook his head. "And?"

"They didn't get lost, William." She rose from the table as the anger she'd held at bay all day washed over her. "Someone took them. Someone deliberately took them."

There was a knock at the front door, and a tearful Vera went to answer it.

"We should tell no one," William warned. "I didn't tell the Van der Veers earlier. We don't want to expose the girls to more scrutiny than is necessary. And we don't know who did it. We need to keep them safe."

And besides, they all thought, how did one announce a resurrection?

Vera returned and said that Jakob Van der Veer was at the door.

"Jakob?" William said, rising. "Is he ill?"

"No. He wants to speak to Elizabeth."

"Elizabeth?"

They all turned to her. "Do you want to, Lizzie?" Amelia said.

She did. She went to the door and slipped outside onto the veranda, where Jakob was sitting on the swing, bundled in a woolen topcoat, a thick muffler wrapped around his neck, black leather gloves covering his hands. He rose when she came out.

"What is it?" Jakob said. "Something's happened, hasn't it? During the flood?" He took her by the elbow and drew her to him, a gesture that yesterday would have been a liberty, but in this newly upended life, seemed more than permissible. They sat down together on the swing. "Did you lose someone?"

She shook her head.

"Tell me, please?" he asked.

"Someone I love is hurt . . ."

"Your aunt, uncle? Not your grandmother?"

"No. Not them."

"I'm happy to hear that. I like them all very much. But I am sorry about whoever this is. Will they be all right?"

That was the question. The essential thing. "I don't know," she said.

"I am sorry. I don't mean to—" He pulled a handkerchief from his coat and handed it to her.

"Thank you. I've gone stupid with weeping. You will think I weep all the time."

He shook his head. "Of course not."

The sun was going down. She shut her eyes against the tears, but they came anyway. She dabbed at her eyes with his handkerchief. He did not ask her any more questions, and she was grateful for his reticence. They sat swaying on the swing together.

Elizabeth turned suddenly. "I forgot. Uncle William told us about your ordeal. How are you? Are you well?"

Jakob indicated his muffler with his gloved hand. "Still frozen. But I'm fine. No lasting effects that I can tell."

"He said you ran across the ice."

"I did. The office seemed about to cave in. I thought I had to, if I wanted to live."

"Did you have to?"

"I don't know. Father hasn't been down yet to inspect the damage. There are reports that the river is already receding. We'll know soon enough whether I was foolish or prudent. Father was hurt, too, though he went out this afternoon. Where, I'm not sure."

"I can't believe you crossed the ice."

"Desperation breeds action." His smile was self-deprecating, endearing. He glanced away and then back again. "There is something else, too. Something I want to tell you."

The night watchman was crossing the street, a lantern and a duffle in his hands. He set them down on the sidewalk and hauled the creaking wrought iron park gates shut. From the duffle he pulled out a long chain and padlock and went to work closing up the park.

Jakob said, "Now I'll have to walk around."

"It seems so."

"Elizabeth, when I was stranded on that rooftop, I thought only of two people. My mother, and you. I don't know whether I was about to die or not. I may never know. But all night, all I could think about was what a shame it would be if I didn't get to see you again. And this afternoon, all I could think was that I wanted you to understand that. Under any other circumstance, what I am about to say would be too forward. But now I've learned how brief a thing life can be. I think you are extraordinary—"

He held up his hand as she opened her mouth to dissuade him.

"I'm not talking about your violin playing. Not even your beauty. Well, perhaps some of it is your beauty." He smiled ruefully. "But I think you are very courageous. You were young when you went to Paris, and yet you survived Monsieur Girard's tyranny. I admire you very much."

She shook her head. "I hardly survived. And you don't know how much you exaggerate. Someone else—"

"No one would have lasted as long."

"I doubt that."

"I adore you, Elizabeth. I've met no one else like you. So, you must suffer my adoration. Will you?"

His gaze was insistent and kind and even, yes, adoring. "You don't know me very well," she said.

"But I want to get to know you well. Will you let me?"

"Your experience has made you precipitate."

"I won't deny it. But what does that matter? May I return tomorrow to see you? We'll have to think of something to do other than the ice regatta. And besides, everyone's sleds were lost in the floe."

"Forgive me, but I can't see you tomorrow—"

"Of course. I'm sorry I don't mean to press. But you must get out sometime. May I call later this week to walk with you in the park?"

She nodded.

"Excellent." And he rose and took his leave.

Chapter Twenty-Five

That evening, in his book-lined study, Gerritt seized the Scotch decanter from the walnut sideboard and poured himself and Jakob each a glassful. Gerritt hadn't changed out of the work clothes he'd donned to go out earlier. His pants' hems were crusted with mud, his canvas shirt sweated through. The bandage on his forehead was ragged and bloodstained. He handed Jakob a glass and motioned him toward the worn leather armchairs that framed the large fireplace. Several logs crackled on the hearth, and the andirons glowed red. Jakob was grateful for the warmth. After returning from Elizabeth's, he still hadn't removed his muffler.

Having summoned Jakob, Gerritt now proceeded to ignore him, staring off into the middle distance with the distracted air of someone who had forgotten his way. Surely, Jakob thought, his father was only gathering his energies to somehow call him to task for the hole in the office roof or for not saving more of their lumber. Jakob hoped not. His visit to Elizabeth, wonderful as it had been, had sapped his energy, and he was ravenous—a function of being exposed to the extreme cold, Doctor Stipp had warned him. The smell of roast beef wafted up the stairs, and with it the earthy scent of roasted potatoes and turnips, a fine dinner that reflected his father's taste.

Now Gerritt turned his gaze on Jakob. "Your mother said you went to the Stipps'."

"I wanted to tell Elizabeth something,"

"I would think you would have spent the day asleep after the night you had. So does this mean that you are still taken with her?"

"Very much."

Gerritt nodded and lifted his glass to study the refractions of the fire through the cut crystal. "Any repercussions for them from the flood?"

"They seem to have had a bit of a shock."

"Shock?" Gerritt cocked his head, his eyes observant now. "Were they upset about your mishap?"

"No, about someone else's apparently."

His father shifted in his seat, concerned. "About whom?"

"She didn't say, and I didn't pry. I probably shouldn't have told you."

"Ah, Jakob the reticent. It's good of you to keep a confidence."

Jakob felt slightly ashamed at this compliment, as if it were really an insult. He changed the subject. "Why did you go out? Doctor Stipp wanted you to stay in."

"I went to see Harley. And then someone had to see about the district. I wanted to see how much trouble we were in. The reports were true. The water is receding fast. If you'd waited another few hours, a boat could have reached you."

"Another few hours and I might have been dead."

Gerritt dismissed this sentiment with a wave.

As sanguine as he had been earlier with Elizabeth, Jakob hated having to defend himself to his father, or impress on him the extremity of his situation. Walking home around the park from the Stipps', the thought of what could have happened had overwhelmed him. In the moment, he had not hesitated to go out on the ice, but the whole thing had been fraught with immense danger. He had been lucky, and not a little foolish to attempt it. But he was alive. And also, he realized now, furious. Harley's abdication of his responsibility had been nagging at him all day. Where had the man been? A hundred other workers had flooded into the district, and Harley had never shown.

"Did you find out where Harley disappeared to during the ice break?"

His father took a sip of the Scotch, keeping his eyes fixed on Jakob. "No. He was heavily medicated, in pain. He took quite a blow."

"If he had met me in the district like I thought he was going to, I wouldn't have been stranded. I could have gone for the books right away and gotten out."

"Nonetheless, Harley's a hero," Gerritt said. "No one can figure out how he got hurt. He might have been unconscious for hours." He set his emptied glass on a side table, resting his case.

"Perhaps, and I'm sorry he's hurt, but why did he go home first instead of going straight to the district?"

"I don't know. He must have had a good reason."

Jakob looked away. His father and Harley together were a bulwark. Jakob's entrance after Harvard into their tight alliance had caused resentment on Harley's part, though his father had dismissed Jakob's concern as imaginary.

Jakob touched his glass, balancing at the end of his armrest. He kept his tone light. "And where were you, Father?"

"Damn this thing itches," Gerritt said, ripping off the bandage on his forehead and revealing the thin red line of his gash and the garish stitches holding it closed. He tossed it into the fire.

"I want to know where you were," Jakob said. All at once, his exhaustion fell away and was replaced by pure, unfiltered rage.

Gerritt glared at Jakob, and his voice turned harsh and remonstrating. "Where was I? Right behind you. But first we had to say good-bye to our guests, and then you'd taken the good carriage, so the other one had to be harnessed and readied, because your mother wanted to come, and that took time, too." He waved a hand in irritation. "A cloak, her hat, some warm gloves. It was interminable. Do you know how long it takes to get her to move? Hours."

"You could have ridden Dolly. You could have been there when the district started to flood. I was alone. It was impossible to do everything by myself." He never opposed his father absolutely. All his life, he'd been careful, respectful, and fearful of exposing his mother to the explosive tirades his father displayed at work, when labor mistakes or shipping problems—things outside of his control—upended his expectations. Jakob doubted he'd protected his mother from much, not when a sherry decanter had become her comfort and confidante. "I thought you were coming to help."

"You did well enough without me."

"You abandoned me."

"But you saved yourself. Son, all this complaining is out of character. Be proud."

Jakob was about to press for a better explanation, but he checked himself. He couldn't tell whether his father was being obtuse or deliberately misunderstanding him. And if he had come, perhaps they both would have been caught, and would his father have been able to manage the ice? He doubted it. He decided to change the subject.

"How much lumber did we save?" Jakob said. "Could you tell? We filled at least one of the barges. Did you find any of them?"

"I didn't go downstream. And by the time the riverfront and roads dry, and we retrieve whatever inventory we can, we may spend the last penny in our coffers."

"I don't think so, not since I last worked on the books, but I can look tonight."

"No need." His father shrugged. "I'll do it."

The books were Jakob's responsibility, though Gerritt understood the business far better than Jakob, who had a good hold on it himself. Lumber was a great generator of cash, but it was also a seasonal commodity, and profits were dependent upon a steady flow of product, which was in turn dependent upon a thousand other things, not the least of which was ready access to one's inventory and a navigable Hudson, which they didn't have, and wouldn't, for a while. They sold most of their lumber downriver, in Manhattan City, and beyond, as far as Boston and Europe, which they would not be able to do for at least a month.

"I can find excess revenue somewhere." Jakob recalled some outstanding receipts they could call in if necessary; Manhattanites tended to be delinquent on their bills unless pressed.

"Not to worry, Jakob. We are better off than most. You saved those books, and I've got them now. Nothing for you to concern yourself with. Your job is to feel better."

A maid tapped on the doorjamb and knotted her hands together in the nervous tic that Jakob had noticed all the maids exhibited when they encountered his father. "Mrs. Van der Veer is waiting for you at table," she said. Her face registered no disapproval of the clumps of dried mud that had fallen from Gerritt's pants onto the Turkish rug, even though she or someone else would have to deal with it as soon as he exited the room.

At table, Viola made no mention of Gerritt's attire. And to Jakob's relief, his mother seemed much more self-possessed that she usually did at this late hour, her gestures more deliberate. Tonight, no sherry glass glimmered in the candlelight, no decanter stood in wait on the pantry sideboard. He caught his mother's eye, and she looked up from her plate and nodded confirmation to his silent inquiry. Dinner often passed like this for them, in mute conversations of subtle nods and glances.

Gerritt never noticed, and he didn't again tonight. "Why didn't you order champagne, Viola? Both of your beloveds have been rescued from Poseidon's grasp. That's worth celebrating, isn't it?"

"Of course," Viola said, and rang the bell.

Later, when she refused to drink even a drop, Gerritt finished the bottle himself and had to be carried to bed.

Chapter Twenty-Six

The next morning, Mary woke to sun streaming through the window of the girls' bedroom. She had slept in an armchair that William had brought up from the parlor. The sour vapor of sleep still permeated the room, though at some point during the long night, she had cracked open a window.

At midnight, when Emma and Claire had stirred, Mary had administered a third dose of narcotic. Above all, she believed they needed rest, because consciousness carried its own dangers; weighted down with intolerable realities, people often gave up. And memory had a way of feeding itself. Starving it through insensibility, interrupting it for a short while, would delay recollection, and she wanted to avoid a repeat of yesterday morning's hysteria.

Mary pulled a shawl over her shoulders and went to the girls' bedside, trying not to wake them. The two sisters lay entwined and inert under the counterpane, their lips and cheeks reassuringly pink, their breathing measured and deep. The strands of their copper hair were damp with perspiration and seemed darker somehow. How much lasting damage the two would suffer was impossible to determine. Over the years, Mary had discovered that the hardest part of being a physician was to wait for possibility to become fact, for the corporeal to repair or declare itself, for a rested soul to emerge from a wounded body—or not.

William brought her a cup of tea and reported that it was eight thirty. Farmers' wagons and carriages were already bustling up and down the avenue, punctuated by the periodic percussions of the sledgehammers still pounding away on the row houses. And still the girls slept on. Amelia and Elizabeth looked in, and they all took turns going down to the kitchen to eat breakfast. Toward ten, they were all there when first Emma's, then Claire's eyes blinked open. They seemed to register nothing of where they were—an effect, no doubt, of the medication. Their bodies roused one limb at a time, first a twitching finger, then a jerk of an elbow, then a shifting leg, until finally they drew themselves sleepily up in bed, their eyes filmed with a glazed, wary numbness.

To Mary's repeated assurances—*You remember us, Auntie Amelia, Aunt Mary, Elizabeth, Uncle William; We're taking care of you; You're safe; We love you*—Emma and Claire said nothing. And they were careful not to draw attention to themselves. Claire's small hand brushed sleep from her eyes, her pale face an unreadable mask. From time to time, she laid her head on her sister's shoulder. They both held themselves very still. It was the stillness of a wary hope, a kind of disbelief that mistrusted itself.

Everyone defaulted to doing concrete tasks, except William, who pretended to read a book in the corner out of fear that his maleness would frighten them. Elizabeth fetched food: buttered bread and chicken broth. Amelia poured tea. Mary tucked a sheet here, smoothed a wrinkle there, while observing the girls out of the corner of her eye, relieved that they displayed no signs of nausea from the morphine. Emma and Claire accepted these ministrations with a wary eye, withdrawing into themselves at any quick gesture. Even the moving of a dish or a walk across a floor threatened. Emma grimaced whenever she extended a leg or shifted in bed. She had not yet discovered her stitches.

Claire pulled Emma close and whispered into her ear, and Emma shook her head. Her eyes, large and round, were socketed above a bony expanse of high cheekbone and deep hollows. Like Claire's, Emma's face was all architectural angle and spare beauty, unmarred even by the yellowing bruise on one cheekbone. Mary could see Emma sorting the past from the present, trying to decide what and who to trust. She recognized the vigilance. Recovering soldiers at Antietam had followed her movements with the same heedful gaze. Whoever had taken the girls shackled them still.

How much to push? Stories of pain never came out straight. They emerged in bits and pieces, and only when the teller could tolerate the telling. Soldiers she had treated often relived their experiences in distracted and disconnected tales that made little sense to anyone but them. Push them too hard, and they broke. Fail to push them enough, and they receded into darkness. Getting to the center of the pain to alleviate it, to free it, took a deft touch.

No one knew exactly what to do or what to say.

It was then that Elizabeth gathered her skirts and sat on the edge of the girls' bed. They looked at her with widening eyes, moving even closer together.

Elizabeth cleared her throat. "Once upon a time, not very long ago, a dragon who lived in a dark cave found two wonderful little sisters. He was greedy and mean and wouldn't let them go outside. He hurt them and scared them and said that no one cared about them anymore."

Emma and Claire turned rapt and attentive. Everyone listened in amazement. Elizabeth was compiling her story from clues: from the girls' pale skin and darkened hair, their mute terror.

"But the dragon was wrong. People who loved them searched and searched. Days and weeks went by. To the girls it seemed like a very long time. They began to lose hope. They feared all was lost. But these were clever girls. Smart girls. Like you, Emma and Claire!

One night they were strong enough and smart enough to escape! They ran out into the night, into the streets. Bells were ringing and it was so loud and they were very afraid and they didn't know what to do. They didn't know where they were." Clever Elizabeth was weaving in details they had gleaned from Officer Farrell. "Then a good policeman found them and brought them to a safe place. A house a lot like this one. But the sisters were still frightened. What if they said the wrong thing and the dragon found them again?

"But I want you to believe me now, girls. That dragon can't ever find you again. You're safe now. Do you understand?"

Claire nodded—an incremental dip of the chin that would hardly register as agreement in anyone else. She nudged Emma, and Emma, her voice scratchy from deep sleep, turned wordlessly to Claire. They looked at one another for a long time before Emma turned and said, "Where are Mama and Papa?"

For the eternity of several seconds, no one said anything. Elizabeth, so competent a moment ago, could find nothing now to say.

Amelia stepped in, kneeling on the floor and reaching for the girls' hands. She said, "Do you remember the big storm? The one when you got lost? Well, your mama and papa got lost, too."

"Did the Other Man find them?" Claire said.

"The other man?" Amelia said, assuming the measured cadence of the master midwife, who had captained hundreds of women through every shoal of labor, and who confronted every disastrous surprise as if it were no surprise at all.

Emma put a restraining arm on Claire, but Claire persisted. "The one who found us. The bad man. Why didn't he find Mama and Papa?"

"The bad man?"

"The one who hurt Emma," Claire said.

Emma tried to silence Claire with a hand to her mouth, but Claire pulled it away.

"There were two men? A bad one and a good one?" Amelia's steadfast control did not falter, even as Mary and William glanced at one another. *Two men.*

"Did the bad one find Mama and Papa like he did us?"

Amelia said, "No, Claire. No, sweetheart. No one found them."

Claire said, "But where are they?" She turned to her sister. "Emma? Emma? Where are they?"

For Claire, there was no leap of understanding, couldn't be one. She was too young. Emma could no longer meet Claire's eyes. She looked as if she were detaching herself from any further responsibility, as if she had claimed too much before and was now exhausted from the effort and could no longer summon the energy to perform one more act of succor for her little sister. She shut her eyes as Claire tugged at her sleeve, imploring her to answer. When Emma opened her eyes again, it was in wide-eyed supplication for Amelia's intercession.

"Claire," Amelia coaxed. "Do you want to come with me? Come with Elizabeth and me. I'll tell you everything. But we'll go outside to the veranda. It's pretty outside. We'll swing. Do you remember the swing? We can talk, and Elizabeth will play her violin. Won't you, Elizabeth?"

"Of course I will."

Claire looked at Emma for permission.

"Don't worry, Emma. I'll go with them," William said. "You don't need to be brave anymore. We are all here to be brave for you. She'll be safe. I promise." He was not a man who gambled, but he was gambling now, all of them hoping that Emma would relinquish Claire to his custody. What trust she could invoke for any man, even one she had called uncle all her life, was unknowable. It was a gamble they all hoped Emma would take, but it was by no means certain that she would.

Emma's glazed eyes focused on William as if she were contemplating every possible outcome of letting Claire go. Then she nodded imperceptibly. William gave her no chance to rethink her decision. He knelt beside Claire and scooped her up from Emma's side and carried her out the door, swaddling her in a blanket as they went, while Elizabeth and Amelia trailed behind.

Mary took Elizabeth's place at the edge of the bed.

Soon, the strains of a Mozart lullaby came through the window, but Emma did not respond to the music. There was not a flicker of relief. Mary wondered what strength or despair it took for a young girl not to cry after she'd learned her parents had died.

"I know we aren't your mama and papa," Mary said. "But you will never be alone. I promise. You'll live here. And we'll do everything to help you. We love you and Claire very much."

Emma lay back down and dragged a pillow over her face and drew her legs into the fetal position.

"I—we all—will take care of you. Last night, I gave you medicine to help you sleep and to help with the pain. I can give you more now. You can sleep. I promise nothing will happen to Claire. And nothing will happen to you, either, except that you'll be safe with us. I will be here or Amelia or Elizabeth. Always."

Emma made small, indecipherable sounds.

"Pardon?" Mary said, leaning down to listen.

"He said, he said—" But her voice drifted off.

"Who said?"

"The Other Man."

"The man who hurt you?"

She nodded. "He said that I needed him. That I'd miss him if—he wasn't always with me."

Deep fury coursed through Mary's veins. "Listen to me, darling. He's gone. He'll never touch you again."

At length Emma whispered, "It burns."

"I know," Mary said, relieved. It was a beginning. All else—who the two men were, what Emma could tell them of their captors, had to wait. "I know it does, Emma. I can fix that. And the medicine will make you sleep, so that you can rest. And when you want to, we can talk."

She mixed a small amount of tincture of choral hydrate with some cider. Emma drank thirstily and lay back down. Mary stroked Emma's hair until the girl fell under the spell of the sedative. From outside, the soft tunes of Elizabeth's violin underscored Claire's occasional chatter and then her cries, as Claire, too, finally understood what Amelia had been trying to tell her.

Chapter Twenty-Seven

Later, in response to a loud pounding at the front door, Mary slipped out of the lying-in room where Emma was still sleeping and leaned over the balustrade, peering into the foyer below, where William had opened the door and was speaking with someone. William was planning to go soon to the hospital to see Mr. Harley and their other patients, and earlier, Elizabeth had taken Claire to her room, and Amelia had just spelled Mary so that she could bathe and dress.

"I just need a word—"

"Darlene?" Mary said, registering the owner of that coarse, insistent thrum. Mary hurried down as Darlene rustled into the dark foyer in a swish of tawdry, nighttime finery—a gown of blue satin that was iridescent even in the entryway's dull light. She was heaving with exertion. Mud streaked the hem of her shiny skirts. Several strands of hennaed hair had fallen from their pins and fringed her face in an uneven curtain. Despite Darlene's garish dress, her face lacked any hint of rouge or paint. Usually, she wore a great deal of the stuff; even this past Thursday, when her wounds had been raw and weeping, she'd drawn kohl around her eyes. Now, her low, square neckline revealed possibly more bosom than had ever been shown in public at noon in the city of Albany. She tugged self-consciously at the dress, but to no effect: it was made to reveal, not conceal. William flashed a glance at Mary that seemed to communicate that he feared locusts might rain down on them next.

Darlene, with another ineffectual tug at her neckline, said, "I didn't get the right house at first. Some of your neighbors might be wondering about me."

The vision of the scandalously clad Darlene dashing from house to house in her opulent gown struck Mary in her exhaustion as laughable. "William, may I introduce Darlene—I'm sorry, Darlene, I don't know your last name."

"It's Moss."

"How do you do?" William said, then nodded and excused himself, leaving them alone.

"He your husband?" Darlene asked, with a jerk of her head, eyeing William as he disappeared up the stairs.

"Darlene, what is it? Are you all right? Is it your arms?"

In response, Darlene thrust them out to show Mary that the slashes, no longer bandaged, were already knitting themselves back together. "I told your husband it's not about these."

"Why, you've taken such good care," Mary said. She took Darlene's arms in her hands and examined the wounds carefully, marveling that she had followed through on all she asked of her.

"I apologize for barging in. I do," Darlene hurried on. "Thing is, I ran all this way. Cut across fields and through the almshouse grounds to avoid the road. That's why I'm fagged, you see. I ran and ran."

"You ran up the hill from downtown?" Mary said. "Why didn't you just take the horsecar?"

"I didn't come from near the river. I'm in a new house now over on New Scotland, past Ontario," Darlene said. "That other house was no good. Thursday, soon as I got back from clinic, with my cuts all bandaged and fixed, Madam fined me for getting cut, as if I'd slashed my own arms. Then she wouldn't pay me what I was owed, another penalty, she said, for not having the good sense to dodge the razor, and when I complained, she busted out with a palaver of screaming and yelling. But I gave as good as I got, then skedaddled. I caught a ride on the back of some farmer's wagon. Paid him like he asked, out behind a tree."

Mary winced at this revelation, but Darlene dismissed it with a shake of her head. "Free is a lot cheaper than the horsecar, and the conductors kick me off anyway, claiming I'm uncouth, even though I'm the picture of manners when I go out."

"I'm not sure that it was actually *free*," Mary said. She was studying Darlene carefully, taking in her disarray, her fatigue.

"Do you mind if I sit down?" Darlene said. "I'm still fagged."

Mary gestured toward the parlor, where the prostitute took in the furnishings, a collection of rather drab but serviceable armchairs and tables, an intentional choice, since the parlor served as the waiting room.

"No offense," Darlene said, "but it's all a sight unhappy, isn't it? We've had far nicer things in the houses I've worked."

"Darlene?"

"Sorry. The new madam took me in right off. She didn't care about my cuts or the bugs in my hair, but she decided I oughtn't to service men till my arms got a little less weepy and I got my hair straightened around. Nice lady. She let me take care of myself, said when I was ready I could start up again.

"Then last night she said she'd thought of a way for me to pay my board right off. She took me back to her private room off the kitchen, where a man was laid out in her bed. He had a fat bandage on his neck. She said he was her friend and that I was supposed to take good care of him 'cause she couldn't 'cause she had to be out front all night. I was to give him food when he asked and dose him up good with liquor when he said he was hurting. She didn't have anything stronger, even though she said someone was supposed to have brought her some poppy syrup. She warned me not to say anything to anyone. And I did what she asked. I took care of him. Anyway, he was already half drunk when I found him, complaining about his neck and moaning."

"That's why you're here? You need a doctor?" Mary said, rising. "Why didn't you just say? I'll tell William—"

Darlene held up her hand, forestalling her. "To keep him quiet—he kept crying out—I asked him questions about how he'd gotten hurt. And Lordy, did that man talk. He started complaining that some little boys just about drowned him in the flood. Then he got all mixed up. One minute he was talking about those boys and the next he was clinging to my wrist and crying sorry about taking those sisters, and God, did he love them, and where were they, poor things, and he hoped they'd made it. *Oh my darling girls.* He said that again and again. It took me a long time to figure out just what he was saying and who he might be saying it about. And then I knew. But I wanted to make sure. So I asked him a couple times, just vague like, so I wouldn't scare him: girls? What girls? *Oh, angels they are,* he said. I kept pressing him, and finally he came out with their names: *Emma and Claire.* I'm right, aren't I? Isn't that the name of your girls?"

An icy chill shot up Mary's spine.

"I think he's the one—the man who took your girls—and he's lying in a bed just down the road."

Mary stared at Darlene. Captain Mantel's warnings returned with a rush. He had said that Darlene would turn up, wanting money in exchange for information, and now here she was.

"Didn't you hear me?" Darlene said.

"Did you say this man has a cut on his neck?"

"Yes. His neck was bandaged as neat as you like. And stitches. Looked as good as if you did it, come to think of it. But it was getting a bit bloody. Just seeping, you know. So I used the soap you gave me on his cut. Seemed to help. But what I really wanted to do was to put my thumb in it to make him suffer."

Darlene's description of the man's injury sounded strikingly similar to James Harley's, whom she had left yesterday confined to his bed in City Hospital. Now she couldn't help but wonder whether Darlene had read the newspaper story about Harley and concocted this tale in hopes of profiting. But Darlene had not yet asked for a penny. Mary wracked her memory of the terrible article. Sometime yesterday afternoon, after the delicate task of sewing up Emma, William had read her the reporter's patronizing drivel. Were it a time any less fraught, Mary would have penned a repudiation. But what had the reporter said about Harley? She recalled no description of his injury—just his name.

"What did this man say his name was?"

"He couldn't say. He was half out of his mind, sick with fever."

"You didn't read yesterday's paper?"

"I can't read," Darlene said, exasperated. "I told you that on Thursday."

She had, Mary recalled now, and banished any further question about Darlene's motives. "What does he look like?"

"Head as bald as an eagle's. Burly like. Hard and strong."

Harley. Without a doubt. Mary sat back, her heart racing. She shut her eyes against the image of that man with Emma.

"Dr. Stipp?" Darlene was peering at her.

"Did he talk about anyone else? Another man, perhaps?"

"No. Just the girls. And those boys, I guess."

"Does he live there?"

Darlene shrugged a bare shoulder freed by the wide neckline of her dress. "I don't know. Can't say. Last night's the first time I spied him. Since I got there, I'd been out back in the damned laundry shed, rinsing my hair with that Lice-Bane." She combed a hand through a loose strand. "Though, I tell you, if he came from somewhere else, he sure didn't get there by himself. The man isn't well enough to put one foot in front of the other. I wanted to come here right away, but I had to watch him. So, I soaked him in more whiskey until he passed out. Near two in the morning, the madam came back. Then this morning, when I woke up, I bolted to come tell you. Slept in my dress and corset so I could get out quick. 'Course," she added mournfully, "none of any of this will tell you where those girls are. I asked and asked. All that man babbled on about was that accursed flood taking them away. Maybe your girls are all right—I hope they are—I wished I'd found 'em for you—but I think—oh, I should have said this earlier—maybe they drowned? Maybe they didn't. But all that water—oh, my heart aches for you, thinking of it."

An excess of caution held Mary back from alerting Darlene to the fact of Emma's and Claire's survival. There were too many variables, too many things she did not yet understand.

"Darlene, would you be willing to tell my husband what you just told me?"

Darlene shrugged again. "Would have told you both if he'd stayed."

Vera did not blink at Darlene's colorful attire. She poured her a cup of coffee, then disappeared into the kitchen muttering something about eggs. As Darlene faithfully repeated the whole story to William, she ran her fingers appreciatively over the fine wool of a shawl Mary had unearthed for her.

The unflappable Vera soon returned with a plateful of scrambled eggs and black bread slathered with butter, squeezing Darlene's wrist in a gesture of affection before retreating again. Vera never betrayed that she heard anything of what was said in the house, but she always knew everything. The other night, when she'd been weeping, no doubt she'd thought no one had heard her.

Darlene ate her fill. William asked a few probing questions that

Mary had not thought of: Was it possible that the man was mixing up the sex of the children, confused about the gender, because he was ill? Had Darlene ever said the girls' names to him before he told them to her? Was she certain she had heard him correctly? Drunken men, he informed her, had a tendency toward ownership of other people's stories.

Darlene scoffed at any suggestion that the vagaries of inebriated men were any kind of mystery to her. And she remained adamant. She knew what she'd heard.

Mary and William exchanged an urgent, puzzled glance. Vera reappeared and demanded that Darlene turn over her shoes.

"Why?" Darlene said.

"To clean them."

Darlene stared after Vera as she toted away her surrendered shoes. William and Mary hardly noticed the exchange, preoccupied with Darlene's news. William implored Darlene to say nothing of the man's disclosures to anyone. Could they count on her?

"Of course. You ought to mind that the madam is with him now, and who knows what he'll say to her."

"We are so grateful to you."

"At least you know now who took 'em. And if they did go into the river, I'm ever so sorry. Now, will you do something for me?" Darlene said.

Mary braced herself.

"If you send the police, can you give me a shout 'fore they come? I don't want to end up in the station house again. It's cold in those cells, and I'm never dressed for it. And I've no money this time to pay a bribe. They don't let you leave till you pay them something under the table. And so you know, that Captain Mantel is the worst."

"Mantel?"

"He's funny, that one. The things he asks for? He always pays well—but none of the girls like to work him."

"Work him?"

"Come now, Dr. Stipp, you can't be shocked by anything now, can you? He's a rough one, too. Likes the young ones. I had a bruise or two from him myself, upon a time."

Mary sat stunned. Captain Mantel, whom she had turned to for help. "Why didn't you tell me this that day at the clinic?"

"That man's trouble. He might have been outside, listening." She was wiping her face with a napkin and dusting bread crumbs from her décolletage when Vera returned with the shoes.

"They'll just get all muddy going back," Darlene said, slipping them on, "but thanks all the same, and for the eggs."

Vera waved her hand and disappeared again.

Darlene shrugged the shawl from her shoulders, but Mary insisted she keep it. A smile of gratitude crept across Darlene's face and then she dashed out the back door, down the wooden steps, into the fenced garden, and through the gate to the alleyway, where Harold was shoeing one of the carriage horses, bent over the horse's rear fetlock. Mary watched Darlene's bouncing flight until she disappeared, then turned to William.

"Emma said there were two men."

"The police captain?" William shook his head. "That's a leap. It can't be true."

"I'm not sure what's true anymore."

Chapter Twenty-Eight

In his scuffed helmet and muddied uniform, Colm Farrell looked a sweaty mess. Mary and William had gone looking for the policeman and found him on Broadway, patrolling for looters at the junction of Broadway and Steuben, where merchants and restaurateurs were shoveling mounds of river sludge into the gutters, piling sodden showcases and furniture onto the sidewalk to dry, and stacking crates of rescued goods high off the muck. Up and down Broadway, the *thacketa thacketa* of steam pumps percussed the air, arcs of dirty water spraying into the street. Warning them that he had little time, he left his noisy post and trudged after them the one block into the quiet relief of Mary's clinic.

There, Mary described Emma's injuries and Darlene's revelations, omitting her remarks about Mantel, still uncertain whether or not they could trust the policeman completely. Farrell listened intently, at one point removing his helmet to scratch distractedly at specks of dried mud on one cheek.

"This is the same whore who suggested they might have been taken in the first place?" he asked.

Mary flinched at the ugly word, but said, "It is."

"And she didn't ask you for money?" Farrell said.

"No."

"So Mantel was wrong about that," the policeman mused, sounding surprised.

At the mention of Mantel, William said, "She mentioned something about the police captain."

Farrell narrowed his gaze. "What did she say?"

"Something about certain appetites."

Farrell's gaze went suddenly flat. He sniffed and hitched up his pants. "Might be the captain's a lonely man. Might be he likes company."

"And he such a crusader against prostitution," Mary said.

"We can't all be as angelic as you two, now can we?" Farrell said, but with respect.

"Listen, we've just come from the hospital," William said. "James Harley is gone, and no one remembers quite how that happened. There is no record of any other physician dismissing him. Of course, a patient is free to come and go as he pleases, but Harley was in no shape to get himself anywhere."

Farrell nodded, the muscles working in his strong jaw. "But why would anyone move a wounded man from a hospital and plop him in a whorehouse?"

"To hide him?" Mary said.

"Maybe."

"Do you know the house Darlene described?" William said.

"Oh, I know it," Farrell said. He thought for a moment. "Could be the man Darlene's talking about read that story about Harley in the paper, and took it on as his own."

This so precisely echoed what William had said earlier that Farrell's repetition of it undermined Mary's confidence. "Please, can you just go and see?"

"I'll try. I have to get permission from Captain Mantel. He'll be furious. I haven't told him yet about finding the girls."

"What? You haven't?"

Farrell shook his head. "Wasn't sure yet that a crime had been committed. Now, though, I'll have to tell him. But just so you understand if—*if*—I make an arrest, you won't be able to keep the girls' survival and situation quiet. You've had a night of reprieve, but as early as tonight it could be all over the police blotter and then the newspapers. People don't often come back to life. It's an event of some note, and with wee ones, it's a story of hope, even if—" Farrell's facade of dispassion fell. He refastened his helmet and adjusted his belt, fiddling with the placement of the brass buckle, gleaming in the shabby grimness of the clinic. "Will the little ones be—will they get better?"

Mary and William exchanged a glance. "We hope so."

Farrell did not seem convinced. After all, he had seen some of what they had seen, though not as intimately.

"There's something else," Mary said. "Claire said there were two men."

"Two? Two men where?"

"She didn't say."

"You've not asked her yet where she was?"

"They're not in a state to talk. But she said there was a good one and a bad one."

"That's important. Or not."

"What do you mean?"

Farrell shrugged, apologetic. "You realize, it's going to be hard for people to believe what those girls say?"

"I beg your pardon?" William said.

"A good man and a bad man? I'm sorry, but unless you can get her to be more specific—what I'm saying is, she's going to have to be clear, do you understand? For anyone to believe her. It doesn't hold. If there was a 'good man' then why didn't that 'good man' help them to get away? It sounds—well, to my ears, it sounds like a fairy tale."

Mary could hardly draw breath. "Fairy tale?"

"I'm just saying. I'm trying to help. All of us know something happened to them, but it's not an easy thing to get charges filed for something like this. Men are accused every day. Sometimes falsely. The courts are sensitive to that. And you have young girls talking about good and bad men—"

Indignation boiled up inside Mary. "I believe them. You saw them."

"Well that's all good and fine for you, and I believe them, too. But I'm telling you, the issue isn't whether or not *you or I* believe them. It's whether or not everybody else will. So, be careful who you tell that to, is all I'm saying. And I'll keep the information in mind."

"Emma has always been a smart girl," Mary said. "She is not frivolous—"

Farrell cocked his head, his gaze once again sympathetic. "Would you rather I didn't tell it to you straight? Would you rather I sugarcoat the whole nasty tangle of something this sordid? You're a doctor. Both of you are. I'm shocked you've not figured this out for yourself. And all I'm saying is maybe she made up the good man so that she could get through it. You see? Someone she could believe in? I've got daughters of my own. I'm not talking out of my left foot here."

Mary swallowed and looked at William, who raised his eyebrows in return. The possibility had never occurred to her, and Farrell's assessment unnerved her. He might be right—what child didn't try to imagine their way out of desperate trouble like the kind Emma had just suffered? If so, Emma was more disturbed than Mary already worried she was. She cleared her throat. "There's one more thing. Darlene doesn't want to be arrested. She says police demand bribes, and she hasn't any money to pay you."

"I'm not one that takes bribes, thank you very much. But in any case, I can't see why I'd arrest one whore over another—"

Mary bristled. "Why don't you call her something less derogatory?"

Farrell stared and then said, "Look. If I took one—*lady*—I'd have to take the whole bloody house. But mind you, there will be other trouble for Darlene. She won't be able to stay where she is after the madam figures out that she's the reason I'm there. Especially if Harley is someone important enough to keep him in her bed."

It occurred to Mary now that if word of Darlene's actions got out, she wouldn't be able to work anywhere in Albany again. No madam would tolerate a whore who caused the police to arrive at her doorstep. She might have to go to a house in Schenectady or Troy, though more than likely she'd have to escape to Manhattan City's anonymity. And if she wanted to escape the profession, she had little hope of doing it here. Few people would hire a woman who'd worked as a prostitute. Unless, Mary thought, she sent her to the House of Shelter. She would ask Gerritt Van der Veer for his help.

Outside, Mary locked the door behind them. Farrell, his long face lined with exhaustion and strain, surveyed the narrow alleyway, his eyes coming to rest on the small red cross beside the door.

He would be in touch, he said. Until then, they were not to do anything or say a word to anyone.

Chapter Twenty-Nine

The precinct vestibule reeked of kerosene and dust, and the lantern had burned low, but it was light enough for Colm Farrell to read Mantel's keen interest.

"But those girls are dead," Mantel said, his dark eyes slit with both challenge and suspicion. The entryway of the police station was uncharacteristically deserted in the aftermath of the flood, nevertheless Mantel beckoned to Farrell to follow him down the narrow hallway to the privacy of his office, a low-ceilinged closet of a room crammed with crates of loose paperwork, piles of tattered arrest logs, and an arsenal of firearms large enough to arm a posse of volunteers, should he ever require one. Farrell ducked under the doorframe and took a seat across from the captain, who had squeezed into his chair, the brass buttons of his uniform clinking against the edge of the desk.

"Now, tell me what the hell you're talking about," Mantel said.

"They're not dead," Farrell said.

"God in heaven, Farrell, if they're not dead, then where are they?"

Farrell told the whole story from beginning to end, including Mary Stipp's assertion that Emma had been raped.

"Let me understand this. You knew yesterday that those O'Donnell sisters are alive and you didn't tell me?"

Mantel's gaze had turned flat and steady, betraying a far cooler mien than Farrell believed the man ought to be displaying under the circumstances, but he found it even more interesting that the captain had exhibited no horror or surprise at what had befallen Emma and Claire, only outrage at not being informed in a timely manner of their resurrection. He returned the captain's taciturn gaze, an effective interrogation tactic; people could stand anything but silence. But Mantel was well acquainted with the technique, too, and he wanted his answer. Finally Farrell gave in. He'd been working since seven in the morning, and he was hungry, weary, and sick to death of the mystery surrounding the O'Donnell girls' disappearance. "I didn't know then that a crime had been committed," Farrell said evenly.

"That excuse is a little thin, Farrell. You find dead girls that aren't dead, that's information, especially since we'd been searching for them. And as if it isn't already a nightmare around here, now the whole city is going to be screaming about this. And you want to go hunting for James Harley in a whorehouse? The city's new hero? The one good thing that happened to Albany all week?"

"If you'll allow me to."

"Why isn't that man in the hospital?"

"I stopped by there on the way here. The nurses said you were there yesterday. Maybe you can tell me why he isn't still there?"

"When half the city of Albany was looting storefronts, we had a genuine hero on our hands. I went to thank him."

Farrell stared at the captain, undeterred by the man's deflection. After the initial wave of unrest had passed, they had arrested all of six men for looting, and one of them turned out to be a shop owner who had been retrieving a dozen blankets from his own store to distribute to the less fortunate at City Hall. "I'm sure Mr. Harley appreciated the visit."

Mantel frowned, hesitating before choosing his next words. "I'm not convinced he's guilty. You can't trust a whore to tell the truth, and everyone saw Harley save those two boys. But go retrieve him, if you can find him. I'm more interested in whether or not those O'Donnell sisters said anything to you about where they've been."

"You haven't asked me yet how they are."

"Who are you? A doctor? Why would I ask you?"

"I'm not sure how old the older girl is. She might be underage," Farrell said, with emphasis.

Mantel made a dismissive notion with one hand. "It happens. Children—it happens. You can't be soft about these things, Farrell, do you understand? It's more important to flush out what those sisters know. Have they said anything about who did it? Did they mention Harley?"

"They're hardly talking, Captain. You should have seen them—I've never seen a child in such a state."

"Get on with it then," Mantel said, waving a hand. "Go find Harley. Arrest him if you have to. But whatever you do, don't arrest that madam."

"Why would I?"

"Don't be coy. One more thing. You're certain that those sisters are going to stay with the Stipps?"

Farrell had already risen. With one hand on the door latch, he looked back and regarded the captain. "Does it matter?"

Mantel offered a nonchalant shrug. "They're orphans. It's our responsibility to find them a home that we can trust. I'm not certain the Stipps are the place for them. She's a doctor who goes out all over town at all hours of the day and night, hardly reliable as a homemaker. We might need to turn them over to the nuns at St. Vincent's."

"I think the good doctors would put up a fight if you tried to take those girls away from them."

Mantel shrugged again and busied himself, shifting piles of paper around his desk. "It was just a thought."

Farrell commandeered a police wagon and took along a fellow officer named Kiernan O'Brien and drove out to New Scotland Plank Road. It was pleasant to be away from the ravages and turmoil of the river cleanup, but the spring road was rough going. Some of the planks had deteriorated after the blizzard and the road company hadn't yet replaced them. After rattling past the forbidding gray stone of the penitentiary and the dark red brick of the almshouse, the officers were happy to reach the newly plowed fields that lay beyond.

When they reached the whorehouse, they followed the lane lined with oak trees down to the picturesque, turreted dwelling painted a pretty shade of pale yellow that gave an incongruous impression of prosperity. It was past five o'clock, and a dozen carriages were parked in the yard. The flood had deterred no one, and may have even spurred those who wanted to escape their watery troubles. Heavily curtained windows prevented prying eyes and provided the discreet cover patrons expected. Admittance through the front door of a bawdy house was usually under control of the madam, but no policeman ever entered through a public parlor. Farrell and O'Brien drew up around back.

The madam, a worn-out slip of a thing who called herself Melody Addison, said, "Early, aren't you?" She thrust her hand between her breasts and fished out a wad of greenbacks, and counted out the regular quarterly bribe for Captain Mantel that Farrell usually collected on the first of June. Farrell palmed the wad of bills and pushed past her into the tidy kitchen. The stove and table and chairs were well scrubbed and gleaming in the waning light streaming through two sets of uncurtained windows. Upstairs, bedsprings squeaked. Evening and its happy profitability was upon the house.

"Maybe you want something extra this time?" Melody said, letting drop one shoulder of her robe to reveal a swath of breast.

Farrell ignored her.

The madam denied everything.

Farrell threatened to knock down every door in the house if she didn't reveal where her special guest was hidden.

Reluctantly she showed him across the back vestibule into a bedchamber. It was handsomely furnished with a brass bed, a tall highboy, and an oak armoire with a rippling mirror set into its door. A stout, bald man lay in bed clutching a cup of tea in one trembling hand. His untrimmed beard gave him the look of a vagrant, and the rumpled bedclothes were rife with the stink of fever and sickness. His eyes had sunk into his cheeks, and a purple bruise curled around his neck, though the bandage at the back of his neck was clean. Someone, it seemed, had been taking care of him. His hands shook as he set the teacup on the bedside table, a flash of alarm lighting up his pale face.

"I don't know why you're after him," Melody said. "Don't you know he is a hero? He saved two little boys. And he's hurt besides. There was an article about him in the *Argus* yesterday."

"So I understand." Farrell eyed the man whom Melody had just unwittingly identified for him as Harley. Farrell ushered the madam to the door and locked it behind her and took a seat in a caned chair. Through a window open to the evening breeze, a farmer was sowing a distant field row, a burlap bag heavy with seed slung across one shoulder.

Farrell said, "Your doctor is worried about you, Mr. Harley. She couldn't find you at the hospital this morning."

"She?" Harley said, his voice guarded.

"You didn't know that your doctor is the famous lady doctor?"

"No. I—I didn't. I didn't notice anything for a while."

"And how are you feeling now?" Farrell said. "Need to go back to the hospital?"

Harley blinked, and Farrell waited, extending the silence until Harley said, "How are those boys?"

Farrell had no idea where the boys were or how they were faring. "You remember rescuing them, but not who your doctor is?"

"Saving children isn't a thing you forget."

"I bet not. They're fine. Back with their mother. You're quite the champion of children, aren't you?"

Harley leveled his gaze and shrugged, wincing as he did. It was obvious that he was in a great deal of pain, but he had his faculties about him. The intoxication of the previous night that had propelled him into confession—if indeed he had made one—was no longer a factor.

"Since you love children so much, you must have been heartbroken when those other children died."

Harley blinked. "Other children?"

"You work for Gerritt Van der Veer, don't you? At least that's what the paper said."

"I do. Yes." Harley shifted in bed, pushing himself up against the single pillow, keeping a wary gaze on Farrell.

"Then you must remember those two little girls, Emma and Claire O'Donnell, who disappeared in the blizzard?"

Harley blinked again.

"Their father, David O'Donnell, was a stevedore in Van der Veer's yard. He died in the March storm."

Harley grimaced, the muscles of his jaw working. "Right. Oh, yes. O'Donnell. Sorry. Yes. We all miss him." Harley gestured distractedly toward his neck as an excuse. "I'm not myself."

"It's a funny thing to leave a hospital when you're not feeling your best."

Harley shrugged and winced again.

Farrell nodded, as if he agreed that leaving a hospital to stay in a whorehouse were a logical move. "Here's another funny thing. Your doctor, when Emma and Claire disappeared? She bothered the precinct captain to distraction about them. Those Stipps looked everywhere for those girls. She wouldn't believe they'd gone into the river after the blizzard. Tireless, that woman." Farrell shook his head, as if to lament what a bother a woman of determined nature could be. "Anyway, we're all proud of you, for taking care of those boys. Shame, though, about your house. You live in the Pastures, yes?"

Harley peered at him.

"Didn't you know that all the basements in the Pastures are completely under water?"

A flicker of panic crossed Harley's face.

"Don't worry. Captain Mantel sent me himself to look it over, secure it." The lie rolled easily off his tongue. "Didn't want the house of a hero looted."

"Flooded? The basement? How high did the water reach?" Harley said, balling a swath of silken sheet into a fist. As pale as he had been, he grew paler still.

In an offhanded manner, Farrell said, "You'll be happy to know, though, that I found those girls."

"You did?" Harley's voice was a strangled mix of dread and joy. "In the cellar—where? Oh, the poor dears. Are they all right? Did they survive the water?"

Farrell paused before saying, "But how could they have survived? They're dead, aren't they?"

An opaque veil drew across Harley's face as he realized his mistake. He sank against the headboard and shut his eyes.

It was difficult for Farrell to contain his loathing. He'd almost missed the sisters in the dark. What would have happened to them if he hadn't found them? "I hear there were two of you."

"Two of us what?"

"Two of you who took the girls."

"How did you know where I was?" Harley managed, his voice barely above a whisper.

"I'll tell you that when you tell me who brought you here," Farrell said. "And if there was another man."

But Harley had gone silent.

Sick as Harley was, there was little chance he would escape, but Farrell was feeling none too generous. He called O'Brien in, who manacled himself to Harley with a pair of nippers.

Farrell next questioned Melody. Locks of her dark hair tumbled across a forehead ridged with worry. "But he's a hero," she said, her tone pleading as she glanced between the chamber door and the policeman. "He's *important.*"

"He's important to you."

She affected nonchalance and failed, finally fixing Farrell with a defiant stare.

"Are you the one who brought him here?" Farrell said.

Melody shook her head.

"Then who?"

She refused to answer, an interesting bit of information that he logged away. "So a sick and injured Mr. Harley somehow just arrived on your doorstep yesterday? Out of the clear blue sky?"

She nodded, dropping the robe again off one shoulder and looking at Farrell from under a thick fringe of dark eyelashes.

"Did Harley say anything to you about two little girls?"

"Little girls? No. It was two little boys. It was in all the papers."

Farrell tilted his head to one side. "You think you know James Harley well, don't you?"

Melody stiffened and yanked the lapels of her robe together with one hand. "I do know him. He's good to me."

Color rose in her cheeks. In the last two years, Farrell had visited this house perhaps six times, having taken over the duties of bribe collection from another officer who had retired, and he had never seen her this discomfited.

"How old were you, when you first started all this?" Farrell said, directing a nod at the closed parlor doors and the world beyond, any evidence of its shiny facade absent in this plain, homey kitchen, with its scarred wooden floors and muslin drapes. "Were you young?"

She lifted her chin, a gesture at once defiant and defensive. "It's not a terrible life, no matter what you think. I have money saved. Enough to live on for a long time. I'm leaving soon. Harley and I—we—" She stopped then, having concluded that she had said too much.

In the relative privacy of a laundry outbuilding in back of the whorehouse Farrell questioned every prostitute in turn in order to obscure that he was interested only in Darlene, who happened to be the last. She eyed the policeman warily, leaning against the edge of a crude wooden shelf lined with several copper washtubs. A beautiful woolen shawl covered her bare shoulders and she worried a tip of the fine wrap against one cheek as she said, "The madam isn't going to be too pleased with me, no matter if you don't tell her it was me. She's not stupid. Now what am I going to do? The doctor promised me she'd warn me before you came, so I could get away from the house."

"And I promised Dr. Stipp I wouldn't arrest you. She wrote a note for me to give to you."

A look of bemused astonishment flooded the bone-weary features of Darlene's face as Farrell held out an envelope.

Darlene shook her head "I'm not good at that reading business. Would you read it to me?"

"Later, after we talk," Farrell said, tucking away the envelope in his jacket pocket.

Darlene cast a longing glance at it before saying, "It was him, right? I was right? He's the one who hurt those sisters?"

"Just tell me what Mr. Harley said to you last night."

She was a loquacious woman, but the bones of her story matched the one the Stipps had reported, though Farrell was surprised when Darlene added that she had been the one who had cleaned Harley's wound.

The prostitute shrugged, as if this were nothing remarkable. "Dr. Stipp showed me how." She held out her arms and displayed a set of healing scars.

"How did that happen?"

She shrugged again. "What does it matter? You won't do anything about it. Hey, you're not going to arrest me, are you?"

"No. Not you. Harley and Melody, yes. And I agree with you that Melody is not a stupid woman. She'll figure out it was you soon enough. I suggest that you go somewhere else, anywhere that isn't here."

"I don't have any money," Darlene said, with a gesture of embarrassment. "I left it all behind in my other house. Haven't had a chance to earn any here yet."

Farrell dug into his pocket and retrieved the roll of bills that Melody had pressed on him—Mantel's monthly bribe.

Darlene gaped at the fat wad, then breathed a knowing, resigned sigh. "So you want to—?"

"No."

She looked skeptically from the money to him, and thrust her chin forward. "I always earn my way."

"You already have," he said. He then read her the letter from Mary, in which she recommended that Darlene go to the House of Shelter.

Farrell gave Darlene a head start down the road before he fettered the madam and Harley to the iron loops bolted inside the wagon bed. Melody spouted a string of epithets at Farrell, though her protest lacked enthusiasm, and soon enough she focused her attention on Harley's comfort, divining a way to cradle his head in her lap without disturbing his dressing as they bumped down the drive in the police wagon, headed to the county jail.

Chapter Thirty

The next morning, at ten o'clock, Viola Van der Veer was doing something she never did. She was listening outside the open door of her husband's study. Moments before, as she finished dressing, her maid had informed her that the police captain had come to see Gerritt, and she had hurried down the servant's stairway to hover in the alcove adjacent to the doorway, pretending a sudden and profound interest in rearranging a bouquet of hothouse lilies enshrined on the alcove's marble shelf. From the study came the crackle of a low fire, along with terse whispers of a conversation. She had never before stooped to eavesdropping, but neither was Gerritt forthcoming, and a visit by a police captain on a Thursday morning merited attention, especially when the city was in such turmoil. Jakob was still sleeping, or he had been an hour ago, when she'd looked in on him. Just after dinner, he had succumbed to deadening fatigue, and this morning had slept through breakfast.

"I thought you would want to know," Mantel murmured.

"Alive?" came Gerritt's incredulous voice, far louder than the police captain's careful undertone. "Are you sure? The two O'Donnell girls?"

Viola's heart leaped in her chest. With a swish of her skirts, she swept into the study.

Gerritt glared at her, his expression a mixture of incredulity and irritation. "What is it, Viola?"

"Did I hear correctly?" She could hardly get it out, disbelieving. "Bonnie's daughters are alive?"

Mantel had been leaning against the back of one of the tobacco-scented armchairs. He turned and removed his brimmed cap. His great coat was unbuttoned, its military-style brass buttons glinting in the low firelight. He had not taken the time to relieve himself of either cap or coat. It was clear that he did not mean to stay long.

"How do you do, Mrs. Van der Veer? Yes. Those girls have come back to life. Found by one of my officers in the Pastures, apparently. On the streets." Mantel swiveled to include Gerritt in the conversation. "And I'm sad to bring the news that it looks as if your Mr. Harley might be involved. I would have come to tell you last night, but it was late when Farrell returned, and I thought a visit this morning would draw less attention. Though I don't know about that now. There were plenty of people afoot this morning. I haven't much time. We're doing double duty, all of us. I slept only three hours last night. I'm ragged to the bones."

"Where are they? Are they all right? Are they in the hospital? What happened?" Viola said.

"Did I hear correctly? The O'Donnell girls are alive?" Now it was Jakob at the doorway. He was dressed in a worsted wool suit, a woolen muffler wrapped around his neck.

"That's right," Mantel said.

"Are you sure?" Jakob said.

"It's verified," Mantel said. "Though I've not yet seen them myself."

"But how were they found? Where have they been all this time?" Viola looked from Mantel to Gerritt, who echoed faintly, "Yes, where have they been? This is astonishing."

Mantel shrugged. "We know very little. But it seems they've been staying in James Harley's house."

"Harley's house?" Jakob said. "No. That's impossible."

Mantel shook his head. "Not impossible. We have a witness—two, maybe. I've been keeping an eye on Harley myself lately. There have been some reports about him."

"You arrested him?" Jakob said.

"One of my officers did," Mantel said.

"But are Emma and Claire all right?" Viola pressed. "You haven't said."

"Respectfully, madam, alive is better than dead, isn't it? Other than that, like I say, I don't know. I'm going from here to find out—"

"But where are they? May I go with you?"

"They're at the Stipps' house, I'm told. On Madison—"

"Do they need anything? Can I help in some way?" She could call for the carriage and be there in an instant. "I'll just go now and get my coat—"

Mantel held up a restraining hand. "Mrs. Van der Veer. I don't know the particulars. But I believe that the girls might require some rest. Better to write the Stipps first, I think, to see what you can do."

The captain was right. She couldn't charge over there and impose herself on them, no matter how much she wanted to help. And she had never met Emma and Claire; she'd only heard Bonnie speak of them. If she rushed over now in her excited state, she might frighten them. Gerritt had poured himself some Scotch—Mantel had declined—and he took a sip now. Viola rarely came in here. Gerritt's study was always dark—at night, clubby, if he were entertaining male friends—but during the day, oppressive. Jakob came to her side and placed his arm around her waist, his presence warm and strong. She might be mourning Jakob today if things had gone differently.

"What will the DA charge?" Jakob said.

"Kidnapping, at least," Mantel said. "I don't know what else, but Farrell—the officer who found them—he suggested to me that

Harley"—Mantel looked away from Viola and Jakob to Gerritt, as if he could not say what he had to say while looking at them—"interfered with them, too."

Viola's knees buckled. She blinked away tears. Jakob walked her to one of the chairs by the fireplace and helped her to sit down.

Gerritt put a hand on the mantel to steady himself. "Are you certain? Did he admit guilt?"

"I don't know. Farrell has no need to justify his arrest to me—only to the district attorney. But mind, Gerritt. Your overseer is in the county jail and you can bet that no magistrate is going to free him without substantial bail, hero or no. That's what I came to tell you. You'd not have reason to know, otherwise. And now if you'll forgive me, I have to be off. I have some apologizing to do. I wasn't exactly convinced that those girls were alive, as you'll remember, Gerritt, from my visit to her establishment."

"Whose establishment?" Viola said.

Mantel eyed Gerritt with a patriarchal gleam. "Should you tell her or shall I?"

Gerritt took another sip of Scotch. It occurred to Viola that it seemed very early to be indulging. "Mrs. Stipp operates a medical clinic for ladies of the night," Gerritt said.

Viola straightened. "Ladies of the night? Do you mean that she treats prostitutes?" She tried to imagine mixing so closely with the unclad women who hung out of the windows of the bawdy houses along the waterfront, and couldn't. "That is a bit of a surprise, yes, but why do you regard the information as something I should be protected from? How is Mrs. Stipp's clinic any different from Gerritt's House of Shelter?"

"The difference, madam," Mantel said, his demeanor revealing astonishment at her unruffled reply, "is intention. Your husband's good work eradicates the city of the scourge of prostitution. But Dr. Stipp was hiding what she was doing. Makes you wonder what else she was up to. Without a doubt, she's aiding and abetting, at least. There's also a rumor that she's been performing abortions. Not that Harley is much better. He was found in a whorehouse out on New Scotland. The one near Ontario," Mantel said, nodding at Gerritt, a sly glance slipping between the two men.

Viola shuddered. This was not the first time she'd heard the two of them make knowing references to the locations of bawdy houses.

Mantel returned his cap to his head. "There's depths to Mr. Harley, it seems, that not even his closest friends were aware of. Now, I probably shouldn't have told you any of this. I want you especially, Gerritt, to be careful. The backlash against you—and your business—for employing Harley is likely to be substantial when word gets out. Folks aren't generally too pleased about situations like this, even though it's more than likely that Harley isn't guilty. What man saves two children when he's been defiling others?" He tipped his head at Viola. "Sorry, Mrs. Van der Veer. But it makes no sense. Now, don't go spreading this news around. Those vulture newspapers will be on it soon enough. It's up to the courts to sort it out."

With a second nod of apology to Viola, the captain swept out the door, his greatcoat open and flapping, his dirty boots trailing mud behind him.

In his wake, Gerritt said, "Shocking. Just shocking. Those O'Donnell girls? And Harley? I can't believe it."

"Will you fire him?" Viola said.

"Of course not. Not yet. Not until I know something firmer. Now, my dear wife, would you please excuse your son and me? I need to ask something of Jakob."

"I'd rather stay," Viola said, feigning confidence, wondering what punishment this bit of insolence would earn her. "These are Bonnie's daughters. I want to know everything."

"What about writing your note to the Stipps?"

"It can wait ten minutes."

"This is business."

When she didn't rise, Gerritt sighed. "Fine, then. Jakob, I need you to go down to the jail and do whatever it is that lawyers do. And post bail if it's been assessed, please. We don't want the poor man incarcerated if we can help it."

"But he can't do that," Viola exclaimed. "These are Bonnie's daughters who have been hurt. And to think, Mr. Harley was in this house for dinner just the other night when all along he had them. And what about Jakob and Elizabeth? They have an understanding. You can't ask Jakob to do any of this. It's not right."

"As far as I can tell," Gerritt said, "all that Jakob and Elizabeth have had so far is conversation. And Harley has been a good employee for as long as Jakob has been alive, far longer than we've known the Stipps or that hatmaker—"

"Hatmaker?" Viola said. "Bonnie was my friend, Gerritt."

"She was a hatmaker, Viola. Don't exaggerate—"

"Father," Jakob interrupted. "These little girls mean something to Elizabeth. She considers them her sisters. And right now, in your concern for Harley's well-being, you seem to have forgotten that because of him I nearly froze to death."

"Are you forgetting that Harley is a hero?" Gerritt said. "What would it look like if we didn't extend him ready legal help? You're a lawyer. He needs one. Much as I deplore what he may have done, at this point he is only accused. What if he is innocent? Think about that. He's been a friend to this family for twenty years. And if we are to get Van der Veer Lumber up and running again, we need him."

The noble words *innocent until proven guilty* careened through Viola's mind, but Gerritt's protestation seemed more a way to manipulate Jakob than a blind devotion to justice at all costs.

"Father, there are a dozen reasons why this isn't a good idea. It is better if Harley has someone who is not his friend—"

"Why, no lawyer would have any business at all if he didn't bail out his friends. How do you think lawyers get clients?"

Jakob strode across the room and pulled a compact volume from a shelf. He leafed through it. Viola could tell by its size and the advertising on the back cover that it was the *City Directory,* a repository of useful information about Albany, from street addresses to the schedule of day boats. It also listed the names of all the lawyers in the city. She knew because she had once gone looking for one, though this being the state capital, you couldn't walk down State Street without encountering a dozen within a minute. She remembered seeing something like 250 names and addresses listed, though not Jakob's. He had been examined and ratified by a judge only this last January, and the book was printed in December.

Jakob thrust the open book into his father's hands. "There are many lawyers to choose from. You could ask any one of these to represent Harley. Or query Abraham Lansing. He's one of the preeminent lawyers in the state. As I recall, he wasn't too partial to Mrs. Stipp, so he should have no qualms taking the case." Jakob's tone was polite, but insistent.

"Don't be obstinate, Jakob. This is really very simple."

"I beg to differ, Father. This is no ordinary case. If what Mantel says is true, then this could be a question of child rape, complicated by the not irrelevant fact that these are children whom Elizabeth and the Stipps happen to love."

Gerritt snapped the directory shut and reshelved it. He was fastidious with his books, careful of them. "Judge and jury, are you? Didn't they teach you anything at that college I paid for?"

"If you want Harley to be well defended, anyone is a better choice than I am. I have never once tried a case in real court."

"You were examined by a judge in January. You're official."

"Why don't we let Harley find his own counsel?"

"Didn't Aristotle say that law is freedom from passion?"

Jakob stared at his father.

"Yes, I know a few things," Gerritt said, his voice imbued with sarcasm. "And I also know that if you pledged yourself to engage in the law, then you believe in morality as prescribed by law—that everyone is entitled to a dispassionate defense, even the loathsome."

Viola chafed, but it was an oddly nuanced argument for her husband to make. Calculated to appeal to Jakob's virtuous—and lawyerly—nature: *What if Harley is innocent?* She studied Jakob's face, his disquiet. She wanted to step between the two of them, ease her son's refusal. "Jakob, you don't need to do this. I think—"

"You don't think anything, Viola," Gerritt said. "Nothing. You are not engaged in this conversation. If you wish to remain in the room, be quiet."

"I will not be quiet," she said, rising. "Jakob, I urge you to do as you wish. You're old enough to do so. Your father is being unreasonable, out of affection for Harley. But you are not his servant."

Gerritt turned solicitous. "My dear, I realize you think I am being rude. In business matters I can be gruff, as you've just seen. I need Harley for the business, therefore I need Jakob to defend him. Give Jakob and me a chance to work this through. You've raised a good son. He'll make the right decision."

Viola turned to Jakob, who appeared calm despite his father's unreasonable demands. Her son nodded at her briefly, to reassure her. Reluctantly she kissed him on the cheek, gathered her skirts, and went out, almost tripping over a ripple in the Turkish carpet.

Gerritt went to a window, shut it, and stood silently with his back to the room. Jakob wondered what his father's next ploy would be, because there always was one.

Finally, Gerritt turned, brushing lint from the lapel of his frock coat with one hand. "You understand, this will be the biggest court case in the entire city—maybe even the state—for a long while."

So, an appeal to vanity. "No, Father. I won't do this for my own aggrandizement. This is Elizabeth's family."

"Don't cloud your thinking with sentiment, Jakob." Now that his mother had gone, his father's voice had taken a harder edge. "Those O'Donnells were only friends to the Stipps, not family. If you're so fond of Elizabeth, defend Harley and find out who really did it. She'll thank you for that. And that would be a challenge worthy of your virtue."

Jakob moved closer to the fire. How was it possible to still be cold? He thought his bones might be cold forever. "I would rather not. You see, I think I could love Elizabeth, Father. After very little time, she already means a great deal to me. I don't think she would understand if I defended Harley. She might perceive it as a betrayal."

"Not if you couch it properly. Isn't that what you lawyers always do? Pitch a persuasive argument?"

"Harley deserves an experienced lawyer."

"You are being self-deprecating."

"I've never practiced, Father. You know that. I haven't been inside a courtroom except for school and my swearing in."

His father scoffed. "There always has to be a first time. And besides, I clothed you, housed you, fed you, saw to it that you were educated at the best college in the nation, and provided you with a job at the biggest lumber concern in the world. Without me, you would have nothing. And now I am giving you one more thing—the chance to do what you say you want. Criminal law. You see, I've been paying attention."

His father could cobble a cogent argument out of anything, even guilt. "You've missed your calling, Father. Why don't *you* defend Harley?"

"I'll tell you what, Jakob. You do this for me, and I'll let your mother divorce me."

Jakob gasped. He sat down hard, the cracked leather cushion giving way with a hiss.

"Isn't that what she wants?" His father stared at him, his level gaze unflinching. "You want the best for your mother, don't you? I believe you want that even more than you want Elizabeth. I'll be frank with you. It can be no surprise to you that your mother and I have our differences. And I've seen you two, scheming together, exchanging looks and conspiring about what to do about me. I'm not blind to your bond. Nor do I begrudge you your love for your mother. It's natural and right. Now I'm providing you with an opportunity to ease her unhappy situation. When the time comes, after the trial, I'll allow someone to find me in flagrante delicto with someone. Then you can file on her behalf. And to sweeten the deal, I'll make sure that your mother is as rich as Croesus. Is that good enough for you? Reason enough to set aside an infatuation to serve your family in the way that will do everyone the best good? Yes, it's a bribe. But Harley is a man who has made my life much easier. And I believe in him."

It was as long a speech as his father had ever made, when sober.

"If you divorce her, Father, she won't be welcome anywhere." The law granted dissolution only in cases of abandonment, usually, infidelity, rarely, and generally only when committed by the wife. It was an ugly, public process despised by those in society and looked down upon by most. One could never remain a member of a church afterward. For the sin of divorce, shunning and shaming were the order of the day, and it was always the woman who fared worse.

His father swirled the liquor in his glass and mused over it before looking up again. "Fine. Instead, I'll give her a generous allowance and she can live apart from me, wherever she likes."

Jakob couldn't believe it. Finally, his mother would be free. "But you are forcing me to choose. My mother or Elizabeth."

Gerritt shrugged. "It's not really a choice, is it? Not for a son as loving as you. And you can easily fix it with the girl. Just explain to her that you are doing your family a favor. That seems easy and clear enough to me."

"Why, Father? Why insist on me? It makes no sense."

His father lowered his voice and leaned in, speaking almost in a whisper. "If you won't do this, then get out."

"What?"

"Get out of the house. Of Van der Veer Lumber. Of Albany." A glint of steel flashed in his father's eyes.

Jakob said, "I don't understand—"

"I've asked very little of you in your life, Jakob. Now I ask you for just one thing—"

"So going to get the company books in the middle of the river breakup was 'little'?"

"I need this, Jakob. I need this very much. Another attorney would have no regard for our family, our fortune, our privacy. But you would. You would be discreet, careful. You would protect our reputation. Our livelihood depends on you. Do you understand? Your mother's livelihood depends on you. And if you are not loyal enough to do this for us—for your mother—then our family, our life, will mean nothing after this. If I am willing to sacrifice the woman I love, shouldn't you be willing to sacrifice a mere flirtation, alluring as it may seem to you now?"

The lie that he loved Viola had tripped off his father's tongue without even a hint of sarcasm.

"Do you swear to me, Father, that you will ask nothing else of me for the rest of my life?"

"Your debt to me is fathomless, but I promise, not so much as an invitation to dinner."

Upstairs, Viola greeted Jakob's news with fury. "Don't do it, Jakob. There are more lawyers in Albany than there are rats. Someone will defend Harley. It's not as if he'll be abandoned with no one to help him."

"I don't understand why Father is so insistent."

"That is the question, yes. Why?"

"He claims loyalty, family duty, honor."

"Rather ironic that he would claim family honor while offering to divorce me in the same breath."

They were sitting on the narrow settee by the window in her bedroom. Sunlight fell on the pink and red stripes of the tufted silk cushions.

"Mother, I know you are not happy. I will help you file, and after it is all done I'll make certain you are not alone. You could live with me, or you could move back to Manhattan to be with your parents."

"That would be social suicide, darling. I would be the disgraced failure, shuttered in the house on Fifth Avenue, suitable only to provide gossip for the house maids."

Jakob grasped his mother's hands. Her fingers were bone thin and ice cold. In the sunlight, her skin looked like bisque porcelain, unmarred by any real furrow. The black profusion of her eyelashes was wet with tears.

"You're more important to me than anything," she said. "Don't do it. Our problems—your father's and mine—should not be your concern."

The real problem, Jakob thought, was that his father was not a stupid man. Nor was he ignorant of the law or human nature. Jakob was aware that his father was manipulating him, but that did not mean that his father was wrong. It was impossible to shake the sordidness of the possible charges, but even so, everyone was entitled to a defense. Everyone. And the real possibility of Harley's innocence remained. With the exception of Harley's puzzling absence the night of the flood, his interactions with Jakob had always been straightforward. While every man was capable of harboring secrets, the truth remained that the right to a fair trial was superior to any repugnance on the part of anyone. It was more honorable to defend Harley than to prejudge him or abandon him. And what was the truth of what had happened? Impossible to know, unless he looked for it.

"I think it's best if your concerns *are* mine," Jakob said.

"Are you sure?"

"I am." But he couldn't imagine Elizabeth ever trusting or forgiving a man who would defend a person she believed had hurt Emma and Claire. Nor could he imagine Elizabeth's face when—if—he told her. What he wanted was to remember her as she had looked at him last night, her eyes shining with happiness and relief at seeing him. But his heart ached for her and all she had been going through. He wished she'd felt free to tell him last night about Emma and Claire, especially since he'd babbled on and on about himself. "But remember, Mother, this whole thing may be a mistake. Maybe charges won't be filed after all. We—all of us—have made a leap. Harley could already be freed."

"Didn't you hear the police captain say that he'd long had his eye on Harley?"

"Yes. But I'm not sure what he meant."

Jakob left his mother writing her note to the Stipps and went out to the stable to saddle Dolly.

He turned the mare down upper State in the direction of Maiden Lane and the magistrate's office. The noontime air was thick with the earthy promise of tulips and daffodils, though it was still chilly. Across the park there was a faint din and a cloud of dust rising above the row houses that were being demolished, but when he looked through the wrought iron fence in the direction of the Stipps' residence, he couldn't make out their house at all. It might as well, he thought, not even be there.

Chapter Thirty-One

Across the park at the Stipps', Emma and Claire held on to Elizabeth's hands as they ventured into the back garden. One of William's patients had presented at the house with an emergency, and Mary and Elizabeth had whisked the sisters outside. There had been no question of turning the man away. A metal lathe had crushed three of his fingers at the ironworks at the NY Central rail yards. Their clinic was closer than any of the hospitals, though in truth there was little William could do for the man here at the house aside from splinting the mangled remains in an attempt to preserve them. Surgery would probably be needed, in the form of amputation, especially if the fingers turned gangrenous. Through the open kitchen windows, Mary could hear Vera humming, no doubt in an attempt to dampen the gruesome noises coming from William's clinic.

It was Thursday. Amelia had gone to the morning prayer service at church, driven by Harold, who had been charged with posting a note afterward on Mary's clinic door, explaining that once again she wouldn't be seeing patients. Mary hated to do it, especially after the kindness they had all displayed last week, but she wanted to stay at home with the girls. Yesterday, when she and William had been rooting out Farrell, Emma had slept under Amelia's watchful eye, helped along by the chloral, but Claire had attached herself to Elizabeth and followed her around the house, asking again and again where her parents were. Elizabeth explained about the cemetery and promised to take her there, but Claire didn't really understand. Claire's misery had been hard for Elizabeth, and Mary didn't want to desert her again. This morning, she'd already had to leave for an hour to make her rounds at the hospital.

Emma and Claire were wandering barefoot, walking gingerly on the cold, green grasses, taking mincing steps, not venturing from Elizabeth's side. Elizabeth had brought out her violin case and placed it on a blanket she had spread under a maple tree. The girls' toes were already turning blue in the dew. They needed shoes, but no cobbler made house calls, and Mary certainly wasn't going to take them out in public. Not yet. Not until she had to. And certainly not today. Hampered by her stitches and bruises, Emma moved with greater caution than Claire, whose step was lighter. The two looked so much like their parents. They had Bonnie's beauty and David's lanky limbs, though their hair was their own. It glowed cinnamon in the sunlight, falling in a warm cascade about their shoulders. After the blizzard, the Stipps had cleaned out the O'Donnells' rooms and donated their clothes to the community basket at the church. Yesterday, when Mary and William had returned from seeing Farrell, Amelia, in search of something for Emma and Claire to wear besides nightgowns, had gone there and discovered two of their dresses still in the basket. This morning Emma and Claire had pulled them on with near reverence. Later, Mary would have a seamstress measure them for some new ones, but she doubted they would love anything as much as they did these remnants of their old lives.

Their resurrection still seemed impossible, yet here they were, making a tentative first foray into the world at Elizabeth's side. Elizabeth seemed to instinctively understand what the girls needed. Her touch, at once careful and affectionate, earned no reflexive withdrawal from Emma and Claire. Elizabeth looked over her shoulder at Mary and smiled her mother Jenny's conspiratorial half-smile, which Jenny would flash as a ceasefire in order to get through a rainy summer afternoon or a long winter evening. Now it seemed a ghostly benediction across time.

Claire loosened her grip and ventured one step, then two, then plopped onto the ground, gathering the skirts of her dress tightly around her ankles. Emma, however, froze. After a few moments, Mary went over and took Emma's hand and coaxed her back to the stoop. Emma had not spoken a word this morning. Seated beside Mary, she made herself small, knotting her hands together, drawing them over her knees and pressing her folded legs to her chest. A single raised vein snaked across the expanse of her right cheekbone and disappeared into the ghost of the yellowing bruise. The dress that Amelia had unearthed was the pink calico that Bonnie had sewn for Emma last Christmas. Dense vertical lines of lace decorated the bodice, along with tiny pearl buttons that Emma used to finger at meals or in the rare times anyone could get her to sit still. But she sat still now. David, Mary thought, would not be able to bear his scrappy daughter—whom he had encouraged to scramble up trees and dig in the dirt and laugh at anyone who scorned her—in so lifeless a carapace. During the war, her patients often wanted to recount the battle to her, to make her understand. But mostly they called for their mothers. Throughout that first terrible night at Antietam, when it seemed as if the entire world was bleeding, calls of *Mother* had filled the air. And in the nights and days afterward, their keening cries obliterated even the battlefield gunfire. Emma had had six eternal weeks of difficult nights. Had she called for Bonnie? And how had she survived, with no mother to answer her call?

A whisper of a giggle drifted across the garden. Claire was plucking early buttercups from a crop growing in the shade of the overhanging maple. Emma watched her sister intently, and Mary remembered Bonnie gazing at Emma and Claire with that same fierce love.

"Emma?" Mary said.

Emma shook her head.

"It's all right. You can tell me."

Emma hesitated, then turned to Mary and said, "Claire told. She wasn't supposed to tell."

"Tell about what?"

"He said—" Emma closed her eyes, as if she were trying to shut out the memory. "He said if we told—"

"About what happened," Mary said, trying to encourage her.

"He said if we told, then something—" A strand of hair blew across her face and she absentmindedly hooked a pinky finger around it and dragged it behind her ears. Before, Emma had been a chatterbox, a lively, bubbling font of intelligence and mischief. Now she couldn't even finish a sentence.

"He said that something terrible would happen to Claire, didn't he?" Mary prompted.

Emma pressed her lips together and nodded grimly, her eyes glazed with fear.

Mary reached over and cradled Emma's pointed chin in one hand. "You're safe now, do you hear me? Nothing will happen to Claire, not here."

"You don't know."

"You're safe now." If need be, Mary would say this every hour, every day, for the rest of her life, so that Emma would believe it, too. "You're safe."

"But you don't know."

"Know what?"

"What he's like," Emma said.

Although Mary knew what had happened to Emma in broad terms, she did not yet know the whole of what she had suffered. However, from Emma's obvious terror she had a suspicion of how they might have survived such a man. "I think I might know, darling. I think he told you that if you did whatever he wanted, he would leave Claire alone. Is that it?"

Emma looked at her, astonished.

Mary pulled Emma close and touched her lips to the top of Emma's head, not wanting to hold her too tightly, not wanting to scare her more. In the garden Elizabeth was pulling her violin from its case. She and Claire were perched on the blanket, Claire leaning against Elizabeth's shoulder, one knee bent, while Elizabeth coated the bow with rosin. A hint of pinesap wafted across the garden.

"You don't understand. I did something terrible," Emma said.

"No, Emma," Mary said. "You did nothing wrong."

"But I did."

"None of what happened to you and Claire was your fault."

"But I killed him."

Mary drew back. "What? Killed who?"

"The good one. I hit him with a shovel."

"With a shovel?"

"He came downstairs when the bells were ringing and I was scared that he wouldn't let us go. I remembered Mama saying that bells like that meant fire or flood. So I picked up the shovel and hit him hard and he fell down and Claire and I ran up the stairs."

The words spilled out of Emma. It was the most she had said since she'd come back. But it still took a minute before Mary understood. At the hospital, she had assumed that something sharp in the water had injured Harley. But a shovel, wielded by Emma?

"Is that how you got away?"

Emma nodded.

How had the girl ever delivered such a devastating blow? "But, darling, you didn't kill him. You hurt him a little, but he's alive." Mary wouldn't mention now—or perhaps, ever—that she and William had treated Harley. "You didn't kill him," she said again.

"I didn't?"

"No."

Emma's eyes widened. "Then I'm not bad?"

"No, Emma. You're not bad. You're the bravest girl I have ever met. You saved Claire and you saved yourself. Hitting him was the right thing to do."

"But he was the good one."

Here it was again. Good man, bad man. Mary had been on alert since Farrell's observation the day before. Had there really been two men? Across the garden, Elizabeth lifted her bow, and the first sweet note of something beautiful lifted into the air.

"Why do you say he was the good one?" Mary said.

"He gave us food. Once, he combed our hair."

"But did the good man—the one you hit with the shovel—ever hurt you?"

Emma shook her head.

"He didn't—touch you—the way the other man—the bad man—did?" Mary said.

Emma shook her head again, adamant.

There were a thousand questions Mary wanted to ask—who was the other man, what did he look like, do you know his name—but to push the girl now would be to suggest that she didn't believe her. And they hadn't heard yet from Farrell. What if Darlene hadn't been telling the truth? What if Harley wasn't the man after all? And two men harming Emma seemed easier to believe than one who stood by and let another assault her.

Emma was yawning. This would be Emma's pattern, Mary thought. She would give up a few details, and then collapse. She seemed to have acquired an extraordinary capacity for sleep, as if she had not slept the entire six weeks she had been gone.

Vera stuck her head out the back door. "Someone to see you at the door."

"A patient?"

"Says he's the precinct captain—Mantel? I made him stay outside on the veranda." When Vera was upset, her accent grew heavier, and it was heavy now. She turned and beamed at Emma. "How is our Emma today? Does she want hot chocolate?"

"I want to sleep."

"Vera, warn Lizzie to keep Claire outside, would you please? Come on, Emma. I'll take you upstairs." Mary led Emma up the back stairway to the lying-in room, the little girl's hand clutching hers with a lassitude that spoke both of exhaustion and indifference. Emma's eyes were already closing as Mary covered her with a light quilt and said, "I'm going outside to talk to the policeman. If you need me, you can go to the window and call for me, all right?" But she wasn't certain that Emma had even heard her.

Downstairs, in the foyer, Mary could hear William in his exam room broaching the necessity of surgery with his patient and the patient's anxious questions, the strain of pain and shock evident in the high, trembling pitch of his voicc. William's even tones seemed to calm him, and their voices dropped to a low murmur. Outside, Mary found Mantel, pacing. He wore his greatcoat though this morning the air had lost all hint of winter. He doffed his policeman's cap and said, "Mrs. Stipp," without any hint of hostility.

"*Dr.* Stipp." She shut the door and stood before it to signal that she would not be inviting him inside.

"Forgive me. *Doctor.* I came to apologize to you. I acknowledge that you were right all along. Those girls were alive, just as you thought. If it's any comfort, I thought you'd want to know that we've found the man who took them—with your help. It was Mr. James Harley who got your girls. Ironically, the man you stitched at the hospital." He seemed to have added the last to share the blame, as if Mary were somehow complicit in his failure to locate Emma and Claire, but his manner remained subdued, with no sign of the bluster he had displayed in their previous interactions.

"Why didn't Officer Farrell come to tell us himself? We waited for him last night."

"It was late when he got it all taken care of. I gave him the day off today. A man's got to sleep sometime, doesn't he? Plus, given how I behaved before, I owed you this courtesy."

Mary gave no indication that she accepted his apologies. She didn't. He'd behaved abominably and she wasn't about to forgive him. "Did Mr. Farrell mention to you that Emma and Claire say that there were two men involved?"

"He did. He also told me Harley needed a doctor. I arranged for Albert Van der Veer to go see him. The jail doctor isn't worth his salt. So neither you nor your husband should go near the man now. He is no longer your patient."

"Do you know that the girls say that Mr. Harley didn't touch them?"

"Well, their imaginations—"

Mary held up her hand. She was tired of everyone saying that Emma had to have imagined something she was so adamant about. Mary was even tired of her own doubts. "If you speak to me again as if I or Emma don't know what we're talking about, I'll report you to the mayor, which is what I should have done the second you dropped your search. You ought to have gone door to door to save those children."

"Your impression of my powers of search and seizure are prodigious, madam, but I assure you I do not possess the right to ransack Albany, no matter what you think. No regulation allows for such a blanket action. Something like that requires evidence of a crime committed. There was no sign of a struggle, no sightings of Emma and Claire that indicated anything other than that a tragedy had occurred, much like the hundreds of other tragedies across the Northeast as a result of that blizzard."

"Tragedies?" William had appeared behind her, having escorted his patient to the door. The man wore a sling positioning his bandaged hand high across his chest. Dazedly, he stumbled past the policeman and wandered off toward the horsecar stop a half block away, where he sank onto the slatted bench to await the next car.

"How do you do, Dr. Stipp," Mantel said to William, after turning to watch the man go. "Your wife seems to be worried I won't be doing the work to hunt down whoever is responsible for what happened to those girls. But I will, you can count on it. And I assure you that we'll be asking Mr. Harley if he had a friend. But he's in no shape to talk just now. Albert Van der Veer went to see him in jail and he reported the man is feverish. Right now, I'd like to talk to your girls, to see if they can describe the man who kidnapped them—if that's what happened."

"It *is* what happened," Mary said. "You just said Harley took them."

"Right. Yes. Well. Everything's alleged until proven in court. I'm just being careful here. Now, can I talk to the girls?"

"Absolutely not. Not yet," Mary said. "Emma can barely stay awake, and Claire is—young. She calls Harley the good man and the second one the bad man. Actually, both of them do."

"Can you tell me anything? How are the girls feeling?"

"How do you think they're feeling, Captain? I examined them both. The evidence is unmistakable. Emma was raped. But Claire was not. She was spared."

"Spared?"

"Completely."

Mantel whistled through his teeth. "I wonder what that's about?"

"Don't be obtuse. You know exactly what that's about," Mary said, unleashing her full anger. He was pretending to know very little, his previous cavalier reference to the matter seemingly expunged from his memory. It was infuriating. "It's just as you said before. Claire is not of age. But Emma is. Whoever raped her knew that and acted accordingly."

Squinting against a sudden shaft of light streaming under the portico, Mantel registered Mary's statement with a vague, grim nod. On the street, the horsecar plodded past and slowed to a stop. They all turned to observe William's patient ascend the open stairs, his gait far steadier than before.

"Well," Mantel said when the car started up again. "The district attorney will probably file charges against Harley soon. He'll need to talk to the girls within a few days, too, so get ready. And he'll be asking you what you want to do. Have you talked about that?"

"What do you mean?"

"Well, if this goes to trial, Emma and Claire will need to testify. Have you thought about that?"

Mary exchanged a look with William. They'd been too busy taking care of the girls to consider the possibility of a trial and what it might mean for Emma.

"Well, I'll be leaving you for now," Mantel said, replacing his cap. "But one last warning. This story is fair game for the newspapers. Get ready. Like I told Farrell, it's not every day two children come back to life."

With that, the brawny man tipped his hat and clattered down the steps, making an ignoble, hasty retreat down the slate walkway and across the street to the uneven sidewalk that ran outside the park fence. As he turned into the park, he passed Harold and Amelia returning from church. Harold dropped Amelia in front. She strode up the walkway, brandishing a copy of the *Argus,* its headlines blaring that the "Winter Sisters" had been found alive, that James Harley had been arrested for their kidnapping and ravishment, and that the girls were so crazed by their ordeal that they had been interred in a sanitarium.

"How can it be announced in the newspapers already?" Amelia said, sinking breathless onto the veranda swing. "How does the reporter even know? Especially what happened to Emma? We told no one. And a sanitarium?"

William and Mary stared at one another. It seemed impossible that the sympathetic Farrell would leak the news before they gave him permission.

Only later that afternoon, when they received Viola's letter with its generous offer of shelter and help for Emma and Claire, did they learn that Captain Mantel, astonishingly, had stopped first at the Van der Veers to inform them of James Harley's arrest before coming to tell them.

Who else, they wondered, had he told?

Chapter Thirty-Two

A letter for Elizabeth from Jakob arrived early the next morning, Friday, April 25, via a Van der Veer footman before any of them had even breakfasted. Jakob had never come to claim her for the walk he had promised her, and she expected that this cream-colored envelope with its clear flowing script was an apology.

She took the envelope upstairs to her room and tore it open.

Midnight
Thursday, April 24

Dear Elizabeth,

I apologize profusely for not coming to call on you this week. I intended to come to see you today, however the entirety of my attention became embroiled elsewhere and I confess that I forgot our engagement until this late hour, so I am writing you now with my sincerest and most heartfelt apologies.

And I fear that after I tell you what occupied my attention so completely, you may never want me to call ever again.

I would prefer to tell you the news I am about to relay in person, however I do not wish to disturb Emma and Claire O'Donnell. Yes. I know now what caused you so much distress the last time we saw one another. Early this morning Captain Mantel came to inform my father of all the news. It is this event that diverted my attentions. My father has induced me to represent Mr. James Harley, therefore today became consumed by a visit to the county jail and then a bail hearing. You may perhaps learn tomorrow that the judge has refused Mr. Harley bail. He is to be held pending charges. The district attorney will soon decide whether or not to file, I expect within the next forty-eight hours.

I realize my involvement in the case will come as a shock. What I pledge to you and your family is that if Mr. Harley does go to trial, I vow to take enormous care with Emma and Claire in court. My own shock upon learning of the crimes committed against them cannot in any measure approximate yours, but I assure you that my heart is with you and your family, even as I pay duty to mine. I will understand if you wish to never see me again, though I am heartbroken at the prospect of losing your regard.

I remain yours most sincerely,
Jakob Van der Veer

Elizabeth laid the letter open on the bed beside her and looked out the window and across the park. She could not see the Van der Veer mansion, and for that she was glad. Even if the park's saplings had not already been budding, the distance was too far, though since meeting Jakob, she had often fancied that she could just make out the mansion's distinctive height. After a few moments, she retrieved the letter and went downstairs into the kitchen, where to Vera's surprise she pried the burner off the cookstove and shoved the letter into the fire.

Chapter Thirty-Three

In the next several days, speculation in the newspapers about Emma and Claire and James Harley echoed a rising hysteria in the city, to be expected perhaps in a place still reeling from the effects of the flood. The Stipps heard nothing from the district attorney. They spent their time at home, tending to the girls, seeing their patients, trying to ignore the clusters of the curious who gathered on the sidewalk across the street, their heads tilted together in gossip, occasionally pointing toward the house. On Sunday, they did not go to church. It was not until Monday that they received a request for an interview from Lansing Hotaling, the district attorney. He arrived at the Stipp house on Tuesday morning, after sending a second note to arrange the time of the appointment. He specifically needed to question Emma, he wrote, to precisely understand the case. It was imperative that he speak with her before she forgot any details. He would not question Claire, he wrote, for she was far too young and unreliable by the standards of the court to provide crucial testimony.

Mary and William met him at the door. Hotaling was about thirty years of age and nearly seven feet tall. He had to duck under the door lintel. When viewed from the side, his long frame resembled a question mark, bringing to mind Washington Irving's lanky Ichabod

Crane. Juggling a sheaf of papers and a carrying case, he shook William's hand with a large, damp grip. His wrinkled frock coat was expertly tailored but bunched at his elbows, and several brown stains marred the yellow silk of its turned cuffs. Though he wore a wedding ring and his trousers were neatly pressed, the overall impression was of a man who needed someone to take care of him.

He took a seat on a chair in the parlor and arranged his papers on the low table marred with the nicks and gouges of years of waiting patients and their restless children. Clasping his large hands in an attitude of prayer, he began, "You have only to read recent newspaper articles to ascertain that if we go to trial, this case will pose difficulties for everyone involved."

"Have you filed charges yet?" William asked.

"No. And I'm not certain whether or not I will. Emma's responses today will give me a good sense of whether or not I can even bring a case, and what sort of case I can bring. Kidnapping is straightforward enough. I'll probe that issue with her first. What is in question is the other charge, which has obviously, in breach of the rules, already been leaked to the press."

"We think Captain Mantel may have been responsible for that," William said.

"The police captain? I'll note that. Now, if indeed Emma is a victim of indecencies—"

"She is," Mary said. "Without equivocation. I can readily detail the injuries I found on exam that directly point to—"

The district attorney stopped her with one long hand. "Please, Mrs.—"

"*Doctor,*" Mary said.

"I will gladly hear what you have to say, *Dr.* Stipp, but only after I speak to Emma. I do not want to contaminate my impressions with yours—"

"They are not impressions. They are facts."

"There are facts and then there are alternate facts."

"That is the most ridiculous thing I have ever heard anyone say."

"Be that as it may, correct procedure must be followed."

"We insist on being present when you speak with her," Mary said. "She has not been talking much. Nor do I press her for details that she cannot yet give. She is in a precarious state. My goal, my mother's goal, my husband's, has been to make her feel safe. It is a minute-by-minute process."

"Fine. One of you may stay, but you will not prompt her in any way, do you understand?"

Amelia escorted Emma in, the girl shuffling, careful of her stitches. She was worrying one of the minute pearl buttons of her dress with her fingers. Yesterday, when they'd told her that someone would come to ask her questions, she'd responded with silence. Mary lifted Emma onto her lap as William and Amelia retreated to the hallway, hovering just out of sight. Elizabeth had again taken Claire to the back garden with a diversionary picnic.

Hotaling's face was a mask of trained disinterest. He explained to Emma why he was there and what he needed her to do. It was important, he said, that she answer every question, because he wanted to understand. Could she do that?

She nodded, her eyes moving from his long fingers to his narrow face.

Hotaling began, balancing a small lap desk he'd brought with him on one thigh, his legs crossed, a notebook open and at the ready, a newly shaved pencil twirling in the long fingers of his left hand.

"All right. We'll begin. How old are you, Emma?"

"Ten."

"How old is your sister?"

"Seven."

"Can you tell me what happened when the blizzard ended?"

"We went outside when the teacher said to go home. But Mama and Papa weren't there," Emma said, her voice breaking.

"I know this is hard, but you must answer every question I ask you, even when you're sad. Do you understand?"

"Yes."

"When your parents didn't come for you, what did you do? Did you go back into the school?"

"No. We thought they were coming. But they didn't. And then we wanted to go home."

"There must have been a lot of people outside, other parents and so on. Did you ask someone you knew for help?"

"They all left us."

"Again, did you think of going back to the school?"

"The teacher said we couldn't. She said we had to go home because she didn't have any food for us anymore. We were hungry. We just wanted to go home."

"How long did you wait?"

"I don't know. It was so cold."

"What happened next?"

"We started to go home, but the snow was too deep."

Mary shuddered at the thought of Emma and Claire trying to maneuver through those terrible drifts.

"Then what happened?"

"Claire sank and I couldn't dig her out."

"Where were you?"

"At the intersection of our street."

"And what happened next?"

"A man stopped. He was in a sleigh. He said he would help us. He dug Claire out."

"Did you know him?"

"No."

Mary was astonished. Emma had barely responded to anything they had asked her.

"What did he look like?"

Emma buried her face in Mary's chest and would not answer.

"All right," Hotaling said. "Can you tell me whether you had ever seen him before?"

Emma shook her head.

"Can you at least tell me his name?"

"The Other Man," she said.

"He didn't tell you his name?"

"No."

"Why did you call him the other man?"

"Because there were two men."

"There were two men in the sleigh?"

"No. Just him."

"Then what happened?"

"He put us in his sleigh."

"Why did you let him?

"He said he would help us." Emma was trembling now.

"Did you ask to go home?"

"I thought he knew where we lived."

"Where did he take you?"

"To a house, near the river."

"Then what?"

"He went inside and left us outside."

"Why didn't you go home?"

"The snow was too deep."

"Then what?"

"He came outside and took us in, and the Man was there—"

"The man?"

"Yes. It was his house. And he fed us and took care of us."

"What was his name?"

"He never said."

"What did the other man do then?"

"He left. But sometimes he came back. And he—"

"What?"

"He—he hurt me."

"What about the one you call the Man? Did he hurt you?"

"No. He never did. He took care of us. He gave us baths and fed us. He was nice."

"How did the other man hurt you?" Hotaling had given off taking notes now. He'd softened his voice, too. "The reason I want you to tell me is so that you and I can tell the court the truth and he can be punished. Do you understand?"

The litany of questions that followed felt to Mary like a battering ram. Hotaling asked questions she had not yet dared to ask for fear of Emma's fragile state. From moment to moment, it was impossible to know whether she would answer even a simple question requiring only a yes or a no answer, to say nothing of more complicated inquiries, but she did. Mary wanted to protect her from all of it, but Emma answered one after the other, sometimes with stilted clarity, sometimes with a despairing shake of her head. Anytime Mary protested—which was often—Hotaling insisted that she allow him to do his job. There are aspects of law that are distasteful, just as there are in medicine. Did he interfere in her work?

He pressed on:

Did this other man come in the day or at night?

How many times a week?

You don't know?

Was he short, tall, fat, thin? What was his hair like? His beard?

Why don't you know? Why can't you say?

Perhaps you played make-believe, because you were bored? Made him up?

Did you fight him off?

How hard?

Most girls would rather die than submit. They would fight until the death.

He threatened your sister?

Did he ever hurt her?

Then why did you believe he might?

He said so? But those are just words.

Show me where he touched you.

You have to, Emma.

All right then. Did he ever put his member inside you?

At this point, William stole into the room and stood behind the district attorney, locking eyes with Emma in an effort to instill courage.

You don't know?

Have you ever had sexual congress with anyone else?

It's when a man or a boy puts his member inside you.

Not at school? Maybe in an alleyway?

No? But did you want to?

Are you telling the truth?

How did you get away?

With a shovel?

Did you want to kill him?

Which man did you hit? Are you sure?

When Hotaling said he was finished, Mary handed over a limp Emma to Amelia, who bore her away in her arms, promising hot chocolate and cake and more sleep if she wanted it.

"What was that?" William raged, after they heard the kitchen door latch shut behind Amelia.

Hotaling was juggling his notes into his carrying case. He looked up, exasperated. "My interest as prosecutor is in convicting criminals, not in protecting witnesses."

"Do you know what you just put her through?"

"You should be grateful I'm even prosecuting, considering the challenges. I was already committed to lodging the kidnapping charge. I just needed to verify, and though it could be argued that Emma and Claire went willingly, it's apparent that they had a different idea of this 'other man's' motivation. My object today was to decide whether or not to pursue rape charges. You understand that to win a court case that alleges rape, I have to prove unequivocally that Emma suffered unwanted penetration. Prove it, in stark, unvarnished, eminently credible, incontrovertible evidence. Sometimes girls say that men have raped them when they have not—"

"That is utter nonsense."

Hotaling held up a cautioning hand. "Let me finish. It was my job today to ascertain the veracity of my witness—*my* witness—not yours. It's interesting that Emma says that whoever it is didn't rape Claire. Rape would be far easier to prove if Emma herself were underage, but she is not. In order to make my case, Emma has to perform perfectly in court. Perfectly. She cannot make a single mistake. She has to be strong enough to undergo the ugliness of a trial like this one, because this one will be ugly. If she cannot withstand the barrage in her own home, then she certainly won't be able to in open court. I would be a laughingstock for bringing the case, and in the end it would all be for naught and then where would we be? No justice, no resolution. So do not tell me that I do not know my job. I had to ask those questions.

"Now, as I see it, there are several extenuating issues with this case, one of which may be difficult to navigate. Emma survived. It's very difficult to justify a rape charge when the girl wasn't killed. In court, survival is considered an indication of acquiescence."

Mary shot out of her chair. "Are you out of your mind? No child would acquiesce to what happened." She then listed, graphically, every detail of Emma's injuries, down to the last stitch, using merciless language intended to unseat Hotaling with its precision. Taking a sheet of paper from Hotaling's pile, William wrote down everything she said.

When Mary finished, Hotaling accepted the sheet of paper from William and added them to his haphazard sheaf of papers. "Unpalatable as they are, doctors, these physical injuries in and of themselves do not in fact prove rape. With a young girl like Emma, they prove only intercourse. Do they not? Her size? The comparative"—he cleared his throat—"ratio?"

"Dear God," Mary said. While it was true that because of Emma's size, she would have sustained the same injuries had the intercourse been consensual, that was completely beside the point. "You've completely missed the fact of her many bruises."

"In court"—Hotaling shrugged—"rape is proved by evidence of concerted and prolonged physical resistance until the victim's death. She was hit, apparently, but one can survive blows. In turn, she defended herself with a shovel, but he did not die. It would be better if he had—a fight to the death. As it is, under these circumstances, the defense could suggest that Emma was not raped. That she participated, then repented her immorality and staged an attempt at full resistance as a ruse, but in reality did not wish to kill her lover, and so spared him. The bruises do help us, but given your relationship to the O'Donnell girls, the defense will challenge your impartiality as an unbiased witness. You should have taken her to another doctor to be examined. But that can't be helped now."

"Emma was raped, Mr. Hotaling. Without a doubt."

"That's my job to prove, isn't it? We will have to see how clever this young pup Jakob Van der Veer proves to be. Do you know him?"

"We do," Mary said.

"Well, he's out of his depth. He's never tried a case before—except as a student at Harvard—where they lean on torts and constitutional law more than trial procedure, as I well know."

"You went to Harvard?"

"I did. The other possibility is that Emma could be charged with assault, however you'll be happy to know that I am the one responsible for filing such charges, and I will not be following through."

"What?"

"This is a complicated situation."

"It is as straightforward as they come."

"It will be my job to make it seem so in court. You'll be happy to know that as a result of this meeting, I have now decided to file charges against James Harley for kidnapping and rape."

"But what of the other man? You heard Emma say—"

"With all due respect, Emma couldn't even tell me what Harley or this so-called Other Man looks like. It's a good thing she hit Harley, because at least we have his wound as identifier."

"But—"

"There is no substantial evidence that another man even exists. This morning, before I came here, I interrogated Mr. Harley. He denies that there was anyone else, which is telling, because usually a defendant will do everything he can to deflect blame. And even though Officer Farrell shares your suspicions, I would be a fool to try to chase down a fictitious second man whom even the defendant swears doesn't exist. And the only evidence Emma has offered is a rather murky description, and I have to tell you, a jury consists of men, and men will believe a man—especially a defendant who could save himself by naming someone else—over a brutalized girl any day. But no matter. I'll craft my questions in such a way as to skirt her delusion that there was another man. Shouldn't be hard."

"Isn't it possible that Harley is protecting someone?" William said.

"Would you have me pursue a ghost or make certain that Harley is incarcerated? At the very least, he kidnapped those girls. And imprisoned them, I think. I believe he raped Emma. I do, or I wouldn't be attempting to convict him." He began stuffing his case again with papers. "There is another thing," he said, folding the flap of his case and setting it on his lap. "I've had reports that you, Dr. Stipp"—he nodded at Mary—"have been performing abortions at that clandestine clinic of yours."

"I haven't!" Mary said.

William stood. "Where did you hear such an outrageous thing?"

Hotaling shook his head. "I can't say. But understand, doctors, that I take such allegations seriously."

"Rumor," Mary hissed. "Not allegation."

"I had to ask. Now, Emma will be a witness. You must make certain that she's ready."

"Ready how?"

"Warn her of what might happen in the courtroom. It won't be comfortable for her."

"What if we refuse to put her through it? What if we drop the charges?"

"They are no longer yours to drop. Your chance to end this has passed. If you didn't want her to have to testify, then you ought not to have reported the crime. Many women don't. But you did. And now it's my job to convict the perpetrator. Good day. I'll find my own way out."

"If this breaks Emma . . . " Amelia said, leaving the statement unfinished.

They had put the girls to bed. Mary was staring off over the table into the back garden, lifting and replacing a spoon from the saucer of her teacup. William and Elizabeth were fingering the gold rim of their cups. Amelia was studying a berry stain on the white tablecloth. Vera had made a strawberry pie from tiny, early fruit that she was growing in a sunny corner of the garden.

The trial was out of their hands, the train they could not stop.

Chapter Thirty-Four

The Court of Sessions tried the county's criminal cases five times a year in the venerable City Hall courtroom that they shared with the supreme court, circuit court, and the Court of Oyer and Terminer, which occupied the chambers at other times, meaning that the earliest Harley's trial could take place was during the Court of Sessions' next residency beginning on the third Monday in June. The charges finally filed against him numbered three: kidnapping, imprisonment, and rape. These charges each carried a sentence of not less than ten years. If Harley were convicted on all counts, he could spend the rest of his life—or at least thirty years of it—in the Albany Penitentiary, which was situated by some mean twist of fate a quarter mile behind the Stipps' home.

The ever voluble Horace Young blared all this information in yet another Extra Edition of the *Argus* that hit the streets at four o'clock in the afternoon on the second day of May, a Friday, three days after Hotaling's first visit to the Stipps. The edition sold out within an hour, helped along by a featured quote from Lansing Hotaling, who, upon exiting the courthouse earlier that day, had declared that the city was after blood. All told, Horace Young's articles had already earned the *Argus* twice its usual revenue for the year. But over the almost eight weeks since Emma and Claire O'Donnell's reappearance, the twelve newspapers in Albany had joined in the scandal mongering. Never had the city's publishing coffers been so full.

Incensed by the unending stream of articles, the Honorable Julius Thayer of the Court of Sessions pushed *The People v. James Harley* to the front of the docket. And so the day was set. On Monday, June 16, the grand jury would hear District Attorney Lansing Hotaling's evidence. And if the jury handed down an indictment, the trial would begin immediately afterward.

On Tuesday, May 6, Jakob met with Lansing Hotaling at his office in City Hall to discuss the possibility of a plea bargain.

Hotaling received Jakob without getting up from his desk. His airless office occupied a room on the second floor of the white marble building and had a north-facing window that he declined to open. The district attorney leaned back in his seat and tented his hands. "Absolutely not. No plea bargain. Insufficient blood is let in plea bargains."

Having discharged the sole reason for his visit, Jakob saw no reason to stay. He rose to leave to make his second visit to Harley in jail, but Hotaling waylaid him. He had a few other things to tell the young attorney.

By the time Hotaling was finished, Jakob was shaking with rage.

Jakob had first visited Harley more than a week before, on April 25, the day his father had charged him with defending Harley. It was the first time Jakob had ever been inside the forbidding county jail, with its thick brick walls and barred windows. There had been a raft of drunk and disorderly arrests, the flood having unleashed extremities of passion normally encountered only on Independence Day, and the place was full of bellowing drunks. Irritated by the caterwauling, the jailer, a scowl of a man named Charles Bahan, did not respond to Jakob's questions about Harley's health as he led Jakob down a dank, central corridor lined with solid steel doors. The gloomy passageway was lit only by a single candle at either end. The jailer carried a third. After unlocking Harley's cell, Bahan handed Jakob his stub of candle then locked him in with Harley, retreating back down the hallway in semidarkness.

The dingy cell was windowless with only a narrow, louvered slit in the steel door. At the outer limits of his candle's flame, Jakob spied Harley snoring on the bare wooden bench that served as a bed. Even on the warm afternoon—the thermometer outside City Hall had read seventy-two degrees—the cell was chilly. Roaches scurried underfoot, dispersing into cracks in the brick flooring. Jakob nudged Harley with the toe of onc boot and Harley swung his legs over the edge of the cot and erupted with a loud, hacking cough. Groaning, he seized the back of his neck and swore. The bandage was a dirty, wrinkled mess. Harley still wore the nightclothes he'd had on when he'd been found at the whorehouse. Jakob made a note to bring the foreman a change of clothes and handed him a blanket and a bag containing the beef sandwich he'd brought for him from home. It was odd to see the powerful Harley in this enfeebled state, grateful for even small scraps of comfort. Every memory of his father's yard from childhood included a clear image of the strapping Harley orchestrating the movements of hundreds of men and thousands of board feet from atop a tower of plywood or lumber.

It was absurd to think he had committed such a terrible crime.

"Has a doctor been coming to see you?" Jakob said.

"Oh, yes."

"Well, he's done a terrible job."

Harley shrugged and unfolded the woolen blanket. He wrapped it around his hunched shoulders then gingerly peeled the waxed paper from the sandwich and took an enormous bite. After quickly devouring half the sandwich, he looked up at Jakob and said, "Are those girls really alive?"

Jakob didn't know what he had expected Harley's first words to be. "They are."

An unguarded look of pure relief crossed Harley's face. "Oh, thank the Lord. Where are they, then?"

"Somewhere being well taken care of." Jakob cleared his throat. "I need to ask you some questions."

"Are you going to defend me? Is that why you've come?"

"Father wants me to. Unless you prefer someone else, in which case—"

"No. You. Your father trusts you, I trust you."

Jakob let go this last hope of a reprieve with a small, ironical laugh. "As I said, a few questions—"

"I didn't kidnap them," Harley started in, fervently brushing crumbs from his nightshirt. "Someone just brought them to my house. I'm fond of children, you know, just like those boys I helped. I took good care of them—"

"Excuse me. Emma and Claire were actually in your house?"

Harley sat straight up, and this defensive posture came at the expense of his cut. He swore again and gestured toward the back of his neck, refraining from actually touching the bandage.

"You had them all that time?" Jakob said.

"I didn't *have* them. I told you. I was taking care of them."

Harley's reasoning was incomprehensible to Jakob. "But didn't you see all the flyers that the Stipps posted? Didn't you see the advertisements in the newspapers? And what about that dinner? Father brought up their deaths. Why didn't you say anything? And before, in the yard, we were all talking about them. Didn't you hear us? Why didn't you tell us all you had David's daughters?"

Harley shrugged and took another bite, taking time to chew and swallow before answering. "Because I thought someone might take them away from me, and I loved them."

"But you had no right to keep them." Jakob began to pace. The dampness was turning his skin clammy. "I don't understand."

"When I heard their parents died, I decided to take care of them. They were safe with me. And if I listened to all the jabber in the yard, do you think a stick of lumber would ever move?"

"Custody doesn't work that way, Mr. Harley. You said that someone brought them to you? Who?"

"Can't say."

"Or won't?"

Harley had finished his sandwich and was wiping crumbs from his lips with the back of one hand and crumpling the waxed paper, stained brown with mustard, with the other. He seemed oddly calm for a man in his situation. "Can't say as I recognized him. He was all muffled up because of the cold. A do-gooder, I expect. I was so focused on the children that I didn't take notice."

"A do-gooder who just happened by your house in the aftermath of the blizzard with two little girls?"

"He may have said he knew O'Donnell, but I can't remember."

"I don't believe you."

Harley waved away this challenge. "It was a blizzard. You know how it was. I was doing my part for the world."

"Captain Mantel told me this morning that Emma and Claire were interfered with."

Harley's face crumpled. To Jakob, Harley appeared well and truly crushed.

Harley began to shout. "They were interfered with? Impossible! No! How? When? It must have happened that night, the night of the flood, after they ran away. That's when anyone could have taken advantage of them—out on the streets like that, all alone? Anyone. Oh, I'm heartbroken. I adore those girls. Oh, how cruel. But it wasn't me. It wasn't."

"You did nothing?"

"Nothing except care for them."

"Was it you who took advantage?"

"You know me. You know who I am. I took excellent care of them. Surely they know that, and you should, too. Surely they'll remember. Surely they'll tell you."

Jakob ignored this appeal. "I need to explain to you that the charges are likely to be steep: rape, kidnapping, imprisonment. Ten years each, minimum charge. Thirty years. That would mean that you would likely die in prison. Since you've already admitted to keeping the sisters, even if you deny the other charges, the jury will extrapolate to the other. I suggest you consider pleading guilty. If you agree, I can probably bargain for a lesser sentence. Of course, a guilty plea means that you admit guilt."

Harley was gaping. "Thirty years?"

"Minimum. But there might be other charges added. I've talked only to Mantel. I won't see the district attorney until after he files charges, if he does. Right now I'm going to see whether or not the judge will post bail."

"But I didn't touch them. I kept Emma and Claire with me out of the goodness of my heart. I had no idea anyone was looking for them. Everyone knows that orphan asylums are soulless places. I gave them a loving home, I did. I was going to send them to school after they recovered from the shock of losing their parents, but they were still fragile little things. I just wanted to protect them. I was helping them."

"Thirty years, Mr. Harley."

Harley's fretful gaze darted away and back again. "But I didn't do anything to those girls. I love them."

Now, seething with rage after his meeting with the district attorney, Jakob hesitated outside Harley's cell. Not only had the district attorney dismissed any hope of a plea bargain, but he had also outlined

Emma's and the Stipps' depositions, including Mary Stipp's detailed summation of Emma's injuries. He fought to compose himself as the jailer once again handed him a stub of a burning candle.

Unlike last time, this time the overseer rose from his bunk to greet him. In the chamois shirt and canvas pants that Jakob had sent to him, Harley looked more like his former commanding self. In the Van der Veer yard, Harley had held exacting standards for neatness, insisting that the rows of lumber were laid out with military precision. And now he had somehow freshened up, and appeared to be no longer feverish. Even his bandage, clean and free of discharge, was neatly secured with a square knot.

As he had done on his first visit, Jakob handed Harley a bagged sandwich, but Harley tossed it onto the carefully folded blanket at the base of his bed and clutched Jakob by the shoulder. "Where have you been? No one will tell me anything."

"They are charging you with rape, kidnapping, and imprisonment," Jakob said. "Just as I predicted. And no plea bargain. Hotaling won't do it. He wants to make an example of you, though in my opinion a plea bargain is just as good as a case won. However, the nature of the injuries that Emma O'Donnell suffered has persuaded him to pursue this case with a vengeance." Jakob could not erase from his mind Hotaling's recitation of Mary's painstaking catalog of harm meted out to the girl. There could be no doubt it was rape. It was difficult even to look at Harley now, wondering whether or not he had done it. Pushing his still simmering rage aside, Jakob cast his thoughts ahead to the trial. He'd studied a few rape trial transcripts to evaluate defense strategies. They seemed to consist mostly of heaping shame on the accuser: *Do you wear underclothing under your dresses? Are you sure? Do you ever go without it? Did you that day? How can you remember? What were you doing alone in that part of town? Isn't it true that you have already had relations with other men? Aren't you flirtatious by nature? How long have you been promiscuous? Did you even resist a little? Did you fight to the point of exhaustion? Why not? You seem strong enough to persuade a man that you're not interested, if you really didn't want to, but you really wanted it, didn't you? Did you scream? No? Why not? If you didn't scream, then any reasonable man would take that as leave to do as he pleased.*

"Are you sure you wouldn't rather have a more experienced attorney?" Jakob said, making one last effort to remove himself.

A momentary flicker of indecision crossed Harley's face. "No. I've decided."

Jakob sighed. "Very well. Before the district attorney turned down our request, he shared some information with me. Since I last saw you, he has interviewed Emma. Just as you claimed, it seems Emma insists that another man—not you—brought them to your house."

Harley's gaze lit up. "But I already told you that, didn't I?"

"But she also says that this other man raped her in your cellar. Repeatedly." Jakob did not mention that Hotaling had summarily dismissed Emma's assertion of another man: "Unreliable, those sisters," Hotaling had averred. "Not right in the head. They developed a fondness for their kidnapper—Mr. Harley—and in order to survive excused his misdeeds on the grounds that he was the one who fed and nurtured them. They were making up stories for themselves to keep their sanity from deteriorating. Happens, sometimes you know," he'd continued. "And you can bet that if there were another man, Harley would name him, just to get himself freed."

Jakob wondered whether it was possible that Emma had imagined this other man. He supposed that it was possible that a girl as young as Emma could drift into confusion and reverie to cope with horrific circumstances, but he didn't know. He studied Harley's stolid expression for any indication of what the truth might be. Today Harley had a hurried, practiced air about him, but Jakob wondered whether his anger with Harley colored his impression of everything the overseer said.

"I swear to you, I didn't touch them," Harley said.

"Tell me the truth. Did you rape Emma?"

"No. Ask her. She'll tell you."

"I plan to." He had sent a note to the Stipps yesterday evening, requesting a formal interview with Emma, but he'd not yet heard back. "Did another man come to the house?"

Harley met Jakob's gaze with the same authority he had commanded in the yard. "See here. No one raped them—not at my house. If it happened at all, it happened the night of the flood, when they were out of my care." Harley sank onto his bench and yanked the sandwich from the bag and began to tear off mouthfuls of bread and meat.

Jakob said, "I need to clarify something else. Was the reason you didn't go to the yard the night of the flood because you went to your house to make certain that Emma and Claire wouldn't drown?"

"That's right," Harley said. "I couldn't leave them to fend for themselves. I had to get them out of the house. Then, something hit me and I don't remember anything after that, not until I woke up in the hospital."

"But why couldn't they walk out of the house by themselves? You didn't lock them in, did you?"

"I couldn't leave them to their own devices. Children get scared. And about you—out there on that ice. I'm sorry about that. I thought I'd make it back in time to help you. I didn't know that I'd get hurt or you'd get stranded."

"Just tell me, Mr. Harley. Were Emma and Claire locked in?"

"I needed to keep them safe!"

Jakob noted the sidesteps. Harley had not completely denied that there was another man, nor had he denied locking the sisters in. "How were you injured? Something hit you, you said?"

Harley shook his head. "I don't know."

"Did Emma hit you with a shovel?"

"A shovel? Emma? Hit me? Why would she do that?"

"Time," the jailer said, peering in through the louvered window in the door. Jakob had heard nothing of Bahan's approach. He had the terrible feeling the man had been eavesdropping outside the cell the whole time.

"Can you give me a few more minutes?"

Bahan said, "I've got seven hundred things to do and being at your beck and call isn't one of them. Time."

On the way out, Jakob asked the jailer, "Has someone besides the doctor been to see Mr. Harley? His manner is a little—let's say changed."

"You mean other than Captain Mantel?"

"Captain Mantel?"

Bahan shrugged, newly reticent. "Can't say, really. I'm not here twenty-four hours a day."

"Does the jail keep a visitor's log?"

"Sometimes."

"May I see it?"

There were pages and pages of visitors scrawled into the ledger, and very few of the entries were readable. The trick, it seemed, was to answer to the letter of the law—sign something—but not to write legibly enough to have anyone detect your name.

Jakob shut the ledger with exasperation and went on to his next appointment.

Chapter Thirty-Five

The Argus

May 6, 1879
By Horace Young

Winter Sisters' Whereabouts Confirmed

Emma and Claire O'Donnell, the blizzard girls, widely believed to be receiving treatment in a sanitarium, are instead living with the Doctors Stipp in their home on Madison Avenue. Can this be prudent in light of the injured girls' situation? Especially since it is now known that Dr. Mary Stipp finances and provides medical care for Ladies of the Night at a clinic in downtown Albany. This reporter wonders whether there might be a connection between the assault on the O'Donnell children and Dr. Mary Stipp's immoral activities. Given these vagaries, we pose a third, more important question: Ought any citizen of Albany County patronize the Stipp Clinic from this day forward?

Chapter Thirty-Six

After leaving Harley at the jail, Jakob had some time before his next appointment, so he went by the Lumber District to see how the cleanup was faring. He hadn't been there since the night he'd spent on the roof. The Van der Veer office had withstood the flood's onslaught, but the entirety of the inside had to be torn out and replaced, several broken windows reglazed, and the axed roof patched. Twenty carpenters were hard at work while Gerritt ran the business from a room he'd rented at the Delavan House. Indeed, the entire Lumber District was picking up the pieces, repairing its docks, relaying its trolley tracks, putting its sawmills to rights, and sorting and restacking salvaged lumber wrestled out of rushes miles and miles away. The place was still a bog of mud, though the Hudson had long ago retreated into its channel. Sloops and tugs and day boats plied the river, and the Erie Canal had reopened to a backlog of packet boats, its infuriated captains losing money by the minute.

He met Farrell at the base of State Street, and they veered down Green Street, covering the quarter mile to Harley's house in more time than they would have liked. River silt nearly a foot deep sucked at their boots as they slogged down the center of the road, which was still impassable to wagons. People were slopping mud from their homes with tin buckets and flat shovels, hanging bedding and clothing out to dry on lines strung between tree branches, and tending to steam pumps chugging brown water and more muck onto the already buried cobbles. The air was thick with humidity as the rivulets evaporated into the summerlike air.

At Harley's house, a bored policeman, very young and pimpled and hot in his wool uniform, blocked the door. "Captain Mantel says that no one is to come in."

"No one but police, that is," Farrell said. He jerked his head in Jakob's direction "And this one's defending Mr. Harley, so he gets to see everything."

Chastened and newly cooperative, the young officer waved Farrell and Jakob in, reporting that they had pumped out the cellar only that morning with a steam rig borrowed from the Albany Brewery and they ought to be careful because the stairs to the cellar were swollen and slippery.

The clapboard house, Jakob noted, was one of the older row houses in the Pastures. The newer brick federalist structure next door was far more elegant, with gabled roofs and dormer windows that Harley's more humble house lacked. Inside, his house reeked of mold and sewage. Heavily tracked river silt sat six inches deep in some places; in others, warped floorboards testified to the river's destructive force. The stove flume in the kitchen hung detached from the wall. The modest furniture—a single chair, two low tables—lay in splintered pieces up against plaster walls. A waterline reached a foot above the floor. Outside, in the narrow alley behind, a wooden privy tilted at a thirty-degree angle.

The door to the stone cellar stood askew, half off its hinges. Jakob noted a set of keys dangling from its lock. Downstairs, the smell of must and mold in the derelict basement overwhelmed them. It was little more than twenty by twenty. One of the cellar walls had partially collapsed, and someone had propped a few four-by-fours against the remaining boulders and wedged several more under the ceiling joists. Two waterlogged mattresses, a ruined couch frame, a Perry coal stove with its chimney intact, a copper tub basin, and a shovel had come to sodden rest on the muddied floor. Farrell took hold of the shovel and tagged it with a slip of brown paper. Orders, he said, from Hotaling.

They came up out of the cellar, and then climbed a narrow stairway to the second floor. There was only one room under the low eaves. A high, neatly made bed rose four feet off the floor. The quilt wasn't even mussed. Harley's shirts and underwear and a second set of bed linens were neatly folded in a chest of drawers. Several pairs of pants hung from nails along one of the walls.

Farrell's lips formed a thin line. "Neatest criminal I ever saw."

"He was careful at the yard, too," Jakob said. "Van der Veer Lumber has the fewest accidents in the district—due entirely to his vigilance."

Farrell touched the counterpane, which was thick with down feathers. "He kept himself comfortable."

Jakob recalled that Harley had only recently bought the house—presumably on monies he had saved from his twenty-year tenure at Van der Veer Lumber—but even so, the home seemed more than Jakob imagined Harley could afford. The Pastures was a far more expensive area to live in than North Albany, where most of the Lumber District laborers resided. The Pastures' denizens were small-time merchants and business owners. Perhaps in addition to his propensity toward tidiness, Harley was frugal, too, though it occurred to Jakob again how little he knew about the man his father set such store by. He leaned against the edge of the bed and looked around the small room. Newly painted. Pristine.

Farrell arched his eyebrows at Jakob. "Why such a high bed?"

Jakob shrugged.

"Get up."

Farrell still held the shovel, and he laid it down. Then he tore off the bedclothes and flipped the mattress onto the floor. Hidden in the bed frame, a hinged wooden box about six inches high bore the trademarked oval stamp of Van der Veer Lumber. A handle was built flush into the top. Farrell lifted it.

Piles and piles of greenbacks in neatly tied bundles lay nestled inside.

Farrell let out a low whistle. "You pay him enough for this at the yard?"

Jakob shook his head, mentally tallying the fortune before him. Fifteen hundred, two thousand dollars?

"Grab a pillowcase," Farrell said. "I'm going to get that stripling downstairs to come witness this."

Jakob did, and Farrell returned with the stripling, who gaped openmouthed at the money.

Jakob and Farrell began the count.

They added up the money twice.

It came to $2,150. A fortune.

Later than night, Jakob searched his father's study, stealthily opening and shutting the many cabinet doors and easing his father's desk drawers in and out with the smooth deftness of a burglar. Methodical and patient, he replaced everything just as he had found it, conscious of his father's acute attention to every detail, noting how similar he and Harley sometimes were. Finding nothing, Jakob carried a lit candle down the stairs and out into the bricked yard and through the stable doors. Six carriage horses slept in their stalls, their heavy exhalations undisturbed by his intrusion. A heavy canvas tarp covered his father's sleigh, which was set on blocks for the off-season. Jakob set the candle on a shelf and picked up one edge of the tarp, folding it back until he could see inside. On the sleigh's leather seat were the books that Jakob had rescued.

He lit two oil lamps affixed to the stable wall and sorted the ledgers by date. There were two distinct sets, duplicates of one another. His own handwriting, small and precise, filled one, its pages and labeled columns listing monies in and monies out, lumber purchases, sales, payroll, and expenditures for maintenance and upkeep. The second set he had never seen: his father's looping handwriting filled these pages with similar tallies of debits and credits, except that none of the tabulations in the two sets of books matched, nor did the source of monies or expenditures.

And all his father's entries were coded.

Chapter Thirty-Seven

Four days later, on Saturday, May 10, William Stipp stepped down from a canary yellow car of the Old Colony Railroad onto a sand-strewn street in Provincetown, Massachusetts, the tiny fishing village at the far tip of Cape Cod. It was one o'clock in the afternoon. A white rush of steam exhaled from the locomotive into a blue sky already noisy with the cries of seagulls and gannets looping over the shingled shanties of the fishing village. The pungent scents of brine and fish carried on a light breeze from the nearby bay, just out of sight. It had been two days of travel from Albany, with an overnight stay in Boston at the United States Hotel, and they were all tired.

They was everyone but Mary, who had stayed behind in Albany.

In the frantic hours before their departure they had scurried to pack. Eschewing the services of the meticulous cobbler, Mary had procured shoes from a shop on State Street that sold them ready-made; Amelia had scared up another pair of dresses for the girls from the church box; Elizabeth had helped Vera to drag trunks from the attic; and Harold had been sent to purchase railroad tickets.

They had withheld from the girls the reason for their swift departure.

On the morning before their hasty retreat, Jakob had come to depose Emma and Claire. Elizabeth had arranged to absent herself. Recently, Madame Hubbard had written to her twice, the first letter expressing exultation at the sisters' resurrection and the second, desolation. Wouldn't Elizabeth like to come for a visit to allow Madame Hubbard to offer her comfort? Seizing the excuse, Elizabeth had gone to call on her French teacher at the unreasonable hour of 9:00 a.m., taking with her one of Vera's strawberry pies as recompense.

At the door, Jakob failed to disguise his surreptitious survey of the foyer and hallway—presumably looking for Elizabeth—before he took a seat in the same parlor chair that Hotaling had recently occupied. Jakob looked as if he had not slept. His waistcoat was wrinkled, his unbuttoned shirt cuffs had been rolled back, and his shock of sandy hair had not been combed in some time. Before beginning, he yawned, rubbing his eye sockets with the heels of his hands. Despite his fatigue, however, Jakob flashed them both a dead-eyed certainty, one that William had come to recognize in the war as the life-or-death resolve of the newly fearless.

"Before you bring in Emma and Claire," Jakob began, "I want to tell you that I've met with Lansing Hotaling and he shared the particulars of his interview with Emma and with you. I want you to know that I will not bother her on points of physical intimacy that I believe will only embarrass her."

Mary glanced at William. Emma had spoken little in the two weeks since the district attorney's bludgeoning visit. It was as if she were just holding on, and despite the rapid healing of her cuts and bruises, she remained withdrawn and lethargic.

"If I may, before we go on, did Elizabeth share my letter to her with you?" Jakob said.

"She didn't," Mary said.

"She told you nothing?"

"We're not interested in puzzles, young man," William said, "so why don't you save yourself an interrogation and tell us what you want to say?"

"I fear that all of you may regard me as a traitor. Indeed, I feel a bit of one myself. I said as much in my letter to Elizabeth, though I expect her opinion of me plummeted the moment she learned that I would be defending Mr. Harley. I expect that yours did as well. I want you to understand that my role as Mr. Harley's attorney is not one I sought out." He stared past them, silent for a moment, his bloodshot eyes watery with fatigue. "Are you aware that Captain Mantel's first name is Arthur? I haven't figured out who 'G' is yet. I have an idea, though."

"What on earth are you talking about?" William said.

He shook his head, as if to clear it of cobwebs. "Forgive me. What I mean to say is that I want to assure you that you can trust me."

"You're defending James Harley," William said. "How can we trust you?"

"I mean Emma and Claire no harm. I promise that I will not bolster my defense of Mr. Harley at Emma's expense. Another defense attorney might seek to discredit them or use shame as a tactic, but I will not. Not today, not during the trial. I hold your family in the highest regard.

"Before I forget, there is one thing I want to warn you about. Be on your guard with Captain Mantel. Take care what you say to him. If you can, avoid him altogether."

William raised his eyebrows, but Jakob would tell them nothing more. Instead he said, "Have you explained to Emma that she'll be going to court?"

They had, in stages. They did not know how much she'd absorbed of what they'd told her, but she seemed to understand that she would have to answer more questions, both now and later. The concepts of a gallery and a judge and jury, however, Emma had greeted with silence.

"Do you think she'll be able to testify?"

"We don't know. She's still not talking much."

"There's still five weeks before the trial. Do you think she will talk to me today?"

"We can't say whether Emma will answer any of your questions. Mr. Hotaling terrified her."

Amelia led Emma and Claire in by the hand and sat between them on the long divan, a protective arm around each. Jakob's sharp-eyed gaze turned kind and sympathetic. He said hello in a soft voice and that he was glad to meet them and most of all that he wanted to help them. He understood, he continued, that they probably didn't want to talk to another stranger like him about the terrible thing that had happened to them. But he wouldn't always be a stranger. He was going to see Emma again at least one more time, in the courtroom. But today, he had only one question for both of them. It was an easy one, but it was an important one, too. They would have to try very hard to remember, and if they couldn't, it would be all right. Would they try?

He posed his question, and at first neither Emma nor Claire responded. It was as if they were digging through eternity to find the correct answer. But the question concerned nothing about their bodies, and Emma exhibited none of the reticence she had exhibited with Hotaling. She considered Jakob's question for a time, her brow furrowed as she glanced around her grandmother to Claire, who was waiting for Emma to answer first.

Emma said, "I do remember. It was bright red. Like a cherry."

The room stilled. Mary, William, and Amelia gaped at one another. Jakob shut his eyes for a brief moment, and when he opened them he said, "Are you sure?"

Emma nodded emphatically.

Jakob said, "Thank you. Now what do you say, Claire?"

Claire nodded in turn. "Red."

"You're sure? You're not just saying that because that's what your sister said? It's okay if you can't remember."

Claire shook her head solemnly.

"Thank you," Jakob said. "You really helped me. Another time, we'll talk again. But not today. I'll wait until everyone feels better."

Mary noted with gratitude that he did not single out Emma as the one who most needed to feel better.

Amelia shepherded the girls into the kitchen, and a second shocked silence permeated the room. William and Mary could think of nothing to say.

"It doesn't prove anything by itself," Jakob said, his voice subdued. "It's just one more puzzle piece."

"A rather significant one," William said. "What will you do now?"

"What I have been doing. Mrs. Stipp, I trust you have nothing more to say about Emma's injuries than what you told Mr. Hotaling?"

"No. Nothing."

There was a knock at the front door, and they could hear Vera padding down the hallway to answer it. She came into the parlor carrying a large crate addressed in neat block letters to Claire and Emma O'Donnell, care of The Doctors Stipp, 714 Madison Avenue, Albany, New York.

The package had no return address.

William pried open the crate with a crowbar he got from the carriage house. Inside, on a bed of fine paper straw, lay two exquisite dolls, dressed in lavish gowns and wearing pale wigs and fashionable hats. Mary lifted them out, strips of the paper falling to her feet like confetti. They were beautifully made. Each one was almost a foot tall. Their heads were crafted of painted porcelain and their glass eyes fluttered open and shut. A single envelope dangled from the wrist of one of the dolls, attached by a scalloped golden ribbon. It was addressed to Emma.

Jakob stole it away with a proprietary motion that bordered on violence. He tore the envelope open and read the note out loud.

Do you miss me?

Jakob looked up and said, "Take Emma and Claire to the edge of the world. Don't wait another day. Saratoga isn't far enough. Nor is Lake George. Take them somewhere beautiful, somewhere far, far away, and don't come back until the trial. Tell no one—not even me—where you've gone."

And so, a mere thirteen hours later, everyone but Mary had embarked from the Boston and Albany Station on Steuben Street on the 2:00 a.m. Express, stealing away in the middle of the night to avoid anyone else taking notice of their abrupt departure. Well provisioned by Vera with a wicker hamper stuffed with meat pies, bottles of ginger ale, wintered-over apples, a small crock of butter, and two loaves of dark bread, they'd easily endured the six-hour trip to Boston, arriving at eight o'clock in the morning. They'd checked into the United States Hotel, a titanic, utilitarian railroad hostelry that catered primarily to excursionists. From a nearby shop, Amelia purchased Emma and Claire broad-brimmed sun hats in addition to warm coats and gloves, unseasonable items she insisted the salesclerk unearth from a back storage room.

Now, at the Provincetown railroad depot, William handed their luggage tickets to the porter and turned to help Claire and Emma down the railcar's steep stairs. Amelia followed behind, balancing her small leather valise and the emptied hamper in one hand and gripping the handrail with the other. She turned to lend Elizabeth a hand, but Elizabeth skimmed down the three steps without any help. She carried a new violin in a cheap case made of pinewood that William had purchased for her in Boston. When he had discovered at the station in Albany that Elizabeth had not brought her own instrument, out of fear that the sea air would damage it, he told her that while she might be willing to sacrifice the progress she had made, he was not. In Boston, he asked after reputable violin-makers and was directed to St. Botolph Street, an hour horsecar ride away. He purchased an inexpensive one over the protestations of its maker, who argued that no one should choose a violin except the person who was going to play it. They are cherished beings, he'd claimed, like children, and to select one for someone without their approval was tantamount to committing a crime. But Elizabeth was thrilled.

Emma and Claire had never been to the sea. William hired a hack to carry their luggage from the depot to their hotel and a second one to carry all of them. The road to the hotel ran past the harbor. The wind was up, and the whip of sail and rope filled the air. A dozen sailing sloops and schooners rode at anchor. Dories, trawlers, cutters, and dinghies crowded a long dock extending a hundred feet into the glimmering bay. At the dock's far end, a steamship was loading day passengers for the bumpy trip back to Boston. It was delicious to watch Emma and Claire gasp at the vibrant scene, delicious to catch them forgetting, even for a moment, the stone walls of that cellar. It was eight weeks since the blizzard, two since the flood. They had buried Emma and Claire, and now they were alive.

In Boston, when they had asked where to stay, the concierge had said, "Provincetown? Why are you going there now? It's all 'Portugee' fishermen and sand and herring. But if you must, there's a new hotel for the tourist trade."

The Whaler's Rest was a shingled two-story inn with a long, covered veranda that faced the sea. This early in the season, the inn abounded with vacancies, and they were assigned choice rooms on the second floor overlooking the endless bay and its strip of shell-pebbled beach. Two rooms connected through an interior door: Amelia and Emma took one side, and Elizabeth and Claire the other. William's corner room down the hall was full of light and furnished with a single bed made up with a white bedspread and two bright blue pillows.

Do you miss me?

William shuddered at the memory. He hoped that Provincetown would be far enough away to keep Emma and Claire from harm, but he didn't know. He might have suggested getting out of town anyway. Horace Young's relentless newspaper articles had stirred up the city so much that none of them could go anywhere without being stared at, which was one of the other reasons why he had hated to leave Mary behind, vulnerable to every curious stare or passerby. He had wanted to be the one to keep the clinic going to save her that indignity, but soon after they had begun packing, a letter arrived for her, the libelous newspaper articles having done swift work.

Dr. Mary Stipp,

In light of developments recently brought to our collective attention, as well as information that you have been performing abortions at a private clinic, you are invited to report on May 12 at one o'clock in the afternoon to Albany City Hospital for examination of the terms of your medical staff appointment to this hospital. Please reply at your earliest convenience to this summons. However, please note that should you be unable to attend, said meeting will proceed without you. Any and all decisions made will be binding and indissoluble.

The Examination Committee
Albany City Hospital

During the war, in the midst of falling shells and dying men, Mary had not shown as much fury as she did when reading that letter aloud to him. *Rumors,* she railed. *Who started them? It is unconscionable.* Never once in the chaos of Antietam had William worried about Mary, but he worried now. The convoluted prejudices of a committee could be far more sinister than the brutality of artillery.

He went to the window. Outside, Claire and Elizabeth were climbing down a set of wooden stairs to the beach. Claire smiled at Elizabeth from underneath the wide brim of her sun hat, and Elizabeth bent low to kiss her cheek. William went down the hall and knocked on Amelia and Emma's door. Emma was in bed, her back to the open door, a small figure curled up under a white candlewick bedspread. Amelia, reading a book, looked up at William and shook her head.

Mary had performed one last exam on Emma before they left. Amelia had held her hand and distracted her with stories, having learned that trick from Elizabeth. Luckily, no sign of venereal infection had manifested itself. Mary removed the stitches and declared Emma physically healed, completely able to undertake the trip. And even if no doll had ever made its way to their door, it had grown abundantly clear that while Emma's body had healed, her mind had not. A place to disappear to, a place to regain her strength, a place where Emma and Claire could venture outside without anyone knowing who they were, was a good idea in any case.

William shut the door quietly. Were they expecting too much of a fishing village and a cheery hotel? Perhaps.

Chapter Thirty-Eight

In the amphitheater operating room of City Hospital, Dr. Mary Stipp sat beneath the bright pendant gaslight that illuminated the surgical arena. The surgery bed had been pushed against the wall. The ten members of the examination committee occupied the two front rows of the theater, the customary province of observing medical students. The physicians constituted the governing staff that oversaw the medical affairs of the hospital, in addition to granting and revoking admitting privileges. This afternoon, their general demeanor was one of censure, though their individual greetings to Mary had betrayed no hostility. As usual, the operating theater was cold, kept frosty to slow patient bleeding during surgery. How many surgeries had she done in this room? One, two a week? A hundred, at least. It smelled strongly of antiseptic.

The committee president, Thomas Hun, adjusted his pince-nez on his long nose as he read through a sheaf of papers on his lap. Mary thought the elderly Hun austere and smugly upright. As current dean of faculty at the Albany Medical College and former president of the Albany Medical Society, he had for years denied Mary entry to the society's ranks, just as a prior dean had once denied her admission to the college. The vice chair of the committee, Samuel Ward, had been a medical cadet in the war, but of the rest she counted only Albert Van der Veer an ally. Mary studied Samuel Ward's fine, impassive face. He kept his gaze trained on Hun, as one would a general, thereby distancing himself from the soldier being disciplined.

"The committee has received several complaints," Hun began, finally looking up. He was a deacon at St. Peter's Church and on Sunday he was famous for reading the liturgy in a thin, quiet voice so that parishioners had to listen carefully. "In fact, I have a list, which I will read for the benefit of all:

"Maintains secret, unsanitary private clinic for treatment of Ladies of the Night, which thereby aids and abets prostitution.

"As yet undetermined possible further connection with said profession.

"Neglect of duty.

"Performs abortions."

He removed his pince-nez and dangled the glasses from a speckled hand that had probed innumerable patients over his fifty years of practice. "What say you, Dr. Stipp, to these charges?"

Mary stifled an impulse to raise her voice. "I beg your pardon, Dr. Hun, but am I in a court of law? Charges? Aids and abets? Perpetrates?"

"You understand the purpose, I presume, of this committee?" Hun waved his glasses at the silent cohort seated with him. "We certify competency in our medical staff. Any medical appointment is subject to review. When a member of the staff is publicly questioned about his—forgive me, *her*—medical practice, it becomes a concern. Staff appointments are not tenured. They can be withdrawn for any reason this committee deems valid."

"Fine," Mary said. "I'll explain, though I shouldn't have to. I established the private clinic as a haven to serve those women that neither this hospital nor any other in town will treat. In fact, this hospital has refused to treat many such women on many occasions."

"We have a budget for the indigent—"

"You know very well that it does not extend to the treatment of women of a certain class. No. Let me be more specific. To the treatment of prostitutes."

The collective committee, with the exception of Albert Van der Veer, winced.

Mary continued, "They are regularly turned away, especially in the aftermath of an abortion—"

"At this hospital, we do not condone immorality—"

"—when they are bleeding to death, in pain, on death's door."

"Answer the last charge, Dr. Stipp," Hun said. "It is the most egregious of the four. In that clinic of yours, do you perform abortions?"

"I do not. That is a savage rumor fomented to discredit me. But I never turn away a woman who has been harmed by one."

"It is the same thing."

"It is not. Hospitals refuse to treat prostitutes even for rape."

"No prostitute is raped. That is impossible."

"They *are* raped. Often. And attacked. It's a hazard of their profession. As is venereal disease."

The men scoffed, and Mary wondered how a purported investigation into rumors had so quickly devolved into what defined the rape of a prostitute. "Do you know what I do at my clinic? The exact things that each of you does every day for your patients. I treat their tonsillitis, stitch up their wounds, and ease the ravages of disease. I deliver their babies. I take care of them."

Hun sniffed and tented his hands. "Naturally as a woman of peculiar liberality, you are sympathetic to these disreputable causes—"

"Tonsillitis in a child is a disreputable cause?"

He ignored her. "But our purpose today speaks to respectability and your fitness as a member of this staff. City Hospital has a reputation to uphold. It has long been the view of this committee—frankly, since you were first admitted—that your status has always been provisional. It was our belief that your husband would intervene should you stumble. However, both of you operated on Mr. Harley, and considering that the man is now charged with the ravishment of one of those sisters, it was a gross conflict of interest that I am surprised you undertook, given your demonstrated affection for the O'Donnells and your many efforts to recover them. We are all therefore shocked that you would give aid and comfort to the man who attacked them. And—"

"That is a baseless charge, and you know it," Mary said. "Neither William nor I had any idea that Mr. Harley had been involved in the kidnapping of Emma and Claire O'Donnell. Had we known and had time, we would have called in another physician, as was since done. Albert Van der Veer has stepped in, as I am certain you are also aware." She tilted her head at Albert, who acknowledged her with a brief nod. "However, in any case, the time required to obtain alternate assistance that chaotic night would have compromised Mr. Harley's already precarious physical condition. Only my husband and I and Albert Van der Veer reported to the hospital that night, and Dr. Van der Veer had already gone home when Mr. Harley arrived. Where were all of you, by the way?"

"Please hold your commentary until I am finished speaking," Hun said. "We also heard from our head nurse, Miss Müller, that you were late on your rounds of Mr. Harley the day after you treated him—"

"Emma and Claire had just arrived and needed care—"

"Thus allowing Mr. Harley to be spirited away and putting him at greater harm."

"It is preposterous to hold me accountable for that. He was taken away without my consent or knowledge."

"If you had not been derelict in your duty, then you would have been here and thus could have prevented that unfortunate development. No matter what the man's offense, he deserved good medical treatment. His life was put at risk, we understand—"

"As are prostitutes put at risk when they are denied care. I—"

Hun forestalled her with a raised hand. "Despite our many points of difference with you, and despite the fact that few of us consider a woman fit to do the work of a physician, we the committee recognize that given your prior profession as a midwife, your sympathies cannot fail to fall naturally into the arena of womanhood. Today you have also denied performing abortions, and though I personally am not yet entirely persuaded, we lack evidence. You will therefore be pleased to learn that I have decided that we will renew—provisionally—your appointment here to City Hospital under the condition that you treat females only, for female problems, with the caveat that you desist in caring for prostitutes. The reputation of the hospital is at stake. Charitable impulses are to be lauded, but not immoral ones." He sniffed again, satisfied with himself. "I think you will find this ruling more than generous."

He offered this compensation prize as he would a box of fine chocolates. To his right and left, his fellow physicians hunched blank-faced, giving nothing away of their own opinions on the subject of Hun's supposed benevolence.

"I am a medical doctor," Mary said. "Educated and experienced. I am careful, prepared, diligent. I have met every criterion of our profession and will continue to do so for as long as I choose to practice. I will treat whomever I wish to treat, regardless of gender or background or societal caste."

"I thought as much," Hun said, gathering his papers. "Of course you may do as you like privately, but you will no longer be associated with this hospital. Your appointment to City Hospital is terminated."

"You understand that my patients will suffer if I do not have access to the surgery—"

"You should have considered that before you refused our olive branch. You may, of course, always refer them to any one of us here, or to your husband."

"He also operated on Mr. Harley, if you'll remember. And yet you do not investigate him?"

Hun rose. "This investigation is now concluded."

One by one, her former colleagues filed from the surgery. Albert Van der Veer put a hand on her shoulder, but she shook it off. She wondered how long they had all been waiting to expel her from the hospital's physician rolls. She gathered her things and exited the hospital through the accident ward. Outside on the street, under a streetlamp, Captain Mantel was talking with Doctor Hun. Mantel caught her eye, a flicker of triumph on his face.

At her downtown clinic, Mary attacked the accumulation of dust and dirt, mopping the floors and chasing away the roaches with buckets of water. She had forgotten her apron, and when she straightened, she wiped her hands on her splattered dress. She loved these grim walls, the blistering work that chapped her hands, the raw humanity that walked through her doors. Three years she had spent here, once a week, caring for women who might now be her only patients. She had no idea what would happen to her other practice once the news got out that she had been dismissed from the hospital. It was a Monday, not a Thursday, but she lit the lantern to hang outside anyway.

When she opened the door, she was shocked to find Viola Van der Veer on the doorstep, looking out of place in the dank alleyway. She was dressed in a fine blue gown that emphasized her tiny waist. Mary recognized Bonnie's fine handiwork in Viola's elaborate hat, decorated with ostrich feathers and a hummingbird perched in a nest of twigs. This was the second time an overdressed Van der Veer had made an unannounced appearance at her clinic, and both times she'd been shocked to see them.

"Jakob told me you might be here," Viola said. "May I come in?"

Mary opened the door wide to admit her, then hung the lantern outside in its usual spot. Viola edged past her, lifting the hem of her gown to keep it from dragging in the puddles of mop water pooling on the uneven floor. Inside, she turned, taking in the musty clinic, betraying no surprise.

"It isn't much, but my patients feel safe coming here. Until recently. Would you like to sit?" Mary said, indicating one of the wooden armchairs stacked in a corner.

Viola waved away the offer. "I'm sorry for the unannounced visit, but I have long wanted to see you in person to say how sorry I am about Bonnie's daughters. I'm heartbroken about what—happened." She pulled nervously at the tips of her calfskin gloves. "I would have called on you, but I wasn't certain how you would have felt, given our family's connection with Mr. Harley."

"I would have been grateful."

"I probably shouldn't even be speaking to you." Restless, she began to walk about the room. "No doubt there is some legal prohibition banning it. And they're maligning all of us in the papers. This morning, that terrible Horace Young pointed out the impropriety of Jakob defending Mr. Harley. Not that I wanted Jakob to do it, but the truth of it is that we are all pariahs now. No one, it seems, will win in this. Least of all Emma and Claire."

"No, they won't."

"How are they?" Viola said, stopping, her voice plaintive.

"I believe Claire will be all right, but Emma—I don't know."

"I'm terribly sick that our family has a part in this. I loved Bonnie. She was kind to me. I had very few friends, and she was one." Her expression darkened. "My heart breaks—but how I feel doesn't matter. Not in comparison to how the girls must be feeling."

Mary noticed that Viola's hands were shaking. She had dropped the hem of her dress, and the silk of her skirt was absorbing the last of a small puddle, but Viola took no heed. Clearly, the tiny woman had something else on her mind besides an apology.

"Jakob is smart," Viola went on. "And good. It was his father who wanted him to defend Mr. Harley. Jakob didn't want to. He was afraid of what Elizabeth might think. But he's clever. I suppose all mothers say that." She looked up, embarrassed. "I'm sorry. I didn't mean—" She gave up talking and ran a gloved hand up the doorjamb.

"Mrs. Van der Veer—"

"Viola, please."

"Viola. What is it that you came to say?"

She sighed and hesitated for a moment. "I collect French dolls. Very expensive. Jumeau. I know to someone like you that seems frivolous"—she nodded at the clinic, in which nothing could be said to be frivolous—"but I like fashion. And the dolls are meant to show off the latest couture from Paris. I miss going there. I used to go with my father. I think I told you that at the party? Anyway, I like to see what is new." She was talking fast now. "The dolls mean a lot to me. They're quite rare and difficult to find. No one in Albany sells them. You have to go to Manhattan—"

"Viola?"

"Jakob told me. About the dolls sent to the girls."

Mary recalled how quickly Jakob had snatched them from her hands. She had caught a glimpse at the bottom of their shoes, the scroll of a French word embroidered into the silk.

"He recognized them—the type of doll—that day at your house. He knows about my collection. I keep them in my bedroom."

Mary fought a sudden chill and reached for the shawl she had put aside when she was cleaning. The content of the note came suddenly back to her: *Do you miss me?* "The dolls are yours? You sent them?"

"No." Viola's hands, perpetually in motion, stilled. "No. They weren't mine."

"How do you know?"

"I counted them. I'm certain. The ones that were sent to Emma and Claire did not come from my collection."

"Then do you know who did send them?"

"I don't."

"Did Jakob tell you there was a note?"

Viola's startled response told Mary that Jakob hadn't.

"What did it say?"

Mary didn't like to think of what the note had said. Its cool arrogance had unnerved her. "I think you'd rather not know."

"I see." Viola swallowed. "I can't even imagine how awful this is for your family. It is for me. It has been for Jakob. I hardly see him anymore. During the day, he hides himself away somewhere preparing for the trial. He won't even tell me where he goes. He never wanted to be involved—but I told you that already."

Viola looked wistfully around the clinic. She was lingering, as if she had nowhere else to go. Mary wondered how she filled her days.

"I think you might like to know," Mary said, "that Jakob was very good to Emma when he interviewed her. Very kind. We—most of us—appreciate his discretion. Very few attorneys would have treated her with such care."

"I'm glad." Viola's face lit with pride, but within seconds her expression fell again. "I suppose it's Elizabeth who is distressed."

"She loves those girls. They are like sisters to her."

"That's what Jakob says. He fears Elizabeth will never forgive him."

Mary shrugged. She couldn't speak for Elizabeth.

Viola nodded ruefully and looked distractedly about the room, her attention flitting from object to object without seeming to register any of them. After a moment, she said, "Are you ever sorry that you married?"

The question startled Mary, but Viola had spoken without self-pity, echoing the clear-eyed attitude about men that was most often voiced in this room. It was the rare prostitute who suffered any romantic notions about the male sex.

"No, I'm not sorry," Mary said.

Viola nodded, envy glazing her eyes. "I thought so. You lead a life different from mine."

Jenny had once made that same observation to Mary. In it, there existed the implication that Mary possessed the courage to act in unexpected ways, while Jenny and Viola did not: Mary Stipp traveled where and when she would; Mary Stipp braved criticism to treat prostitutes and perform surgery.

"Viola," Mary said. "Who else knows that you collect those dolls?"

The petite woman blushed, looking more childish than ever. "I expect you think it's foolish."

"Not at all. But I do wonder who else knows. Do you ever show them to people?"

"All the time. If I suspect someone might be interested, I offer them a tour. Before the dinner party, I showed them to Catherine Lansing. But the maids know about them, of course, and could tell anyone, I suppose. And the footmen."

"You said they aren't sold in Albany. Where do you buy them?"

"At a store in Manhattan City."

"Do they know you? Have you been there, or do you send for them?"

"I've been there any number of times."

"Do they keep records of who buys them?"

Viola's face lit up, and then she ducked her head in embarrassment. "They do. Every once in a while, they send me a letter to alert me that they've received a new doll, or that they are expecting a shipment and do I want to reserve one? They know I can't resist. I always buy one. Lately, I've had a standing order."

"When was the last time you visited that store?"

"A year ago."

Mary raised her eyebrows, and Viola, understanding her unspoken question, said, "But my husband doesn't let me travel without his permission."

"You could leave him a note," Mary said evenly.

Later that day, as the 5:10 Express rocked over a causeway stretched across a small bay a third of the way downriver, Viola studied an island lying midchannel and buttressed at one end by a warning lighthouse. Some wreckage was splintered against the boulders at its northern tip. It took her a moment to understand that what she was seeing were the remnants of her husband's ice-yacht, the *Honey Girl.* The battered runner, its mast snapped, was wedged in a crevice, its unfurled sails shredded and lapping on the rising tide. Viola could just make out the fanciful looping letters *H* and *G* above the waves, the bright red paint having already crackled and turned dull. She shifted in her seat to point out the wreckage to Mary Stipp, but the doctor was staring straight ahead, resolute.

Chapter Thirty-Nine

William woke to the sound of breaking waves. A thin gray light peeked through the louvers of the closed shutters of his corner room. In the four weeks they had spent in the Whaler's Rest, he had rested little. Often, he woke in the dead of night trying to think of a way to reach Emma. Loud noises startled her. She flinched at the slightest touch—even from Elizabeth or Amelia. With the trial date looming ever closer—it was less than two weeks away—she could not meet even the gaze of the people who loved her.

To establish a semblance of ordinary life, Amelia had established a schedule. Emma and Claire spent each morning reading and writing, and after luncheon William helped Emma review her numbers. Only then did a spark of interest flare in Emma's eyes. He paced her through the complexities of long division, heartened that at least one part of her mind had not dimmed. But invariably, afterward she turned listless and retreated to her room to nap, fully clothed, the counterpane drawn up to her neck. By contrast, Claire reveled in the sea and sun. On the rare occasion when she could persuade Emma to join her on her afternoon visits to the beach, Emma evinced no joy in the exercise. Not even Elizabeth's daily violin practice could pierce Emma's armor. Emma had become a halting, flickering ghost, and William was terrified.

He rose, dressed quickly in shirt and pants and muffler, and crept down the stairs to the dining room. The hall clock read five. In the kitchen, the cooks bustled about, baking the day's bread. He begged a cup of coffee from them and took a seat beside a drafty window and stared through its leaded panes at the bay. Usually, the gray burned off by ten, revealing a clear blue wash of sky, but this early, the cape remained cloaked in a gunmetal mist.

With a sudden rustle of skirts, Amelia, pale eyed and serious, appeared at his elbow. He retrieved another cup of coffee from the cooks, who donated a plate of warm rolls and jam to their impromptu breakfast.

"I have an idea about Emma," William said, after ferrying this bounty to the table.

"And I have one about Elizabeth."

Emma did not own a riding habit, nor had she ridden much, being a city girl. Amelia borrowed a close woolen jacket from the innkeeper's daughter for Emma to wear over her pink calico dress. Then, to protect Emma from the sun, they tied the ribbons of her sun hat so that its brim lay flat against her cheeks. Elizabeth pinned a makeshift veil of lace to the crown, and she was ready.

The herring fisherman who rented William the horse held the bay mare by the bridle as William lifted Emma up on his shoulder so that she could pet the animal's long neck. The mare nuzzled her in return, nickering softly.

"See how gentle she is?" the fisherman said. "My children ride her bareback."

William mounted first, and then the fisherman helped settle Emma on the saddle in front of William. She submitted to the fisherman's grasp, but went limp as he lifted her. William tucked her sidesaddle between him and the pommel, secured his arm around her waist, and whispered, "I'm here."

"Head into the sun," the fisherman said. "It's only two miles to the backshore. When you reach the beach, you can turn either way, but southerly would be best for what you have in mind. Don't worry about the scrub. The mare will pick her way through it."

The scrub turned out to be squat live oaks that clustered together on the low, sandy plateau between the eastern and western shores of the narrow tip of the peninsula. The trees grew close together, their twisting branches intertwined and gnarled by the salt wind. Gooseberry vines clung to the furrowed bark where they weren't usurped by wild grape. There were a few freshwater ponds, but no one lived up here. Throughout the ride, Emma remained silent, her reaction to this forced expedition and the landscape shielded from his view by the obscuring veil. She had not asked where they were going or why.

They breached the headlands after only a half hour's ride, emerging from the salted forest out onto a dazzling plain of sand. Breaking waves hurled themselves at the beach from a great distance out, their constant roar prohibiting any conversation. Here and there, broken masts and wrecks marred the great, frothing expanse. To mark their point of entry, William made note of a bulky heron's nest perched on a high branch of one of the oaks. Then he steered the horse down a shallow switchback of sand and glacial till to the deserted beach. As recommended, he turned southward, veering toward the shore until the mare was wading at the ocean's edge. William guided the animal around bobbing flotsam and mats of sea grass as mackerel gulls hovering on the steady wind followed them like pilot fish. Plovers sprinted across the glassy shore. Far wilder than the bay, the ocean heaved up again and again, the dark, roiling waves rimmed with sparkling white foam.

After riding for several miles, they reached a bluff that soared a couple hundred feet above the beach. William found shelter from the constant wind at its base and drew Emma off the mare. He tethered the horse to one of the heavier pieces of silvery driftwood flung up against the dunes. Amelia had persuaded the cooks to pack them a lunch, and he spread out a blanket and unwrapped meat sandwiches and scones and bottles of ginger ale. The ocean magnified the sun's rays, and Emma blinked as she chewed, for she'd had to remove her protective veil in order to eat. But after a while she lay aside her unfinished sandwich and lay back on the blanket to doze in the sun, a light breeze ruffling the lace on her dress and the ribbons of her hat. Even in repose, she looked battle weary. William looked out toward the sea, biding his time.

The immense watery vista reminded William of the wide desert of Texas and the lesser charms of the Rio Grande. Before the war, he had enlisted and served in an army outpost there, trying to recover from his own paralyzing grief after his first wife, Genevieve, died in a cholera epidemic in Manhattan City. But nothing lifted him from his despair, not until a young Mexican girl named Lilianna, who worked as a laundress, entered his life. Fourteen, thirteen, she was pregnant by a soldier there, and whether she'd been raped or not William had never been able to determine. He had delivered her child and then been parent to them both. Then the war had broken out and he had had to leave them behind. Loving Lilianna and her son had saved him.

Now Emma needed saving.

She slept for a good hour before she stirred. She sat up, resting her elbows on her knees and squinting out to sea.

William feared her great silence might kill her. He didn't need to coax from her the details of what had happened to her; he'd heard them once already when she'd told the district attorney. And he doubted she would want to repeat them now without Amelia or Elizabeth at her side. And to what purpose anyway? Reliving the horror would only rekindle her smoldering fear. He was just gratified that she was not afraid of him. He wished Mary were here. She had already formed a great bond with the girl.

"Come with me, Emma."

He took her small hand and she rose obediently—too obediently. He wanted her to refuse, to fight for herself, but she did not even ask where they were going. He headed up the steep escarpment behind them, following a shallow crevice riven into the hillside. Reedlike sea grass gave some purchase, but it was hard going, for Emma had little strength and the sand gave way beneath their feet and filled their shoes. After fifteen minutes, they'd only gotten a quarter of the way up. She sank to the ground, and he had to reach out and catch her so that she wouldn't somersault backward.

"I can't," Emma said, close to tears. It was the first thing she had said to him all day. "It's too hard."

"It is hard, isn't it?" He perched beside her, a bit out of breath himself, grateful for the cooling wind. Emma's refusal contained the hoped-for spark of defiance, but it also contained a miasma of defeat. He would have far preferred that she had screamed, *I won't!*

"Can we go back?" she said.

"Sure," he said, nodding. "We could go back. But then we'd never know what it looks like up there or whether all this hard work is worth it. But I'm told that up there you can see as far as forever. But we won't know unless we go up and see."

Emma untied a boot and tipped it over. A waterfall of yellow grains blew away in the breeze. She tugged off the other one and repeated the process, unrolling her stockings and tugging them off, too. Her movements were precise, orderly. Wind rustled the dune grass and the ocean pulsed with the rhythmic pounding of a heartbeat. Below, the tethered mare munched on a bunch of beach grass.

"Do you remember from before, Emma, when you climbed trees?"

The girl squinted at him from underneath her hat, her gaze wary.

"Well, that cliff up there is higher than you've ever been in your life. You might see ships. You might see all the way to England."

She looked at him doubtfully.

He grinned. "I'm exaggerating. Not England, of course. But ships, maybe."

Her tentative nod predicted nothing.

"I want to ask you another question, Emma. You don't have to answer me if you don't want to." She neither granted nor withheld permission, so he forged ahead. "I wonder whether you don't want to keep going because you're scared or because it's too hard to keep climbing?"

She stared for a while into the distance, then looked back at him and whispered, "Both."

"I see. This cliff is pretty steep. But I bet everything feels hard and frightening to you right now."

She looked away.

"Emma, do you remember that I told you that when we go back home you have to go to court to tell a judge and jury about what happened to you and Claire?"

"Yes."

"And do you remember that I told you that there will be people in the courtroom?"

She nodded. He had relayed all this in their first week on Cape Cod, one afternoon on the veranda when they had the place to themselves. But he had not been certain that she had understood or remembered his descriptions of the workings of a courtroom or the roles of a judge and jury, or even that she would have to testify.

"You remember that in a couple of weeks Mr. Hotaling and Mr. Van der Veer will ask you questions, just like they did before, at the house? The reason that it's important that you answer them is so that we can find out who the other man is. And you are the only one who can help the judge."

She turned attentive, watchful.

He hesitated now. He wanted neither to coddle nor push her, and he certainly did not want to coerce her. But there was no way out: she had to get on that witness stand to testify, and they all had to help her do it. There were times when he wished they'd not reported a damn thing, because in the end, what purpose would the trial serve if Emma was destroyed by it?

"You see, Emma, I'm just a little worried about you."

Her eyes grew hollow and fearful but also darkly luminous. *Someone had noticed her. Someone had seen her.* At least, this is what William hoped she understood.

"I brought you out here today not just because it's beautiful, but also so that you could practice doing something really hard. This is a tall hill, the tallest one around. It's not a great big mountain, but the sand in our shoes and the wind are going to make it pretty hard to get up there. It's already hard for me, and I'm a grown man. But one of the things about life is that when you do something hard and succeed, then you learn that things aren't as scary or hard as they seem. And when you're done, you feel like you can do anything. It's one of those important things people have to learn. And you already did a very brave thing once. You saved yourself and Claire by hitting that man with a shovel and escaping. I'm so proud of you for that."

A ghost of a smile flickered across her face. He would leave it at this, if there were more time before the trial, leave her with no other challenge for the day than to regard herself as admired. But there wasn't more time.

"No doubt about it, you're a soldier, Emma. As brave as they come. In fact, I brought something for you." He fished in his shirt pocket for the Medal of Honor he'd earned at Gettysburg for meritorious medical service. Exhumed now from its velvet box, the brass eagle and star flashed in the bright sun, and the flag's red and white stripes shone vibrant against the pale yellow sands. He was breaking several army regulations for what he was about to do, but he didn't care.

"I earned this in the war, for doing some really hard things, and I want you to wear it now, because you've done some really hard things. May I pin it on you?"

She nodded, and he took great care affixing it to her dress. She fingered it and looked up at him. Once during the war, at Fairfax Station, surrounded by thousands and thousands of dying men, he had said to Mary, *Choose who you are, choose who you'll be.* He could not say that now to this ravaged child, but the situation was just as dire, the choice just as necessary.

"I just want it all to be over," Emma whispered. "I don't want to think about *him* anymore."

"Do you think about him a lot?"

"All the time."

"I can tell. I thought you've been awfully scared and unhappy. And now it seems as if you want to hide forever. I don't blame you one bit. It was awful what happened to you. But I'm sorry to tell you that you have to save yourself one more time. Now, I'm not going to tell you to climb that hill. You have to want to, for yourself. But I think it will help you later."

He wanted to say, *It's either hide forever or see forever.* He wanted to say, *You need to choose.* He wanted to say, *Follow me, I'll show you.* Instead, he held his breath, nodded solemnly, and looked out to sea, pretending to watch the hundreds of seagulls whirling in flight.

The sun was behind them now and the cliff was casting long shadows onto the beach. They didn't have much time before they would have to return to the hotel. And this gambit would only work once. After this attempt, he had no idea what else he could do for her besides protecting her, which he would do no matter what. But that would shore her up for only so long. Every inch toward courage was a decision. Even ten feet on her own would be a triumph. The line between coercion and choice for her was the line between darkness and light. He would never push her, but she needed to choose to climb this hill. If she didn't, she wouldn't have the courage to climb onto the witness stand or perhaps even to walk down a street on her own.

Emma tugged at his sleeve. "Do you think I can do it?"

He pretended to consider this very important question, as if in fact there were two answers, when there was really only one.

He nodded solemnly. "I do. I think you can."

The sprinkle of freckles on her face had darkened. He should have remembered to pin her veil back on, but if he moved one inch either up or down the hill, he would influence her decision. She searched his face, her blue eyes reflecting the clouds scudding along on the wind. She fingered the medal instead of the pearl buttons of her dress. Then she climbed to her feet and shot up the hill, her skirts bunched in her hands, her shoes and stockings forgotten in the dune grass. William climbed to his feet, gathered her things, and started after her up the sandy path. Here and there grasses were uprooted where Emma had grabbed for a handhold. At each twist and turn, he expected to find her slumped on the sand, but as he slipped and fought his way up the unforgiving verge, her footsteps grew more fleet. He found her perched on the precipice of the headland, her legs dangling over the cliff edge.

Thoreau had once said of this very place, *A man may stand there and put all America behind him.*

Well, a girl could, too.

The brilliant light dazzled. The wide beach stretched to the north and south. Beyond the long sandy bar, the sea sparkled in the sunlight.

William sat down next to Emma. She was winded and breathing hard, but her cheeks were dappled with sun and exertion and pride. The medal glinted in the sun.

They were the only people for miles.

They could see forever.

"We could count the waves," Emma said.

And so they began.

Chapter Forty

After William rode away with Emma, Elizabeth and Amelia abandoned Claire's schooling for a morning constitutional along the beach. There was an ebb tide, and low waves were breaking in a soothing, gentle rhythm. Claire found a piece of driftwood and began to poke at the bubbling clam holes dotting the sand. She wore a pair of rubber boots they'd purchased for her in a shop on Commercial Street, and they peeked out from underneath her dress when she leaned over to inspect the effect of her labors. A light breeze smelled of brine and sea foam.

Out of the corner of her eye, Amelia studied Elizabeth. The sea air and daily practice had done them all good, but Elizabeth was not herself. She had freckled some in the sun, despite their wide hats, and she was attentive to the girls, but she lacked luster.

"You're sounding wonderful on your instrument, Lizzie," Amelia said. And she was. The whole town was enthralled. Her practices had transformed into impromptu concerts, and townspeople found reason to abandon dinner preparations and chores to be seated outside the veranda when she played.

"The violin goes out of tune so quickly in the sea air."

"Well, I can't tell. I think you may sound even better than when you left Paris." They walked on, following Claire, who was chasing a seagull. Amelia said, "I've held off asking you, Lizzie, but can you tell me now why you wanted to leave Paris?"

"The girls," Elizabeth said, her answer swift.

"But you were unhappy before. You were on the verge of quitting before we left. I could tell."

Elizabeth's mouth set in rueful embarrassment. "You think I play well because you love me, Grandmama, but I don't. And they knew it at the school. Monsieur Girard—he made me understand that. He told me every day that I might as well not even be there, since I was taking the place of someone far more talented."

A wave of fury washed over Amelia. She recalled the man's cool good looks, the arrogant cant to his shoulders, his ingratiating bonhomie. "He said what?"

Elizabeth held up her hand. "Don't make me tell you any more. It's humiliating."

"Every day?"

Tears formed in Elizabeth's eyes, and she looked away, tight-lipped. "He said I have no talent. That I am not technically versatile. That if I ever dared try to join an orchestra, I would garner no success. He advised me to go home. To give up. And then Emma and Claire—died." They both watched Claire skipping along the beach, flicking at the wet sand with her stick, sending ribbons of seaweed flying into the sky. "Monsieur Girard was relentless with his criticism, and punishing. And cruel."

"Cruel? Did he hurt you?" Amelia said, instantly alert.

"No. No," Elizabeth shook her head. "It's nothing like that."

Amelia exhaled. She would never forgive herself if Elizabeth, too, had been harmed the way the girls had been. "He had no right."

"Charles Girard is the preeminent violinist of France. I think he knew what he was talking about."

"Listen to me. He had his own reasons to discourage you. The director himself told me that you might soon surpass him in skill. No doubt that small man feared your ascendance. And you, a girl. He must have been humiliated."

"Grandmama—"

"Do you know that your Aunt Mary had the same difficulty? No one wanted her to be a physician. The Albany Medical School rejected her out of hand. To get what she wanted, she had to go to war. And even then she had to fight everyone—Dorothea Dix, even William. Yes," she said, to Elizabeth's incredulous look. "Obviously William came around, but my point is that it wasn't easy for her. Darling, you can't just let one man undermine your life."

"But he's the one who would know—"

"I'll grant you that Monsieur Girard is a great violinist. But that does not render him free of prejudice or jealousy or even malevolence."

Elizabeth stopped abruptly.

"Paris is not the only conservatory in the world," Amelia said. "There is Boston. You could audition while we are here."

"I can't. I won't leave the girls."

"It's just one day, darling. Write, why don't you? Take the train over, or we'll even hire a boat. It's a day trip. I'll go with you. And if the conservatory doesn't accept you, then in turn I'll accept your assessment of your own playing, but not until then. Because I know that some men don't like to be usurped. And I also know that when you play, darling, it's the most beautiful sound in the world."

Elizabeth shook her head and closed her eyes. "But how could he have said those things, Grandmama?"

"Envy and fear make people unkind. I wish I'd known what was happening to you in Paris. Write Boston today, Elizabeth, when we get back to the hotel. Will you?"

Elizabeth nodded, and they turned and walked across the beach to where Claire had scampered to the ocean edge and was letting wavelets lap over the tips of her boots.

"And what of Jakob?" Elizabeth said quietly, so that Claire would not overhear her question. "Why has he betrayed us?"

"Perhaps he has no choice."

"Of course he has a choice. Who could defend such a man as Mr. Harley? How can Jakob look at Emma and Claire and then make an argument in his favor? I will never understand."

"Lizzie, in the last few months, you've lost a lot—Bonnie, for a while Emma and Claire, the conservatory—but what I think you've really lost is your heart."

Elizabeth turned. "But I can't love the girls and Jakob at the same time."

"Maybe you can," Amelia said. "Maybe you already do."

A few days later, Elizabeth stood in the studio of Julius Eichberg, the director and founder of the Boston Conservatory. A German violinist, he had granted Elizabeth an audition by immediate return letter. His nascent conservatory could not have differed more from the bustling Paris Conservatoire and its marble, colonnaded home on the rue Bergère. The Boston Conservatory, operating now for only twenty-two years, did not have its own building. It rented rooms on the second and third floors in the Mason & Hamlin Organ Company's factory. Its marble dolomite facade fronted the Boston Common, but one gained admission to the school by a back door off an alley and up a wooden stairwell open to the workshop floor, from which emanated a great deal of hammering and sawing.

Upstairs, Eichberg's drafty studio had been arranged like a parlor, with a brocade settee, mahogany tables, and rich tapestry hangings on the walls. Overlapping Turkish rugs in hues of red and blue carpeted the entire floor, buffering any sound from the factory below. A jury made up of the three members of the core violin faculty occupied three ladder-back chairs arranged in a semicircle. They each rose when she entered and offered her their hands in greeting. Julius

Eichberg had a kindly face, not unlike the director of the Paris conservatory, but there was something far less challenging in his expression.

"Begin when you are ready," he said.

His genial greeting to both Amelia and Elizabeth had put Elizabeth at ease, and as she lifted her bow, she strove to banish M. Girard's voice from her mind.

She had chosen to play Viotti's Violin Concerto no. 17 again, the piece that had earned her entrance to Paris, for despite its brevity—just over ten minutes—no other music in her repertoire demonstrated a player's dexterity and phrasing in as little time. Noble, gripping, but deceptively light and bright, the solo alluded to the darker orchestral underpinning that the jurists would not hear, for there was no orchestra to mask the tones of her instrument. And she would be handicapped by the fact that this new violin was not nearly as expressive or sensuous as her instrument at home. But therein lay the challenge. If Emma could summit a cliff, then Elizabeth could coax eloquence from lesser wood.

With the first note of the allegretto, Elizabeth slipped into the concerto's strains. She did not hear the music as much as she saw it, shimmering and changing with each stroke of her bow. Once, she had tried to explain this to her early instructors, but no one understood what she meant, and so she stopped explaining it to anyone. But this was how she remembered music. She *saw* it. And this piece of music—in D Minor—looked like the colors of hope. She shut her eyes, giving in to the luster and brilliance of the melody emanating from her instrument. Playing was effortless. She forgot Monsieur Girard, forgot Paris, forgot her fear. There was only music and joy. When she finished the piece, she came back to herself slowly, the last note lingering in the air as the colors dissolved.

She was still catching her breath when Mr. Eichberg, glancing first at the other faculty, who each nodded, said, "Miss Fall, I don't know how the Conservatoire ever parted with you. But I will happily take their loss as my gain."

Book Three

Chapter Forty-One

On Monday June 16, the first day of the Court of Sessions, the city's working classes awoke at dawn conscious of the immensity of the moment and decided en masse to flock to City Hall. From first light, they elbowed for position in front of the white-pillared cake box of a building, spilling onto Eagle Street and down the slope of Maiden Lane, in hopes of either being admitted to the courtroom or catching a glimpse of Emma O'Donnell, who they were now calling "the sullied girl." Since Emma and Claire's miraculous resurrection, the mystery of their whereabouts had become a question of sport, debated with passion in every tavern, prayer circle, factory, horsecar, railroad depot, restaurant, brewery, shop, and home, because despite the newspaper report that the Stipps were housing them, there hadn't been a single sighting. Patients reported that William Stipp was "unavailable," while Doctor Mary Stipp deflected even the most timorous inquiry. A cobbler's claim of an order for shoes sized by penciled outlines created a frenzy but was dismissed as implausible when he could not produce a bill of sale. A porter of the Boston and Albany Railroad claimed that he had seen them depart one May night, but his superiors, fearful of a mob, immediately discounted him. A tantalizing rumor of the female doctor Stipp taking a holiday in Manhattan City emerged to some acclaim; however, this, too, was quashed. The only place civility reigned was among Emma and Claire's classmates, who would answer no one's questions, a decorum modeled for them by their teacher, who was still mortified by her role in the sisters' disappearance and who, upon hearing of their reappearance, had wept for a day. The family of the former principal, hobbled by a dual amputation for frostbite and since confined to a wheelchair, was gauging her laudanum consumption carefully and had since the blizzard, for she had threatened to end her life over her disastrous decision that had imperiled Emma and Claire O'Donnell.

As the crowd waited to see the sisters for themselves, a general camaraderie prevailed, along with the consensus that the Hero of the Flood was still a hero. It was not clear whether or not Emma would testify. That prospect, too, had been bandied about in the newspapers, as if she were an injured prize thoroughbred slated to race in the Travers Stakes at Saratoga. There had been hints of a subpoena, soundly denied by the prosecutor's office. But the longer people shivered in the cool of the early morning, speculation was stoked into avid fervor. By seven o'clock, the night watchman, who usually slept in the doldrums of the early dawn hours tucked into a comfortable corner of the mayor's office, was roused by the noise and went to unlock the great iron doors. But before he did, he perceived the enormity of the waiting crowd and instead telephoned the exchange, a step he had never once taken in his sleepy five-year incumbency as nocturnal protector of one of the prettiest buildings in Albany. He implored the operators to call the City Building at Hamilton and Pearl to send as many policemen as they could, because the citizens of Albany had declared themselves newly besotted with justice, and he was afraid for his life.

Within half an hour, mounted policemen circled the throng and herded the restive crowd onto the grounds of the Albany Academy, pinning them there with billy clubs and shields while grand jurors and prospective trial jurors and witnesses and court officials slipped inside unobserved and undetected via the lowly back door normally used only for the transfer of prisoners to and from the jail next door. Officer Farrell drove to the Stipps' house and escorted them to the courthouse via a circuitous route and snuck them inside by the same method.

With every passing hour, the racket in the streets mounted and invaded even the stately chambers of the courtroom on the third floor, giving the impression of impending revolution.

Nonetheless, by ten in the morning an efficient grand jury handed down a swift indictment of James Harley, and by noon the task of choosing trial jurors had turned out to be an expedient and surprisingly harmonious march through the available jury pool. At noon, the judge called for recess, and it wasn't until one o'clock that an army of guards opened the doors to the public. The mayor was tagged with the onerous duty of choosing who was to be admitted, a job he accomplished on the basis of elevated stature in the community, a prejudice not unmarked by the unruly crowd, who jeered as police barred the doors behind the final candidate.

At one thirty, William Stipp and Elizabeth entered the courtroom, having spent the morning with Mary and Emma in a holding room across the echoing mezzanine. A hush fell over the overflow crowd that packed the pews and jostled for position two deep along every wall. The wide wings of Elizabeth's bonnet served as blinders, but William saw every curious stare following them up the aisle. The presence of the Cornings and Ten Eycks and Schuylers surprised him. Madame Hubbard waved a handkerchief at them, oblivious that her plumed hat was causing a great deal of trouble for the spectators seated behind her. Horace Young caught William's gaze and dutifully recorded something in his notebook. But Gerritt and Viola Van der Veer, curiously, were not among the crowd. William steered Elizabeth into the pew directly behind the prosecutor's table. He was glad that as witnesses, Emma and Mary were excluded from the courtroom, and that Amelia had stayed behind to take care of Claire, who hardly even knew that the trial was taking place.

The district attorney and Jakob were already in their seats, studying sheaves of documents and notes, feigning oblivion to the gallery. James Harley met no one's gaze. He sat slumped in his seat beside Jakob. His time in jail had wizened him, and his beard had gone completely white, though he wore a new linen frock coat and thin vest that unfortunately had already wrinkled in the heat.

A door opened behind the bench and the jury filed in. The smattering of laborers—stonecutters and masons and the like—drew sharp scrutiny from the gallery, but it was the presence of Harmon Pumpelly that was greeted with a collective inhalation of astonishment. As president of the Albany Gas Lighting Company, Albany Savings Bank, and Albany Insurance, Pumpelly was known to everyone. The rest of the jury threw self-conscious glances at the crowd, but Pumpelly, chosen as foreman, nodded to the assembled as if he were the judge himself, lending a further air of gravity to the trial.

"All rise." At the bailiff's reedy cry, Judge Julius Thayer, attired in a voluminous robe and powdered wig, marched into the courtroom and with an impatient wave commanded everyone back into their seats. Throughout Albany, Thayer's adherence to the law had achieved legendary status. At nearly fifty, the big man was stone-faced and glum, his visage cemented in impassivity. A bulbous nose, thick jowls undisguised by a thatch of beard, and a heavy forehead gave an impression of rigorous authority that his tired gaze did nothing to dispel. His wife, Alice, had died six weeks ago during childbirth, but not before producing a fifth daughter. The wet nurse was rumored to be unreliable in her milk, and neighbors reported that the child frequently cried all night. Now Thayer's exhausted gaze raked courtroom and spectators alike before calling the courtroom to order with a sharp rap of his gavel.

"I want to take a moment to make clear that this court is fully cognizant of the infamy of this case." Thayer's was a rumbling growl of a voice, thick with catarrh but loud enough to rise above the din outside. "If there is any misbehavior on the part of the gallery, I will not hesitate to clear this courtroom. During this trial, there will be revelations that will prove shocking to some, particularly any ladies who have been foolish enough to attend, though presumably that is why many of you are here. I find your interest especially to be suspect." He glowered at them, and the women ducked their heads, embarrassed to be singled out. "Nevertheless, here you all are. I warn each one of you to hold your tongues. I care nothing for your standing in the community or any privilege you may feel you possess. This is my courtroom and I will kick out the lot of you if you even so much as peep."

He swept the courtroom again with his eagle-eyed gaze, reinforcing his avowal of intolerance. "I now call the case of the *People of Albany County versus Mr. James Harley*. Will the clerk please swear in the jury?"

The twelve men charged with Harley's fate wobbled to their feet, seemingly stunned by the judge's stern warning and then by the oath they took, with the exception of Harmon Pumpelly, who seemed pleased after Thayer's rebuke to have official cause to be present.

Though it was only June and the real swelter was at least a month away, the afternoon sun was already boiling through the five tall south-facing windows. Several men had removed their hats and were fanning themselves against the heat, but Thayer seemed unperturbed. He nodded at Lansing Hotaling, who strolled to the jury box to make his opening statement.

The district attorney was known for doggedness, not eloquence, but despite this tepid reputation, this afternoon the entire courtroom hoped for oratory. Unlike Jakob, who appeared to great advantage in a cutaway coat and white waistcoat, crisp even in the rising heat,

Hotaling's formal jacket hung on him like a sack. The two stood in odd juxtaposition to one another: the polished novice and the rumpled veteran.

"May it please the court, Mr. Foreman, and each of you gentlemen, the defendant in this case, one James Harley," Hotaling said, nodding at Harley, "is indicted for the high crimes of rape, kidnapping, and imprisonment. These are egregious crimes. Unconscionable. A bane on good society. Even just one of these terrible acts would give rise to abhorrence in the most hardened heart. Now, some of you may recognize Mr. Harley's name in connection with the recent flood. A certain member of the press has dubbed Mr. Harley a hero in connection with his rescue of two little boys. Well, I adjure you to banish that accolade from your mind, because Mr. Harley is not a hero. Mr. Harley is a wolf."

Though Hotaling's intonation was workmanlike and plodding, the courtroom was entranced, breathless at his every turn of phrase. No one pulled even a handkerchief from pocket or reticule, even as tiny beads of sweat formed on their foreheads.

"Members of the jury," Hotaling continued, his voice as dull as a broken bell. "At the conclusion of this case, his Honor the Judge Julius Thayer will charge you with the law, and explain to you in detail just what the laws are governing in this case. He will explain definitions by Penal Law and you will make a judgment. My job is to recite the facts as I intend to present them through the witnesses I call to the stand. The victims in this case are Emma and Claire O'Donnell, ten and seven years old. On March twelfth of this year, at about noon, their principal expelled them from the Van Zandt Grammar School into the aftermath of our recent and devastating blizzard. The going was treacherous. Emma O'Donnell will tell you that her sister had trouble navigating the high drifts and soon sank, whereupon an unidentified man pulled Claire from the snowdrift and took them both to James Harley's house, where Mr. Harley secreted them in the cellar of his home at 153 Green Street, and thereafter kept them against their will for six weeks. They escaped from his basement the night of April twenty-first, the night of our recent great flood. The policeman who found them on a nearby street will tell you that upon hearing their names and recognizing them as the missing sisters long declared dead, he took them to the Stipp residence. They were bruised, troubled, and in a state of shock. Dr. Mary Stipp later examined them and informed the policeman that one of the two girls, Emma O'Donnell, had been interfered with in a sexual way."

The jury shifted in their seats. No one in the courtroom uttered a sound, not even a cough. A thick silence hung in the air, a bated expectancy that governed every move, twitch of eyelid or mouth.

"The defendant, James Harley, was apprehended two days later. Gentlemen of the jury, if I establish the facts of the case, the county expects you to return a verdict of guilty on all counts in accordance with the evidence and what the facts in this case will warrant. And though Emma O'Donnell is at the age of consent, she in no way consented to the activity forced upon her."

Hotaling finished and ambled back to his table, appearing quite satisfied with his delivery.

Judge Thayer turned to Jakob. "Does the defense wish to make an opening statement?"

Jakob rose. In his beautifully tailored clothes, he cut a fine figure, but from his close vantage point, William noticed that the boy's hands were shaking, as if he were acutely aware that his smart attire could not disguise his age or inexperience. Jakob riffled through some papers, laid them down, then took hold of them again. Where, William thought, was Gerritt Van der Veer, or for that matter, Viola? Were they indeed going to leave the boy without even an ounce of familial support? William supposed things had grown complicated for them at home. When Mary had related her overnight excursion with Viola to Manhattan City, she had hinted of some family discord. Later, Mary had tried to see Viola again, but an impolite footman had snapped that Mrs. Van der Veer no longer wished to have any relations with anyone in the Stipp family. Nor had Viola answered any of Mary's letters. Mary had grown worried. Still, if Viola did harbor some animosity toward them, it seemed impossible that a mother who adored her son as completely as Viola did would abandon him, even as a grown man, to a legal debut of such momentous consequence.

The irony was not lost on William that he was concerned about a young man defending the person who at the very least had knowingly kept Emma and Claire from them and who had perhaps even been the one to harm her. And even if what Emma said was true—that someone else and not Harley had raped her—Jakob's allegiances were reason enough to abandon any concern for the boy's well-being. But for some reason, he couldn't. After all, it was Jakob who had warned them to leave Albany after the dolls had been sent to the house, and Jakob who believed Emma and her avowal of a second man.

With a slightly halting gait, Jakob crossed to the jury box, his shock of blond hair highlighted by the harsh rays of the relentless sun. He seemed not to know where to look or what to do with the papers he had brought with him from his desk. In the packed courtroom, his voice sounded hollow.

"Good afternoon, gentlemen of the jury and members of the court. The charges filed against my client, Mr. James Harley, are indeed egregious. I will now address all three."

He fingered through his papers, read a few lines, looked up again. He appeared a schoolboy, nervously consulting his notes.

"First, we the defense do not dispute that rape occurred."

Gasps echoed throughout the courtroom and the sharp crack of Thayer's gavel split the air. "Don't tempt me," Thayer said to the crowd. "I meant what I said. Hold your shock for the dinner table."

Silenced, the gallery nonetheless exchanged looks of disbelief at what they had just heard. The customary defense in rape cases was to claim that no crime had occurred. The defense would maintain that the victim was not a victim at all, but a siren who, having either seduced or acquiesced to the accused man, feigned accusations of exploitation in a nefarious bid to repair her reputation. Emma being at the age of consent made this defense fair game. But for Jakob to assert that Emma had indeed been raped, he had in one fell swoop both destroyed Emma's reputation and undercut his defense of Harley.

He may as well have entered a plea of *Guilty*.

"Rape occurred," Jakob said again, his gaze darting to the jury. "I'll say it one more time: someone raped Emma O'Donnell. Yes, she is at the age of consent. But that will not be my defense. My defense is that it was not James Harley who raped her.

"Evidence will show that someone else is responsible, a man whose corruption, deception, deceit, and greed reveal a far more complicated story than the district attorney is willing to assert.

"The defense also does not contest the claim that Emma and Claire O'Donnell stayed in Mr. Harley's house after the blizzard. Mr. Harley readily admits this. What he denies is the charge of kidnapping. Mr. Harley claims that a stranger delivered Emma and Claire to his door during the storm's aftermath and that, overcome with compassion, he took them in.

"Later, when he learned that David and Bonnie O'Donnell had perished in the storm, he resolved to give Emma and Claire a home. He also chose not to tell them of their parents' deaths because he did not want to upset them and hoped that with time they would forget them. Perhaps that is not the way you or I would handle the situation, but this is what Mr. Harley did. He also readily states that he did not allow them to go to school out of concern for their grief.

"Whether or not this answers to the charge of imprisonment will be up to the jury to decide.

"What I will tell you is that he was so concerned about Emma and Claire's safety that he stranded me in the Lumber District on the night of the flood in order to return to his home to evacuate them. All that he recalls of that chaotic night is descending to the cellar and then waking the next morning disoriented in two inches of water. He fled outside into an alleyway filled with floodwaters and rescued two boys, a selfless action Mr. Hotaling dismissed. Within minutes of delivering those boys to high ground, Mr. Harley would collapse and be transported to the hospital to be operated on for a grave injury to his neck.

"What does this tell us about my client? Do the fullness of his actions reveal mendacity or compassion?

"It is my duty to present evidence in my client's favor. I will contest all the allegations. But I do it less out of allegiance to Mr. Harley than in the interest of justice. Someone raped Emma O'Donnell. Brutally raped her, robbed her of innocence, and cavalierly took advantage of the fact that she and her younger sister, Claire, had been rendered orphans by the very blizzard that delivered them into his hands.

"But it was not James Harley who did this.

"You the jury will decide whether or not to hold Mr. James Harley accountable for this crime. The question is not whether or not a crime occurred. That we already concede. The question for you—and for me to prove—will be *who* committed the crime. And I tell you now, the answer is not a convenient or easy one."

Jakob's unexpected assertions stilled the room. While it was not unusual for an attorney to point fingers at someone else, it was brazen confidence in a case as cut-and-dried as this one. Not a cough or sniffle or shuffle broke the silence. William could see that Jakob's hands still trembled. As he returned to his desk, Jakob slid his gaze Elizabeth's way, giving William the impression that Jakob had been speaking only to her.

"Call your first witness."

The bailiff, a short, unexpressive man hobbled by a limping gait, led Emma toward the stand from the side door. A slow rustling permeated the courtroom as the gallery strained to form an impression of the ravaged girl about whom they had been talking for weeks. The collective perception was of a small-boned, slight figure, demurely dressed in white, with lace edging wide cuffs and a pristine collar that set off a complexion recently exposed to too much sun. Her long red hair, secured with a bright green bow at the nape of her neck, hung in a single plait down her back. On her dress she wore the Medal of Honor that William had given her, and those in the courtroom who knew what it was murmured their disapproval. Thayer, too, seemed surprised and did not hammer his gavel to quiet anyone.

William and Elizabeth marked Emma's entrance with pronounced apprehension. They had instructed Emma to look for them in the gallery, describing to her exactly where they would be—*directly behind Mr. Hotaling, just look for us*— but she had trained her gaze on the floor as she crossed the endless expanse of marble to the witness stand and did not seem to see them.

Jakob leaped to his feet. "Your Honor, I urge you to clear the courtroom of spectators."

Thayer raised his eyebrows, unperturbed, as if he had expected this stratagem from one of them. "On what basis?"

"The comfort of the witness."

Lansing Hotaling flung a look of begrudging acknowledgment Jakob's way even as he rose to object. "I object on the grounds of public interest. It is of significant importance that the people of Albany understand the nature of the crime, so that when the proper conclusion is reached, the entire city will be under no misconceptions.

I believe that my witness, given due consideration, will suffer little or no distress."

"Your Honor," Jakob said, "need I point out that Emma O'Donnell is ten years old?"

Thayer regarded Emma, who clutched the railing around the witness chair.

Thayer said, "As I made clear in my earlier statements, the court recognizes the sensitivity of the subject matter. And while I am more than willing to clear the courtroom for any hint of disrespect on the part of the public toward the reverence and gravity due the court, the right of public oversight in this instance outweighs any perceived discomfort the witness might experience. In addition, the defendant's right to a public trial exceeds that of the witness's right to privacy. Overruled."

The clerk duly swore Emma in, and she climbed onto the witness chair.

Hotaling took her through the preliminaries of name and birth date and place of residence, all questions that she answered dispassionately even when he coaxed from her an acknowledgment of the death of her parents.

"And can you tell us how long you have lived with the Stipps?"

"Since we got away."

"Objection," Jakob said, rising. "Nothing has yet been proven about anyone's need to get away from anything."

"Sustained."

Hotaling threw Jakob a second look, this time of irritation. "I'll rephrase. How many weeks have you lived with the Stipps, Emma?"

"I don't know exactly."

The prosecutor assured the jury that later he would establish the precise time frame with another witness. "And where did you live with your parents?"

"At 46 Elm Street."

"Do you remember the day you left school after the blizzard?"

"Yes."

"Tell us what happened."

Emma recounted being dismissed from school and starting home, and her terror when Claire dropped into the drift. The stranger who rescued them did not seem a stranger when he rescued Claire. He took care of them and promised to take them home. No, she couldn't describe him because his whole face had been covered by a scarf except his eyes. She wasn't even frightened at first when he took them to Mr. Harley's. She knew it was Mr. Harley's because he told her it was.

Hotaling shot a look over his shoulder at Jakob, as if he expected him to object, but no such protestation was offered.

Hotaling went on. "What happened that first night?"

"Mr. Harley kept us by the fire and wrapped blankets around us. He cooked us dinner."

"Did you ask to go home?"

"Yes."

"What did he say?"

"He said it was too dangerous, but that he would take us when the snow melted."

"Did he ever take you home?"

"No."

Hotaling turned and faced the jury to emphasize the point he was about to make. "So no matter how many times you asked Mr. Harley, he never let you go home. How many times did you ask? Three? Four?"

"I don't know. Every day."

"Every day," Hotaling parroted, rapping his fingers on the jury box for emphasis. "Every single day. Now, where did you and Claire sleep?"

"The first few nights, he let us sleep in his bed upstairs but—"

"Did he sleep in the bed with you?"

"No. He slept on the floor. Then, a few days later, after the snow began to melt and people were out on the street, he moved us into the root cellar."

At this, quiet gasps of disbelief reverberated through the gallery. This detail was one of the many that had never been made public.

"Did he ever let you go upstairs?"

"Not me. But Claire."

"What was it like down there?"

"It was always cold and dark and it smelled like a privy. After a while, he brought a bed downstairs, and later a settee so we could sit somewhere. Sometimes, he brought us water so that we could wash ourselves."

"Did you try to leave by yourself?"

"Yes. But the door was always locked."

"The door to the cellar?"

"Yes."

"In all the time he imprisoned you—"

"Objection." Jakob rose to his feet. "That language is inflammatory."

"Mr. Van der Veer," Thayer said, looking at him over the top of his glasses. "The definition of *imprisonment* is keeping a person against his will. Miss O'Donnell has just stated that she wanted to go home and that Mr. Harley wouldn't let her. And the door was locked. Overruled."

"Emma," Hotaling said, suppressing a smile, "in all the time that Mr. Harley *imprisoned* you, did he ever inform you that your parents had died?"

"No."

"When did you learn that?"

"After—when Auntie Amelia told us."

"When was that?"

"After the policeman found us."

"How many days were you in the cellar?"

"I don't know exactly. From the blizzard to the flood."

Hotaling said, "As asserted in my opening statements, let the record show again that the date of Emma and Claire's disappearance was March twelfth and their reappearance April twenty-second, a period of almost six weeks, a point of fact which will also be verified by another witness.

"Now, Emma," he said, turning back, "when you were there in that cellar, did a man put his member in your private parts?"

An explosion of revulsion rippled through the courtroom. Emma's searching, panicked gaze found William. Elizabeth gripped the bar and stood so that Emma could see her. Thayer was pounding on the bench. In the pandemonium, no one seemed to register that Hotaling had said "a man" and not "Harley," but William did not miss the sleight of phrase.

"Did I not make myself clear?" Thayer said. "Another outburst and I will clear the gallery. Quiet. Quiet in the court. You will sit, miss, you will sit," he said, pointing his gavel at Elizabeth.

Elizabeth took her seat and turned to William with a beseeching look.

When the gallery finally quieted, Jakob rose. "Since the defense has already conceded that a rape occurred, is it not possible to bypass any explicit questioning of the witness? Especially under the circumstances?"

"While your sensitive suggestion is admirable, Mr. Van der Veer, you must understand that in order for anyone—Mr. Harley or anyone else—to be convicted of the crime, there still has to be actual evidence presented."

As Jakob once again sat down, Hotaling said, "Can you answer the question, Emma? Did someone do to you what I just described?"

She nodded.

"You must answer out loud."

"Yes."

"Can you describe this man for us?"

She opened her mouth and made a vague motion with one hand. "He was big and bald. He smelled like sawdust, like my father used to smell when he came home from work. His shirts had pleats in them. His mouth tasted like the doctor. He had a beard. Sometimes, all his words ran together."

"Smelled like sawdust. Had a beard. Big and bald." Hotaling gestured at Harley, the stout, bearded lumberman now slumped in his seat. "Can you tell us anything else about him?"

"No. It was always dark when he came."

"No candles? No gaslight?"

"No."

"You couldn't see him?"

"No." Emma's mouth was working now, chewing the sides of her tongue.

"How many times did the man put his member inside you?"

Emma flinched. "I don't remember."

"More than once? Twice? A dozen times?"

"I don't know."

"Why not?"

"I wanted to forget."

"I see. Tell us, did you resist? Scream? Try to fight him off?"

"Yes, but he hit me when I wouldn't do what he wanted."

Thayer held aloft his gavel in stern warning, eyeing the courtroom with a steely gaze, but Emma's revelation was met with breathless silence. Rigid lines of grief, newly impressed into the smooth young skin of her face, deepened. She yanked out a loosened strand from the rope of her braid and twined it around one finger.

"How many times did he hit you, Emma? Every time?" Hotaling said.

She stared at him, twining and untwining the one strand of hair.

"You're a strong girl, Emma. You're alive. Did you fight him? As much as you could?"

Her eyes glazed, and she whispered, "Yes, but it was hard. It felt like he was tearing me apart, like he was breaking me."

A note of grim determination had set into the deep parentheses around Hotaling's mouth and he leaned onto the railing of the witness stand with a confiding air. "You know the difference between right and wrong, don't you? Are you sure you didn't really want it? Weren't you secretly excited? Weren't you curious? Didn't you ask for it?"

"No!" she screamed, and buried her face in her hands.

And there it was, the smear of accusation and blame hurled in courtrooms and police stations everywhere at rape victims, though this time, perversely, it was not the defense attorney doing the hurling, but the prosecution. But Hotaling had maintained that his job was to dredge up every nasty suspicion a jury might entertain and mitigate each one before the defense could manipulate those same doubts in their favor. It was the way of rape trials, he'd insisted. It was imperative to make the jury understand that Emma was a target of brutality. An unwilling participant. Prey to a predator. And unfortunately Emma was the only one who could persuade them. That certitude was a repetition of what William had said to Emma on Cape Cod, but Hotaling's ugly manipulation of Emma's emotions sickened William now. Elizabeth lay her hand on his forearm to forestall him from leaping out of his seat.

Hotaling let Emma hide behind her hands for a moment longer, then softened his tone and leaned forward. "Emma, you and I need to make this very clear so that the jury understands everything that happened. Look up. Look at me, now. Take your hands away from your face. That's right. Did you fight him every time?"

Emma had gone blank-faced, and her response was desultory, dull. "Only at first."

"Why only then?

She looked down at her hands, which she had folded on her lap. "I didn't want him to hurt Claire. He said—he said if I did what he wanted, he wouldn't hurt her."

"Help me to understand. You didn't fight so that he wouldn't hurt your sister?"

"Yes."

Hotaling deliberately paused and eyed the gallery. Several women were crying. There was a rustle as men, clearing throats suddenly thick with emotion, handed handkerchiefs across pew backs. After waiting for the stir to die down, Hotaling turned back to Emma. "We have only a little more work to do, you and I. Just one more thing. You got away from Mr. Harley. I want you to tell the court how you did that."

Emma swallowed convulsively. It took a moment before she could speak. "I hit him with a shovel."

Hotaling pulled a long-handled shovel from underneath the prosecution table. "Is this the shovel you used, Emma?"

She nodded, and he reminded her again to answer out loud.

"Yes."

"I introduce this shovel, taken from the basement of the home of James Harley at 153 Green Street, into evidence."

"Who took that shovel from that basement, Mr. Hotaling?" Thayer said.

"Officer Farrell, a policeman in the Fourth Precinct, who found the sisters."

"You will later authenticate this, or any testimony related to this will be stricken. Is that understood?"

"I plan to authenticate with my next witness. Now, Emma, why did you hit Mr. Harley with this shovel?"

"I wanted to get away."

"When did you hit him?"

"When the bells were ringing."

"The night of the flood?"

"Yes."

"I want you to come down here and show us what you did."

The bailiff shambled over to offer Emma his hand, but she shimmied off the chair by herself. Hotaling handed her the shovel and backed away.

"Go on, Emma, now. Show us," he said.

Emma heaved the shovel up over her head and then swung it downward with surprising force. Its tip struck a corner of the bench and a wedge of mahogany flew through the air and skittered past Hotaling's feet. A titter of excitement trilled through the gallery as Emma lost control of the shovel and it clattered to the floor. The judge smoothed the collar of his robe and without resorting to his gavel waited for the crowd to quiet.

"Mr. Hotaling," Thayer said. "In the future, please ask the permission of the court before you execute such an exciting display. Emma, you may return to your seat, unless Mr. Hotaling wishes to excite us all further?"

Hotaling handed the shovel to the clerk and Emma traipsed back to the witness chair. She seemed to have taken new energy from this physical exertion, as if the demonstration, awkward as it was, had unleashed the belief that her ordeal would soon end.

"Emma, where did you strike Mr. Harley?"

"In the neck."

"Was Mr. Harley hurt?"

"I don't know, but he fell down and he didn't get up."

Hotaling said, "Will the defendant please rise and show the jury the scar on the back of his neck?"

Jakob indicated to Harley to stand. A sheepish Harley rose and untied his necktie, unbuttoned his shirt, and pulled aside his collar to reveal the curved angry ribbon of a scar.

"Show the jury, Mr. Harley," Thayer said.

Harley had not looked at Emma and he did not look at her now as he scuffed to the jury box and the jurors craned their necks to get a good view.

"Thank you," Hotaling said. "You may return to your seat. Now, Emma, did you think you had killed him?"

Emma again eased her braid over one shoulder and nervously played with the loose hair at its end.

"It's all right," Hotaling said. "You can tell the truth."

"Yes."

"That is a kind of fighting to the death, isn't it?"

Her eyes took on a livelier expression, understanding him now. "Yes."

"Then what happened after that?"

"Claire and I ran upstairs and out of the house."

"Where did you go?"

"I don't know. Down an alley. Across a street."

"Then what happened?"

"We slept for a while, I think. Officer Farrell woke us and put us in a wagon and took us to our house."

"To your parents' home?"

"Yes."

"But they weren't there, were they?"

"No."

"Where did he take you next?"

"To Aunt Mary and Uncle William and Auntie Amelia's house," she said, looking up at Elizabeth. "They all took care of us."

Elizabeth nodded at Emma as Hotaling declared Emma to be Jakob's witness, and Emma, believing herself excused, scrambled down from the chair and ran toward Elizabeth and William, but the bailiff, newly nimble, caught her around the waist and said, "Not yet, missy. Not yet."

Stricken, Emma burst into tears.

For several minutes, the sound of muffled weeping infiltrated every corner of the otherwise silent courtroom. The bailiff had used the break in between questioning to open one of the windows, and the restless murmuring of the crowd outside drifted in.

"Emma," Judge Thayer said. "Do you need to be excused for a minute?"

Emma hung her head and covered her face with her hands. She did not look up or answer. William sprang to his feet and tapped Hotaling's shoulder, but before Hotaling could even turn, Jakob rose from his place, took the handkerchief from William's hand, and put it unfolded into Emma's. She buried her face in the linen. The courtroom clock read three. Emma had been on the stand for an hour.

"Do you wish to be excused for a moment?" Thayer said again.

"Would I have to come back?"

Thayer regarded her from the full height of the great mahogany bench. "Didn't someone explain this to you? That both lawyers have to ask you questions?"

Emma nodded.

"All right then. Now it is Mr. Van der Veer's turn to ask you questions. But Mr. Hotaling might want to ask you something else when he is done, and then Mr. Van der Veer might need to again."

"I want it to be over."

"I understand. It will be, soon."

She made no reply. Someone coughed. The sun went behind a cloud, casting a welcome shadow into the courtroom.

Thayer nodded to Jakob to begin, and he approached the stand, a kindly bent to his long, lean frame.

"Hello, Emma," Jakob said. "Do you remember me? We met once, and I asked you several questions. Do you recall that?"

It was impossible to tell whether or not she did. She appeared removed now, shell-shocked, not really seeing him or anyone.

Jakob linked his hands behind his back. "Emma. I am Mr. Van der Veer. Do you remember me? We talked before."

She looked up and nodded.

"All right then. I'm going to ask you a question. Do you remember that you promised to tell the truth?"

Emma's gaze searched the room, again seeking out William and Elizabeth, and this time she found them and did not look away. "Yes."

"Here is my first question. It's very important." Jakob turned then and surveyed the gallery and with this hesitation compelled the courtroom to train its collective gaze on him. "Can you tell us about that medal you're wearing?"

The hint of a smile crossed her face and she wiped her face with William's handkerchief, now bunched in one hand. "Uncle William gave it to me. He said I was very brave."

"And so you are. Now I have another question. Did Mr. Harley ever hurt you?"

"No. He never hurt us. Not once."

Emma's quiet assertion provoked no outburst, though spectators craned their necks to get a glimpse of Harley, who looked more cornered than exonerated. Despite the opened window and the brief respite from the sun, it had grown ever warmer, and now people were fanning themselves with their gloved hands.

"If Mr. Harley didn't hurt you, then who did?" Jakob said.

"The Other Man."

"Can you explain to me about this other man? I'm a little confused."

Emma bit her lips and then wiped them with the handkerchief. "Claire and I called Mr. Harley the Man, and the other man the Other Man."

"So," Jakob said. "Before, when you were describing being hurt to Mr. Hotaling, were you talking about Mr. Harley, who you call the Man, or were you talking about the Other Man?"

Emma braced herself against the seat of the chair. Her mouth was working again, the muscles in her cheek churning away as she chewed the edges of her tongue.

"The Other Man."

A murmur ran through the courtroom, and Thayer frowned, silencing everyone.

"So it was the other man who hurt you and not Mr. Harley?"

"Yes."

"Is the other man the one whose words slurred together, the one who tasted like the doctor?"

"Yes."

"Where did Claire go when the other man hurt you?"

"Mr. Harley took Claire upstairs."

"And that was when all the things you told us about before happened?"

Emma ducked her head. "Yes."

"Since you ran from the cellar, have you ever encountered the other man on the street or anywhere?"

"No."

"Is he here?"

She shrank again back into the chair, her expressionless gaze focused straight ahead. "I don't know."

"Why don't you know?"

"I never saw him. It was always dark."

"You couldn't see his face?"

"No."

"Not once?"

"No."

"Just a couple of questions more, Emma. Did you hit Mr. Harley on the back of the neck because he was the man who hurt you?"

She blinked and shook her head. "No. I just wanted to get away."

"That is all. Thank you, Emma." Jakob returned to his table and sank into his seat.

Thayer raised his eyebrows at Hotaling. "Redirect?"

"Emma," Hotaling said, not bothering to rise. "You were away from home and afraid. Maybe you didn't want to believe that the man who was kind to you and your sister was in fact the same man who was hurting you."

"That is not a question, Mr. Hotaling," Thayer said.

"I'll repharase. Isn't it possible, Emma, that it was too difficult for you to believe that Mr. Harley—who fed you and took care of you—would also hurt you?"

"But he didn't."

"But it was dark, wasn't it? How could you tell?"

She shook her head. "I just could."

"Perhaps Mr. Harley returned after he took Claire upstairs?"

"No."

"Tell us what you did when the man was attacking you."

She looked up, uncomprehending.

"What I mean is, what did you think about, during the attacks?" Hotaling said.

"I went away."

"What do you mean?"

"I shut my eyes and pretended I was somewhere else."

"You pretended that you were somewhere else? Then how could you notice anything?" Hotaling paused, waiting for her to answer, letting her nonanswer speak for itself. He said, "Nothing further."

William looked at Elizabeth, who answered his grave glance with one of her own.

Thayer sought out Jakob, who held up three fingers, indicating he would ask three questions.

"Emma?" Thayer said. "Mr. Van der Veer needs to ask you something else. Just a few questions. And then it will be over. Then you can leave. Do you understand?"

Emma wiped one cheek with the flat palm of one hand, the handkerchief having been wetted through. She turned toward Thayer and nodded.

Jakob rose, but stayed at his table. "Where were you in the house when Mr. Harley took Claire away?"

"Downstairs. In the cellar."

"And where were Mr. Harley and your sister?"

"Upstairs."

"And then the other man would come downstairs?"

"Yes."

"I want to ask you just a few more questions, all right?"

Emma nodded.

"You said before that you *went away* when the other man was with you. That you pretended you were somewhere else?"

She regarded him warily, conscious that she had stumbled before. "Yes."

"But could you hear anything?"

"Leading the witness," Hotaling said.

"I'll allow."

Emma's eyes lit up. "Yes. Footsteps."

"Upstairs? Heavy ones?"

"Yes. And Claire's, too."

"Always?"

"Always."

"So, there had to be two men, didn't there, one man upstairs—Mr. Harley—and one downstairs—the person you call the Other Man—because you always heard footsteps?"

Emma uttered a breathless, relieved *Yes.* Jakob turned to the jury, to make certain they registered Emma's bright certitude.

"Then afterward, when the man who was hurting you left, what would happen?"

"I'd hear voices upstairs. Then the door would open and shut."

"Which door?"

"The one to the outside of the house. There were always three footsteps, then the door would open and shut, and that was how I knew the Other Man was leaving, and that he wasn't coming back that night. When the Man—Mr. Harley— came home, it took him three steps, too, to get from the front door to the stairs."

"Three footsteps? Exactly three?" Jakob seemed surprised. He leaned forward, alert.

"Yes."

"Tell me, Emma, did you count anything else?"

"What do you mean?"

"I mean that contrary to what the district attorney said, you seem to notice quite a lot of things. Did you ever count other things?"

She shrugged, relaxing a little. "I counted the walls."

"Really? How do you count a wall?"

"They were made of stone. Round, gray, big stones, with loose dirt between them. There were fifteen on the bottom row, and then fourteen, and then sixteen. They weren't all the exact same size."

Jakob narrowed his eyes. "Do you know how many stairs there were?"

"Ten. They went up to a door that was always locked—"

"There were ten stairs? Exactly ten?"

"Yes." As halting as Emma had been before, she spoke fluently now. It was as if Jakob's logic had unlocked a dam inside her. "They were wood and they weren't painted. The settee was covered in fabric that had pink and brown flowers. There were seventeen pink ones and only twelve brown ones. And the coal stove said PERRY on it, in block letters with little rectangles at the ends of the lines. The bedspread had little blue and brown flowers and vines. And the cellar always stank." She was repeating details, but Jakob didn't stop her. "It was like we were inside a privy. It made us stink, too. There were two windows high up, and boxes outside that blocked most of the light in the day, but we could still see." She ran out of breath and looked at him expectedly.

"Like I said before, it seems as if you notice a lot of things, Emma," Jakob said. "You are good with detail." He turned and raised an eyebrow at the jury, and Thayer let him get away with this small commentary. "Do you like numbers?"

"Yes," she said.

"Anything else you want to tell us?"

"There were always boat and train whistles. And the trains went by—they were so near. I kept thinking I could touch them and that we could climb on them and get away." She nodded in Harley's direction but did not look at him. "Always, after the Other Man left, Mr. Harley would come back down with Claire. And he'd give me water to wash with. And he'd—help me. Then he'd leave us alone. I'd wait till Claire was asleep and then I'd hope my father would come." Behind her, the afternoon sunlight revealed small fissures in the white marble wall. "And I'd think all night about Elizabeth's violin. She used to play for us. And I would think about that, and I wouldn't be so frightened."

All heads turned to Elizabeth, who ignored the rustle of attention and kept her gaze trained on Emma.

"Now, I want you to try to recall one more thing," Jakob said. "I want you to tell us something specific about the other man. I know you don't want to think about him. But try, Emma. I know you couldn't see him. But something, maybe, that you didn't need eyes to see?"

She blinked and touched the back of her hand to her mouth, drawing her small knuckles across her lips. "His voice was cold."

"His voice? Cold, you say? I'm going to try a little experiment. Mr. Harley," Jakob said, turning. "Could you please say something to Emma?"

Harley looked up. His gaze darted between Jakob and the judge, who nodded.

"Say something? Like what?" Harley said.

"That will do. Now, Emma, is that the voice you remember?"

"No. The Other Man sounded different."

"Do you think you would recognize this other man's voice if you heard it again?"

Emma's new ease evaporated. "Don't make me see him."

"He's not here. Don't worry. No more questions, Emma."

A shaking Emma was led from the courtroom by the limping bailiff, trailed by Elizabeth, who had risen from William's side and fled after her, her lithe figure crossing paths with Jakob, their fingers touching for a brief moment as he headed toward his seat, though no one noticed, because everyone was watching the small girl who had spent her days and nights counting stairs and steps and stones to the shriek of endless train whistles and dreaming of escape.

Chapter Forty-Two

It was three thirty. The air stifled. The temperature inside the courtroom had reached eighty degrees. Albany was a city of bells, and now a dozen clarions marked the half hour, ringing from all quarters of the city. People shifted in their seats while Thayer tugged at the wilting pleats of his robe. His wig had slipped, and he pushed it up with one finger. Even Jakob seemed limp from the heat.

Farrell's Irish accent turned out to be far less broad when constrained by giving testimony. He chronicled for Hotaling his discovery of the girls and Harley's arrest, which was dramatic enough, but the revelation of the money hidden under Harley's mattress proved even more riveting. But when Jakob coaxed from Farrell a description of a system of bribes enforced not just at the New Scotland address, but also at all bawdy houses in the city, a collective gasp of astonishment rocked the room. A surprised Hotaling scribbled something on a piece of paper and gave it to the bailiff, who limped from the courtroom with it. The district attorney slipped another into his assistant's hands. Thayer raised his eyebrows at Hotaling, who said he had no need to cross-examine.

Darlene Moss's ample figure was contained by a low-necked rose-colored dress, of far more modest cut than the ones she usually wore, but still revealing. She identified herself as a former prostitute and described her conversation with Harley to Hotaling in her usual voluble way. In turn, Jakob extracted an admission from Darlene that she had been dosing Harley with whiskey throughout the night and that he was suffering from a fever during his so-called confession. When she flounced out of the courtroom at the end of her testimony, her unabashed gaze ran over the gallery, causing several men to shrink in their seats.

It was now five o'clock. Long shadows from the elm trees outside fell across the gallery. The bailiff had opened more windows during Darlene's testimony, and bluebottles buzzed the room. Men fanned themselves with hats, women with their gloves, which they had peeled off out of desperation and now flicked back and forth in seizures of overheated agitation. Ordinarily by this time in the evening, a judge would have adjourned the proceedings until the next day, but Dr. Mary Stipp was the final witness for the prosecution, and Thayer agreed with Hotaling that it was in the interest of efficiency to allow him to complete his case in one day.

Mary took the stand with her customary authority in spite of whispers of suspicion and curiosity. Somehow the news of her dismissal from City Hospital had been leaked to Horace Young, and in a sly piece bordering on slander, he raised the question of whether or not she ought to be seeing any patients at all. What cautious respect her wartime service had earned her in the eyes of the general public completely eroded. In the past weeks, the number of patients who came to be treated at the Stipp clinics had dwindled to a handful.

To the gallery, Mary's plain black skirt and white overblouse seemed drab and lifeless compared to Darlene Moss's peacockery. As Mary answered the perfunctory questions of identity, residence, and credentials—she had served as a nurse in the War of the Rebellion, trained as a physician in New York, practiced for fourteen years—her hair, silvered and curling, fell carelessly from its pins around a face that was serious, intent, and wholly unreadable. Hotaling led her through the preliminaries, establishing the close nature of the relationship between the Stipp family and the O'Donnells, the fact that Mary, as both midwife and physician, had delivered both Emma and Claire, the Stipp family's relentless search for the sisters in the aftermath of the blizzard, and their sudden reappearance on their veranda.

"Now let us get to what happened inside your home after they arrived. What did you notice when you brought Emma and Claire inside?"

"Both Emma and Claire were very frightened. They appeared almost to be in a trance. It wasn't until my niece Elizabeth played her violin that they allowed us to take them inside, but they had to be carried. Then they seemed to come to themselves, but when we ran a bath, Emma exhibited extreme modesty. She got into the bath with her nightgown on. She didn't want us to touch or see her. She wouldn't look at us."

"Did you subsequently examine both girls?"

"Yes."

"Can you tell us your findings?"

"Claire exhibited no evidence of physical harm."

"And what of Emma?"

Mary cleared her throat. "Emma's torso was bruised in multiple places: along her right shoulder, bilaterally on her rib cage, along the anterior iliac crests of her pelvis, and on each of the spinous processes. A splinter was embedded in the flesh of the right inner thigh. Several deep scratches had been made on her upper thighs. Her forearms were covered with scratches. Her vaginal opening was swollen, inflamed, dilated." Despite moaning from the gallery, Mary did not stop her clinical recitation. "The general appearance of the vulval tissue spoke to recent and frequent traumatic vaginal penetration by the male organ as evidenced by multiple labial tears, some fresh, and others in the process of scarring. I stitched two of the recent injuries, eleven stitches total. The others, due to abundant blood flow to those tissues, were already healing. All spoke to Emma having been forced into sexual congress against her will."

A dozen men in the gallery averted their gaze as Mary finished. She lifted her chin, daring the district attorney to ask the next question. A breeze stirred the heavy air in the courtroom.

"Did you call for the police after that exam?"

"No."

"Why not?"

"I didn't need to. Officer Farrell instructed me to alert him to any problems. We told him the next day."

"Not immediately?"

"I had given Emma and Claire sleeping medication. I was trying to come to terms with things myself."

"What did Emma tell you of these injuries?"

"That she had been forced to engage in intercourse, and hit when she refused."

"Did she use that language?"

"Of course not. She's a child."

"And what did Claire tell you?"

"Claire has said little of her internment."

"Did you take Emma to another physician for verification of your conclusion?"

"Why would I? Everything was apparent. There was no reason to put her through more scrutiny. A second examination of that sort would have been brutal in her situation."

"Why didn't you ask your husband for verification?"

Mary exhaled, and her eyes showed the slightest flicker of anger. Thayer removed his spectacles and wiped them with the billowing edge of a sleeve of his robe.

"The last thing those girls needed was to be touched by a man, even a man they consider to be their uncle. And my husband does not have experience in the area of female medicine. In these matters, I am the expert. I was a midwife for many years. My mother, Amelia Sutter, is also a midwife. She was with me during the examination. She can corroborate my findings if you need further confirmation."

Hotaling cleared his throat. "A crime of this nature is personal. Might you be more affected by Emma's injuries because of your own vulnerability as a woman—"

"Absolutely not. The rape did not happen to me. It happened to Emma. If I were describing someone's broken arm, would I be rendered inarticulate because I might someday break one myself?"

"Yes, but isn't it possible that your closeness to her clouded your medical judgment, or may have caused you to exaggerate Emma's injuries in any way?"

"I never exaggerate, and I certainly don't have to in this case. The girl was torn and battered. Emma's precarious mental condition after the fact, the multiple wounds of various ages, the fact that she herself described to me her terror, all lead me to state without equivocation that she was raped. The only thing that is saving her is her youth, because tissue in the young renews itself more readily than in an adult. But I have no idea how her heart will fare. I lay the responsibility for that at the feet of the man who raped her."

Only the reporters' scraping of pencil on paper broke the silence as they bent to the task of recording the doctor's statements word for word.

"How often did you say you shared a meal with the O'Donnell family before the blizzard?"

"Weekly. Sometimes more."

"Did conversation around the table include medical talk?"

"Medicine is our life."

"Did it include information regarding sexual congress between men and women?"

"Don't be ridiculous. We are physicians, not pimps."

A frisson of censure rippled through the crowd, but Mary Stipp did not blink.

"On any occasion in your home, could Emma have perhaps overheard something about childbirth and then extrapolated and imagined that she might have been interfered with?"

"Are you mad? No child imagines rape."

"No further questions, Your Honor. Your witness, Mr. Van der Veer."

Jakob leaned over to whisper something to Harley, then rose.

"Dr. Stipp, I would like to speak to your credentials, if I may. Recently, you have been assailed in the newspapers for maintaining a clinic for prostitutes. It has also come to the public's attention that you have been dismissed from the medical rolls of Albany City Hospital for this reason. How can you possibly defend yourself as a physician competent enough to offer testimony in a case of this kind?"

Mary bristled. It took her a moment to begin, and when she did, Jakob sat down, and as Mary talked, he let himself fade into the background.

"When a vagina is penetrated, it never appears the same way again. Especially in children. The average age of menarche is fifteen. Girls' bodies before that are neither capacious nor elastic enough to accommodate the male member." There was a stifled cry from the gallery, which she ignored. "A girl of this age is always physically wounded during the act; any intrusion causes labial and vaginal tears. And may I point out that any so-called desire of a prepubescent girl is a phantom of men's imaginations, because no one—and certainly not a girl of ten years of age—would ever consent to being so damaged. In addition, because of that private clinic treating prostitutes, I weekly see evidence of the same constellation of injuries in grown women who have been abused.

"I have also from time to time come across young girls with a certain type of vigilant and withdrawn demeanor, like Emma's. These are children of good homes and families. I then discover that they have been raped." She folded her hands and looked at the jury. "Raped. So you see, I am better acquainted than most anyone in the city with the effect of rape on female genitalia."

There was a long silence.

Jakob finally rose and said, "The defense concedes that Dr. Stipp is an expert witness, more than qualified to speak to this issue. In fact, it appears that she might be one of the premier physicians of Albany. We would all do well to remember that."

Thayer let this commentary go, too. He was no fan of libel.

"Dr. Stipp," Jakob said, "I have one other concern to address before we get to the salient point. Do you consider it a conflict of interest to have treated both the victim and the alleged perpetrator of said incident?"

"I recused myself from Mr. Harley's care as soon as I learned that he was a suspect in Emma's case. I did not, however, recuse myself from caring for Emma, because I trust no one but myself."

"Can you tell us about how you came to do surgery on Mr. Harley?"

"Directly upon learning that a flood was imminent my husband, William Stipp, and I went to City Hospital to treat any victims that might arise. We worked through the night. Toward morning, Mr. Harley was brought in."

"Can you describe for us Mr. Harley's injury?"

"He had suffered a sharp cut on the back of his neck, slightly curved, deeper toward his right side. The skin was completely broken, the trapezius muscle on the right side of his neck severely contused. The sternocleidomastoid, too. Had the blow been made with more force or a sharper object, both muscles could have been severed, and his spinal cord ruptured."

"Could the blade of a shovel have made such an injury?"

"The outline of the wound perfectly matches the side of a shovel blade."

"Thank you. Now, can you describe the conversations that you had with Emma and Claire regarding the number of men involved in assaulting Emma?"

"On several different occasions, Emma and Claire described two men. They called them the Man and the Other Man. It soon became clear to me that the one she referred to as the Man was Mr. Harley. The matching wound is enough to confirm his identity. She said that Mr. Harley never assaulted her. She said it was the Other Man who had raped her."

"Did Emma ever say who the Other Man was?"

"No."

"I have no further questions for now, but reserve the right to recall Dr. Stipp at a future time."

"Redirect?" Thayer said, almost as a dare.

And Hotaling took it.

"In your experience as a physician, would you say that it's possible for a young girl to imagine things that did not in fact occur?"

A light breeze blew through the open windows, carrying with it more flies. Mary pushed aside an errant curl. "I believe her."

"I'll ask it another way. You are a physician, and it is to your rational expertise that I apply. Do children in distress sometimes make up fantastical tales to remove themselves from a present, difficult occurrence? Say, imagining themselves somewhere else in order to mitigate an oppressive incident, like a rape?"

The color drained from Mary's face. "Sometimes. Yes."

"And if that is the case, isn't it possible that Emma may have protected herself in other ways? Say, disbelieving what was directly in front of her because it was too difficult to accept the reality of her situation?"

"Emma is a bright girl."

"But you are a physician experienced with battlefield cripples, are you not? In the war, weren't there men after a battle who did not remember the particulars of how they were hurt? Or where? What is it that you doctors call that?"

Mary swallowed, discerning the direction of his inquiry, as did the entire courtroom, many of whom shifted in their seats, sensing the battle to come. A moment ago, there had been a general stirring, as if everyone were eager to be out. Now, though, all thoughts of departure had been abandoned. It was stifling in the room. Jury members, some of whom had shown signs of nodding off in the heat, now mopped their sweaty faces with already damp handkerchiefs and leaned in.

"I don't think that is relevant here," Mary said.

"Come now, Dr. Stipp. I didn't ask your opinion of relevance. I asked you to reveal a well-known affliction. Many of our veterans suffer from it." He turned. "I could ask the gallery to name it. Everyone knows it."

"You are trying to make an implication that I believe is unjustified in this instance."

"Perhaps this display of stubbornness on your part is what your colleagues objected to at City Hospital." Until now, Hotaling had kept his face professionally impassive, his tone respectful. But now he allowed a sneer of contempt to drift in, prompting a tittering in the gallery.

Mary shot a fiery look of defiance at the district attorney. "What my colleagues objected to was mercy, Mr. Hotaling. To unprejudiced medical care delivered to needy women who have been denied even the most elemental care—"

Thayer groaned. He was leaning back in his seat, his head thrown backward in disgust. He slapped his hands on his bench and drew himself forward, his face a shade of pale crimson in the afternoon heat. "Stop this nonsense, Mr. Hotaling. You are arguing with your witness. And, Dr. Stipp, if the district attorney asks you a question, you are to answer it or you will be held in contempt. Is that clear? To both of you?"

Mary shut her eyes and appeared to falter as she reached into her reticule for a handkerchief. Her cheeks had turned a high, hot pink, though it was unclear whether the coloring was from fury or the closeness of the room. But it was very apparent that she understood that Hotaling had goaded her into an outburst.

"Soldier's heart," Mary said, in a tight voice.

"Ah," Hotaling crooned. "Such a poetic term, is it not? And please enlighten us. What exactly does it mean?"

"It describes a nervous state of being, a kind of separation from reality, a skittishness."

"I see. A separation from reality." Hotaling paused and turned, nodding to the jury as he leaned nonchalantly onto the railing of the witness stand. "Could you equate the recent event in Emma's life to the same kind of difficulties that soldiers suffered in battles?"

She swallowed. "One could, yes. But—"

"So, if a grown man could be confused about what exactly happened in a difficult situation, might not a young girl?"

"Emma's situation differs in that while she was battered, she exhibited little to no signs of mental derangement other than exhaustion. And every day she improves. Only a soldier who does not improve is said to be suffering soldier's heart."

"You were in seclusion when Emma testified, but it may surprise you that not only did she try to leave the courtroom, but she wept a great deal."

Mary drew herself up. "Weeping is a normal, healthy reaction to intolerable events. I believe that if you had been raped, you too would weep, Mr. Hotaling." She ignored the quick inhalations of breath, the reverberations of staggered disbelief. Someone in the gallery blurted, *A man, raped? Nonsense.*

"Enough!" Thayer roared. "Ask a question, Mr. Hotaling. And the rest of you are to silence yourselves or I will muzzle every last one of you."

"Then I repeat my earlier question," Hotaling said, "which I would like to point out, with all due respect, Your Honor, that the doctor refused to answer. Dr. Stipp, if a grown man could be confused about what exactly happened in a difficult situation, might not a young girl?"

"Of course, it's possible, but—"

"Even when grounded in all other particulars, say for instance, where it happened, or even other minuscule details?"

"Often minuscule details, but—"

"Thank you. That will be all. The prosecution rests, Your Honor."

Mary did not at first rise when she was dismissed. Even as Judge Thayer hammered his gavel and declared the court in recess until nine o'clock the following morning, she remained stolidly in place. She turned to watch the jury filing out of their enclosure, their sidelong glances expressing a chary disdain that she had not detected earlier when she had taken the stand. Even Harmon Pumpelly allowed himself the indiscipline of raising his eyebrows at her. Hotaling had succeeded in baiting her, as had the hospital committee, taking easy aim at her deepest passions. What a fool she had been to let them.

And to what purpose was Hotaling working? To make a case that a distressed Emma could not possibly tell the difference between one man and two. Hotaling didn't want the truth. He wanted *his* truth, which was a far simpler thing to prove.

And it seemed he was even willing to jeopardize his entire case. For why wouldn't the jury then disbelieve Emma about everything? Would they even convict Harley of rape? Even after Jakob's concession that a rape had occurred? Would they declare Harley not guilty and would a defeated Hotaling then refuse to search for the real culprit?

After Emma had testified, Elizabeth had whisked her away. Mary had not even seen her or had word of Emma's demeanor on the stand. The information that Emma had tried to run away had come as a shock.

From the gallery people were throwing surreptitious glances her way as they shuffled out the door. Now freed of Thayer's censuring gavel, snippets of their conversations floated toward her. *A woman who talks like that in public? Can't even tell the difference between imagination and reality when a child tells a tale? Thinks so much of herself she doesn't even ask her husband for help?*

And, *That Harley's obviously as guilty as Satan.*

Jakob and Hotaling were stooping over their desks and shoving papers into carrying cases. Hotaling finished first and left without a word.

"Tomorrow," Jakob said to Mary, then tucked his case under one arm and acknowledged William with a crisp salute and disappeared into the vanishing gallery.

William and Mary waited to leave until everyone had cleared the courtroom and the clerk was surveying the pews for lost belongings. They exited by the side door and went into the witnesses' room and retrieved Elizabeth and an exhausted Emma. Then they went out to the street via the back door, where Harold awaited them on Maiden Lane with the carriage.

Unnoticed by anyone, Gerritt Van der Veer, having left the courtroom earlier with the crowd, drew back behind one of the stately oaks on the courtyard grounds, a workman's cloth cap slung low over his forehead, a pair of smoked spectacles hiding his eyes.

Chapter Forty-Three

EXTRA

WHO IS THE OTHER MAN?
PROSECUTOR BADGERS
EMMA O'DONNELL
THE BRAZEN FEMALE DOCTOR MARY STIPP
LECTURES JURY THEN IS PUT IN HER PLACE
DEFENSE CLAIMS SO-CALLED
OTHER MAN RESPONSIBLE

The newspapers had produced, within an hour of the end of the day's proceedings, a riot of Extra Editions that made their way into the ravenous hands of the city's occupants, who devoured them with their evening meals, reading aloud to their families and arguing over whether or not James Harley was the true attacker. One of those readers was Gerritt Van der Veer, who tossed aside his copy of the *Argus* without reading past the headlines. Jakob studied his father from across the dinner table. Only he and Gerritt were at table tonight. Viola and her maid had disappeared earlier that morning. The cowering staff claimed ignorance of her whereabouts, and none could make eye contact with Gerritt. The staff reported that at one o'clock that afternoon Mrs. Van der Veer had called for a hack and into it had packed a trunk, her maid, and herself, then driven off to an unknown destination. After every servant echoed this story, the cook asked whether Mr. Van der Veer wanted dinner served in the dining room at eight, as usual? Mrs. Van der Veer had arranged for roast lamb.

Now Gerritt pushed a dollop of mint jelly around his plate. "You know where your mother is, don't you, Jakob?"

Jakob pushed back from the table. He'd torn into his meat, and now it sat in his stomach like a stone. The afternoon had been an agony of concentration. "Mother has a mind of her own."

"She never did before. She's still furious about that black eye I gave her when she got back from that unannounced trip to Manhattan City."

Jakob had found Viola hysterical, locked in her bedroom, holding a wet cloth to a red welt below her left eye. It had taken all Jakob's self-control to rein in his fury. Then hours and hours to help his mother to formulate a plan.

Jakob reached for the decanter of wine, poured himself a glassful, and downed the burgundy, wrinkling his nose at the sour taste after the sweetness of the jelly. "You ought not to hit your wife, Father. Then perhaps she won't leave you."

Gerritt had gotten up from his chair and was pacing, practically trotting from one side of the dining room to the other. At any other time, he would have sharply rebuked Jakob for that remark. Instead he said, "I'll find her."

"Why? You don't love her."

This, too, elicited none of his father's usual rage. "It's not a question of love."

"You said you would free her if I defended Harley. You readily agreed. What does it matter to you where she is?"

"It's about control, Jakob. I can't have my wife flittering off like a lightning bug whenever the notion comes to her. If you know where she is, then return her to me. And I think I made it clear that her freedom was contingent upon you winning. Now, tell me how you think you are going to save Harley after such a poor performance today?"

Jakob put down his knife. "You were there?"

"Yes, in my best laborer's costume. I must say that it was a pleasure to go incognito. No one recognized me."

"Then you know that my saving Harley rests on the fact of finding the man who actually raped Emma."

"Possibly."

"How possibly?"

Gerritt contemplated Jakob over the long expanse of table, littered now with their half-finished meal and guttering candles. "It's an odd thing to have to be a detective, isn't it, in order to save a man from prison? But in this case, of course, your only edict is to save Harley. Cast doubt on him as the perpetrator. There is no need to point any specific fingers, no need to make another man's life miserable. If you are successful in proving that another man is the rapist, then you are in effect condemning that man to prison, aren't you? Provided, of course, that he is brought to justice. But that would be a criminal undertaking, wouldn't it? The Albany Penitentiary is a cesspool. No man belongs there. By saving one man, you in effect save two if you are skillful enough to save Harley without ruining another man's life in the bargain. And as long as you save Harley, you will have fulfilled your promise to me and earned your mother's freedom. Isn't that all you wanted in the end? Her freedom?"

"Yes, but it seems Mother has earned her own without any help from me."

"I doubt that, Jakob."

"I thought by now that you would have learned not to underestimate women. Or your son."

"Then you have already reached your goal."

"Perhaps."

"I know who you are, Jakob. I know you will act in the best interest of this family."

"Yes, Father. You have my word on that."

Gerritt eyed Jakob through heavily lidded eyes. "Shame about Captain Mantel and all those bribes. Did you know he was taking money under the table like that?"

"I think it was a shock to everyone."

"You've already perfected the lawyer's tool of deflection, I see. What do you know about it?"

"That was Farrell's thing. I think he was tired of being the captain's shill."

"You don't seem to mind being mine."

Jakob smiled evenly.

"But don't Captain Mantel's actions call into question everything he does? In certain circles it's known he has a taste for young girls."

Jakob said, "I thought you favored not pointing fingers."

"Fine. We can talk about Van der Veer Lumber. The new office is finished. Good profits, despite the flood." Gerritt lifted his eyebrows. "And you'll be glad to know that we saved the safe and I've put the books back."

"Glad to hear it. Good night, Father."

Later, in his study, Gerritt proceeded to slowly empty his decanter of Scotch. He had flung open a window overlooking State Street. They were out there, the Stipps and the O'Donnell sisters, across the verdant blackness of the park. This unimaginable rift with Jakob and Viola was their fault. But for the blizzard, none of this would have happened. He should never have gone to the cemetery for their funeral. If he hadn't, the two families' lives would not now be entangled and all would be as before. He paced back and forth before his fireplace. A breeze riffled the scattered papers on his desk. He stopped midpace and took another swallow of Scotch. The alcohol burned. Why was Jakob forcing the issue? His sole job had been to defend Harley. Emma had been his gift to Jakob, a high-profile case meant to catapult him out of lumber and into the dirty business of justice, as Jakob had wanted. It was a father's task to aid his son, as it was a son's task to aid his father. But the ungrateful boy would tell him nothing. Over the last eight weeks, Jakob had revealed not one iota of his strategy, plans, or evidence, not even the identity of his witnesses. He had all but disappeared from the house, too, though Gerritt had heard that he had been frequenting the State Library, using it as an office in lieu of a comfortable perch in his own home. Over the past weeks, the boy had rarely returned in the evening until long after the sky had faded into that twilit gray of late spring. On the few occasions Jakob had deigned to return early, he had sequestered himself with his mother, who'd also deserted Gerritt, taking her meals in her bedroom. Jakob, Gerritt had learned, had been taking most of his at Jacob Morgan's restaurant on State Street, hunched over midday and evening bowls of soup like an ill-paid clerk or secretary.

And Viola. God. That churlish woman.

Since Viola had returned from that little trip of hers, he'd become a ghost in his own house, relegated to dining alone or at his club, sending messages back and forth to her through the servants, who tiptoed through the house uttering one-word answers to his inquiries about whether she had gone out (yes), and where (a shrug). She had left him—at least in any way that mattered—and though he'd long ago left her, Viola's defection battered his general sense of dominion. Nothing, not even his shameful loss of control when she returned from that jaunt with Mary Stipp, had moved her. She was simply indifferent to request or provocation. For incomprehensible reasons, recently she had instituted a standing quarterly order for new dolls to be sent to her from some shop in Manhattan City. He'd been there with her once. That overheated and perfumed box was located somewhere on Broadway near Union Square. Damned expensive things, those dolls were, too. French, Viola said. Special. She had bushel barrels of them. Thirty, forty, he didn't know. He'd indulged her. She kept them locked and private in that cell of hers upstairs, and he doubted she ever even looked at them after she'd enshrined them behind glass.

And where was she now? It was a relief not to have to suffer her tonight, but she'd left without his permission. He ought to feel well rid of her, but there was something about having her, even hiding in that bedroom of hers, that allayed his unease, much as he didn't like to acknowledge it. He preferred to couch it in terms that most men would understand. *Control.* Task one when the trial was finished was to find her, if only to appease his sense of self. He wandered upstairs with his highball glass newly refilled, the liquor sloshing over the glass rim as he pushed open the door into Viola's room. The air was cold and dark, the windows shut against the night. He felt his way to her bed, half expecting to discover her asleep. His eyes adjusted a little to the darkness, and he sat down, his head bleary with alcohol. His rage had exhausted him. He lay back on the cool pillows, letting his arm extend over the edge of the bed. His eyes fluttered shut. He felt the highball slip from his grasp, heard the dull thud of the tumbler hitting the carpet, even imagined the slow wash of Scotch flooding its fibers, all without noticing the glass eyes of a curio cabinet full of staring dolls.

Across the park, Mary and William were again sitting up the night in Claire and Emma's room, something they had not done since the first few nights of the girls' return. All evening, William had bolstered an exhausted Emma with reassurance. She had grown confused under Hotaling's deliberate diversion of the truth, as had half the courtroom and probably even the jury. It had taken great effort to convince Emma that she had done well. Now it was late evening and he and Mary were huddled under blankets in a pair of chairs, watching Emma and Claire sleep. It was the first moment they'd had to speak privately, though throughout dinner and afterward they had sought out one another's gaze repeatedly. In the hallway, Elizabeth was playing a Brahms lullaby. Every night Elizabeth lulled the girls to sleep with the hypnotizing strains of Brahms.

Mary and William whispered under the soft tones of the music.

"Thank God for Jakob," William said. "Another defense attorney would have torn Emma to shreds."

"She did well, yes?" Mary said. "As well as you told her she did? Why did Hotaling say she'd tried to leave the courtroom?"

"That was infuriating. Emma thought she had been dismissed, so she was just coming to see Elizabeth and me. I think Hotaling told you that just to see what you would do."

"What is the matter with that man?"

"He wants to win."

The window was open and the abrupt hoot of an owl sounded above the girls' shallow breathing. The park harbored one or two during the summer months, when mice overran the open ground.

Mary said, "I think I derailed everything."

"Anyone with a child knows that children imagine themselves somewhere else all the time. It's the joy of childhood. We're on a pirate ship! We're in a palace! Hotaling knows that, too. He just made it sound as if she were out of her mind. His is a dangerous game."

"I'm worried, William. If nothing comes of this trial, if Harley is freed and—"

"It's the same outcome anyway, Mary, no matter what happens or what you said today. The girls can't stay here in Albany after the trial. They'll be the object of curiosity and rumor for the rest of their lives if they do."

"But where will we go?"

"I haven't any idea."

Uncle William's and Aunt Mary's voices whispered through the gentle strains of violin and Emma's half-sleep, but Emma wasn't listening to what they were saying. She liked having them there. Somehow they always knew when she needed them and what she needed them to do. She hadn't even had to ask them to stay with them tonight. After dinner, Uncle William had carried in the extra chair and blankets and then Aunt Mary had read to them and tucked them in and now they were sitting with them as the sky grew dark.

Earlier, in the courtroom, when everyone was staring at her, Emma had kept a running count. Two eyes for each person. Two; two four; two four six; two four six eight. It was a way to distract herself from paying attention to what she was having to say in front of everyone. Elizabeth and Uncle William had said to look at them, and she had, but it was better to count. It ordered her mind. Two four six eight ten. She hadn't been able to count them all. She couldn't see everyone. And there had been the moments when she could see nothing.

Of course, she had lied to them all. She knew exactly how many times the Other Man had come. *Eleven.* She knew exactly how many days she and Claire had been inside that cellar. *Forty-two.* She knew exactly how many times she'd begged to go home. *One hundred five.*

She knew how much she missed her mother and father, too, but that was too much love to count.

She didn't tell what she knew because she was embarrassed that she couldn't describe what the Other Man looked like. It seemed ridiculous that she couldn't tell them that. They all wanted to know. But it had been dark. Not even a candle. All she could remember was that voice. That cold clutch of pain.

In the witnesses' room, after Emma had testified, Elizabeth had stayed with her until they could leave. Elizabeth hummed to her because she didn't have her violin. She said it was one of Mozart's numbered concertos. Prolific composers almost always use numbers, Elizabeth explained, instead of names to title their pieces of music, for two reasons. One, because they write so many that it would be impossible to come up with names, and two, because music is a matter of count: 3/4 time; 7/8 time. So, Piano Concerto Nos. 1, 2, 3. Violin Concerto Nos. 21, 22, 23. Symphonies Nos. 1 through 9.

That's why music lasts forever, Elizabeth said. That's why we remember it. It's about time. It's about eternity.

Now Emma decided that if enough days passed from when she and Claire had gotten free to when she felt safe again, she was going to compose a piece of music and name it after the number of days it had taken her to stop being afraid.

But right now she would have to name it the Eternity Concerto, because she couldn't imagine a time when she wouldn't be afraid. On that cliff on Cape Cod with Uncle William, there had been a glimmer of possibility, but it hadn't lasted.

Through Claire's quiet breathing and Elizabeth's playing, Emma could hear Uncle William and Aunt Mary discussing something about her, but she had already given sleep permission to soften the edges of her world.

The next morning at 7:00 a.m. Gerritt Van der Veer awoke to a fresh-faced maid kneeling beside the bed, gathering the broken shards of the highball glass.

"Beg your pardon, sir. There's a man at the door for you."

"Who is it?"

"Don't know," she said, rising.

"Send him away."

"He won't go."

"Well, have whoever it is meet me in my study."

"He won't come in, sir."

Gerritt wiped a line of drool from his beard, straightened his wrinkled vest and crumpled shirt, combed a hand over his bald pate, and stumbled down the stairs, holding a hand to his head to try to subdue the crippling headache shooting flashing stars across his vision. It took a long moment to recognize the bailiff from the previous day, even after the man identified himself. He wore not his uniform but a lumpy tweed jacket, twill work pants, and a rough, high-collar shirt with a narrow string tie. Around his waist he had holstered a Colt, and from a ring dangled a pair of nippers. From the shadows at the side of the door, a young policeman emerged. Dark circles under his eyes suggested that he'd been up all night.

"Are you Gerritt Van der Veer?"

"What of it?"

"You are under court order to come with us now." The policeman presented Gerritt with a subpoena.

"Holy hell," Gerritt said and tried to shove the door shut, but the young policeman put out a hand and stopped him.

"Jakob!" But Gerritt's bellowing did not summon his son. "Holy hell, what is this for?"

"Can't say."

"For God's sake, at least allow me a chance to clean up," he said, managing to get hold of a cap hanging from a hook.

"Sorry, sir," the bailiff said. "I can't."

Chapter Forty-Four

"Dr. Stipp, can you describe for me what occurred at your home on Thursday, the eighth of May?"

Jakob Van der Veer had recalled Mary Stipp to the stand as his first witness for the defense. It was nine o'clock, and the courtroom overflowed again. Outside, barred onlookers required a near cavalry troop to control them, and occasionally shouts of *Free Harley!* and *She's of age!* penetrated the courtroom.

Jakob stood at his defense table, one hand resting on a wooden crate. He'd not slept except for a few fitful hours before dawn. When the bailiff had come for his father, Jakob had not answered his father's fury. He'd gone to the window, watched them cart him away, and then dressed in a new frock coat and gone down to the Delavan House to visit his mother. She had taken a corner room under her maiden name of Van Wyck and hidden herself away with her maid, who ferried meals upstairs from the dining room so that she wouldn't be seen. His mother had already dressed for the day in a sunny-yellow frock and a matching hat, a disguise of optimism. He took the wooden crate she had hidden for him and tucked its bulky weight under one arm.

Viola touched his elbow the way she used to when he was younger. "I'm frightened, Jakob."

He had kissed her on her cheek, unwilling to tell her that he was frightened, too. For both of them, after today nothing would ever be the same. There ought to have been hope in that statement, and maybe there was, but it was still all before them and everything depended on him.

"Do you know where to go?" Jakob said.

"I do."

"All right, then. I'll see you later."

Now, in the courtroom, as Jakob awaited Mary Stipp's answer, he fought to keep his gaze on her and not look again at Elizabeth, who sat as she had yesterday directly behind Hotaling. He wished he could banish the look of distress that enveloped her. Yesterday when their hands had briefly touched, he'd wanted to believe that the gesture had been deliberate on her part. It had been on his.

Mary said, "On May eighth, you had come to our home to question Emma, and while you were there, a pair of dolls was delivered to our home, addressed to Emma and Claire."

Had he eaten this morning? Jakob couldn't remember, but now he tamped down a swell of nausea and touched his hand to the wooden crate. "Is this the crate they came in?"

"Yes."

Jakob made a show of opening the case and withdrawing the dolls, much as William had done that day in the Stipps' parlor when they were delivered. Jakob held them up for the crowd and the jury to see. That day at the Stipps', they had given him permission to take the dolls with him and he had hidden them under his bed until his mother had taken them with her to the Delavan yesterday. "Are these they?" he asked Mary.

"They are."

He carried the dolls to the prosecution table and gave them to Hotaling, who held them at arm's length.

"Objection," Hotaling said. "These dolls were not collected by a policeman. Provenance cannot be authenticated."

"Will both counselors approach the bench, please?" Thayer said. Thayer narrowed his eyes as he tapped the end of a pencil on his desk. This morning, his face wore a haggard look of concentration. Earlier, Jakob had heard Thayer ask the bailiff to replenish his tea at regular intervals.

"Mr. Van der Veer," Thayer said. "How did you come to be in possession of these artifacts?"

"I took them from the Stipps' home that day. I recognized them—at least, their type—and believed them relevant for reasons that will soon become clear. I kept them hidden in my home until I could present them here today."

"Why was I never told about them?" Hotaling said.

No defense attorney needed to provide the prosecution any evidence unless they asked for it, and Hotaling hadn't, a point of procedure that Hotaling was well aware of. Jakob began to explain for the record, but the judge was already waving his hand in approval. Hotaling exhaled loudly and turned on his heel, making for the prosecution table in disgust.

Ignoring him, Jakob said, "Dr. Stipp, can you please describe these dolls?"

"I know very little about them except that they are from a French manufacturer named Jumeau. Your mother knows far more than I do. What I do know is that they are very expensive and very rare."

"Do you know who sent them to Emma and Claire?"

"I do not. There was a note included, but it wasn't signed."

"And what did the note say?"

"*Do you miss me?*"

Jakob had not expected the same dread from the gallery as had hit both him and the Stipps, but the polite silence that greeted Mary Stipp's answer unnerved him. He retrieved the card from his desk and showed it to her. "Is this the note?"

"Yes."

"What did you understand its meaning to be?"

"I thought it was sinister. Emma told me that the man who raped her told her that she would miss him."

"And you believed this note was a direct reference to that?"

"I did and do still."

"What did you do after you received the note and dolls?"

"The trial wasn't to begin for more than a month, so my husband, mother, and niece took Emma and Claire away. We were worried that the person who had sent it might mean them harm. I, however, did not accompany them. I stayed behind to care for our patients. Then, one day I went to Manhattan City to see about the dolls."

"Which day?"

"May twelfth."

"And with whom did you undertake this trip?"

"With your mother, Viola Van der Veer."

"Objection." Hotaling shot to his feet "Does the defense lawyer regularly use his mother as a private detective?"

"Your Honor," Jakob said. "Neither Dr. Stipp nor my mother alerted me to their journey before it was undertaken, but as you will soon learn, their trip uncovered a fascinating turn of events."

"It had better be fascinating," Thayer said.

Jakob preferred the more alert Thayer to this exhausted, scolding shell. It was ten thirty-five. Morning shadows still cooled the courtroom, but the bailiff was heaving open the windows anyway, hoping to preempt the noontime swelter. A sleek crow squawked in protest from the branch of the majestic elm tree across the street as angry wrens in the upper branches scolded the interloper. The jury hunched in their places. It was these men Jakob would have to convince of everything he believed to be true, which in this moment was also everything he feared to be true.

"Now then, Dr. Stipp," Jakob said. "Why did you and Mrs. Van der Veer both go to Manhattan City, and what did you discover there?"

"As I said, Mrs. Van der Veer collects Jumeau dolls. No one in Albany sells them. She knew of just one store that did, in Manhattan City, where she purchases hers. The store is Arnold Constable's, near Union Square. It was logical to assume that the same shop may have sold the dolls to whomever had sent them to Emma. So we went. Mrs. Van der Veer is well known there. She asked them whether or not they would look through their receipts to see who had sent the dolls, and because of who she is, they obliged her. It did not take them long to find the bill of sale in their records. It was from late April of this year, purchased via mail, paid in cash."

Jakob went to his table and fished in his case for the slip of yellow paper that Mary and his mother had given him the night they had returned from Manhattan City. He showed it now first to Hotaling, then to the judge, then to the jury, then to Mary. "Is this that bill of sale?"

"Yes."

"And who does it say was the purchaser?"

"Captain Arthur Mantel."

Hotaling shot to his feet. "Objection. This witness is not on the list the defense attorney delivered to us."

"Viola Van der Veer will address the issue of authentication," Jakob said. Hotaling sighed and sat down again.

To those few in the gallery who had never encountered Gerritt Van der Veer's wife, she appeared on first assessment to be diminutive and self-conscious. However, to the many who knew her, she carried herself with far more self-possession than usual. The pleated silk of her dress gathered in cascades of folds in a modest bustle and drew envious glances from every woman in the room. Her doll-like face lacked the unsettled fear that usually characterized her, too, and her voice, though hushed, carried a new note of determination during the particulars of residence and identification. Viola, like Emma, was barely visible from the back of the room when she took the stand, but her tall, elaborately decorated hat gave the latecomers occupying those rows a focal point.

"Can you tell the court how many Jumeau dolls you own?"

"Fifty."

A loud murmur greeted this pronouncement, and Viola hastily added, "They are not playthings. These are collector items."

"Can you tell us, is one more exceptional than all the others?"

"Yes. One of the ones that you have there on your table. She was released in Paris earlier this year. I own one of the very few of that type sent to the United States. That is another," she said, nodding toward the dolls.

"Can you describe her particulars to us, please?"

"She was designed by a famous French sculptor named Carrier-Belleuse. What distinguishes this doll from others is the remarkable detail of her porcelain face, which appears very human, and the expressive beauty of the glass paperweight eyes."

"Paperweight?"

"They open and close with the movement of the doll. She has an eight-ball body, made of wood, which means that she can be put into various positions when held up by a stand. It makes her appear more lifelike. As you can see, her dress is stunning. It's made of rose silk, with exquisite pleating and Belgian lace and fine ruffles. The detailing is as subtle and cultured as the most expensive ball gown. Her hair is human. Her hat is finished with a white plume that mimics an egret's. Baroque pearls close the shoe tabs. The hat, dress, and shoes are all made of the same rose silk."

Her voice had taken on a serious, educated tone, as if she were describing the various physical attributes of a prize horse. The men in the audience stirred with interest, responding to the unspooling details, recognizing expertise when they heard it.

Jakob held up a second receipt. "Is this your bill of sale?"

"Yes."

"And how much did this doll cost?"

Viola hesitated before saying, "Thirty dollars."

Everyone in the room gasped. It would take most people half a year to make that sum, and few could spare that to buy something as frivolous as a doll. A laborer might make fifty cents a day if he was well paid, and far less if he was not, which included most everyone.

"Who knows that you have this collection?"

Viola lifted her chin. "My maids and a few acquaintances, the few people I invite to see them. Most of the women I am acquainted with would not understand my interest. So I am careful not to throw my pearls before swine."

Everyone registered the covert dig, including several Pruyn women, who had hidden themselves beside their husbands in an effort to remain inconspicuous.

"And in the family?"

"Oh, yes, everyone knows."

"Including your husband?"

"Yes."

"Tell us what happened to you when you returned from your trip to Manhattan City, Mother."

Viola locked her hands together on her lap, her white gloves taut against her knuckles, one thumb moving rapidly against the other. Something like shame flashed across her face as she hesitated a moment before saying, "Gerritt hit me."

Shock rippled through the courtroom as spectators jostled one another to get a look at her. While it was a common sight in Albany for women to be cuffed in the tenements and alleyways of the city, intimate violence was not supposed to happen in the homes of higher society.

"Where did he hit you?"

"On my right eye."

"Did you suffer any injury?"

"Yes. Bruising and a deep cut."

"That will be all. Thank you, Mother."

Judge Thayer's voice, husky with concern, carried over the now silent courtroom. "Mr. Hotaling?"

Taken aback by Viola's revelation, Hotaling leaned back in his chair and made a tent of his fingers. "Mrs. Van der Veer. Are you at all estranged from your husband?"

"We've been married for many years. My husband has many business concerns that keep him from the house. He is often gone from dawn until long after dark."

"Do you resent these absences?"

"On the contrary. I find the freedom refreshing."

A round of strangled titters fluttered through the gallery.

Hotaling sighed. "No further questions."

On the stand, a red-faced Arthur Mantel, subpoenaed yesterday afternoon from his office at the precinct house and held overnight in a jail cell pending charges of accepting bribes, glowered at the whispering gallery, reserving his fiercest hatred for Jakob, who stood to one side of the witness stand. Mantel was holding himself very rigid. After the usual establishing questions, Jakob showed Mantel the receipt for the purchase of the dolls sent to the Stipp house.

Uncomprehending, Mantel shook his head. "I don't understand."

"You've never seen this before?"

"No. What is Arthur Constable?"

"This is the receipt for the purchase of two dolls sent to Emma and Claire O'Donnell. And that is your name, listed as purchaser. The date is April twenty-sixth." Jakob went to the jury box to retrieve the dolls, which the jurors had been passing among them, and gave them to Mantel, who also held them at arm's length.

"Did you send a request to purchase those dolls and send them to Emma and Claire?"

His face took on the bewildered affect of someone who believes he is being tricked. "No. Of course not."

"Then how did your name come to be listed there?"

"I have no idea."

"How can you account, then, for the fact that your name is listed as the purchaser?"

"I can't." He shifted uncomfortably in his seat and laid one doll in his lap so that he could pull at the high-buttoned collar of his jacket.

"Perhaps you purchased those dolls as a proxy for someone else?"

A flare of indignation mottled the skin of his face. "I did not."

"Say, for instance, James Harley?"

"Absolutely not. I am not an errand boy for suspected felons. And besides, no transactions of that type would ever occur in our jail. The jailer reads every letter that goes in or out."

"Perhaps you allowed someone else to use your name?"

Mantel waved his hand in dismissal at such a ridiculous suggestion. "I did not."

"Perhaps you sent those dolls to the girls as an apology for abandoning your search for them?"

"Don't be absurd."

"Tell us, why did you abandon that search?"

Mantel glared at Jakob. "Do you go looking for ghosts?"

"You understand, Captain, that you are under oath."

"Listen. We looked. We couldn't find them. And I have never seen those dolls. I did not send them. How many times do I have to say that?"

"Perhaps you are being literal? Did you have the store send them?"

Mantel's round face flushed a deep crimson. He leaned over and laid both dolls at his feet and jabbed his finger at Jakob. His voice came out in a hiss. "Let me be clear. I had nothing to do with those dolls. At all. I'd never even heard of them till this moment."

"Perhaps you would like to know that there was a note. It read, *Do you miss me?*" Mantel startled as Jakob pushed on. "Maybe you have business dealings with someone who may have had reason to send them? Or maybe you're repaying the debt of a bribe?"

"Objection," Hotaling said, leaping to his feet, his confusion apparent. "Leading questions. This is harassment and innuendo and conjecture. There is no prior basis for this testimony."

"Sustained," Thayer said. "Mr. Van der Veer, you will restrict your questions to fact and only fact. You have not established Captain Mantel as a hostile witness, and he certainly doesn't appear to be one to me. And if you cannot establish that Mantel purchased the dolls, then move on to something you can prove."

Jakob turned away. "I'll ask one final question. Captain Mantel, do you know who sent the dolls?"

Mantel exhibited only the slightest flicker of indecision. "No."

"Let me ask another: Perhaps you suspect who may have sent them?" Jakob said.

Hotaling sighed, not even rising to his feet. "Objection. Suspicion is not fact."

"Sustained."

"Forgive me, Captain," Jakob said. "I do have just a few more questions for you. Would you please tell the court where you spent last night?"

Mantel's face flushed a deep crimson. "You know where. In jail."

"Yes, that's right," Jakob said. "In jail. Now, Captain, are you aware that yesterday one of your police officers testified that you are taking bribes from whorehouses?"

"I was not aware," he said.

"Are you taking bribes?"

"That is a scurrilous charge and wholly unsubstantiated."

"Your witness, Mr. Hotaling."

Hotaling tapped his fingers on his desk, eyeing Jakob out of the corner of one eye before saying, "How long have you been a police captain in Albany, Captain Mantel?"

"Twenty years."

"Until this moment, have you ever been suspected of committing a crime?"

"No."

"Is purchasing dolls a crime?"

"No."

"Is writing cryptic notes a crime?"

"No."

"Is forging someone else's name on a document a crime?"

"Yes."

"And bribing a police officer? Is that a crime?"

"I don't know what you're talking about."

"Thank you," Hotaling said. "That will be all."

"Mr. Van der Veer? Any cross?"

Jakob said, coolly at ease. "Not at this time, Your Honor. He may be dismissed."

"Captain Mantel, you are released on your own recognizance. I trust that you will answer any and all summonses from this court? And that you will remain in the courthouse should you need to be called again?"

Mantel gave a resentful nod, and Thayer released him.

Mantel was on the way out the door when Jakob said, "I call Gerritt Van der Veer to the stand."

The captain turned and gaped. The courtroom erupted. Thayer hammered and hammered and finally stood, pointing out the worst offenders to the bailiff, who took two men by the elbows and forced them out, causing the entire room to hush.

Thayer called both attorneys forward.

"Mr. Van der Veer," Thayer said, his eyes sharp with fury. "I understand that this is the first case you have tried and I understand that you may not be adequately versed in trial procedure, which I am sorry to say, may prove a liability for your client. However, let me help you. Lawyers don't usually call their parents as witnesses."

"To say nothing of irrelevant discussions of the origins of dolls—"

Thayer glowered at the district attorney, interrupting his tirade with a gesture of irritation.

"Your Honor, I am aware of the irregularity," Jakob said. "But Gerritt Van der Veer is Mr. Harley's employer. Up until Mr. Harley's arrest, they worked closely together for many years. He is here to attest to many things, among them to act as a character witness for the defendant."

"Gerritt Van der Veer was excluded from my witness list, Judge," Hotaling said. "Mr. Van der Veer had only Harley listed. I prepared for Harley."

Thayer narrowed his eyes and tapped the end of his pencil on his desk again. "I'm not fond of incestuous complications. This had better have relevance, Mr. Van der Veer."

Gerritt Van der Veer sauntered into the courtroom in the company of the limping bailiff who had subpoenaed him that morning. No one could remember ever seeing Gerritt Van der Veer less than impeccably turned out. This morning, however, he had the rumpled appearance of having slept in his clothes. His wrinkled shirt was stained, and a small razor nick on his neck had bled onto the hastily buttoned collar of his shirt. However, despite his disheveled appearance, he made a show of seating himself, removing a hat to reveal a scalp flushed pink, and balancing it on his knee. He was regarding his son with ill-concealed rage.

Jakob swallowed hard as a strained silence fell.

"Can you state your name for the record, please?" Jakob said.

"I will when you tell me what I am doing here."

Jakob blushed, heat rising to the roots of his hair. "Unfortunately, we cannot proceed unless you state your name, Father."

"Why the drama of a subpoena, Jakob? We had dinner together last night. You could have asked me to come to court then. It certainly would have been more polite."

Thayer said, "Mr. Gerritt Van der Veer, we are all aware of the singularity of this situation. But I caution you. You have been subpoenaed in a court of law to answer questions on behalf of your employee James Harley as a character witness. You will be in contempt of court if you do not answer the questions posed to you."

"Then I'll enter a plea of contempt of my own. I was dragged here this morning against my consent. I would like to go home."

"Impossible. Your son has subpoenaed you, using his newfound authority as an attorney to the hilt," Thayer said with a hint of amused respect. "I suggest that if you don't want to be jailed that you answer the questions posed to you, and then you will be set free to go about your day. Your choice."

Gerritt tossed a sour look at Jakob and addressed himself again to Thayer. "My name, as everyone knows, is Gerritt Van der Veer. Jakob knows very well where I live. It's the house I built for him and his mother at 411 State Street."

"I am not the one asking you questions, Mr. Van der Veer," Thayer said. "Answer your son, which is not something I ever envisioned saying from this bench."

Jakob clasped his hands behind his back and turned away, his heart pounding in his chest. All his life, he had managed his father, working to prevent his volatile eruptions. Jakob's daily goal had been to provoke the least amount of conflict and to protect his mother where he could. He had skirted, hazarded, wondered, flattered, eased, and had largely been successful, though the effort at appeasement was an exhausting dance, one he had hardly recognized he'd engaged in. It was simply his way of maneuvering in the family. But he had never opposed his father absolutely. For sound reason, he'd been careful, respectful, and above all fearful of exposing his mother to the explosive tirades his father displayed at work, when labor mistakes or shipping problems—things outside of his control—upended his expectations. But now, he was about to abandon years of careful calculation for another kind of careful calculation. "Father, can you tell us how you know the defendant?"

"Again, something you know. He was—is—my head stevedore. My overseer."

"And how long has Mr. Harley been in your employ?"

"Twenty years or so. Let's see," he said, gazing at Jakob with a mocking look. "I think you were one year old then. So, yes, twenty years."

"Is Mr. Harley good at his job?"

"He was the envy of my competitors. I don't know how many times another yard tried to hire him away. I had to pay him well."

"How much did you pay him?"

"Ten dollars a day. Six days a week. That's sixty a week. Three thousand one hundred twenty a year."

"So much? For an overseer. You're certain about that?"

His father seemed to gather focus. He studied Jakob with that familiar look of benign bemusement he adopted whenever Jakob questioned him about some arcane contract stipulation, common in the lumber industry, whose agreements with landowners had been forged long ago, before the world had grown so complicated. "Harley is good. And I know my books inside and out."

"Define *good*. He was punctual, trustworthy?"

"He ran that lot like a general."

"So you were a good team?"

Given a chance to boast, Gerritt warmed to his subject. "Van der Veer Lumber makes more money than any other enterprise in the district."

"And part of this was due to Mr. Harley's efforts on the lot's behalf?"

"It was."

"Was Mr. Harley privy to all your concerns about the business?"

"I allowed Harley access to almost everything, except that he never balanced the books." Gerritt straightened and pulled at the creased lapels of his jacket. "I am meticulous about those, in strict control of them."

"Can you tell us about your work for the House of Shelter?"

Hotaling raised his hand to object. "What does this have to do with Mr. Harley?"

"This attests to character," Jakob said.

"Whose?" the judge said.

"Mr. Harley's."

"Then make a connection, please," Thayer said.

"Your work at the House of Shelter?" Jakob prompted.

His father's voice carried a false lightness. Dissembling was the single tactic he wasn't good at. "I founded and funded it. It is a house of reformation for prostitutes."

"How long ago did you establish that home?"

"Twelve years, I believe."

"Did Mr. Harley participate in the House of Shelter?"

"He found me girls, persuaded them to come to the house."

"Found you girls?"

Gerritt shifted in his chair. "Found the *house* ladies of the night."

"How very interesting. How was the House of Shelter funded?"

Hotaling's chair scraped against the floor as he hauled himself up. "Objection. I fail to see how the funding of a charitable endeavor has anything to do with this case."

"Mr. Harley was involved with the House of Shelter," Jakob argued. "Again, it will speak to character."

"I'll allow," the judge said. "But be specific, Mr. Van der Veer."

"How was the house funded?"

"By money from my enterprises."

"Why are you so interested in the welfare of prostitutes?"

"I am interested in the moral welfare of our collective society and of fallen girls especially."

"Objection. How is this specific?" Hotaling said.

"Mr. Hotaling, if you are going to interrupt every two questions, then Mr. Van der Veer will never finish questioning Mr. Van der Veer, and we will be let out late again today, and I for one want my dinner." He flicked his hand impatiently, and Hotaling dropped to his seat to a chorus of laughter. It seemed that in his fatigue Thayer no longer had the will to threaten the gallery with expulsion, however little he had enforced his dictum of silence.

"Tell the court more, Father, about your interests in young prostitutes," Jakob said.

If his father was irritated, he did not show it now. Instead, he shifted in his chair, batting back Jakob's parry with pleasure. "A woman can fall and it is her own fault, but when a child falls, then society has failed. Children need help. They need a true friend. They needed me. So I created the home to care for them. I enjoy being around children. I love their energy."

"Does the House of Shelter care for only girls?"

"No. There are women there, too, but my primary interest is in the welfare of the young ones. They are so helpless out on the streets."

"Did Mr. Harley 'like their energy,' as you say?"

"I think so, yes. Childless men often do."

"In all the time that Mr. Harley has been in your employ, have you ever known Mr. Harley to harm anyone?"

Gerritt snorted. "Never."

"To abuse children?"

"He better well not have."

"Have you ever heard him intimate a desire to do so?"

"Never. I would have forbade him if he had."

"Forbade him?"

Gerritt sniffed. "I would have explained to him the consequences of such actions. I wouldn't have tolerated it."

"Would you have fired him?"

"Yes."

"And if he is convicted of these charges?"

"Then I'll fire him, but then that would mean that you had failed."

A light chuckle carried through the room.

"Now, can you tell me what you did on the day after the flood? I'm asking specifically what you did the morning after the flood?"

"The morning of the flood?"

"Yes, you came home with an injury to your forehead, which William Stipp treated."

"Oh, that." Gerritt shrugged. "After waiting in vain all night for you, I happened to recall that Harley lived down in the Pastures on Green Street, which as everyone knows is prone to flooding. I grew worried. He'd left with you the night before from a dinner party at our home. He is my most valuable employee—a friend—so I wanted to see whether he was all right. I went down there—"

"Where exactly?"

"Franklin Street."

"And?"

"What does this have to do with anything?" Hotaling said from his seat.

The judge pivoted on Hotaling. "If you have an objection, you must state what the objection is."

"He needn't bother," Jakob said. "I'll explain what I'm after. This questioning will speak to the close nature of the relationship between Mr. Harley and my father, and to Mr. Van der Veer's own character and trustworthiness as a character witness."

Hotaling sighed and Thayer waved Jakob on.

Jakob resumed, "And what did you do when you reached Franklin Street?"

"I waded into the water. I wanted to get to Harley's house, to see whether or not he was all right. But the current grabbed me and pulled me off my feet. It was a near thing. I only saved myself by catching a streetlamp. I smashed my head against it. I only just crawled out of there."

"You did all that for Mr. Harley?"

"I did."

"That is a risk few people would take."

"I suppose. But I was worried about him."

"And where was I that morning?"

"Still at the Lumber District as far as I knew."

"And was the district at that time flooded?"

Gerritt eyed him through narrow slits, suddenly cognizant of where Jakob was going. "It was."

"I see. So, let me clarify for the jury. Your first thought that morning was not for whether or not your son had survived the breakup, but instead for your head stevedore's well-being?"

Gerritt shot him a sullen look.

"Answer, please," Jakob said.

"I fail to see—"

"Tell the court, how did you know where Mr. Harley lived? Had you been to his house before?"

A flicker of hesitation crossed Gerritt's face. "No."

"In all your years of friendship, you didn't once share a meal there?"

"No. I can't remember."

"Is it *No,* or *I can't remember*?"

"No."

"But you knew his address well enough to know that he was in danger of the floodwaters?"

"I remembered Harley mentioning once that he lived close to the river in the Pastures."

"And what was your plan? To wander around the Pastures

shoulder-deep in floodwaters and hope that you happened on the right house?"

"Something like that, yes." Gerritt's voice had gone steely.

"That seems rather complicated. More complicated than alerting the police that your son was trapped in the Lumber District."

"It was an extraordinary day."

"Did you check on other employees that day?"

"No."

"Why not?"

"Because I'd nearly drowned down in the Pastures."

"You called for a doctor, didn't you?"

"I object." Hotaling's features had gone slack with boredom. "I fail to see how any of this reflects on the case at all. Why does it matter that the witness saw a physician for an injury?"

"Does it?" Thayer said to Jakob.

"The extent of his injuries speaks to the lengths Mr. Van der Veer executed in an effort to reach Mr. Harley's house, which speaks again to the close nature of their relationship."

The judge nodded. "Overruled."

"So, while I—your son—was fighting my way across the frozen river, you went down to the Pastures to wander around in river water looking for a house whose address you didn't know in order to save James Harley whom you did not even know was truly in danger, thereby nearly drowning yourself and requiring stitches?"

"Yes," Gerritt said, drawing his lips into a tight grimace.

"I'm still curious about something. Why didn't you think Harley would be with me in the district? We both left the dinner at the same time with what I thought was the intention of saving as much Van der Veer lumber as we could. I had the additional charge of retrieving the books. Why did you even think Mr. Harley would be at home if I had not returned?"

"I didn't know where either of you were. For all Viola and I knew, you could have gone home another way and been asleep in your bed. Harley's house was nearby."

"Interesting assumption on your part. And then the next thing you did was what?"

"I read about Harley's heroism in the paper, so I went straight to the hospital to see him."

"Because you had read that he had saved two boys in the flood?"

"Yes."

"What happened at the hospital?"

"The place was in an uproar, no place for a man to get well. So I told a nurse that I would take care of him."

"How did you take care of him?"

"Harley asked to go to his sister's, so I ordered my driver to take him there."

"And is this driver still in your employ?"

"I had to fire him. I'd learned he'd not taken Harley to his sister's, but to some brothel somewhere."

"So he is unavailable to testify to this action on his part?"

"I don't know where he is."

"Are you responsible for taking Harley out of the hospital to a brothel?"

"No. My fired driver is."

"You didn't want to get him out of the hospital for another reason?"

"No."

"Not to keep him from being questioned, for instance?"

Gerritt's gaze locked on Jakob. "No."

"I see. Now, can you please describe to the court the nature of your financial dealings?"

Hotaling heaved a sigh and climbed to his feet. "Objection."

"What is this about, Mr. Van der Veer?" the judge said, his chin now propped wearily on his hand.

"As we have heard, Mr. Harley is third in command of Van der

Veer Lumber. The inner financial workings of the company are relevant since it will also speak to his standing in the community."

"Be brief," Thayer said.

"Father?"

"I own Van der Veer Lumber and *Son,* along with you, I might add," Gerritt said. "And I want to make clear, despite what some might believe, that Van der Veer Lumber suffered very little financial devastation as a result of the flood."

"You have had no financial difficulties of late?"

"None."

"Is this because you have other business interests entwined with the company?"

"No."

"Are you certain?"

"Yes."

"Are you not the owner of ten brothels in Albany?"

"Objection!" Hotaling thundered over the resulting tumult. The judge banged his gavel several times before the shouts faded into a restless silence. "The defense attorney is sensationalizing. What does any of this have to do with Mr. Harley?"

"Your Honor," Jakob said, "if Mr. Harley and Mr. Van der Veer are as close as Mr. Van der Veer attests, it is possible that Mr. Van der Veer trusted Mr. Harley in all his ventures, not just his lumber interests. This may give us some insight into Mr. Harley's guilt or innocence. And again, his character."

Thayer narrowed his gaze at Jakob, ignoring the fury directed his way from Gerritt. "Overruled."

"Mr. Van der Veer," Jakob said. "Do you own ten brothels in Albany?"

Gerritt's smug sneer became a rictus of contempt.

"Your Honor," Jakob said, "I'd like to introduce into evidence the property ledgers of the city of Albany." Jakob hauled from his table three large leather-bound ledgers. "These range from 1865 to this current year, 1879."

Thayer took them, turned them over in his hands, then handed them back. "I'll allow." They were unwieldy things, and Jakob had flagged several pages with bookmarks. He returned to the defense table with them and Harley fingered their bindings, curious.

Jakob opened one and read: "787 Quay Street, owner Gerritt Van der Veer. 795 Montgomery Street, owner Gerritt Van der Veer. 976 Broadway, owner Gerritt Van der Veer." He replaced one ledger and picked up another and read four more listings. "The last is the most recent. 289 New Scotland Plank Road, near Ontario Street. Are you aware, Father, that at each of those addresses resides a brothel?"

"Objection," Hotaling said, his suspicious demeanor now warped into attentive interest. "Counsel has not proven that statement."

"Sustained."

"I'll focus on the New Scotland Plank Road property, where Officer Farrell arrested Mr. Harley. Mr. Farrell has already testified that it was a bawdy house. The property ledgers state that you own this property, Father. Will you please verify that it is yours?"

Gerritt eased one elbow over the back of his chair. "Fine. I own brothels." He talked on over the explosion of astonishment and the hammering of Thayer, brazening it out with a sneer of disdain. "So what? For years, I've provided a necessary service to the city of Albany. Some of my best customers are in this room. What does this have to do with anything?"

The room turned suddenly, oppressively quiet as a dozen men in the audience squared their shoulders and stared straight ahead, and the women with them pressed their lips together and planned questions of their own.

"Can you explain to us, Father, why it is that you own both brothels and a reformation house for prostitutes? Isn't that a contradiction?"

"I'm a practical man. The city needs both." He was spitting out his words now.

"Isn't it true that the court cannot rely on anything you say to be true?"

"What the hell is this?"

"Wouldn't Van der Veer Lumber be bankrupt now if it wasn't propped up by money made in your brothels? Hasn't it been for years? Are you not more pimp than lumber baron?"

Gerritt exploded. "Why am I being subjected to questions about my life, when it's Harley who's on trial?" He twisted in his seat to rail at the judge. "I am an upstanding citizen. Yes, I give the city whores, but I also give the whores a way out if they want it. That's just fair footing. And what do I get for it? Treachery. From my own son." He turned on Jakob. "My affairs are my affairs. So take your self-righteous condemnation and ask me a question that matters."

No one in the courtroom moved, except the reporters scratching furiously in their notebooks.

"I have a second set of books, Your Honor," Jakob said. "These are from the safe at Van der Veer Lumber. I personally removed them this morning." Gerritt watched with black suspicion as Jakob made the rounds of prosecution, jury, and judge, showing off the set of ledgers. Then he held open a page for his father. "Can you verify, Father, that these books are yours, and that this is your handwriting?"

His father's face turned to stone. "Yes."

Jakob said, "On page eighty-five of the latest volume, on a page dated the day after the sisters' disappearance, is a line item with the notation, 'Payable to James Harley, two thousand one hundred dollars. Cash.' What is this payment for?"

"I don't know."

"A month later, there was another payment made for two hundred dollars, this one to a 'G.' Was it for Mr. Harley at Green Street?"

"Sometimes our accounting is wrong and I have to make up for errors."

"But did you not just say that you are meticulous in your books? Shall I have the court recorder read your statement back to you?"

Gerritt opened and shut his mouth like a fish. He looked toward Jakob for help, but Jakob's impenetrable mask remained as blank as the surface of a still lake.

"No need," Gerritt said.

"To clarify, you did say that you are meticulous, did you not?"

"I did."

"Thank you." Jakob squared his shoulders. "Now, there are other entries, payable to other people. Can you tell me who 'M' is?"

"That is Captain Arthur Mantel."

Hotaling snapped his head up and looked to the judge, who said to the bailiff, "Can you please ascertain whether or not Captain Mantel is still in the building?"

The bailiff, who had already received far too much exercise that day for his tastes, waved an order at another officer, who slipped out a side door.

"For what were those payments made?"

"I can't recall," Gerritt said.

"Bribes, perhaps?"

Gerritt merely glared in reply.

Jakob said, "Fine. That might be a question for another trial. Tell me, Father, did you go to Franklin Street on the day of the flood not to rescue Mr. Harley, but instead to divine whether or not Claire and Emma O'Donnell were still in Mr. Harley's house?"

"Absolutely not. They were dead! We'd just seen their memorial in the cemetery."

"Had you not visited Harley's home many times in the past, for the purposes of visiting Emma?"

"Never!" Gerritt roared.

"Aren't you the man who picked up the O'Donnell girls in the blizzard and brought them to Mr. Harley's house?"

"What a ridiculous notion."

"Aren't you the man who sent Emma and Claire those dolls?"

"No! It was Mantel!"

A hush fell over the courtroom. During Gerritt's testimony, Jakob had not mentioned the dolls, nor the receipt, either. How could Gerritt have known about them unless he was the man who had sent them? Still, nothing had been proved, but by now an inference had been made. The dolls had something to do with what had happened, and the meaning of the note had taken on a much more sinister aspect for everyone. Coupled with the suggestion of bribes, the whole picture was widening. Now, no one moved, except Jakob, who approached the witness stand as his father glared at him.

Jakob leaned in and hissed, "Do you miss me?"

Gerritt reared back, the smear of guilt on his face unmistakable. Instantly, he checked his reaction, but everyone in the courtroom saw it. Gerritt gripped the railing, his face gone white, a vein at his temple throbbing wildly.

"One more question. Tell me, what is the color of your sleigh?"

Gerritt gaped at Jakob with the icy furor of a man who knew he was trapped. He could not lie. Everyone in Albany knew the singular color of the Van der Veer sleigh—the only cutter in Albany that the James Goold Company had ever painted a solid cherry red, on Gerritt's orders, forgoing the firm's trademark gilt scrolling and black trim. Gerritt had paid handsomely so that the plain design would be exclusive.

Through clenched teeth, Gerritt said, "Cherry red."

"Cherry red?" Jakob said. "Did I hear you correctly? Did you say cherry red?"

"You heard me."

"Actually, I didn't. Can you say it louder?"

"You heard me, goddamnit," Gerritt shouted.

"That will be all for now," Jakob said. "Mr. Hotaling, your witness."

From across the courtroom, Hotaling said, "I have no questions for now."

"You are excused, Mr. Van der Veer," Thayer said. "But you are to remain in the courthouse, do you understand?"

Gerritt snatched his hat and crushed it to his chest as he strode toward the exit, his chin jutting, his face and scalp beet red, ignoring the excited rustling and murmuring as he pushed through the door and into the corridor. James Harley watched him go with mouth agape. He rose slightly, as if to follow him, but Jakob raised a finger at him in warning, and he collapsed into his chair with a groan.

Jakob took some time to shut the open ledger, his hands trembling. He walked all of them across to Hotaling's desk. He seemed to be buying time. The bailiff returned and nodded at Thayer.

"Your Honor," Jakob finally said. "I recall Emma O'Donnell to the stand."

The side door opened. William Stipp stood there with a wary Emma, who was led in by a second bailiff. She was dressed much the same as the previous day, though this time she lacked the jaunty bow and her face had gone completely pale. All eyes followed her halting progress across the room to the witness chair.

Jakob waited until she had settled in before he said, "Good morning, Emma. I need to remind you that you're still under oath, which means that you have to tell us the truth. I have only two questions for you, Emma.

"I asked you the first once before, at your house. It's about that day when you were picked up by the stranger and taken to Mr. Harley's. Can you tell me what color sleigh the man drove? Do you remember?"

"Red. Like a cherry."

A collective gasp filled the courtroom, but Thayer hammered that down.

"And one more, and then you are done, Emma. Just now, a man made a rather noisy exit from the courtroom. Could you hear his voice?"

She nodded. "Yes."

"To whom did that voice belong?"

"The Other Man."

The room ignited. Jakob returned to his seat as Thayer attempted in vain to gavel the room to order and failed. He began to shout. The other officer had yet to return with Captain Mantel. "Bailiff, please return both Captain Mantel and Gerritt Van der Veer to the courtroom."

The bailiff fled as fast as his limp allowed. William rushed to take Emma in his arms and lead her away before Thayer could dismiss her.

"Mr. Hotaling," Thayer said, shouting through the din, "do you wish to ask further questions of Emma?"

Hotaling shook his head. It took the bailiff just half a minute to return with the news that neither Gerritt Van der Veer nor Captain Mantel was anywhere to be found.

Chapter Forty-Five

The brewery hand cast a surprised glance at Gerritt's rumpled clothes and said, "It's not like you to show up looking like you've been to the dog fights. You're welcome to the taps, though, as usual, until the bartender comes in. Five cents a glass. You still got money?"

Gerritt fished out a wallet fat with bank notes, and the grizzled man lifted one eyebrow in approval. He left Gerritt alone in the factory tavern of the Story Brothers' Malt House, more than a mile away from City Hall in South Albany on Broadway, at the corner of Cherry Street, close to the Hudson. Out of force of habit, he had come by way of Harley's house, but had wrenched himself away from the doorstep when he grew cognizant of the curious stares of Harley's neighbors. From deep inside the warehouse, you could hear ship blasts on the Hudson and train whistles high and soulful over the South Bridge. Only railroad men from the nearby Albany and Susquehanna roundhouse and the brewery's cellar hands patronized this workaday tavern, but when a stranger stumbled in and pleaded need, he was admitted without ceremony. Of course, Gerritt was no stranger, though he'd not been in since the flood. The warehouse and factory had been inundated, and eight weeks later, the musk of bottom silt still breathed in the tavern's rough-hewn walls. But the river hadn't breached the brewery's machinery, and it churned on in the warehouse, overriding the tang of mold with the familiar sweet odor of yeast and spiky hops. Gerritt availed himself of a chipped glass from shelves behind the bar and downed his first two glassfuls of warm ale in quick succession. He then perched on a stool and took his time with the third and fourth.

The first time Gerritt had visited Emma, he had come here afterward, to this tavern, and since then he had sought oblivion here more than once, always after *her.*

His hands still shook. He'd charged out of City Hall, humiliation boiling in his ears, Jakob's rancid question hammering again and again: *Do you miss me?*

A pool of yellow light splashed onto the floor from a single, high window, but the barebones tavern was menacingly dark and lonely. Gerritt took heart now that no policeman ever made his way to this blighted place. Even Mantel would never guess where he was: a boon today, for Gerritt knew he ought never to have used Mantel's name on the receipt.

What a damned foolish mistake that had been. He'd used Mantel's name as a decoy, yes, but as a joke, too, because he'd never believed that anyone would ever trace the dolls. And sending Emma that note had been another mistake, a miscalculation. But he'd needed to let her know that he knew where she was. He'd sent it so that she would keep her mouth shut. In a moment of weakness he'd forgotten that she couldn't possibly identify him. He'd always made certain that it was too dark for her to make him out. And how clever his son had been, delaying his question about the dolls until the end, when he was rattled enough to react. Still, as he thought about it now, fortified with alcohol, Gerritt realized that the only thing that Jakob had truly established was that he, Gerritt, possessed a penchant for sending gifts attributed to others and was the owner of several brothels and a cherry red sleigh.

Jakob had never drawn a straight line between him and Emma. Still, if Jakob hadn't drawn a straight line, he'd drawn a crooked one. Allusion and association, while not proof, were suggestion. And suggestion might be enough.

Do you miss me?

How did Jakob know? Viola, of course, on that lark of a trip to Manhattan City with that Mary Sutter. Mary *Stipp.* No fool, that woman. No doubt she had ferreted out that receipt, though Viola deserved that black eye he'd given her.

Or maybe Jakob had figured out everything on his own from that second set of books. He ought never to have sent Jakob for them the night of the flood. That boy was too curious by half.

But the truth was, if Emma had found a way to identify him, he'd be arrested by now.

Jakob had proved nothing. With an unsteady hand, Gerritt hefted the glass to his lips and took another draft of the hoppy ale. It tasted bitter, cheap.

Gerritt pushed aside the memory of blurting out Mantel's name, blaming him for sending the dolls. That had been a mistake, too.

So many ways to betray. So many ways to be betrayed. *Do you miss me?* Gerritt's heart had stopped when Jakob had said that.

Gerritt lurched off the stool, rounded the end of the bar, and pulled another glassful from the tap.

Emma. Dear God, *Emma.*

That ungrateful girl. Where would those girls be now if not for him? They'd been lucky that he'd seen them floundering in all that snow. If he hadn't come along at just that time, they would have met the same fate as their parents. And he'd be safe now. But, God, what a lark it was to have found them.

He'd been on his way to Harley's to get him to come take a look at the district with him to see if anything needed to be done. Had he been heading the opposite direction, toward home, he might have taken those girls to Viola for safekeeping. It was only at Harley's door that he realized the opportunity before him. He'd not even figured out that they were David O'Donnell's daughters until days later. It had just been happenstance, really, and then after that, luck that David hadn't survived the blizzard. That turn had been so convenient. Except for those Stipps looking for them. Then later, when he'd learned that Emma and Claire had escaped the flood, he'd reminded himself a hundred times that they could never identify him.

Except for that damn note he'd felt compelled to include, no one would have ever questioned the gift of the dolls.

But there had been too much to account for. He'd been shocked to pass Captain Mantel on the way into the courtroom, shocked that he had been called as a witness. Had Jakob questioned Mantel about that receipt? What had he said?

Mantel was the variable.

It had been easy to bribe Harley into compliance. All he had had to say was that he would keep taking care of him, keep sending him money. It had been easy enough to get him away from the hospital. And easier still to dupe the night jailer after Harley had gone and gotten himself arrested. But it had been an inspired choice to impersonate a physician at the jail. The subterfuge had been unnecessary, but he'd liked the game; he knew that the jailer was amenable to bribes—a tidbit he had once heard and stored away for future use.

Harley had been asleep when the jailer admitted Gerritt, luckily, or it would have taken some clever footwork to keep Harley from blurting out his name. He'd thanked the jailer and lit a candle and nudged Harley awake. The bandage on the back of his neck was a dirty, wrinkled mess, and for show, Gerritt leaned over it and inspected it, pretending interest, in case the jailer had snuck back and was on the opposite side of the door, peering in through that narrow window.

Gerritt addressed Harley in a whisper, leery of other prisoners who might be listening from surrounding cells, though there was so much shouting and chaos that precaution was probably unnecessary.

"How the hell did you get yourself arrested?" Gerritt hissed. "You were in a whorehouse on the outskirts of town, by yourself, in a room, with orders to shut the hell up. And now you're in the county jail. What happened?"

Harley shook his head. "I don't know. I don't remember. A policeman tricked me."

"He tricked you?"

"I don't know. Somehow he knew."

"How?"

Harley winced as he tilted his head to look up at Gerritt, his eyes bleary with exhaustion. "I said nothing."

"Christ."

"But at least they're alive."

Yes, Gerritt thought, they were, and lucky for Harley, too. "Yes, but you lost them. You owe me compensation."

"I won't say anything. I told no one about you. I swear it."

"How am I supposed to believe you?"

Harley closed his eyes and sighed. "I won't say a thing. The girls, though. They'll say there was someone else besides me."

"But yours is the face they know," Gerritt said, primed for this. "They can't identify me. And if you expose me, you won't save yourself and we'll both be in jail. Outside though, I am free to manipulate the situation. Jakob's agreed to be your lawyer. He'll never cross-examine Emma on the stand. He can't do it. It's not in his nature. And I'll pay your bail."

"If there is any."

"Listen to me, Harley," Gerritt said, leaning down to whisper directly into his overseer's ear. "I'll take care of you. You just have to take care of me. Keep your mouth shut. That's all you have to do. No one can make you talk."

"But I'm not the one who had relations with Emma," Harley said.

"Which will protect you in court. And if there's a trial, and it begins to look bad, then I'll get you out, and you can take all that money I paid you and skedaddle downriver on a night boat if you want—or buy a train ticket—then board any damn boat in Manhattan harbor leaving the country."

"How will you get me out?"

"How do you think I got in here tonight? I'll bribe the jailer to look away for as long as necessary. Or someone will hit him over the head and steal the keys."

Harley peered at him, disbelieving.

"You have enough money, for Christ's sake, after what I paid you for your silence. And I'll send you more. You can live forever on what I'll give you. Head to Paris, for God's sake. It's cheap there. You'll be free."

"I don't speak French."

"Jesus. Go to Argentina then. No one will find you."

"The money," Harley said, burying his head in his hands. "Oh, my money."

"What?"

"It's in my house."

For a moment, Gerritt didn't understand, until he did. He groaned. "You kept the money I gave you in your house? The police have already been there. My God, you are careless."

"This isn't a trick, is it? If Jakob does a lousy job defending me, then you are scot-free and I take the punishment. He is your son. I'm nothing to him."

"I can control Jakob. Easily. But you're free to ask anyone else to be your lawyer. Go ahead. You think you have such a good chance? Do you want to answer questions you don't want anyone to know about?"

Harley cradled his head in the palms of his hands. "What do I tell him, then? Doesn't he need to know something?"

"You tell him that some stranger brought those girls to you in the blizzard. You knew their father, and when you read in the papers that their parents had died, you vowed to take care of them. You had no idea that anyone was looking for them. You were going to send them to school when they recovered from the shock of losing their parents, but they were still fragile. When the flood bells rang, a mysterious object hit you in the head and you don't remember anything else. What? One of them was interfered with? How dreadful. It must have happened when they were away from your protection. You're heartbroken. You adore them both."

Even to Gerritt, this litany was a creative wonder, anchored by one truth and contaminated by untruths that made far more sense than what had really happened. He marveled at the story's sinuous beauty, and as Harley recited it back several times, perfecting his recitation, Gerritt congratulated himself on his ability to manipulate anyone to do anything.

The door at the end of the hall clanged open.

Gerritt leaned over and said, "Remember now, I'm a doctor."

The jailer shoved two inebriated men into a nearby cell before stopping at Harley's.

"I think it's best if you have the jail doctor see you from now on," Gerritt said, snuffing out the candle. "Good-bye, Mr. Harley. You'll be fit in no time."

At least, Gerritt thought, lifting his glass to his lips, Harley had kept his part of the bargain. He'd said nothing about him all those weeks in jail, when he could easily have saved himself by telling the truth. Such was the power of money. It bought loyalty where none was deserved. It bent minds and curated behavior. It solved problems.

But what Harley might say about him now, he didn't know. And there was no way of extracting Harley from the courtroom or Albany, which was something Gerritt had never planned on doing anyway, and which Harley must now realize.

Fodder for betrayal, Gerritt thought. And seeking oblivion in malt and hops was not the answer to his problem. The only answer was to extract himself from the city immediately. He had money enough and could easily get more.

A train whistle sounded. Yes, of course. He would take a train. He wouldn't even need to buy a ticket. He'd just hop on it after it left the station, purchase a ticket on board from the conductor.

His thinking was growing muddled, but it was a pleasant sort of muddle, an easing of the throbbing pain at his temples.

His glass was empty. He staggered to the tap to draw himself a final swallow.

The tavern door flew open and a crowd poured in, raucous with news.

The jury had gone out and come in again. Harley had been acquitted.

"Of all the charges?" Gerritt croaked from behind the bar, shocked that it had all happened so fast.

A few men turned, surprised to see him in the gloom. Someone was lighting a gas sconce high on one wall, dissipating the shadows.

"Oh yes. Not the kidnapping and not the deflowering. Not the imprisonment, either." Laughter all around. "The girl was a liar. We all knew it."

Someone leaned across the bar and slapped Gerritt in celebration on the chest, spilling the beer Gerritt had just poured himself. The man apologized, came around, and drew Gerritt another. The place was teeming with brakemen and warehouse hands.

Harley had been acquitted.

Gerritt gave a derisive laugh, because his clever son had cast just enough doubt to earn Harley a reprieve.

Do you miss me? His son knew, had perhaps known for months. What a cool man he'd raised. Jakob had probably spirited Viola away, too, in anticipation of today. And how long would it be before Jakob found a way to persuade Harley to tell the truth? Especially now that Jakob had saved him from the worst?

Gerritt threw back a good portion of the ale, lowered his glass.

Across the bar stood the stocky figure of Arthur Mantel, dressed, surprisingly, not in his uniform, but in the ubiquitous brown cloth suit of the working class, which made him, in this part of town, invisible, giving him free rein to go places he never would otherwise in his official role.

Gerritt set his glass on the bar. "I said nothing about you," Gerritt lied. "You're going to be fine."

"Why did you use my name for the receipt?"

So, Mantel knew. Jakob must have told him on the stand. Mantel had known when they had crossed paths in the echoing hallway outside the courtroom, reason, Gerritt now understood, for Mantel's frosty look then. Gerritt ran his hand over his vest, conscious of his disheveled appearance. He opened his mouth but could think of nothing to say to appease the police captain. "Did you follow me? And how the hell did you have time to change your clothes?"

Mantel's gaze roved from Gerritt to his half-empty beer stein, then back to Gerritt. "I thought we had an understanding, Gerritt. I stopped looking for those girls; I looked away; you kept me paid; and you said nothing to anyone about the money."

"But I didn't say anything." Lying seemed to be the best strategy Gerritt could muster. He threw coins on the bar and staggered out the back of the building, onto Broadway.

Mantel followed and took Gerritt by the shoulder, spinning him around. The workday had ended and the streets were full of workers hurrying home, their empty lunch buckets jouncing against one thigh, their attention bent on dinner and home, or booze and brawling, dictated not so much by familial situation as preference.

"Somehow your son knows about our arrangement," Mantel said. "Did you tell him?"

Gerritt needed his ale-soaked brain to work, but he was dizzy and drunk. He lurched away, down Cherry to Quay Street, where he plunged northward along the river shore, forcing himself not to look back. There was nothing pretty about the south end of the city, choked with industry and mired still with detritus from the flood. Black silt still coated Quay Street, and Gerritt's boots sank two inches deep. At the open doors of an icehouse Gerritt caught the familiar smell of sawdust smothering blocks of harvested ice. He sold this icehouse his sawdust. He could sell anything to anyone and had, for years. He had even sold everyone on his innocence. Until now.

Mantel caught up and glued himself to Gerritt's side.

"Did you keep books on me, too? Did you write down what you've paid me all these years?"

"Are you as stupid as Harley was? Where is all that money I gave you?'

"Safely under the floorboards of my kitchen."

"You idiot. They'll find it. If I were you, I'd leave with me. I'm going to catch the six o'clock NY Central. We'll be in Manhattan City by nine o'clock. We could draw a draft from any bank in Manhattan City in the morning before anyone—Jakob or Hotaling—thinks to freeze my funds. And I'll pay you more."

"I wouldn't go to a train station. It's likely they are looking for us both by now."

Gerritt whirled on him, feeling a rising panic loosen the last of his moorings. "Why are you here?"

Mantel said, "Why did you use my name on that receipt?"

Gerritt turned away, trudged on. The solid hulking structure of the South Bridge was coming into view. He could make it to the railroad bridge. Climb up onto it. Grab the caboose of the six o'clock.

Gerritt was gathering courage. Surely Mantel could be persuaded that leaving was the only choice now.

A black river snake darted out from the rushes and ran over his boots and wriggled back into the reeds. Gerritt stopped to empty his bladder and plodded on, heavy with sloshing ale, trailed by Mantel. It took only another ten minutes to reach the south edge of the Basin, where a jutting dock adjoined one of the bridge abutments. Gerritt set his sights on reaching it. He'd climb the safety ladder to the bridge deck and onto the pedestrian walkway. The trains trundled slowly over the bridge—five miles an hour—a safety precaution—and a boon for him now. He would step onto the back platform of the caboose as the train chugged past, then sail downriver to the freedom of Manhattan City.

This *river*, Gerritt thought. This damned river had stolen everything from him. Especially Emma. Oh, Emma. He had given her that doll so that she would always think of him and she'd not even brought it to the courtroom with her. And this city, his domain to rule these past twenty years, had turned on him, too. Well, he was done with the place now.

"Come with me, Mantel," Gerritt said over his shoulder at the policeman, who was still following him. "Europe. Paris. Prague. Anywhere. By now I've given you enough money to pay off God for all your sins and mine, too. Because of my generosity, I might add."

In Albany, the risks of punishment for taking bribes were few. Even the state legislature wouldn't make a decision unless it had been greased at least twice by opposing sides. The city ran on graft. Mantel had been taking money for years—and might still, after this, no matter Hotaling's fury.

At the base of the pediment, Gerritt clambered up the ladder. The six o'clock had begun its slow ascent up the incline. Gerritt crawled through the circular opening at the top of the ladder and lurched upright. The walkway was separated from the tracks by a railing. He looked back down through the hole. A grim Mantel was climbing up after him. The bridge was vibrating under the weight of the passing train. The cars were passing close to the walkway—a foot on the other side of the wooden railing. Gerritt left Mantel to his own devices. He edged along the walkway, on which VAN DER VEER was stamped in red on every joist and tie. He counted the ties emblazoned with his name—a dozen, two dozen, fifty, a hundred. He was over the middle of the river now. The height was dizzying, satisfying. In the twilight, the river had gone gray and the sun hovered over the city in a pinkish ball.

Mantel, who had scrambled to his feet, was shouting at him now over the rumble of the train. "All I did was ask to be kept out of it. I took your money and stopped searching for those girls when you told me to. That's it. You're the one who ruined them."

Behind train windows, startled passengers were turning their heads to stare at the two arguing men on the bridge. It was rare for pedestrians to cross and chance being covered in soot and ash, to risk the noise and danger of such close proximity to the heavy cars.

"Stay then," Gerritt shouted at Mantel, who had caught up and now stood an arm's length away. "Tell them about me if you like. You can talk anyone into anything. You convinced the Stipps those girls were dead. Pull the same magic. Save yourself. I'll be on a ship to Europe by tomorrow." Gerritt threw one unsteady leg over the railing separating the narrow walkway from the tracks. He needed to watch his balance or he would fall under the train. He had only to launch himself onto the caboose's platform and then he'd be away.

The caboose careened into view and Gerritt reached for it.

One minute he had a hold of the caboose's platform, and the next he didn't. The train slipped past, oblivious as Gerritt teetered on the railing. Mantel caught him by one arm and hauled him backward onto the walkway. Smoke from the locomotive lingered over the bridge, and the two faced off opposite one another, each of them heaving with exertion.

"We can get the next train, Mantel," Gerritt said. "Go to Europe together. We could—"

Mantel's shove might not have had the same effect on a man less intoxicated. This was what Gerritt thought as he sailed over the bridge's outer railing and the black water of the Hudson. It took him a bleary moment to register the fact that he was falling, his limbs flailing for purchase but finding only air. He observed his hat sailing beside him, a boon companion as below the river surged, licking and hungry.

He hit the surface, fast and hard, out of control. The glacial bite of the frigid water stunned him and he sank like a stone, his limbs splayed out, bile shooting up from the pit of his stomach. For a long moment, Gerritt was too stunned by the impact to move, his thinking muddled by the alcohol still coursing through his veins. Immediately, he thought of his son, of how Jakob had ever managed to survive that night on the roof of the lumber office, soaked through, alone in the bitter cold. Had he suffered this sickening, frozen palsy? How had he managed to save himself, to move, even? Spurred by the terrifying notion that he must now take action or die, Gerritt flailed his arms, but the river dragged him under, sweeping him southward from the ungrateful city that he had ruled for decades. Though it was June, the river was still running fast and high—a consequence of the lingering snowmelt from high in the Adirondacks. How ironic, Gerritt thought. The blizzard that had given him that girl was drowning him now.

He had no sense of whether he was up or down or sideways.

Pressure was mounting inside his chest. He believed his lungs would burst, but he resisted the clawing urge to breathe.

With a deep shiver, he suffered an acute sense of loneliness, and then a final clarity as his last coherent thoughts took hold. It was Mantel who had betrayed him—more than Jakob, more than Viola, more than those Stipps, more than Emma. Mantel, whom he had kept in fine financial fettle all these years, had manhandled him over the bridge's railing without a second thought.

He could see nothing. It was black as pitch.

Do you miss me?

Instinct gave in to need. Gerritt gulped for air, inhaled water, gagged, and frantically kicked in a final attempt to reach the surface—in whatever direction it lay. But the current kept dragging him deeper. The river began to peel away his jacket, unbutton the buttons of his shirt, strip him of his pants and underclothes. A hiss roared in his ears. The chorus swelled into shrieks and howls and then a thunderous bedlam.

But when the Hudson finally squeezed the last vestige of air out of him, the quiet was as flat and soundless as a cellar in the deep of night.

Chapter Forty-Six

That night, at eight o'clock, an exhausted Jakob came calling at the Stipps'. He brought with him an Extra, but an enterprising young newsboy had already sprinted all the way from downtown to their house with a copy, for which William paid him ten cents. The boy had danced away to spend his prize at Ebel's Ice Cream Emporium, which sold the newly invented concoction of an ice cream soda for a nickel.

HARLEY ACQUITTED ON ALL CHARGES
YOUNG VAN DER VEER IMPLICATES
LUMBER BARON FATHER
IN OUTRAGE OF O'DONNELL GIRL AND
IMPLICATES POLICE CAPTAIN MANTEL
IN BRIBERY SCHEME
GERRITT VAN DER VEER AND
CAPTAIN MANTEL DISAPPEAR

The article by Horace Young detailed every facet of the trial, and finished with:

> This reporter concludes with an apology to the Doctors Stipp for the impact of my enthusiastic pursuit of this story on their extended family. They, and Emma and Claire O'Donnell, were highly inconvenienced by the curiosity engendered by the press in general, and more important, by my zealous reporting in particular. I was one of those who had a major hand in besmirching Dr. Mary Stipp's heretofore fine reputation. To my chagrin, I misrepresented her character. I state now that I believe that she is and always has possessed the finest moral integrity and that the good city of Albany ought to be proud of our eminent native daughter and her accomplishments.

"It's about damn time," William said, after reading the apology to the group out loud. They had gathered in the parlor, all of them, except Emma and Claire, whom Vera had set to rolling out the crust of a pie on the kitchen table.

"I came to apologize, too," Jakob said.

"For what?" William said. "Much as I loathe Harley, he is not the one who raped Emma."

"No, but he ought to at least have been convicted on imprisonment."

"Where is he now?"

"I don't know," Jakob said. "They released him. I expect they will return the money we found in his house and that he'll disappear. But that's not the most important news."

"What is?"

"That newspaper article is already outdated. This evening, my father jumped from the South Bridge into the Hudson, and no one has seen him."

"What?"

"Captain Mantel found me an hour ago. Apparently, he hadn't

meant to defy the judge and walk out on the trial, but he'd spied my father leaving the courthouse, so he followed him, intent on bringing him to justice. He found him down at the Story Brothers' Malt House of all places. When Mantel confronted him, Gerritt made a headlong escape to the South Bridge. Mantel says he climbed over the bridge railing and jumped right before his eyes, but before he did, he confessed everything. Mantel says he'll swear in court that Gerritt was responsible for raping Emma. And he said he didn't know a thing about any bribes. The district attorney could look in his bank account if he wanted. He had no idea what that entry in Gerritt's books meant. He was innocent of everything except having become the object of some nervous whores' generosity, which in the end was less than nothing. Especially in Albany.

"And I'm afraid that's true," Jakob said.

"Also, it seems that Harley and Father had a plan to get Harley out. Harley said my father offered to send him to Paris. I didn't know anything about it until afterward. Harley told me before the verdict came back. He was furious at my father for abandoning him. Can you imagine? *He* felt abandoned."

"Where is your mother?"

"At the Delavan House. I'll stay there tonight, too."

"Does she know?"

Jakob nodded. "She is so ashamed. I don't know what Herculean strength allowed her to testify this morning. She went straight back to the hotel. I can only apologize for both of us, but it will never be enough. I came to tell you that we—my mother and I—whatever you think of us—we are both acutely ashamed. She thinks she ought to have known. She's sick about it. She told me"—he swallowed hard—"that when they first married, he would call her *his child, his darling little one, his girl.*" Jakob looked away. "How much he was able to conceal. He was deranged and yet he walked among us and lied to us and carried on as if the things he wanted and did were normal.

It is unconscionable. And my mother and I are sorry. We are sorry for everything. I did as much I could, but it wasn't enough."

"I don't know very many sons who would have done what you did," Mary said.

"Well, he's gone now. I hope. Maybe he was able to kick free. Maybe he climbed out and he's somewhere . . ." Jakob rose to his feet. His face had aged a hundred years. He stole a tired, hopeless glance at Elizabeth. "I just wanted to say we are sorry."

"Jakob," Elizabeth said. She had stayed silent until now. "Do you have a moment?"

On the veranda, they sat side by side on the slatted swing. In the distance, through the spiked pales of the park fence, fireflies roamed like possibility, and crickets and katydids croaked a symphony. At their feet, her violin lay in its rosewood case, the strings still reverberating from the Brahms lullaby she had just finished playing for the girls. She was brushing rosin dust from her skirt when he said, "You do play beautifully."

"Thank you."

"I am sorry," Jakob said again. "My father—you are all being very gracious, but I can't imagine why. And if there is anything we can ever do—but I won't trouble your family or you anymore, I—"

"Please trouble me." Elizabeth looked at him across the small gap between them. As confident as Jakob had appeared in the courtroom—a miracle of composure and machination—he did not look that way now. What had it taken for him to face down Gerritt, to reveal their family's ugly secret for all of Albany to judge and despise?

"We are grateful to you."

He dipped his head in acknowledgment.

"Do you know what you will do now?" Elizabeth said.

"Go to Boston, perhaps."

She stirred. "Boston? Why there?"

"Mother wants to leave the city, and she is the one I'm worried about. We can't stay here. Especially if Father survived." He nodded in the direction of the park, toward their home on the other side. "If he didn't, I'll eventually sell the house, if I can, though who would buy it now? It's an accursed place." Jakob glanced her way and colored. "Actually I'll sell all the houses, if I can. Unfortunately someone will buy them and carry on the sordid side of the family business—without interference from the police, no doubt. As for the lot in the district, that's easy. No doubt one of the other lumbermen will want it, or I'll just stop paying the rent. I'll easily sell the rest of the lumber. Then, after that, what Mother doesn't need to live on, I'll donate to the House of Shelter. She says she can get by very well on less. Until then she'll sell her doll collection, which will fetch a good enough price to allow us to live for quite a while."

"But isn't the lumber business yours, too? Surely that's not—tainted."

"I don't want any of it. And I'd rather earn my money through law. There's a professor of mine at Harvard I could apply to for help in finding a position. He knows a lot of people in Boston. I'm sorry. I ought not to be imposing on you, ought not to be talking about my problems to you. But I needed to tell you that I was sorry. I needed you to know." He made to rise, but didn't. The crickets persisted. The fireflies were blinking on and off, oblivious.

"Anyway," he said again. "We cannot stay in Albany. They"—he waved his hand at the city, blinking out of sight beyond the houses on Willett Street—"would eviscerate us. But first, may I ask? Do you plan to return to Paris for more study?"

"I can't go back to Paris. They defeated me there. So we are exiles, the two of us, from places we have loved. But while we were in Cape Cod, I auditioned at the Boston Conservatory and was accepted."

"Boston?" Jakob said. "You will be in Boston?"

"Yes. I will."

"I see," he said, as if he couldn't believe his luck.

He said again that he had to go. He said it again in ten minutes, and then again in another ten minutes, when he finally did go, but not before he had kissed her. Twice.

Upstairs, in Claire and Emma's bedroom, the strains of Brahms faded away. Amelia held Emma in her lap in the rocking chair, while Claire slept under a summer counterpane dyed blue, her choice, to match the sea at Cape Cod. Emma had wanted a corresponding golden burst of yellow, so it would always be light, she'd explained, though she'd not had to. They had told her, however, that the trial was over. Had even told her that Harley was not going to go to jail. To Emma, Harley remained the one touch of benevolence in those six weeks, and her young mind was happy for him.

"But what about the Other Man?" Emma said. "Where is he? If he comes for Claire—"

"He's a coward, darling. He'll never come for you. We will always protect you. You're safe."

"Grandmama?"

Grandmama. It was the first time Emma had called her that. Amelia smiled and stroked Emma's hair. "Yes?"

"Why?"

So, it was beginning. The first of a thousand *Whys*, the impossible question without an answer. One day, Emma would be angry—beautifully, righteously angry—but for now, it was *Why?*

"I don't know," Amelia said. And she didn't. She was sixty years old and had delivered hundreds of babies and she could no more answer that question than solve the riddle of humanity's existence. "I don't know, my sweet girl. I wish I did. But I'm here. I'll always be here." And she pulled her close and kissed the top of her head.

Chapter Forty-Seven

Emma and Claire O'Donnell, wearing new summer dresses of white lawn, knelt beside their parents' graves in the Albany Rural Cemetery. The minister had just said a second funeral, and the girls were laying bouquets of blue cornflowers and white daisies, unaware that close by a statue of two cherubs had once marked their own deaths. The week before, William had hired a man to dump that statue into the Hudson, Emma and Claire's once purported grave. The day of this second burial—a ritual to help Emma and Claire say good-bye—was a beautiful summer day. The vivid blue sky sparkled, insects buzzed between bloom and sepulcher, and dandelion seeds drifted across the cemetery like snow. The blizzard's mayhem had yielded a season of extraordinary fecundity. All that moisture had spawned color and blossom in abundance, and nowhere more so than the cemetery, that haven of grief and remembrance.

It would take an army to breach the protective perimeter constructed around Emma and Claire this morning. At a respectful distance a good fifty feet down Bower Hill, Viola and Jakob Van der Veer watched as Elizabeth, Mary, William, and Amelia comforted the kneeling Emma and Claire. Gerritt, whose body had washed up on Middle Ground flats next to the shards of his ice-yacht, had been buried on Jakob's instructions in the town of Athens, opposite the flats and far enough away from Albany to hasten the erasure of his father from the collective memory. Jakob had not even set a stone. And soon, Van der Veer Lumber would be no more. There had been plenty of offers to buy their stock and take over the rent for their lot. In addition, he had hired painters to blacken out every advertisement for the company in the city, so that the Van der Veer name was obliterated.

On the top of Bower Hill, Elizabeth was waiting to play her violin, glad of this second chance to honor Bonnie and David the way she ought to have done the first time. Amelia and Mary drew Emma and Claire into their laps, securing them with arms wrapped around their waists and kisses planted atop their white straw hats adorned with sunny yellow ribbons. William stood secure and attentive guard beside Bonnie and David's joint tombstone, placed in the weeks after their burial and that read, *NEITHER SHALL THERE BE ANY MORE PAIN, FOR THE FORMER THINGS ARE PASSED AWAY.*

The first strains of Heinrich von Biber's Passacaglia for Solo Violin in G Minor immediately wrapped Emma and Claire in its consoling spell. No numbered concerto this—this was a composition without echo or match in the entire musical canon. Mournful and sublime, the desolate composition somehow acknowledged everything and everyone they had lost. For Emma and Claire, it was as if their parents had returned for a moment to say good-bye. Mary, William, and Amelia wept, too. Elizabeth's evocative playing drifted from their small circle to Viola and Jakob, then farther down the hill to Harold and Vera, then beyond, to mourners at nearby gravesites. A pair of gravediggers paused in their exertions and rued the necessity of their vocation. With each variation, each eloquent turn of phrase, people throughout the cemetery lifted their heads and were comforted, even passing sightseers, who halted their carriages to listen.

When Elizabeth finished, there was a long moment of ineffable silence, and then birdsong erupted from the branches of the surrounding white oaks and dogwood trees, warblers and wrens and titmice chorusing in appreciation. It broke the spell, and laughing, Elizabeth curtsied, and Emma and Claire, their faces newly alight, wiped their cheeks and tugged at their dresses and stood. William helped Mary and Amelia to their feet, and then they all descended the hill together. Halfway down, Viola and Jakob joined them, and they walked together to Indian Lake, where Vera had gone ahead to set up a picnic in a grove of oaks and Harold had taken the horses to water. Vera laid out quilts on a bed of fallen leaves. They all settled there and passed around sandwiches and ginger ale and summer strawberries.

After they ate, Emma and Claire pulled off their socks and shoes to wade in the lake.

"Lizzie, come with us," Claire begged.

"All right," Elizabeth said, "but Jakob has to come, too."

The younger quartet started off toward the water, Emma and Claire holding hands, Elizabeth and Jakob following, fingers touching, while the older quartet, Viola, Amelia, William, and Mary, watched them go.

Yesterday, Elizabeth and Jakob had married in Judge Thayer's chambers, the same room where eighteen years before, Elizabeth's mother and father had married. Both marriages had been hastened by extraordinary events: Jenny and Thomas's by the War of the Rebellion, and Elizabeth and Jakob's by the repercussions of a hideous crime. It was odd how pain could either annihilate or accelerate love: pain had driven Viola from Gerritt, but the collective pain of all of them had formed a new family, forged by newlyweds who would not wait, who had felt a need to surround Emma and Claire with support and love, and who knew the value of forgiveness.

From the lake came the sound of Emma squealing with laughter. Claire had waded in and tied up her skirts and was cupping cool water and tossing it at her sister. Emma, her dress hem lifted to her ankles, bent down, drew her hand through the water, and retaliated with a tentative splash, dousing Claire in turn. Watching them from the quilts, the older foursome turned to one another with relief. When they'd told the girls that Gerritt had died, the news had seemed to give them both a great measure of relief. Jakob and Viola had apologized, saying how sorry they were about what Gerritt had done, and explaining that they hadn't known. Then, before Elizabeth agreed to marry Jakob, she insisted that they also inform Emma and Claire that the Other Man had been Jakob's father and Viola's husband. It was an impossible fact, but one Elizabeth would not conceal, even if it meant her own unhappiness. She was adamant that the wedding would not take place if either Emma or Claire exhibited any distress. She would do nothing to make them afraid.

Who knows what confusion the news had aroused? But Emma and Claire had nodded solemnly in reply and the marriage had taken place.

And now Emma was playing: accepting teasing taunts from Claire, splashing Jakob and Elizabeth, no longer looking hunted. With her hat askew, her long red hair tousled by the breeze, her toes sinking into the mud, she looked like any child anywhere pleased to be on an outing,

It was noon now. At one, they would all travel back into the city, gather their trunks, and go to the train station, where at six that evening, Viola, Amelia, Jakob, Elizabeth, Emma, and Claire would all board the train for Boston. Jakob had leased a house for them near the Boston Common and had found a position, thanks to Judge Thayer's recommendation, with a firm located near Faneuil Hall. Elizabeth was to start at the Boston Conservatory next week. And Viola and Amelia would look after Emma and Claire. Viola was still shy among them, brittle with shame, but Amelia had taken over the work of making her feel welcome. They were quickly becoming friends. Viola's solemn guilt had begun its release with that welcome, though under what undeserving banner of goodness she had fallen she would not come to terms with for years.

Mary and William were staying behind in Albany. Their fates were no less clearly defined. Jakob had asked Mary to direct the House of Shelter, and she was going to relocate her clinic for prostitutes there. She had already applied for hospital privileges at St. Peter's, and there were promising indications that they would accept her. Thomas Hun had written her a formal letter of apology and asked her to come back to City Hospital, but she had refused. William too had resigned, leaving them short the best orthopedic surgeon in the city.

Now Mary and William watched Emma stooping to inspect a bed of moss on the lakeshore. She had not once looked over her shoulder to make certain of their whereabouts. She showed a new ease in the world. They would miss her. They would miss all of them. It would be one more leave-taking in a lifetime of leave-takings. Of course they would visit them in Boston, and often. They trusted Jakob to take care of them—Jakob, who had discovered the truth and unmasked his father and now must live with the horror of it. It was lucky that he did not resemble his father in any way. And it was fortunate that he had the courage of a man twice his age. Or maybe the young have more courage than the old. Mary and William could name a thousand reasons why this new family, founded in despair and trouble, might go wrong, but how different was this regrouping from the strange regroupings of families that the war had forced? When love drives change, doubt can have no place.

Mary reached over and touched William's face. For the first time in their married lives, they would live alone, without extended family to worry over or care for. Theirs was a tenacious kind of love, as solid and true as granite. Neither of them could think of a time in their life together when either had let the other down.

The miracle of that eclipsed even the miracle of Emma's and Claire's resurrection.

Another chorus of laughter echoed from the pond. Emma had fallen into the shallow water, and her dress was soaked through, and Claire was trying to help her out, and then she too fell in. Sunlight dappled the ruffling surface of the lake as Jakob plunged in to haul each one of them out. Emma took his hand without recoil. She bent over giggling, and the adults all looked on, astounded.

And then it was time to gather up the quilts and wrap the soaking girls in them and pack them into the carriage to be carried away, back along the river gleaming in the summer sunlight, to the house to change clothes and bid Vera good-bye, and then on to the train station, where they huddled together before the train was called, conscious of the moment of leaving everything behind. And then at the conductor's whistle, William and Jakob went ahead and stowed food hampers and Elizabeth's violin in the overhead luggage racks and then the rest followed, save Mary, who observed their progress through the opened windows of the train, until the conductor called all aboard, and William hurried off and Emma and Claire leaned out and Mary and William lifted their hands to touch theirs.

"Try not to be afraid," Mary and William said to Emma together after Claire had drawn her hand back in and climbed into Amelia's arms.

And Emma, alone in the window, answered, "One hundred thirteen."

They shook their heads in confusion.

"The name of my concerto is one hundred thirteen," she said. The train began to pull away. They walked alongside, still touching hands.

"What do you mean, darling?"

"Yesterday was one hundred twelve days since we were taken and today is one hundred thirteen and today is the first day I'm not afraid. One day, I'm going to write a violin concerto and call it Number One Hundred Thirteen, and Elizabeth will play it." Emma drew her hand in and pressed it against the glass until the train pulled out of the station to begin its crawl over the South Bridge, the bridge that had rid them all of Gerritt.

Unable yet to say good-bye—how silly, they were going to Boston next week, would stay with them in their new home on the Common, would get to see their new lives—Mary and William dashed into the street and hurried southward to watch the train cross the Hudson. The evening sky had gone pink and light blue and the paling sunlight outlined the caboose as the train snaked away to the other side of the river and was gone.

On the train, Emma looks out the window. She counts the iron struts of the bridge as they pass and then forgets the number as soon as the train breaks free. They are heading south and the sun is setting over the western hills. The light is golden and full and it makes the river, seen through leafy thickets, so peaceful and beautiful that she cannot imagine leaving it behind now. It came to their rescue, hers and Claire's, a watery hand in the darkness when she was so frightened that nothing seemed real anymore, not the present, not the past.

But now this is what is real, Emma thinks. Not that other thing that happened to her, but Elizabeth, who is smiling at her now, and Jakob, who helped her in the trial, and Mrs. Van der Veer, who likes to read to them and who looks at them both with such kindness, and Auntie Amelia, who can make anywhere feel like home, even a rattling train car. And Aunt Mary and Uncle William love her, too, and they will come to see them every month. And Claire is already asleep, her head nestled in Elizabeth's lap, her hair combed back from her face.

Her mother and father are gone. Gone. This, too, is real, but she will never forget the last moment she saw them, when she turned at the top of the school stairs and the falling snow was still just a lark, before everything terrible that followed, and they looked back at her, holding hands, and said to her, "Emma, take good care of your sister."

And she had.

Author's Note

In 1888, a blizzard engulfed the entire Northeast, arising without warning in that age of little forecasting, killing four hundred people. For the purposes of this narrative, I moved that deadly blizzard to the year 1879.

In 1879, the age of consent in New York State was ten years old. The NY State Statute regarding rape read, in part: "Every person who shall be convicted of rape, either, 1. By carnally and unlawfully knowing any female child under the age of ten years; or, 2. By forcibly ravishing any woman of the age of ten years or upwards; Shall be punished by imprisonment in a state prison not less than ten years."

In 1883, the first fledgling attempts were made in the New York legislature to raise the age of consent. It wasn't until 1886 that the state raised the legal age for females from ten to sixteen, though no mention of the same protection was yet afforded to males.

Acknowledgments

A lucky writer is never alone. The following women provided the best kind of support an author needs to thrive: the freedom to explore and a helping hand when needed. Marly Rusoff, my extraordinary agent, is always my earliest and best reader. Her suggestions on the first six chapters of *Winter Sisters* sent the manuscript in a much more hopeful direction. My wonderful editors Kathryn Court and Sarah Stein provided astute editorial feedback on the very long, very wordy first draft I submitted. Their feedback was instrumental in helping me to reshape the story into a stronger, better version of itself. I am indebted to these women. They, and all the Viking team—from the president to the marketing department—have astonished me with their enthusiasm for *Winter Sisters*. Sarah Stein's assistant, Shannon Kelly, helped immensely with some of the technical complications of copyediting and production. And Kathryn Court's assistant, Victoria Savanh, always answered my innumerable questions, no matter how random or ill-timed.

While writing this book, I met weekly for more than a year with two brilliant women writers who were also working on their own novel drafts. Joan Leegant and Randy Sue Coburn have become the dearest of friends. This book would not be what it is without their abundant generosity, multiple kindnesses, and shrewd observations.

Rich Farrell, Julie Barton, and Rena Pitasky read different forms of early drafts, providing much needed feedback and perspective. Before I sent my final draft to my editors, Rena went through it with a very red pencil. Amazing the number of typos and inconsistencies a fresh set of extremely sharp eyes can find.

I am equally indebted to Louise Crowley, former director of the Vermont College of Fine Arts MFA in Writing program, for arranging for me a much-needed retreat at the eponymous Crowley Center, named after her because she is and always has been a true friend to writers. Melissa Fisher, Miciah Bay Gault, Ann Hagman Cardinal, and Ellen Lesser kept me sane during my long days of writing there. And I must mention, as I do in all my books' acknowledgments, that the MFA in Writing program at Vermont College of Fine Arts is among the most convivial and supportive educational environments I have ever been a part of.

My great thanks to the research librarians at the Schaffer Law Library at Albany Law School for their tireless help with chasing down arcane trial procedure and 1879 New York State law statutes. Profound gratitude to David Danielson, JD, for his eloquent elucidation of the right of any person, no matter how despicable, to legal counsel. I am also grateful to the members of the Listserv of the American Musical Society, especially Styra Avins, Jonathan Bellman, and Geoff Chew. *Merci* to the kind people at the Le Conservatoire National Supérieur d'Art Dramatique, who admitted me to the old concert hall of the Conservatoire de Paris and let me poke around for a while. The research librarians at the New York Public Library were of great help. The research assistants at the Albany Institute of History and Art are unfailingly generous when I have questions. Thanks to Colleen Ryan of the Preservation League of New York State for leading me to Stuart Lehman, assistant curator of the Office of General Services for the

State of New York, who pinpointed details about the construction of the capitol building. And to Anthony Opalka, the Albany City Historian, my deep and abiding thanks for our discussions about the transportation system of nineteenth-century Albany.

And always, thanks to my husband, Drew Oliveira, who supports me in everything.